MY SILENT HOUSE

Also by Jane Murray MacCallum

❤

Children's Stories:

The true story of Sophie

Florence and Winifred Emily

❤

MY SILENT HOUSE

by

Jane Murray MacCallum

Boiler Island Air Systems Inc.

First published 2014 by **Boiler Island Air Systems Inc.** with no financial assistance from the taxpayer.

My Silent House is a work of fiction. Names, characters, places and incidents are either the product of the author's imagination or are used fictitiously. Any resemblance to actual persons, living or dead, incidents or locales is entirely coincidental.

Cover design by Colin MacCallum.

Front cover picture by Brigitte Mattei, Hornby Island, BC.

Printed and bound in Canada by Printorium Bookworks on 100% recycled paper FSC.

Library and Archives Canada Cataloguing in Publication

MacCallum, Jane Murray, 1931-, author
        My silent house / by Jane Murray MacCallum.

ISBN 978-0-9738529-3-6 (pbk.)

    I. Title.

PS8625.C359M9 2014   C813'.6   C2013-907119-9

For David

Introduction and Author's Note

Emily matures in the late 1940s, 1950s and 1960s, my era, an interesting era. There were huge differences in the boundaries imposed by society on the lives of young women then and now. Emily experiences love, sadness, happiness, joy and fulfilment, from the age of 18 to her old age, sixty years later. The story explores the emotions and difficulties a woman encounters on her journey through life in a way that invites the reader to empathise and to understand how different the world of women was then.

Emily's life mirrors mine sometimes, although any resemblance to persons living or dead, other than to my son David, is purely coincidental. Emily's is a long life, in which many characters come – and go. We feel her joy at the birth of a child, her pleasure with Christmas morning and her small children, her growing dissatisfaction with her husband whose transformation from an eager suitor to a tight-lipped, unresponsive husband exasperates her increasingly, her sorrow at the death of a friend, her haunting longing for a son who disappears and her hallucinations in the course of her grieving. The story is enhanced by glimpses into the thoughts of Emily's husband, her relatives and her lovers.

There was of course no sexual freedom; nice girls did not let boys "go too far". It was alright for boys to do this - but not with nice girls. Mother was absolutely adamant that a woman should be in love and certainly married before making love, anything else in her view was wrong and unacceptable. A nice girl was expected to be a virgin when she married. No Love, No Marriage, No Sex, that was the unwritten rule. I believe most of the girls I grew up with adhered to the rules. Vancouver at that time was a very provincial town where families were known and gossip got around very quickly – a pregnancy out of wedlock was considered shameful and would cause great embarrassment to one's family. I made up my mind that this was never going to happen to me. I wasn't a total "goodie two shoes" though, because I secretly and rather daringly danced in the chorus line in a few night clubs whilst still at school. When, many years later I told my mother of these secret events, she had a good giggle, but her ideas of how a young lady should behave were at that time very strong and definitely did not include dancing in a chorus line in a night club!

West Vancouver, BC
December 2013

QUANDARY

The skeleton had given him a real fright, coming across it suddenly the way he did, lying there staring at him with those empty eyes and the hole where the nose should have been and the sandals hanging on the fleshless feet below the tattered remains of blue jeans. Maybe he should have got closer and really looked at it, but, anyway, he couldn't and didn't. He wondered if it was still there; he had often wondered about it. Perhaps he should have told someone, but how would he have explained it? All he had wanted to do was to get away as quickly as possible and enjoy the rest of his hike; it had disturbed him, made him feel sad and very uncomfortable.

He tried to put the unpleasant picture of the skeleton out of his mind and got busy lacing up his hiking boots. He remembered the peace and quiet of the woods and the sound of the sea which he could glimpse through the trees. It was a beautiful place to hike, not a soul about, a place where he can forget about exams and noise and people, maybe the skeleton won't be there, that would be excellent, after all it was a whole year ago that he saw it.

He gathered together food and water and packed his pack.

It was still very cold as he climbed over the rocks and walked along through the woods, but he was well-clothed and the cold didn't bother him. Perhaps as it was nearly spring he would see some of those little wild flowers he had seen before. All of a sudden he felt the tension of the last while leave him, he felt good, really alive, full of energy. Maybe he would pass his exams, but he was not going to think about the "If I don't pass stuff" - not yet.

He began to watch where the path was leading him, remembering quite well which one to take if he wanted to see if the skeleton was still there. In a way he didn't want to see it, but he had to know, he really couldn't think why, but he knew he wouldn't be able to keep away.

Carefully now, he picked his way along through the leafy mulch; he was sure it was near here, yes, he remembered it was under a big tree. He thought he saw it, a slight mound, yes, he could see what looked like bones, poking through some winter-withered leaves; as he came closer he could see most of it.

The clothes were almost all gone now but the leather sandals were still holding together, in places.

He stood looking at it, could it be a girl? He had always imagined it to be a guy but it could be a girl, he hadn't thought of that before. Maybe he should tell the police. He wished he hadn't looked; telling the police will spoil his whole day and, not only that, he will never want to come here again. Why had he come, the person was dead so what good would it do to tell anyone? What would the police do? Would they be difficult with him? He didn't like the police, never had, with their batons and guns, they would just take it away and then what? Perhaps that person had wanted to lie there, undisturbed in the peace and quiet? But what if he had been murdered? Somebody could have killed him out here where there was no one to see. He could have been stabbed in the back or something. Poor guy. He's pretty sure it is a guy, it's something about the shoulders, just something he can't quite define, he is pretty sure it isn't a girl. Of course if she had been an athlete or swimmer she could have had that sort of physique. How would he know really, girls get raped and murdered all the time so it definitely could be a girl now that he thinks of it.

Murder, he hadn't thought of that before.

THE TRUNK

It took him many days to collect her things. It was strange how he would remember something he knew should go into the trunk, but, when he went to look for it, it was never where he thought it would be and of course sometimes it wasn't there at all. He chose her school trunk although he knew he wouldn't fill it, there really wasn't that much left. He thought he had everything now. He hoped he had bought enough tissue paper. He liked the idea of the tissue paper - it somehow seemed more appropriate than anything else. He certainly could not have put her things in newspaper, he smiled to himself, no, that he could not have done!

He picked up her pointe shoes: they were well worn – he fingered the ribbons as he wound them around the faded pink satin, then carefully he folded them in the tissue. She had danced for him a few times a very long time ago, lovely, it was. He picked up the figure skates; tissue wouldn't do for these so he put them aside, deciding to find a towel to wrap them in. He had never seen her skate. He chose next, the velvet evening jacket; he touched it, gently folded it and laid it on the paper, then he closed it up and put it in the trunk. The evening dress he remembered well, although it had been many years since she had worn it; there had been others but this had been her first and she had kept it for its memories. He folded and wrapped it and placed it next to the jacket. Next was the blue velvet case, he opened it and lifted the tiny golden bell from the little satin nest and cupped it in his hand; it was almost impossible to read the inscription now. He put it back in the case and wrapped the tissue around it; he set it aside, he had changed his mind, he would put it with his will, he decided that would be better.

The white silk rompers he had found in an envelope in the linen cupboard. He took them out now and carefully folded them in the tissue paper. He guessed silk wasn't used much anymore for babies; she had said at the time that they were a lot of work but she hadn't minded that.

The one little piece left of her Limoges, (the lid had been broken long ago) he wrapped carefully; it really was too bad so much had been broken. He had felt very sorry when she had been so upset about it. He couldn't understand at the time why it had been so important to her. He had not been very sympathetic, the broken china had seemed unimportant at the time, after all it hadn't been so long before, during the war, that he had witnessed a lot worse things being broken than china. She had tried to explain it to him, that the china had somehow been a symbol of her childhood, her time with her great-aunts, he couldn't really understand, he had never felt all these sorts of emotions. When the aunts finally died, her grief had been very disturbing to him.

The puppets, he couldn't remember their names; he never did get them straight, not many happy memories about them. He could still feel the irritation he had when she and Martha had spent hours and hours in that room making them and their costumes, then writing plays for the wretched things. So many evenings she had been out giving performances at children's birthday parties and Christmas parties. All the same, he had to admit it had been quite an original enterprise; their children and all the village children had enjoyed it. He wrapped each one carefully because their paper maché faces were quite fragile. Teddy (that was all they had ever called him, just plain "Teddy") with his worn-out ears and paws and no growl, they had removed that with their usual curiosity, funny how they had loved that bear so much. He laid him on the paper and carefully folded him in it. Sad business.

The nightie did not need wrapping as she had kept it wrapped in tissue even though it really was in shreds. He undid the ribbon and, without lifting it, touched the creamy silk and fingered the delicate lace, so much lace. He remembered putting it on her, watching it slither over her and settle in a filmy cascade of mist over her body. In the soft evening light she had looked unbelievable to him, ethereal, dream-like when she stepped towards him. His hand fumbled a little as he refolded the tissue and retied the ribbon then placed it in the trunk. The memory of her as she had been then, gave him a feeling of happiness and renewed the memory of his love for her. He didn't allow this memory to include his feeling of horror when she had told him her shocking, strange and upsetting story with tears rolling down her lovely face, although it was not something one would or could forget easily. Poor Tink, so sweet and so innocent and to think she had been afraid he wouldn't believe her, of course he believed her because he knew her, he knew her very well. He can remember how sad he had felt, that she had gone through such a horrible experience, all he had wanted to do was to help *her forget, he had done his best, it had been easy for him, with his heart so full of love for her. They had never mentioned it again.*

He looked around him, had he got everything, then he saw her book, her treasured book "Baron At The Ballet" - a boyfriend had given it to her long ago. He read the inscription again "For my beautiful green-eyed dancing damsel". He remembered looking at the book when they were first married and asking what had happened to this boyfriend; she had said she did not wish to talk about him. Then he had dared to ask her if she had loved him and her answer had been a so-definite "yes" - she had said, "Oh yes". Well, he supposed most people had had a few love affairs before they found the right one, but loving had not been easy for him and when he found Emily, his love for her filled him, he had never felt like that before, no, there had never been anyone but Emily. Maybe that was why he could not really forgive her for what she did, her betrayal had been devastating and to forgive her had seemed impossible. He had come across the book accidentally in the old bookcase in the dining room and had been surprised to see it there as it usually was in her desk. He put it on top.

At last he was finished; he closed the trunk. He was quite astonished at how long it had taken. He could feel that aching sadness fill him once again. He should have forgiven her long ago and released himself from the torture of loving her so much and hating her at the same time. Yes, hate had filled him at times, ugly, angry hatred. Sometimes he would be free of all these emotions for a spell but of course he had expected these feelings to return - that was why he had put off doing this for so long. He was tired now and thought that he would make a pot of tea and perhaps put the telly on, take his mind off the whole thing. But first of course he will hide the trunk, he must do so, right away. Difficult, his first idea was no use at all. Perhaps he should have that cup of tea now after all and think about it some more.

Finally it was done, hidden from prying eyes forever, no one but Emily had known about the secret place where once long ago they had stored their wine. Now with the wine gone it is the perfect place for these memories to lie unseen and untouched forever, even after he is long dead they will still be there. For some reason he likes that thought.

NEW YORK – 1950

I opened my eyes. Carefully I put my hand out to touch my face - it felt sore when I touched it, and hot. My head throbbed unbearably. I turned and lifted my head to look around me. I could see my kimono on the chair and felt a huge surge of relief, it was alright, I was in my own hotel room, I could even see my suitcase. I gently laid my head back on the pillow and tried to turn over but it was too painful - I seemed to be sore all over. I closed my eyes and drifted in and out of sleep trying to remember, trying to piece the fragments together. I was on my way to England, yes of course, I remember saying goodbye to everyone, mother, Stanley, yes yes, but what has happened to me? I lay back again, forcing myself to think, to remember, yes and Edgar was there with Madeleine, everyone was there to say goodbye.

Why am I so sore, did I fall? Yes, that must be what happened - but where? I tried to turn again to get up, I lay back, suddenly dizzy. I remember getting on the aeroplane – yes, I remember the tiny Vancouver airport and waving goodbye to everyone and I remember that chap remembering me and yes, I had booked into the hotel. I lifted my head a fraction; how did I get here so banged up, so sore? A terrible feeling of unhappiness filled me. Exhausted, I drifted back to sleep.

The next time I woke up I realized I was very hungry.

I called room service and ordered a small breakfast, an egg, toast and tea. Gingerly I put my feet on the floor and stood up. My head still ached and throbbed. However, although I was so sore I could walk without much difficulty; there was an occasional stab in my back but it was bearable and would probably go away before long. I was just sore really, nothing much more than that. I ate breakfast, lay back on the bed, and was soon sound asleep.

Unfamiliar sounds of traffic stirred me into consciousness. I touched my face, it was cool now. I pulled myself up, I tried to focus on what I could remember.

I had found the studio as the streets began to darken.

The young man who smiled as he advanced towards me. "Well Miss, what can I do for you?"

Yes, I remember telling him that I had been told that the dancing taught here was the "Katherine Dunham" technique and I wanted to see for myself as I had studied that type of dancing and loved it.

"Really now, that is interesting," he had said, "well you just sit yourself down right here and see what you can see, rehearsing will soon begin, no actual class today." He smiled, he seemed very friendly.

I had watched as the dancers began to arrive and arrange themselves in groups. They were all encased in black tights with tight, brightly-coloured tops; their feet were naked. Very little hair escaped the bands and bandanas.

I remember the beat of the music filling the room, the dancers flowing and floating, curling and uncurling, their arms and legs graceful extensions of their bodies. Formations formed and diffused, bodies drifted as fronds of ferns, gently curving into the music as it filled the dancers with its melodic rhythm.

I had been fascinated, I watched the exquisite freedom of this form of dance.. I wanted to dance with them, my body longing to move to the music, the feeling had been so strong, I had known I could do all of this, I had learned exactly this from my teacher in Vancouver who had studied in New York. This particular rehearsal was for a very special show I was told. If I liked I could come along and he would have a look at me tomorrow morning. "Be here sharp at nine. Vancouver eh? Larry was your teacher?"

"Oh yes, for a long time, two years!"

He had laughed "Yeh, two whole years. Can't say I've ever heard of him but New York is a big place! Well, you come along tomorrow and I'll look at you, see what you can do."

I remembered all of that quite vividly, what happened next? Did I go back? Did he see me? Did I dance for him? I was too tired, my back ached. I couldn't remember, all I wanted to do, was sleep.

"'Bye Sis - don't forget to come back, will you!"

Madeleine (my brother's wife) hugged me, "Do write to us Emily, we want to hear all about everything - don't we Edgar!" (She whispered in my ear, "Are you Okay? Really?") We hugged each other again, "Sure I am", I told her.

"Oh Emily, we are going to miss you, you know!"

My brother gave me a wink, "Well, not everything Sis!" He laughed. I thought to myself that no, not everything, the only person who would be told everything would be Madeleine as I had already told her the plan, my secret plan.

As he looked at his little sister he thought she looked very pale and unhappy, not at all like her usual self, and he could tell she had been crying and a lot too, as much as she had tried to cover it up with stuff. He still couldn't figure out why their mum had got this bee in her bonnet about Emily going to England to study ballet, ballet, always ballet as far as mum was concerned. If one were to be a dancer one had to be a ballet dancer, he knew that Emily wasn't totally committed to just ballet, she just loved to dance, all forms of dance! He looked over to see Stanley looking very forlorn indeed, those two were so crazy about each other, how were they going to survive this huge separation he wondered. Well his guess is that they won't, poor Sis, she doesn't look exactly over-joyed about her trip, with her pale, sad face.

Stanley watched her walk to the aircraft, her ballet body so erect and proud; no-one would ever guess that she really didn't want to go away. He didn't want her to go, no, not at all. He was dreading it, but even if he had been further along with his studies or even finished, to even suggest that she not go, to interfere with her life now would have been wrong - this was a great opportunity for her and once she got there and got started with everything she would probably be very happy, but he would miss her. He knew he would miss her far more than she realized. He should have said more about how much he loves her, how important she is to him, how he hopes to marry her someday, somehow he just couldn't get the words out. It was so wonderful that night, loving her the way that he did and the way she had said how wonderful it was to love him. He just hopes that his letters will be enough to keep her for him.

I went up the steps and into the aircraft to find my seat. When I looked out the window, there was mother crying and dabbing her eyes. By the look of her, one would think that she really didn't want me to go but I knew that she did, although I didn't know why she was so keen, not really, her decision had been so definite. Every time I said that I really didn't want to go, mother seemed to get quite agitated, so where was the sense to it - crying now as if she didn't want me to go at all, when it was all her idea!

I waved from my little window and mother waved her handkerchief and dabbed at her face some more and waved again with a weak little smile. Stanley stood very still. He wasn't smiling; was he thinking about that night when he held me so close and kissed me, whispering my name over and over and I started to cry? I wished he would smile, that would have made me feel better. I felt that excitement get hold of me again, thinking about that night, it was so wonderful when he kissed me, saying my name like that, then he had tilted my head back and gently dried my eyes with his handkerchief, looking into them, telling me not to cry, that everything would be alright, that he would write to me. I could hardly hear him, my heart had been pounding so hard; then he had said that I was his girl and I wasn't to forget it, he sort of laughed and gave me another hug. I wondered if he was thinking about those things right now, the way that I was. I supposed it was silly to think he might give me an engagement ring before I left - that would have been wonderful. Then I would have known for certain that I would be coming back to him, a sort of seal to our promise; it would have made our promise more real somehow. I opened the parcel he had given me (if only it had been a ring!). A beautiful book! I knew about this very beautiful book, all about famous dancers and choreographers with such wonderful photography, all the girls at the ballet school were talking about it and here it was in front of me! I read the inscription "For my beautiful green-eyed dancing damsel". That was all, not, Love from Stanley, no never that! At least he did say "my" green-eyed dancing damsel, that was very special!

As the aeroplane bumped along the runway and took off, my stomach gave a lurch as the climb began, steadily upwards and the little farewell group faded into the distance. I closed my eyes with the image of mother still there, Stanley too, so serious and sad. I was frightened, to be away, so far away and for so long. I looked out of the small window. Why had it been so important to mother that I went to England to study, why?

A tender aching sadness filled me when I hugged mother for the last time and suddenly the tears came. "Now now dear, everything will be wonderful, you just wait and see! Think of how lucky you are!" She had already told me this a million times, "And be sure to write as soon as you arrive - we will all be waiting to hear about the voyage! Don't forget to write to Nellie and Lily too". I had swallowed my tears, kissed her again, hugged her and said nothing. How could I ever forget to write to Nellie and

Lily, my great-aunts, who were such an important part of my life.

I still had to open the package that our neighbour had given mother to give to me.

When I opened the package I quickly realized why mother had said I wouldn't like the gift! Nestled underneath layers of tissue paper was a brown and beige furry coat. There was even a corsage pinned to it! I loathed corsages. I didn't think flowers looked right, stuck on clothes. Even if it had been in good shape (but it wasn't) I would not have wanted it as I just did not like fur coats, not for me. They were fine on my mother and my great-aunts or movie stars, but I had never ever wanted one. It was very surprising to realize that this woman possessed even a mangy fur coat as my only memory of her is seeing her standing on our porch in her grey raincoat looking like a tombstone with her long mournful face (also a greyish colour) hoping to borrow something, sugar or coffee, something that one eats or uses up without noticing, whatever those are. Anyway, what in the world was I going to do with the wretched thing – I couldn't possibly take it with me? No, that was out of the question.

I put it on the floor by my feet. It truly was a horrible-looking thing. Looking at it down there by my feet it looked like a poor dead animal, which was what it had been of course! I would just have to get rid of it somehow. Suddenly my thoughts were interrupted.

"I think we know each other, don't we?" The voice came from the chap in the seat next to me, there were just two seats on each side of the aisle. I looked at him. It seemed most unlikely that we would have ever met as he looked even older than my brother, and my brother was six years older than me. He could have been at least thirty. How would I have met anyone that age? No, I really didn't think that was possible. I smiled at him. "I don't think so."

"Well, you certainly look most familiar. Where are you off to?" I explained where I was going and why.

"You haven't by chance been studying at the Vancouver School of Music and Dance have you?"

"Oh yes I have, why do you ask?"

"Our office is in the building next to you - our window looks right into your ballet class! We, my partner Mark and I, we're lawyers, lots of lawyers in our building y'know, we've been watching you dance every day for a very long time! So it's no wonder you look familiar, although I must say you do look a little different, all dressed up! Imagine that! Meeting you on an aeroplane! We have our coffee downstairs too, same as you - I've seen you there as well of course, many times - in your ballet rig." He turned and held his hand out to me, "Name's Brian, Brian Wilcox. How do you do." We shook hands and I told him my name.

"Well well Emily, you *are* going a long way, all the way to England and all by your self! Brave girl!"

"It wasn't my idea, in fact I really didn't want to go at all - especially alone. It would have been more bearable if mother could have come with me. Anyway it wasn't possible, so here I am!"

She does seem young to be travelling alone to go so far away. Well, she seems confident enough, a little upset and sad but that is understandable, maybe it will be fine for her, I wonder how old she is - rather young I guess, but it would be fun to take her out in London, take her to a show, dinner, yes, show her London Town. I'll have to get her London address before we land. It will be quite amusing to see the expression on Mark's face when I tell him I have actually met the "dancing girl" and might even take her out! That's what I call real luck!

Brian smiled, "My goodness, I expect many girls would be thrilled to be going on such an adventure. Where will you be staying? In London?" I told him about mother's plans, the visit to Jersey in the Channel Islands to stay with my uncle and aunt for a while before going to London to a dance academy; it was a school of pure ballet and, although I loved ballet classes, I had really wanted to do more of the Katherine Dunham technique and cabaret as well so, apart from the holiday in Jersey which I was really looking forward to, I was not thrilled with the idea of the ballet academy in London. I of course didn't mention that secretly I had made my own different plans. I guessed I sounded a bit gloomy because Brian just laughed, "Well buck up Emily – I think you are pretty darned lucky myself! Why didn't your mum want to come with you?"

I tried to explain about the public trustee and the family money being in England and that it was only to be used for my brother and me and then only for education until we were 25, that my mother had a business and couldn't leave and couldn't afford the trip anyway. Mother had always told me not to talk about my inheritance but I didn't think there would be much harm in telling Brian as I would never see him again and I didn't tell him everything about it anyway, like how much it was and when I would get the full inheritance, so I was sure it was alright to tell him that little bit about it.

"Well," he said, "too bad about that, but you really are a very lucky young woman y'know and I'm sure it will all turn out just great. Anyway Emily, you looked pretty good to us - wonderful to watch, my partner and I certainly enjoyed watching you! I'm sure your mother will be proud of you. So, work hard now and good luck! By the way, you wouldn't mind, would you, if I gave you a call next time I'm in London?"

I laughed, of course I wouldn't mind, I told him, but couldn't help thinking that it was highly unlikely that he would ever remember me. And that actually I wasn't planning to be in London - in fact I was hoping I wouldn't be! I told him he could telephone my mother to get my address if he liked, I gave him Mother's telephone number.

When I looked out the window I realized we were coming in to Seattle and getting ready to land. This is where I was to change planes for New York. I looked down at the mound of fur by my feet and suddenly realized that this would be the perfect chance to dump the coat. Brian shook hands and gave my hand a little pat, "Goodbye Emily and good luck" he said and left the aircraft. As I saw him go through the door into the terminal he turned and gave me a little wave. Funny to think that he had been watching me for such a long time! He did seem very nice.

I rushed along to the Ladies' washroom clutching the coat and hating the feel of it and the smell of it. I lurched into the lavatory and hung it, complete with corsage, on the peg. Out in a minute, I rushed away, praying that the attendant wouldn't spot the coat and run after me with it. Rather breathless, I boarded the aircraft, greatly relieved, congratulating myself on the brilliant idea!

Several hours later the sadness and feeling of loneliness began to fade. As the aircraft approached New York, I could see the garden of lights sparkling and twinkling in the night sky. Excitement swelled inside me. Unknown to everyone except Madeleine, I was hoping to get an audition to join a school that taught this special dance technique and hopefully an audition to do some cabaret work at a night club to top up the finances. Whenever I thought about my secret plans I felt nearly ill - it all seemed so unreal and yet I told myself - why should it be unreal?

Yes, now I remember - his name was Jason he said, as he shook my hand.

I remember wriggling into my tights and little velvet shorts and tight black sweater.

"Take your shorts off Emily - I have to see your whole body. I'm sure you don't wear those at your ballet class or in Larry's class."

I admitted that I didn't and went to take them off. I thought they were so cute and had been dying to wear them for an audition as I was sure that was what the girls wore for auditions, in places like New York, or perhaps Hollywood. I had seen that in the movies.

He sat at the piano and played some Rachmaninoff, then Bartok; he didn't seem to look at the keys at all as he watched me dance. At last he stopped; I wasn't at all tired, I was a little nervous.

He came and stood in front of me, "Look, how would you like to do some cabaret work for a while, you've got the legs and stuff for it, I don't have room for another pupil at the moment for the Modern Dance Group but I know someone who could probably find a spot for you in a night club - twenty-five dollars a show, five nights a week. I felt my heart sink, this was not the right order - not at all how I had planned it. I looked at him and wondered if I could talk my way into the modern dance class. "Why didn't you like me for the class? I really want to do that more than anything. You say you haven't a place for me now, but I am going to Britain for a month or two anyway, so would there be a chance for me after a couple of months? I would need the night club work as well to help with finances? If you tell me when there will be a space for me, I could be here when you say."

"Really now, how come you're going to England then?"

I told him mother's plan and how I had hoped to change it.

"Look, why don't you let me take you out for dinner this evening and we can talk about it. I could introduce you to my friend, nice guy, always looking for girls for night clubs. You're all alone here aren't you? All alone in New York for how long?"

"I have one week that's all and then I leave on the SS Media for England and then I fly to Jersey for my holiday and I really want to get my plan in place before I leave." "Come for dinner. I'll take you to Radio City too. We'll talk. I'll give Rob a buzz - see if he will have time to see you. Meet me at the drug store, the one near your hotel. I don't like waiting around, so be on time, seven on the dot."

He seemed a bit gruff and tough but it was New York and people in show business were, I guessed, a little different.

His manner frightened me a bit but I didn't want to lose a chance to complete my plan.

I put on my silk dress; carefully I put on my precious and only pair of silk stockings, then my only pair of high heels. I looked in the mirror, yes, these things definitely made me look more sophisticated, like a New Yorker!

Trying to ignore the uncomfortable feeling I had, standing on the street corner in front of the drug store, I saw someone coming towards me and it wasn't Jason - it must be his friend. Maybe Jason wasn't going to come at all. Panic filled me as the thin, smiling man approached. "Jason tied up, can't come, you're Emily?"

"Yes, I am, but it was Jason I had the appointment with."

"Yeh that's right, but you'll have to make do with me young lady, he might come along later. So first of all you had best come to my place and let me have a look at you."

This was horrible, nothing was as I thought it would be and I was frightened. "We were going to have a meal and I am very hungry."

"Umm, yeh, Jason did mention that, well come on then and we'll grab a bite first."

I trotted along beside him, wishing I could run away but if I did that I would lose my chance. I couldn't give up now!

"Look, Emily I think I'd rather have a look at you and see you dance a bit before we eat, but I can grab you a sandwich if you like and we can take it with us to my place. Okay?"

I agreed, what else could I do? Nothing was happening the way I had hoped.

We climbed the stairs to "his place", a sort of studio, a piano, a large floor space and not much else.

"Here," he said, "put these on, you can go behind that screen."

The shorts were like the ones I had bought, thin black velvet, elastic waist and very short, the blouse was white satin. No shoes. I went on to the floor.

"Not bad, good legs. Let's see a bit of dancing, see how you match up to the music."

Then he began to play "Tea for Two". That was really lucky! I had a great routine for it from my night club experiences!

Suddenly he got up from the piano and began to dance with me. He was full of rhythm and swung me around effortlessly, I seemed to float.

After a few minutes he put the record player on. "You sit down and eat your sandwich. I have a few things I must see to for a few minutes, then you can do a turn or two to the record player."

"What about the class?"

"Class? The only class I have is for night club work, learning routines, you already know how to dance. Jason is the pure dance person, not me. All I do is get you ready for night-club work. Okay?"

I ate the sandwich, the music played on and as I listened I felt very lonely and frightened. Suddenly the music changed, Rob was back. He came over and took my hand. He was a very good dancer, but he held me too tightly and began pushing himself at me, grabbing at my breasts. "Come on, come on, give us a little fun eh?" I tried to push him off but he was very strong and suddenly angry. "What's all the fuss about little girl, I thought you were night-club material, right?"

I twisted out of his grip but he was determined, pulling me, yanking at my blouse.

He kept saying, "Come on baby, come on, give us a bit of fun eh."

I could hear my blouse rip as I struggled and twisted to get free, I lost my balance and fell backwards, and heard the terrible thud as my head hit the floor, he was on top of me. I screamed at him to leave me alone, to let go, struggling and wriggling, clawing at him, no more words would come out of my mouth, I couldn't breathe. I could still hear him but he sounded far away, his snarling, angry voice yelling "get the hell out of here, go on get out, get up and get out, no use being conked out around here, get up and get out!"

My head was throbbing. How long had I been lying here! In a blur, feeling sore and bruised all over, I grabbed my dress, it stuck stickily to my body as I pulled it over my head. Where were my panties? I found my garter belt and stockings and pushed them into my purse, my panties were not there. As I ran to the stairs I saw him half naked, tipping a bottle into his mouth. I nearly fell as I ran down the stairs, my feet in the high heels seemed to slip and fumble out of control, I slid the last few stairs and as I finally came to a stop I felt the edge of the last stair thump my lower back, the sudden terrible pain took my breath away. For a moment I thought I was going to be sick, my dress had ripped and was caught up around my waist. It was then I saw a streak of blood on my thigh. Oh God. Crying, clutching my purse, my heart whirling and pounding, sweat soaking my face and hair, I somehow got to the hotel and to my room, hopefully, unnoticed.

My dream had crashed. I felt used and ashamed as if I had done something wrong and bad. How would I ever forget it all, how! Every time I closed my eyes I saw his mouth coming at me, fear would curdle my stomach and again my body would shake in sobs, sobs of sadness and horror. How could such a thing have happened to me? In a sense it was unbelievable, but however unbelievable it seemed, I knew it was real and I would have to get over it and stop thinking about it; it was not something I could ever tell anyone. I would just have to forget it. I could never really forget but I had to get over it somehow, put it all out of my mind, put it in a corner and let it all die out. No one must know, no, not ever.

JERSEY

I had hardly had time to look around when standing right in front of me was my uncle. "I'm sure I'm your uncle! You're Emily, right?" I laughed and agreed, he took my hand in both of his, "So you don't need to look any further, I'm right here." He put his arm around my shoulder as we walked along, "How was the trip?" "Terrible - very bumpy, fog was the problem and it was horrible." "Too bad, too bad, yes, it can be pretty uncomfortable" he said, smiling the whole time. He was a handsome man with a narrow face and deep-set brown eyes, a prominent beak-like nose and jutting chin topped with a mop of grey hair. He appeared to be a big man, but he was not really big, not tall, not fat, somehow big, wide.

"So," he said, with his very English accent, "here is my brother's little girl! Not so little are you, quite tall in fact. You certainly look like your grandmother, I would have known you anywhere!"

At the car he said he hoped I wouldn't mind lifting my suitcases into the car as he had a bit of a heart problem, nothing at all, he said, but all the same he had been advised not to lift anything. "Have to do as I'm told - mind you, I don't usually pay any attention to these doctors! A lot of nonsense they talk, a lot of the time I think" he went on, as he lit his pipe, sucking and puffing.

Driving along the twisty lanes beside green fields and meadows of flowers, the shimmering sea was never far away. I noticed that some of the lovely old stone houses seemed to have a rosy glow to them; I mentioned this to my uncle. "Yes, some do have a pinkish tinge; that's the colour of some of the stone here which is used for a few of the houses. There's an old wives' tale that says certain minerals gradually seep out of the stone and can drive a person insane! Just an old wives' tale of course. Anyway," he laughed, "you will be pleased to know that our house isn't built with that particular stone!"

He pulled into a long driveway, "Here we are, then!"

Coming across the drive, was a small, rather bent, elderly woman, wearing a shapeless woollen dress and thick stockings; she waved vigorously when she saw us. When I got out of the

car she took my hand and, smiling into my eyes, greeted me.
"How nice to meet you Emily, we have heard so much about you.
I'm Mrs Woods, Ann's mother, but you must call me Mama as
Ann does. Tell me dear, what was your trip like, it can be very
bumpy, that crossing?"

"Yes it was very bumpy because of the fog, maybe it would be
easier by sea?"

"No, it can be a dreadful sea voyage dear, dreadful. Ah well,
it is one of the difficulties of living here. Come along in and we
will have a nice cup of tea. As you know, Ann has been in Paris
but she will be back tomorrow, so then you"ll have more
company."

She took me to my room. Through the wide window the sea
sparkled and danced in the sunlight, with a few wisps of fog here
and there.

"The land you can see over there," she explained, "is France."

"How far away is it?"

"Not far - about 15 miles - and this property goes all the way
down the hill as far as you can see. Hard work for the gardener.
The kitchen garden 's around at the back and that's where I keep
chickens. We have lovely fresh eggs and now and then we have
one of the hens to eat. Things aren't as scarce now of course,
but when we first came here, not very long after the Germans left,
having chickens was really essential and to be able to make a
nice chicken stew was quite a treat, but, as I say, things are much
better now although some things are still rationed. You come
along down when you are ready and Mattie will bring us tea, I am
sure you will be ready for a cup."

It was thrilling to be here at last, far from Canada and New
York, on this little island closer to France than to England -
France was so close I could actually see it. The island seemed
peaceful and beautiful, thank goodness. It was a relief and
comforting to be with family after New York and the long sea
journey, surrounded all the time by total strangers. My uncle so
jolly and pleasant, Aunt Ann was bound to be nice, like her
mother. I relaxed and that wonderful feeling of happiness began
to seep back. I wondered if there had been a letter from Stanley
yet. I must never ever tell him what happened, never.

I will have to stop thinking about it, There are so many nice
things to think about now and it doesn't really matter that my
secret plan didn't work out, maybe once in London I will be able
to arrange something that will fit in with the ballet academy.

I looked again in the mirror. As far as I could see I looked the same as before. Fortunately no one could see the huge bruise across my lower back and luckily the horrible scratches were so high on my thigh no one could ever see those either, even in a bathing suit and anyway they were nearly invisible already. My back still hurt and sometimes if I moved a certain way the pain was terrible but eventually it would all heal and I would be fine again. The important thing is to forget it.

After I was shown the other downstairs rooms, my uncle joined us in the drawing room, Mattie brought in the tea and we were introduced.

"I suppose you would like coffee for breakfast - all Americans like coffee according to the films!"

"That would be lovely! Yes - but I'm Canadian! We're a little different from the Americans you know, but I do like coffee!"

Mattie laughed at this and said she had seen lots of American films and they had given her a good idea of what life is like over there - and Canada is so near it must be nearly the same. Mama clucked and said "That will be all Mattie, thank you."

"What time will Madam be in tomorrow?" Mattie asked, as she turned to leave us. Late afternoon was the reply, she would be in for the evening meal. "It will be nice to have her back," said Mrs Woods, turning to me, "we have missed her. Shall we go out into the garden for a spell?"

It was late in the afternoon the next day when we heard Uncle Cedric's car pull up. The front door flew open - a gust of woman rushed into the room! This was Aunt Ann, stunningly elegant in a very chic, black, tweed suit with a black velvet collar, her hair, dark and glistening in clouds, framed her vivacious face - she effervesced! Her smile was warm and her shiny chestnut eyes were penetrating as they fastened to mine, then she grasped both my hands "My dear," she exclaimed, "it is so lovely to have you here, we have been looking forward to it, haven't we Mama! Won't we have fun! We'll do all sorts of things, I hope you like walking, it is so beautiful here, and this time of year there are very few holiday people about, we can walk for miles and never see a soul - and the vistas!" She laughed then and said what fun it would be to have company on her long walks.

She moved quickly about the room, laughing and saying how wonderful Paris was, at the same time tossing her silky furs from around her neck on to a chair. "We must go there together someday" she said, looking at me with her wonderful smile. Uncle Cedric said little. He offered her a cigarette from his gold cigarette case then held the matching lighter for her, Ann raised her arm gracefully in an elegant arc, tilted her head back and smiled warmly at her husband as he lit her cigarette. Her eyes seemed to glow with happiness as she thanked him and carefully blew smoke into the air beside him.

Next morning, the good smell of brewing coffee greeted me as I came down the stairs to have breakfast, which Mattie served in the "Morning Room", a bright cheery room with the sunlight streaming in the windows. Ann was pouring the coffee, "Are you going to have some now or would you rather wait and have it after you have a bite to eat?   Suddenly the smell of the coffee made me feel ill and I felt a little dizzy. Are you alright honey? You look a little pale. Well it's not surprising really, all that travelling and strange places and people, I expect you need a little rest time, but you should eat a little you know."
She passed me a piece of buttered bread, "eat this and you'll feel much better, I know you will."
I took the bread and slowly nibbled at it and did feel a little better. As Ann sipped the strong coffee and ate the buttered French bread with fruit conserves, she explained how she usually spent the mornings. "After we do the household shopping" she said, "we will go and have our Elevenses - Elevenses are an important part of our mornings here - not just important - essential! There's a wonderful pâtisserie in the town, called "The Buttery" where all sorts of people get together to chat, drink delicious coffee and of course eat the gorgeous French pastries that are made on the premises. Do you have Elevenses in Canada?"
"Not really; people at business stop for a coffee break but they don't call it elevenses and I guess not many people have access to French pastries in the mornings."
"What a shame!" she said, "Coffee break sounds so dull! Having the right name for it makes such a difference, don't you think, even without the pastries?"

Having finished the morning's shopping, we linked arms and Ann propelled us to the pâtisserie. Still linked to me, she rushed us over to chat to one of the chaps sipping coffee. "Look," she said, "just look John, who I have brought you! Isn't it marvellous - she is all the way from Vancouver. Meet Emily! Emily, this is John."

"Well," he said, smiling and friendly, "so you are from Vancouver Emily, a place I have always wanted to visit; some of the   architecture, especially in the west is so different and interesting. Maybe I'll get there yet, one never knows. You must tell me all about it someday. How would you like to come sailing with us? We're racing around the Minquiers on Sunday. I have room for you if you'd like to come and crew for us? You do know something about sailing don't you - I mean, living in Vancouver, I would expect you to?"

Ann piped up, "Oh yes, I should have warned you Emily - John here, would like to sail all the hours of the day, the passion of your life, isn't that right John?"   He laughed, "Yes, so far! I have a small sloop - a pretty thing, very sea-worthy. We do some great sailing you know, sometimes we go to France. Would you like to come?"

I looked at his pleasant, weathered, round, brown face, the sparse fair hair sprinkled unevenly on his head and his faded blue eyes, crinkled at the corners. Nice eyes.

"I'd love to, but I've done very little real sailing. I used to sail in the summers with my brother, but that was ages ago and in rather calm waters, not the English Channel, but I guess I could learn!"

"Fine!   Be at St Aubins Harbour at eight, don't forget now, Sunday morning."

The early morning air was sharp and clear and the sunlight dazzling as we drove along that Sunday morning beside the still and silent, deep-blue sea. The tide was out. At the far end of the quay we saw some chaps stowing and setting up.

"I'll leave you here, I must say I'd rather you than me, honey!" Ann said, as she gave me a farewell hug, "Have fun!"

I walked along to the end of the quay.   It certainly was a beautiful day, and I was feeling better. I called to them, "Hi there! Hi!" I waved and called again.

They all stopped what they were doing and waved back "Hello Hello!". One of the chaps came over and told me to come down the ladder at the end of the quay. "You'll have to jump the last few feet! Think you can manage that!"

I laughed, "Of course I can!" (I did wonder how my back would react.) He came and stood at the bottom of the ladder. I jumped the last few feet; as I landed a terrible pain shot up my spine, I managed a smile, as he grabbed my hand, "Well done! Well done! Umm - you smell nice, what do you call that? I'm Lawrence - and you must be Emily."

John came over, "I'm glad you're on time! By the way, although your aunt calls me John, most people call me JB. B for Briggs."

We walked along to the boat where the other two chaps were. John introduced me. "Peter's my brother, a sculptor, lives in the south of England. Philip lives here, owns a men's clothing shop and of course you've already met 'Lawrence the architect' same as me."

"Is this the whole crew?"

"Yip!"

"I'm the only girl then?"

"Yip!" They all laughed.

"She's a pretty thing isn't she? Gets quite cold sometimes - no cabin for shelter you notice, hope you brought a woolly."

"Actually I didn't."

"Never mind - it looks to be a warm day and I have something you can wear if need be."

The name of the boat was Josephine. I was curious to know who it had been named after as it seemed an unusual name for a boat. It turned out it had been his mother's name. I thought that was lovely to name it after his mother. Yes, he said, she had been thrilled to have the boat named after her but she had since died. He said he still missed her.

Because there was very little wind, the sail to the Minquiers was slow. As the morning progressed it became very warm, my smart navy-blue slacks and pink- and navy-striped cotton-knit shirt that I had bought in New York were far too warm for the day as it turned out. JB offered me an old pair of his swim trunks and a large thin cotton shirt which I was very happy to accept.

There were several yachts trying to catch a breeze, all milling about. The Sea Dolphin (a large white yacht with mahogany trim) was near and the captain shouted over that they were floating over some beer. Peter passed around hunks of French bread and chunks of cheese. The weather was the main topic, as, although it was a race, there was not any racing being done. The Sea Dolphin picked up a trickle of wind and gradually left us behind. I was wishing I hadn't partaken of the beer as I was desperate for a loo! An embarrassing situation, but I knew I would have to think of something and soon!

Stowed in the bow, I saw a blanket and a bailing can and realized that this would be my salvation! I asked JB if he would pass them to me, then I wrapped the blanket around my waist, positioned the bailing can.

"Now then, will everyone turn their heads seaward and whistle or sing! I have to spend a penny - if I don't I shall burst!"

There was much laughter and joking as they all looked seaward and sang some college shanty.

Although it was an embarrassing situation for me, no one seemed to be at all perturbed, in fact they seemed to find the situation highly amusing.

Lawrence, who was looking after the tiller, was a handsome man, tall, well-built, with dark, curly hair, brown eyes and a moustache! His voice was deep, cultured and he had a very precise way of speaking. He caught me looking at him, smiled and sort of winked. "Would I be allowed, Emily, to take you out sometime do you think?"

He looked very old to be dating! "Are you a married man?"

"Goodness me no! What in the world made you ask that?"

"I don't really know, except that you look like you could be. I would hate to go out with anyone who is married!"

"No need to worry about that, I certainly am not. Not yet."

"Then I'm sure you would be allowed to!"

"When would suit you? How about a Sunday? I could pick you up and we can go to the beach near where you live. There is an especially lovely little cove there called Rozel, my favourite actually. We can swim, go for a walk and then have a little dinner together at my flat. How does that sound?"

"In your flat?"

"Yes that's what I thought and then I would take you home, not late you know." He chuckled, "Mustn't keep you out past your bed-time must I?" She looked at him, he looked so nice, pleasant and so polite she was sure it would be alright and yet the idea of being alone with him in his flat might not be approved of, Aunt Ann might not like that. I didn't say anything but thought that I could make an excuse when the time came if I didn't feel comfortable doing that.

We arranged for two o'clock on the following Sunday.

"So Lawrence has you all booked up!" JB was saying as we drove away from the harbour. "Quick off the mark, I would say! Beat me to it, he did! Nice bloke Lawrence, very nice and clever too, well liked around here, hasn't bothered with girls as far as I know, so you must have caught his eye! It was nice having you with us today Emily, I hope you'll crew for me again, will you?"

"Oh yes I should love to, any time, and thank you so much for inviting me to-day! There certainly wasn't much to do though, was there, but I enjoyed it."

The chosen Sunday was a grey day. Underneath my navy-blue, short shorts, I was wearing my brief, bright, buttercup-yellow bathing suit. The little cove that we went to was small and sheltered, with a sandy beach. A few stone cottages were tucked amongst the trees, higgeldy-piggeldy on the hill, coming right down to the shore. There was a little tearoom too and some people were carrying trays with teapot, cups and saucers and scones down to the beach where there were deck chairs dotted about. It seemed sort of old-fashioned, like something people would have done fifty years ago or more. I had never seen anything like this before and thought it all charming. Nobody at home took trays of tea to the beach, only hotdogs and hamburgers, or fish and chips, or pop, things like that. I loved the idea of having tea and scones on the beach, which is what we did after our rather chilly swim, but I had to talk Lawrence into getting it as he said it was really too late for tea and bound to be very expensive. Anyway it was lovely sitting there on the beach on the deck chairs having proper afternoon tea from cups and saucers with scones and thick Jersey cream and jam. Lawrence had fetched the car rug so we tucked it over our legs and were quite cosy. I didn't mind a bit when Lawrence said that because we had tea so late, the meal at his flat would have to be postponed to another time. I was a little relieved even though JB had said what a nice chap Lawrence was, I was still glad I wasn't going to his flat; after all, I didn't know him at all yet. He didn't mention the expense of the tea again so maybe it wasn't so expensive after all.

He swam the way old men swam at home! The side-stroke and the breast-stroke! My mother too swam like that. "You swim the way my mother swims - and old people" I said. "I suppose you don't like to get your face wet!" He laughed, sort of. "I'm sure it was very different in Canada", his voice was prim. "You see, here in England, we went to the sea-side for only two weeks in the summer when I was young. At boarding school we didn't swim of course, I really learned to swim during the war." "The war? Were you in the war? Were you a pilot? My brother wanted to be a pilot." "Yes I was in the war Emily - people my age had to go to war whether they wanted to or not! No I wasn't a pilot - anyway, the war is not something I wish to talk about now, or ever really. By the by, how old are you?"

I told him I was eighteen going on nineteen.

"I thought you were very young Emily, but perhaps not quite as young as that! Never mind, I find you quite charming. You certainly wear your hair in a most unusual way, it is very attractive and I must say you do have a beautiful figure. I'd like to take some photos of you, you wouldn't mind would you?"

"No, I guess I wouldn't mind - although I really don't like having my photograph taken."

I was flattered that such a man of the world found me so attractive. Stanley had never said anything like this, ever. At the end of the day he asked if he could see me again. "I shall give you a ring, it will be during the week, Tinkerbell!"

I laughed, puzzled, "Tinkerbell?"

"That's you - you know - definitely Tinkerbell!"

I thought it rather sweet that he wanted to call me Tinkerbell - maybe it was because of my haircut.

He got out of the car and held the car door open for me and as I turned to run up the path he caught me to him. He didn't kiss me, it was a sort of hug and then he held both my hands, "Nice day" he said, "I hope you enjoyed it too and you do swim beautifully!" He turned then and got into his car, "Cheerio" I heard him call as I ran up the path. I waved.

I knew now that Lawrence was a nice honourable man and that I needn't be afraid of him. I was so glad he had not tried to kiss me. I still felt sick when I thought of kisses, but not Stanley's kisses – no, they were so sweet and full of love and tenderness.

"How would you like a trip to France," JB asked when he telephoned. "Come and crew for me - there'll be another couple, they are friends of mine from England? You'll be away one night, maybe two - depends on the weather, of course. Bring some francs!"

I didn't ask if Lawrence would be going but I rather gathered not. I accepted, thrilled at the invitation.

It was not a very strong wind that pushed us across the Channel, but strong enough to give us a good sail and keep everyone busy! My uncle had warned me that the English Channel could be a very frightening place even for an experienced sailor. I had never been in weather that had frightened me. In the late afternoon the wind changed and suddenly the rigging rattled wildly. The little boat came alive as the sky darkened, the water looked cold and sinister as it tossed us about and rolled in over us. The woman from England was feeling squeamish, she told me she thought she was going to be sick, her face was very pale and she looked miserable. I tried to reassure her by smiling, but I was pretty frightened; she had come more for the trip to France than the sail, she told me. I looked over at JB, he was calm and full of smiles. "Quite fun!" he chirped. I didn't think it that much fun although I did not feel ill, but in this tiny boat it was certainly scary. He went on to tell us that we were near Chausey, a small island off the coast of France. All the yachts would be stopping there - "We often stop there if the weather looks difficult. There's one small inn where we can dry off and have a good meal and if the weather 's reasonable the following day we'll go straight home, no pottering about I'm afraid, as the weather looks as if it's changed - not terrible though." The English couple were visibly relieved.

It was peaceful as we walked up from the little harbour, seemingly everything undisturbed by the passing of time - tiny, whitewashed cottages; here and there, goats strolled about companionably with hens and cows on little, green fields. Tall trees shaded small farmhouses tucked in little hollows. It was so peaceful, but only a few years before, the Germans had marched around in their warrior helmets and uniforms, frightening the inhabitants of this tranquil oasis. It was truly a delight to experience this unusual, tiny island. I imagined immediately that I would like to have been a farmer's daughter and lived right here forever!

JB said he would like to order my dinner. "Something you'll love - I guarantee it!" he said with enthusiasm. "Lobster á la mayonnaise and we'll have a bottle of champagne to go with it!"

The lobster arrived in its pink shell with the flesh covered in a creamy-looking sauce. I took a mouthful, delicious - and the bread, freshly baked, still warm, all crunchy on the outside and soft and milky on the inside. I thickly spread the creamy, deep-yellow butter on it and took a bite; it was so good I thought I would like to eat the whole loaf! I didn't much like fizzy drinks but I liked the wonderful dreamy, floaty and a little dizzy feeling in my head as I sipped the sparkling champagne. A pastry oozing caramelized apples that smelled strongly of cinnamon, topped with clotted cream was our dessert. As we were drinking our coffee, the proprietress came to the table. Small, looking frail and bent, in sombre black, she said that someone had told her that there was a young lady here from Canada - "Yes?"

"Yes, I am Canadian." I told her. Then, with a big smile showing many gaps in her teeth, she said she would like me to go with her - she had something she would like to show me.

Puzzled, I got up from the table and went with her. I looked back at JB, he just gave me a wink and shrugged his shoulders. The old lady took me through the dining-room then into a large pantry where she pulled up a worn, rag rug from the floor. She then lifted a trapdoor and beneath it there was a ladder. Quickly and neatly she went down first and then beckoned to me.

"Come now!" she said as she shone her torch for me. At the bottom of the ladder I jumped and landed on hard earth. The sudden jump jarred my back and took my breath away, a worry I had tried to avoid thinking about. The smell of stale, damp air filled my nostrils, making me feel a little sick and the thick darkness was horrible. Out of the darkness, I heard her quietly speaking, "I keep Canadian soldiers. I hide them until they can be picked up and taken to safety. I do this all in war. Nobody know. Germans come but no suspect. I never get caught, soldiers never get caught."

She laughed a little. "Not nice down here - but safe, very safe. They get away! All get away. I happy woman!"

I imagined our soldiers in that dank, dark cellar with Germans stomping around upstairs looking for them, such desperate fear they must have felt as they froze, frightened to breathe. She smiled at me, "I am happy woman - très heureuse, très! I did all I could for them. Very safe here. Canadian soldiers good men, I want to help."

I thanked her for showing me this hide-out, "Such courage," I told her, "you must have been very frightened!" She just smiled and chuckled, "We fooled those Germans, Yes! Very good, yes!" "Yes," I said, "very very good." We shook hands, she kept on smiling and shaking her head, "Yes good, very good!" We climbed up the ladder and I went back to the table and told JB the story.

"Quite remarkable. You were lucky to hear her story, makes one stop and think doesn't it, how very brave some people are, so completely unselfish, quite wonderful. If she had been found out she would most probably have been shot. I don't suppose she has told many people her story and probably never shown anyone else her secret hide-away - it would have been too dangerous. Maybe someday her story will be told, not that she would want any recognition for her heroic actions I'm sure.

"Now then Emily, I have booked a room for you for the night. The others will be staying here too. I shall sleep on the boat. No cabin, you know, wouldn't want anything to be meddled with - best to be on the safe side I always think. I'll see you at breakfast. Good-night, my dear, sleep well. Unless of course you would like to sleep on the boat as well!" He laughed!

The morning was bright and clear with a strong wind - excellent sailing weather. So a taste of France was all I was to have, a very small taste. I was a little disappointed!

When JB dropped me at the house, he said he would like me and my aunt and uncle to dine with him one evening.

"I'll ring your uncle in the morning." He thanked me for coming, "You did well" he told me, "Were you nervous?"

"Well, those waves did look huge as they came towards us and I was pretty frightened I guess. My uncle had warned me that the English Channel could be very rough."

"It looked worse than it was you know. I have been in seas a lot worse than that one!"

"Well I'm glad I wasn't with you!"

"I am too, It can be frightening even for an experienced sailor like myself but I respect the sea and my long experience has made me a very cautious sailor. Well, it was a pleasure to have you on board, so I hope I haven't frightened you away!"
"No, not yet - but it was getting close!"

My aunt and uncle accepted JB's invitation. The yacht club was not only the place where his boat lived, it was where he lived as well. His apartment overlooked the harbour and was furnished lightly, with modern furniture. He explained that all of his meals were prepared for him in the club's kitchen and that the stewardess would bring the dinner and that she would serve.

"So," he said, "we have nearly an hour until then. Now then Emily," he looked over to me with his twinkling eyes, "would you be very sweet and obliging and dance for us before we have our dinner? I love ballet and would love to see you dance a little."

I was surprised at this request; after all it was a dinner party, but I was rather pleased too, I always loved to dance and anyway, how could I refuse? I hadn't done any dancing since New York, I just hoped my back would be alright, not hurt.

I looked over to my uncle, wondering what on earth he thought of this idea! "Come on Honey, have a go!" Ann all smiles and enthusiastic.

My uncle then lit his pipe, "Yes, yes - let's see what you have been up to with this dancing business!"

"I'll put some Tchaikovsky on, Emily – Waltz of the Flowers, will that suit?"

"Yes perfect." I said. "But only a bit of it you know."

"Of course. Of course, I'll turn it off as soon as you decide to finish."

I took my shoes off and stood up. I was glad I was wearing my dress with the pleated skirt - it was not a large room so my performance would be very limited. My arms in first position, I stood still for a moment waiting for the music to take me into the dance. Pleasure filled me. I moved around the room in gentle turns, glissade to the right and the left ending in an arabesque ordinaire, a few more turns, a petit jeté ending in the waltz step, after which I dropped into a deep curtsy. The music stopped, my uncle clapped with vigour and gave me a big smile. "Well done, well done! Most enjoyable!"

"Honey, that was sheer pleasure to watch, wasn't it, John?"

JB was sitting very still, looking at me. "Yes," he said, "yes it was, now dinner. Thank you, Emily."

At home the next day, Uncle Cedric said he would like a word with me. "Come in, come in, Emily, sit down, love. You've been here quite a while now haven't you, what about your dancing? We enjoyed your little performance last evening and of course I suddenly realized that nothing has been done about it. Your mother will wonder what has happened! What are your plans, apart from all this sailing and socializing! We have some friends just outside London and they say they would love to have you stay with them whilst you get yourself sorted out at a dance academy with lessons and a place to live. How would that suit you?"

A little embarrassed, I said that I really would like to stay right through until the end of the summer. Then in September go to London. I told him I had been thinking that I would like to find a job of some sort here on the island.

"Well Emily, that is not necessary you know. Your allowance from the family trustees is more than adequate. What would you need more money for? If you would like to stay here a bit longer, that is fine with us. As long as you like - but you'll have to do the explaining to your mother! She will be expecting you to be getting on with your career, you shouldn't worry her you know. Is it a good idea to be taking the whole summer off? I thought dancers had to be at it all the time."

"Well you are right, they do. I probably really shouldn't take the summer off, but perhaps I won't be able to ever again. I don't think mother will mind too much - I shouldn't think it would worry her really, after all, one summer isn't that long of a delay is it? I'll write and tell her all about it. I know I don't really need the money either but I would love to get a job here and the extra money might be useful when I am in London. Would you mind if I did, Uncle Cedric?"

"No, Emily, it is entirely up to you. Would your mother approve?"

"Oh yes, she would definitely - she doesn't approve of young people sitting about doing nothing and if I am not going to dance classes she will be wondering what on earth I am doing all day. I have had lots of summer jobs, I like the feeling of independence I have with my own earned money and mother wants me to be an independent type of woman, she has always said that."

"Well then, it's fine with me, love, if you are sure this won't upset your mother. We mustn't do that you know. You should write to her immediately and tell her your plans so she is fully aware of what you are doing and make certain that she understands you will be carrying on with the original plan in September. I don't want her cross with me because of your shenanigans."

I wrote the letter.

And so it was arranged, a whole summer here, I thought, it was going to be great fun.

Now I must write to Stanley and tell him my plans, his letters had been disappointing, not at all what I had hoped for. I had really expected him to write more lovingly but somehow all he ever writes about is what he is doing at university or his exams or the latest record he has bought and of course there is always stuff about his car. When we were together he was so different from that.

Ann had taken me to a small exclusive shop in the centre of town which sold silk lingerie and French perfume on the main floor and, upstairs, dresses were modelled and sold as well. I hadn't given any thought as to what type of work I should try for, but as I was near the shop I decided to go in and ask. Instead of being taken to the manager's office, the manager came to meet me, holding out her hand and introducing herself. "I am Madame Corbette. So then what can I do for you, young lady. You say you want to see me?"

"Well yes, I wondered if there were any openings here for a sales clerk?"

"Have you experience?"

"No," I told her, "none."

"Well, well I suppose we could try you out, see how you like it with our busy season coming up. Have you done modelling?" Only for artists I told her, in my ballet leotard and things like that for them to draw.

"Oh I see, ballet, that explains your posture, I am sure you would make a good model. We have a sewing room at the very top of the building where we make up some of our own dresses. It could be useful if you were to model these for us - you look to be a nicely-proportioned size 10 - very popular size. Let me see you walk, just a few steps. Yes, you walk well too, so important. Why don't you come in tomorrow, be here at nine - I will show you around and take you to the work room, then if you think you would like to give it a try, you can stay. How does that sound?"

It sounded fun. I accepted, but in the excitement I forgot that Saturdays were often sailing days and I would have to work Saturdays. Still, I was pretty excited about getting the job, a new experience, different from anything I had ever done before and I would learn how to model as well.

"I shall miss you! And how will JB get along without you?" Ann was quick to realize what I had completely forgotten about in the excitement.

"Oh Ann, I thought about that after I had accepted and it is a shame, but maybe I won't miss all of the sailing Saturdays and maybe there will be some sailing Sundays as well! And I did get the job and I have never done anything like it before, I have never worked in a shop and I have never modelled before except at the art school, so it will be a completely new experience for me."

"Yes honey and I'm pleased for you and I'm sure there will be lots of sailing Sundays and there are always the Bank holidays too. I'm sure that John will be sailing on all of those, so don't fret honey. It looks like some of our long walks will have to be taken on non-sailing days but there are bound to be some of those days too."

In the morning I took the early bus and arrived at the shop at eight thirty. Madame Corbette greeted me quite enthusiastically. "I am so glad that you came early. Now I can show you everything without interruptions. Are you American?"

"No, I'm Canadian, from Vancouver."

"What in the world brought you here?"

I explained it all and told her about my uncle and the art gallery he owned in the town. I didn't mention my ballet plans.

"I see, really just visiting, so how long will you be here then?"

I told her I was not sure at all, but certainly for a couple of months.

She nodded approval, "I guess you were bored then?" After she had shown me around the whole shop, we went up the stairs to meet the seamstresses who did all the alterations and made many of the dresses that were sold in the shop. "You will like them, only with silk we make" Madame Corbette told me. She went on to say that visitors from many countries came here to purchase "because of no tax you see - even very exclusive dresses inexpensive here.   Now, I shall leave you here to be measured and I know you will enjoy modelling them and if you decide to purchase one yourself I can give you a bit of a discount."

I hadn't been working there long when a dress was ready for me! I put it on, a simple white silk with princess lines. Madame Corbette came to inspect.

"Yes," she said "with your tan, this is perfect! There is another dress being made for you now in a different style. We will see how they sell before we make any more of these."

Being a saleslady was not much fun at all, as some of the clients were fussy, hard to please and difficult to fit into the outfits they wanted. I found it rather tedious and uninteresting, apart from the modelling. I was also noticing how my back ached when I stood for any length of time. Sunny Saturdays were difficult to endure! When JB phoned and asked me if I would like to go shrimping with him at lunch time I didn't hesitate, what a wonderful way to spend my lunch-time. "We'll take the shrimps to the yacht club and the stewardess will prepare us a delicious lunch!"

"I mustn't be late back though!"

The seamstress overheard the conversation as the telephone was in the work room.

"If you're a little late, come up the back way, our entrance - and no one will know. You can slip into the showroom, pretending you have been up seeing me. Don't be too late though!"

JB was parked down the street. I saw his car and ran to it. "Don't you ever walk anywhere?" he teased. "Even when you walk, you nearly run! Hop in and we'll go and find those shrimps. By the way, what is that perfume you wear, it's rather nice, I enjoy getting a whiff of it from time to time."

I told him it was "Je Reviens", the only perfume I ever wore. He turned then and looked at me, "I do like it - I've never heard of it before, I don't usually like perfume." He reached over and patted my hand. "You're a nice young thing Emily."

The shrimps were plentiful, it took no time at all to have enough for our lunch. While we waited for the stewardess to prepare them we sipped a gin and tonic. It was heavenly sitting outside in the sun with the sea right there, blue and beautiful, eating and chatting, but time was running out and I began to get a little nervous.

"I really must get back - I don't want to get fired!"

"Why not, you could marry me, I'll look after you!"   He laughed! I laughed too!

"Come on then, we had best get you back.   How about Sunday for a sail?"

"I would have loved to but I did promise I would go to the beach and swimming with Lawrence again, he seems to love to take me swimming - although he's not a great swimmer he loves to swim."

"Mmmm - I see, that's nice, I'm glad - well then, how about the Sunday after?"

"Yes, perfect! I would love to."

"Do you really like your job?   Why don't you learn to type and then you could work for me?   No work on Saturdays - or any other day you feel like doing something else!"   I wasn't sure whether this was a serious question or not.   I liked the idea of not working on Saturdays but the idea of working in an office - even a very nice architect's office - did not appeal to me.   I had to admit though, that selling dresses wasn't very exciting, but I wasn't planning to do it forever, I told him, and I wasn't.

"Yes of course, I forget that you will be leaving us, too bad that is, too bad, but don't go too soon Emily, will you, you want to be here for the Battle of Flowers you know, has your aunt told you about it?"

"No she hasn't actually."

"Well, I can't do it justice with my simple words but it's a parade of flower-covered cars, lorries and wagons - a luscious mass of flowers moving down the streets, every flower you have ever known or thought of is there in glorious abundance.   A celebration one could say, of flowers.   I don't know the date of it exactly but I shall let you know when I know."

"What a wonderful sort of celebration, I would love to see it!"

"Yes you must and what's more, after the parade is over the flowers are torn from the vehicles and tossed everywhere!   Great fun, and it's definitely a party night!"

Sunday with Lawrence was quiet, peaceful.   We went swimming in one of the beautiful small coves that he liked so much. I loved these quiet coves, the empty beaches, the feeling of freedom that always captured me when I was near the sea, it was like a huge surge of life that electrified me, that made me leap and run with abandon but I had to be a little careful now as lately my leaps and landings had been accompanied with a sharp pain low in my back that was beginning to be hard to ignore.

He loved these days with her. He loved to watch her in her bright, sunny-yellow bathing costume, dancing and leaping into the air - so uninhibited in her joyfulness. He loved to hear that clear, open laugh and waited for her to call him. He ran to her, but she had gone! Skipped off laughing, then dived into the water and swam away from him, her long graceful strokes cutting neatly into the water. He waited, watching her with pleasure. He called to her, "Photo time!" He knew she didn't really like having her photo taken but he did want to capture her in that joy - she just exuded happiness - and in that bathing costume, what there was of it. He must ask her about that mark on her back sometime, he had not noticed it before, maybe some sort of birth mark.
He took as many pictures as she would allow. He put the camera down and she came to him.

We drove all around the island. He showed me the different areas, places that he particularly liked. Afterwards we went to his flat where he prepared a little meal: scrambled eggs and toast, ice cream and coffee. We listened to some music. "You seem to be going about with JB rather a lot?" he said, looking at me very seriously, no smile, "He's nearly forty you know."
I was annoyed. "It's not what you think, Lawrence - we are good friends, that is all. Everyone tells me this, even Mattie has mentioned it! I am truly sick of hearing it. It's not like I am going to marry him, you know! After all, I enjoy crewing for him and he likes to have me."
He looked at me and frowned, "I certainly hope you are not going to marry him, Emily! He really is much too old for you!"
"Actually, I don't like this conversation Lawrence and it's time I went home! All I do is crew for him." My voice started to escalate.
He got up quickly, "Yes yes of course," he said, as he pulled

me to my feet and put his arms around me, "dear Tinkerbell," he whispered, "I didn't mean to annoy you."

He kissed me, but I pulled away, I wasn't sure if I wanted his kisses, "Come on," I said, "come on!"

He went to get the car keys and when he came back he put his arms around me again. I ducked out of his arms and ran to the door. "Oh do come now Lawrence, do!"

He thought she was probably too young for him, but he felt very drawn to her, to her youth, her energy, her joyfulness, the way she moved was so beautiful - so lovely to watch. It was exciting to be with her. She is so refreshing. He loves to hold her and kiss her soft young skin and feel her supple body close to his. She however, cools very quickly when he allows his emotions to run away and it is becoming harder and harder for him to hold back. She said she's a virgin and intended to stay that way until she married. She apparently wouldn't be going to bed with him! That was a bit of a blow, but then what could he expect with such a young thing. Really, although he would love to make love to her, he is quite glad that she is such a moral sort of person - it pleases him. He has never been attracted to anyone before, not like this, and if he were to be honest with himself, he is already more than a little in love with her, yes much more than a little, much more.

"I'll ring you during the week" he said as he let me out of the car. "How about your day off?" He took hold of my hand.

I told him that I was going to spend the afternoon with Françoise, my new friend from the shop who had just been moved into my department.

Although Françoise was 28, married with a little girl, one would never have guessed she had such responsibilities. She was so vivacious, and seemingly carefree. I thought she was very exotic with her black, curly hair, dark-brown eyes and olive skin. I loved her strong French accent. Often we had lunch together, laughing and chatting like schoolgirls.

We had planned our Sunday at the beach early in the week and she had invited me to have supper with them at their farm, I was really looking forward to the occasion, I told him.

"A pity - I guess I shall just have to do without you for once, won't I?"

He looked at me in such a way I was sorry I had not let him

kiss me more, I felt suddenly I would have liked it, and in my heart I knew it would be alright and yet sometimes the thought of anyone at all kissing me made me shudder.

The day at the beach with Françoise was not a great success as it became cloudy and quite chilly. We returned to the farm early to find that Françoise' husband Pierre was in the kitchen preparing the meal. "He loves to cook, he is very good at it too, aren't you cheri" Françoise said happily as we left him in the kitchen and entered the huge living-room. The table was set, ready for the meal, a stone fireplace occupied the length of one wall. I had never seen a fireplace like that before. "We put whole trees in that fireplace! Emily, wait until you are here at Christmas, you'll love it, I know! You must visit us for Christmas, even if you are living in London, you will have to come; you must."

"Come in, come in," Françoise beckoned to the fair-haired girl waiting politely in the doorway. She looked about 14. "This is Louise, my daughter."

"But she is so grown up!" I said.

"Yes, I was married at 16. I got pregnant!"

She giggled, "It wasn't all my fault, was it, cheri", she called to her husband.

"Of course it was all your fault! Anyway what are you complaining about, you have a lovely daughter. You should stay at home and be a proper wife and mother instead of working and gallivanting about, the way that you do!"

"Oh phphphhp, don't start all that now, Pierre! He does not like me to have a job! I like to have a job, I do NOT like to be stuck here all day! I get so bored."

"You wouldn't get so bored if you did a little work now and then!" Pierre called out.

At dinner Pierre told us that there was to be a dance - a fund-raising dance, one of the Royals would be there but for the life of him he couldn't remember which one. He had bought four tickets. "Emily, why don't you and your boyfriend, Lawrence isn't it, come with us? That would be nice, wouldn't it Françoise?"

"Yes - Emily, do come."

I would love to go to the dance. I would ask Lawrence. It would be nice to go to a dance with him; he is probably a very good dancer, he being so much older and so sophisticated. I told them I would ask Lawrence and let them know right away.

That evening I telephoned Lawrence and invited him to escort me. To my surprise he said no, he did not want to go to the dance.
"Why ever not?"
"I don't care for such occasions." he replied.
"Well if you won't come with me, there are plenty of other pebbles on the beach!" I was very angry, how could he refuse! Then to my astonishment he said, "I dare say there are."

As soon as the words were out of his mouth he regretted them. He could have gone this once, just to please her and it no doubt would have been very pleasant to dance with her. Just because he was tired of dances from his Army days he should not spoil her fun. A mistake, he quickly realized, but not quickly enough. Before he had the chance to tell her he had changed his mind, she had said good-bye and had hung up!

I could not understand anyone not wanting to go to a dance! I telephoned Françoise and told her how disappointed I was, as I would really have liked to have gone, I felt I should not ask JB as second choice, it would be rude and might hurt his feelings. Françoise, laughed, "You know, I am glad, very glad! We know the perfect escort for you! Perfect! You'll like him, I know it!"
She chuckled with delight! "I can hardly wait to tell him what I have found for him! Is that fine with you?" I said yes, of course it was, but I was hurt and disappointed, I had expected Lawrence to want to come with me.

My evening dress still fitted but it seemed a little tight, all the Jersey cream beginning to show! The white silk strapless bodice did look good on my suntanned skin and the flowing black silk skirt accentuated my still neat waistline, although it was definitely a little larger than it had been. Françoise was wearing an all-white dress and with her dark hair and brown eyes she looked stunning!
Waiting at the table was my escort! He stood up as soon as he saw us approach. Françoise introduced us. "Emily - Paul,

Paul – Emily." He held out his hand and looked right into my eyes. "How do you do, Emily." He smiled, very pleased with what he saw, she was like no one he had ever seen before! And her voice! "Where on earth did you find her, Françoise?" he jokingly asked! "Where?"

I laughed and told him about my visit with my uncle and aunt. "Have you lived here long, Paul?"

"Yes, all my life, apart from a spell in England at boarding school of course. My parents have lived here all their lives too and their parents and so on! Well, we don't go back to the stone age exactly, but William the Conqueror perhaps! We are the authentic Jersey French, aren't we, Françoise! We were here during the German occupation too."

"Really? How frightening it must have been, I would love to hear all about that."

"Any time you like -" he said, smiling, "although it is not a very pleasant subject I must admit". He wanted to dance all the time - every dance!

"Your hair cut." he said. "Rather unusual isn't it? Do all Canadian girls wear their hair like that?" He didn't wait for an answer! "Shall we dance? Are your feet nearly dropping off?"

"No, never!"

"Would you let me take you home Emily when you're ready?"

"Yes that would be lovely."

In the car, which was a small sports car, he turned me towards him and kissed me, suddenly I was kissing him back and it was wonderfully exciting and for that short moment I had forgotten about that horrible man. "I don't mean to jump the gun you know, but you are hard to resist and I couldn't! Sorry about that, well I'm not really sorry. How about you?"

"I guess I'm not sorry either but I think we had better be going."

He saw me to the door, "I'll call you in a few days - will that be alright?"

"Yes, that will be alright" I said. I could hardly speak, I was so churned up. I looked up at him, he smiled "Lovely, lovely evening Emily." Then he was gone.

When I got to bed I started to think about Stanley and I felt guilty somehow, although he had not written many letters and they were not like I had expected either, just telling me boring things that he had been doing at university or what new record he had bought, things like that. He probably goes out with girls at the university and wouldn't expect me to stay at home and not go out with anyone at all. So really there was no need for me to feel so guilty. If I had been engaged to him it would have been different, but we weren't engaged and although we had sometimes talked about how many children we wanted to have and the sort of houses we liked, Stanley had never actually asked me to marry him - in my heart I knew we were really too young for that, he had all of his university to get through and I had only just finished my first professional year of dance. I felt better after I had thought it through, any guilt I had been feeling, lifted. Now I could let my thoughts go where they wanted to go, I closed my eyes and thought of Paul - how exciting it had been with him and how he had wanted to dance so much, and it was such fun. I thought about the kiss and felt good that it had been alright and had not made me feel frightened at all, maybe at last I was getting over that horror as I had also been alright when Lawrence kissed me. I went to sleep.

I awoke, my whole body soaking wet, I was crying and choking all at once, shuddering with heaving sobs, shouting, "leave me alone, leave me alone" as I struggled to free myself from that horrible man's claw-like grip. I could still see his face so close to mine with sweating pores, laughing and coaxing, then angry and nasty. I sat up, my back was aching badly, then I realised my back ache was really my period. I had lost track of them with all the travelling and changes in my life but now I realized this one was late, very late. Suddenly the cramps were agony I rushed to the bathroom as everything seemed to be flowing out of me in gushes, I hurt so much, I started to cry as I stumbled back to the bedroom, I needed my mum, how I wished I could see her smiling face come in the door. Oh how I needed her and Oh how I missed her. Thinking about her made me cry more, I couldn't stop. I got up and took an aspirin and decided to take two. In the morning I still felt terrible and just couldn't make the effort to get up when Ann knocked on my door. I told her what had happened, she came in and plopped down on the bed. Poor sweetie, I'll get you a hot water bottle and you just stop there until you feel better. A cup of tea is what you need. I lay back and thanked God for my wonderful Aunt Ann and cried some more and hoped and prayed I would never have another period like this one!

Paul telephoned during the week, but I had to tell him I was busy on my day off and on the Sunday.

"You are a busy girl! Tell me then, when can I see you?"

"Friday evening would be fine, if that suits you?" I felt excited just talking to him.

"I shall pick you up at seven sharp. Will your aunt and uncle be there?"

"Yes, they will - why?"

"I should like to meet them, that's all. See you at seven then!"

I put the phone down.

"What's up?" my aunt asked as I came away from the phone. "You look a little pink!"

"Paul wants to meet you, I told him you would be in when he comes to take me out - you will be, won't you?"

"Yes Honey, we will! So we are going to meet another Prince Charming! You are getting quite a collection! Well - enjoy yourself - you are only young once!"

Friday finally came. I had felt impatient for the day, wondering all the time if Paul was as nice as I had thought. When he arrived, we were all in the drawing-room, he was charming to everyone.

As we left he called back "I'll take very good care of her, don't you worry!"

We had not been driving long when he pulled over to the side of the road.

"What's the matter?"

"Nothing - well, that's not quite true; there is something the matter and I must tell you right away."

"What is it?"

He turned toward me, "Emily, I am married."

"Married? Really? Oh dear, oh dear. Why on earth are you taking me out then?"

"I'm separated - and have been for five years, but the horrible part is that although I have tried to get her to agree to a divorce she will not give me one. Not yet."

"Why not, if you really want one?"

"She thinks that some day I will take her back. She lives in Germany and consequently it makes it all very difficult. If you would like not to go any further with this, it might be best to stop it right now I think. I know I would love to carry on, but the decision must be yours. I am not free at the moment and it is doubtful when I will be free."

All I could think was - what a shame! And he was so nice too!

"I suppose we could be friends," I said at last, "couldn't we?"

"We could," he said, "but I don't think it possible for us to have a platonic relationship, not really, not honestly. So shall I take you home then?"

This was just too horrible, I did not want to go home, I wanted to go out with him as we had planned.

"I don't suppose it matters that you are married, if you are separated does it? I mean it is almost like being divorced."

"When you put it like that, you are right, but on the other hand - well never mind - if you are happy with the situation as it is that's fine, but you must tell your aunt and uncle. I would not want them to find out and think I was taking you out under false pretences. Now are we off? Are you happy? Truly?"

I said that I was and tried to feel comfortable about the situation. All I wanted to do was to go out with him anyway and if he wanted to take me out, what could be the harm in it. I thought it nice that he told me right away. It showed that he was honest and straight-forward.

As Paul took up more of my time, he wanted to spend every evening with me and every Sunday. Lawrence gradually became less important in my life. I explained to Paul that I couldn't be with him all the time as it would be rude to my uncle and aunt "But if you would like to come over and play whist with us some evenings, that would be nice. We would like that."

"How old are you?" I had wondered, but thought it would sound too young and silly to ask him but he did seem a lot older than me.

He laughed, "How old are you?"

"I asked you first!"

"I am 27, just, turned 27 in April, now it's your turn!"

"I'm just 18 - but I will be nineteen this year."

"You are very young, Emily" he replied. His voice was serious and he was not looking at me - he was looking out of the window. *But then I knew that really, right from the start.* Then he said, suddenly, abruptly, "I'm in love with you, Emily. I should like to marry you. If, that is, you would have me? I have written to my wife again. Life is full of surprises. Maybe this time she will give in! What do you think Emily? Would you marry me?"

I was shocked. Marriage? The only person I had ever thought about marrying was Stanley and that was a far-away thing, a sort of dream life 'way off in the future. I knew I would get married someday. Stanley had his university to finish and I had my training to complete and I wanted to continue to dance professionally - it had been my dream, my ambition for such a long time. Although I found Paul exciting to be with, I had known all along that it would not be a permanent relationship - after all he was still married and I was committed to my dancing. The feeling of shock suddenly turned to excitement, I was thrilled, it *was* wonderful that he had asked me to marry him. Lawrence who was so serious and seemed so fond of me had never mentioned marriage and of course Stanley had never asked me! Without thinking at all, I burst out "Oh Paul! I think I would love to marry you!"

He turned then and took my hands in his, "You would? You would, really?"

"Oh I think so, Paul. But of course it is impossible - apart from the fact that you are married already!"

"But Emily, you know I am trying desperately to get out of that miserable marriage."

"Yes I do know, but I am expected to go back to ballet school this September - you know that. I have to go because this was the purpose of the trip! Already I've put it off too long. I've put on weight and I'm out of training! I do love to be with you Paul, we do have fun together, but after the summer I will be leaving. My uncle is making the arrangements for me right now! I have to go!"

I had started to worry and wonder about the plans. I had missed my dancing a lot, my routine at the ballet school in the mornings and rushing off to other studios in the afternoon, dancing until I dropped! Then I was so busy I had put it out of my mind but I had known all along that I was going back to it soon, that this was just a holiday. It would be hard to leave this lovely island, my wonderful aunt and my new friends Lawrence and JB,

Françoise and Pierre, it was not a place one could come back to easily; it was too expensive and also took too long. Once in London I might never see Paul again or anyone else. I had not really thought about that nor had I thought that Paul would love me - not enough to want to marry me! I had never imagined that he would be serious about me, not like that, to talk of marriage!

"That Lawrence chap - do you still want to see him?" he asked me. "We are together so much I am surprised you can be bothered with the chap at all! I am surprised that he can be bothered with you really; I mean, he hardly has any time with you nowadays."

"Yes I know, but he is not at all serious about me, not like you, so the fact that I am with you so much is not important to him. It doesn't bother him one scrap I'm certain! He couldn't have been serious could he, or he would have taken me to that dance where I met you! Anyway, he is a nice person - bossy though and not terribly generous, but I would hate to hurt his feelings because I do like him. I think he is a very kind man and we like to do the same things too, we met sailing which he enjoys and so do I, we go for drives and walks and to the beach and he loves to swim you know and actually so do I!"

He looked at this young girl, with the very green eyes. He was completely taken with her. She was so different from the girls he knew - from anyone he had ever known or met. She was full of energy, laughter and fun! The way she loved to dance! All night if she could! And that time at Pierre and Françoise' when she did her chorus girl act! "Tea for Two" - why, that was incredible. Her hair, straight, bobbed like a girl of about 10! No one her age wore their hair like that. It's marvellous - like a cap of gold silk. Her legs! And what's more she had read many of the books he had read! Amazing that. He can tell that Pierre likes her, the way he calls her the golden girl and now wants her to crew for him since he heard about her crewing at the yacht club and how good she is at it.

He does not like the thought of her going out with this Lawrence chap. So they like doing the same things – well, he likes reading the same books as she reads, and he likes to dance with her and although sailing and swimming are not his favourites, as time goes by there will be lots of things they will like to do together. Doesn't she realize that he is very serious about her? For God's sake, he has just asked her to marry him!

Well, he supposed it didn't count as he was not free, not yet! All the same, he was going to have this girl! If she goes to London, he will just have to go and get her, that's all. He has made up his mind. He knows he wants no other and, as for her boyfriend at home, he is certain that can be dealt with - after all he is thousands of miles away and she hasn't seen him now for months.

Aunt Ann was becoming very concerned about my uncle's health as his breathing seemed to become much more laboured and frequently his hand would go to his chest where he felt the pain. She knew that to tell him not to get excited was a waste of time as he was a very excitable man and he did everything at great speed. His Scotch and his pipe were part of his daily life, so no doctor, no matter how good a friend, was ever going to get him to give those up and, as for resting, well it just was not his nature to lie about, so he just laughed and said "It's no use, I can't change!" As he said this, we knew it to be true - he couldn't and wouldn't, so although Aunt Ann told him to be careful and made him go to the doctor quite often, she realized that there was little she could do about his health.

Mama was going to England to settle some business matters, Mattie was off too, for her yearly holiday in England, so there would be only the three of us. The house would be quieter - perhaps the quiet house would give my uncle the rest he needed. Ann was sure this would be a wonderful opportunity to restore my uncle's health; she was going to cook him special meals, cosset him as much as he would allow her to.

It was a beautiful summer. The shining sun delighted us daily with warmth and brightness, the gentle breeze smelt clean and fresh as it blew in from the sea. The town was busy with holiday-makers, but not crushed. The visitors gave a happy, festive atmosphere; they were jolly, enjoying themselves, spending their well-earned money on their tax-free luxuries! Food was plentiful. The island was paradise and people were enjoying the freedom and easy living. For the islanders, the horrors of the German occupation were behind them – but never forgotten.

It was a pleasant, easy life. Of course I knew it could not last, but I tried not to think too much about the changes that would soon be taking place. Uncle Cedric had made all the arrangements for me to stay with his friends outside London and to attend a ballet academy. He also had arranged an audition for me at a television studio where they were planning a programme of dance, modern dance. "This," he had said, "will get you back into the dance world; from there you'll be able to sort yourself out. I'm sure your mother will be very pleased to know you are back on track", he had added.

The plans were all in place. Paul had said he would come to London to see me every month. He was not going to let me out of his life, he said. I still thought about Stanley. It was getting difficult now to remember how it was with Stanley now that Paul was with me so much, the times with Stanley had faded and I thought of him less and less. Paul took up most of my thoughts and I hated the thought of leaving him. Lawrence didn't call me very often now, he had seen me with Paul, he had been at the yacht club when Paul and I had gone in for a drink one time so I guess he had given up. In a way I was sorry and in a way I did miss him, he was such fun to be with on the beach and he did love the sea and nature the way that I did, he always noticed the various flowers when we went for walks and the birds, the night sky, things like that. Paul didn't see them, not the way that Lawrence and I did.
    Ann was philosophical about it all. "Honey, what will be, will be. Time will work things out - it always does. You have known all along that you would have to give him up more than likely. He has known it too. Time heals, and when you are busy with your dancing again, you'll get over it, I know you will. Don't forget how fond you are of Stanley. You are still so young, Emily. You have your whole life ahead of you, a wonderful career that you have looked forward to and worked for, for years. Try not to fret. There are still a few weeks left, so just you enjoy them and let time look after everything else."
    I listened to Ann and tried to see things the way that she did, but I really didn't think it was going to be easy.

Lawrence had said he would pick me up at the bus stop in the town. "Takes far too much petrol to come and fetch you", he said. I immediately thought that Paul would never say such a thing! Anyway, there he was at the bus stop, all smiles, waiting for me. We walked down to the sands and strolled along the beach. There was a breeze but it was not cold, the water was gently lapping the sand at the edges, we took off our shoes, I dashed off laughing, he ran after me and caught me to him, "Emily, Emily," he was laughing and happy. Holding hands, we resumed our walk, it was then I told him that I wouldn't be seeing him much anymore, I didn't tell him the most recent plans that had been made for me. Something made me hold back.

"Why ever not? Just because you are going about with that island chap shouldn't stop you seeing me. I heard that he was married anyway. So I don't really understand why you are bothering with him. You are much better off going about with me. Why don't we go for a swim?"

"But Lawrence, I've not brought my bathing suit. You didn't mention a swim on the telephone!"

"We can drop back to my flat and I can lend you my old trunks. I expect we can fix up a top for you, out of a towel or something. I'm sure you'll think of a way to do it. Then we can come back and have a lovely swim when nobody is about, in this lovely soft evening light when all is still and the air has a touch of warmth in it. Are you game?"

"Of course I'm game!" I liked doing things on impulse!

At the flat, we tied a towel together with string and somehow, when I put it on, it worked! I wore a pair of his old flannels over his ancient woollen swimsuit with an old white shirt on top, to the beach. He had brought his camera!

"You can't possibly want a photo of me in this outfit", I laughed at the thought! "I won't let you! Anyway, you must have hundreds of me by now - nearly enough for an album!"

"However many I have, I don't have enough! Now be a good girl and do as I say!" He smiled at me with such warmth in his eyes I had to turn away. He held his camera this way and that way, catching me, I imagined, in the most awful positions and probably looking terrible.

"Oh Lawrence - that's enough - do let me go!"

At last he put his camera down. *Off she went, he had hoped she would. It was wonderful to watch her dancing into the air like that - with that joyfulness.*

I called to him "Are you not coming? Do come!"

He ran to me and caught my hand, "You really are a Tinkerbell, you know!"

I laughed, "Come!" I said, "Come Lawrence, let's swim!"

I ran ahead of him into the water, leaping, laughing, splashing, I felt such joy in my heart even though I knew my back would ache as I lay in my bed that night.

He paused to watch her in the dim light, he loved to watch her and to hear her. Her laughter, that sprang out of her at any moment, unexpected.

She called to him again, "Oh, do come, do! It's marvellous! You'll love it! Look! Look! Lawrence! I can see the moon! Look there!"

He looked at her and then he looked at the moon and then he looked at her again, he knew he loved her, he had known at the beginning, he wanted her for himself and for always.

Back at the flat, he prepared one of his little meals - scrambled eggs and toast. "Now then, don't say you won't be seeing me again - that would be foolish. I thought you were to go to London eventually for your dancing?"

"Yes I am - and I am not sure I want to!"

"Well, surely you don't want to work in a shop for very long, do you? That is not a career, Emily! To be a shop girl? Waste all that training, you told me that you had studied dance for years. You should carry on with what's planned for you. I can see you when I go to London which is quite often as you know, and I won't be living on this island forever, in fact I might have to leave much sooner than I had thought. I''ll take you home now. Be sensible, Emily."

I thought he sounded nearly as old as my uncle when he talked like that. But sometimes he was rather nice to be with and it was fun going swimming like that on the spur of the moment and he did love the outdoors - walking, sailing and swimming, and he had told me that he played tennis too, things that Paul didn't seem interested in at all. He didn't make me feel the way that Paul did though and that was a pity.

"I'm going to miss you JB", I told him, on the way home from another sailing trip. "I guess I really don't want to leave!"

"Well," he said, "don't!"

"I have to go. I promised my uncle and all the arrangements have been made now. The real problem is that I'm not sure that I want to go on with my ballet and I have known that for ages but I just don't know how to tell anyone - I'm so confused. Everyone expects me to go on with it and I dare not tell mother after she sent me over here for just that reason! Anyway, I must go to London and see what happens - maybe they won't like me at the academy!"

"People have been known to break promises Emily. Things change, situations change. But if you feel you must go then you must and you do love your dancing I know and it was certainly a pleasure to watch you, but I will be very sorry to see you leave. We have had some lovely times together. You will probably feel quite different once you are there."

I looked at his serious, weathered face and sad eyes, "I know we have, I have loved every minute. Perhaps you are right though, maybe once I am there I will feel better once I am back in the routine."

As he drew up to the house he said "You and your and aunt and uncle must come over before you leave, Emily. I'll ring you."

"That would be lovely, JB. Are you going to ask me to dance again?"

"I might - wait and see! You didn't really mind that much, did you?"

"No of course not, it was fun! I still love to dance you know, that hasn't changed one bit!"

"Off you go then. Do I get a little kiss?"

I poked my head through the window and gave him a little peck on the cheek. "Will that do?"

He laughed, "It will have to, it seems! Cheerio Emily!"

My aunt was in the drawing room, smoking. "Honey," she said, "I'm frightfully glad you are back - it has been the most ghastly day."

"What's happened?"

"Your uncle suddenly felt terribly ill and went to bed. I called the doctor - luckily, being a friend, he didn't mind coming over on a Sunday. There is nothing to be done about it - your uncle is dying."

"*Dying?*"

"Yes, he is and there is nothing to be done but wait. He's now unconscious."

"But Ann - how could this happen so suddenly. I mean, I didn't think he was so ill?"

"He was, Honey, but he simply didn't want anyone to know. He wanted to live his life his way. The doctor knew, and your uncle knew, but I didn't know! He is, as I say, unconscious, but if you would like to go up and see him it would be wise to do so now I think. He's not expected to live through the night."

"Oh Ann - how terrible! What should we do?"

"Nothing, just wait. I'll sit with him. I haven't made anything to eat, can you manage, Honey?"

"Of course; I'll scramble us some eggs, would you like that?"

"Perfect."

My uncle's breathing was very noisy. It filled the warm, stuffy room. He was not conscious of my presence. I said his name a few times, but there was no response. I left and went down the back staircase to the kitchen to prepare the eggs. My Aunt came in, "Let's eat in the morning-room. That would be best - then I can trot up and down the back staircase to his bedroom."

We ate our eggs and, as she left to sit with him, she suggested that I brought the tea upstairs so that we could sit on the stairs and drink it. "That way" she said, "I can hear if there's any change in his breathing."

I washed up and set the tea on a tray and took it up. We sat on the stairs drinking tea.

"Do you want me to take a turn in there?" I asked.

"No, dear, I'll go now. Would you fetch my cigarettes? I'll come and have one with you after a bit."

I took up another pot of tea and we sat on the stairs and had a cigarette. My aunt's hand shook and her voice trembled. "Oh, my God, Honey - isn't this terrible, terrible." She put her arms around my neck. "I am so glad you are with me, so glad, Honey. It's terrible to sit here and not be able to do anything! I'll go now; would you make some more tea in about a half an hour or so?"

"Is there anything you would like me to do Ann?"

"No dear, I can't think of anything thank you. I'll be out shortly."

"Isn't it a good thing Mama is not here."
"What a blessing!"

We were now drinking our third pot of tea and Ann had smoked numerous cigarettes. We looked at each other and Ann reached out her hand to hold mine; she shut her eyes, "Oh God, this is awful." She pulled out her handkerchief, "This won't do, will it, Honey!" She managed a smile. Out of the night stillness there was a sound - a long, low, moaning sort of groan, a terrible sound. Ann jumped up, "My God, my God!" She ran across the hall. All was silent, there was no sound. I knew what had happened. After some time my aunt came out of the room. "He's gone."
"Yes."
"Make us some more tea - there's a dear, will you; in the meantime I'll phone the doctor."

"I think we should go to bed now, Emily."
The house so still - it was strange to think of my uncle, dead, across the hall. I never got to know him well, but I liked him. He had a gruff way with him, but he was gentle too and kind. My poor aunt, a widow so young. They never seemed that crazy about each other, not like my brother and Madeleine. All the same, married only a few years and now he was gone. I must write to mother, she didn't know him well but all the same I knew she had liked him a lot when she visited him in England many years ago.
There was a knock on my door, "May I come in, Sweetie?"
"Of course."
"I just cannot sleep, would you mind if I popped in beside you to-night? I seem to be so cold and I can't get warm somehow."
"Oh Ann, do!"
She jumped in beside me and we cuddled up together like two spoons.
I felt her shivering and shaking subside after a while, then I heard her steady breathing, it was comforting to have my aunt there beside me, sound asleep.

I telephoned the shop to tell them I would not be in. I explained the situation, but Madame Corbette was not at all pleased.

"How much time do you need?" she asked.

I wasn't sure, I said maybe a week would do.

"That is rather a long time, Emily - just at the end of the holiday season. Try to make it less than that."

I didn't think that would be possible but I did not say so.

The funeral was small, Uncle Cedric had been married before, when he was a young man many years ago, but only briefly and there had been no children. Mama wouldn't be back until after the funeral, Ann thought it would be better that way. There would be only a very few close friends. Ann was pale and tense. She had many concerns. The art business, how would she manage that and the house. It was large and needed repairs. There was not a lot of money.

Suddenly, everything had changed. Mattie had to go; there was really no need for her. Although Aunt Ann hated housework we decided that we could do it together and that way it wouldn't be too bad. The gardener would have to carry on to keep things in order - the garden was far too large to be left to its own devices. There was much to see to at the gallery. Ann asked me to do the banking and also to look after the reception desk from time to time. It was two weeks before I thought it would be suitable for me to return to the shop. But after I had made the decision I realized that there would be no point as I would be leaving the island soon anyway. I rang Madame Corbette to tell her my decision. "Well," she said, "that is too bad Emily, and I am sorry about your uncle of course, you weren't the greatest sales lady we have ever had! You were quite a good model though! I wish you well Emily and Bon Voyage, my dear."

At supper that evening my aunt asked me if I still wanted to go to London.

"Not really, but I did promise."

"How would you like to stay here with us and help me with the business? I need help and we get on so well. I need your company, Emily! If you want to carry on with some of your dancing there is one studio here - you might be able to help there

with the young ones - and the little shows they put on from time
to time are really quite sweet."

"Oh, I would love to do that, Ann - really love to! I'll write to
mother and I'm sure she will be quite happy for me to do this."

This was a miracle, I thought, now I won't have to leave at all!
Ann gave me a big hug, "Are you happy, Honey?" How could
I not be? I couldn't wait to tell Paul! And it would be nice to get
back to some dancing and with children - it might be perfect for
me.

Ann was trying to learn about the business, but she was not
at all keen. Because we were economizing on fuel we didn't use
the drawing-room anymore, just the morning-room and the
kitchen. The large AGA kept the morning-room comfortable. We
dressed warmly in many layers, with woolly vests the first layer.

The dance studio job worked out perfectly. I helped with the
children at the barre and led the older girls. Recital time was
coming up and I was delighted to be helping with the
preparations. It was not a full-time job, but it was a pleasant
occupation and although my back bothered me at times I was not
really straining it with my present routine, I was careful to avoid
certain positions and was beginning to think it was really on the
mend.

*Ann very soon realised that the business was not making
enough money, her accountant confirmed her assessment and
added that it really never had. She decided not to do anything
until after Christmas. The house and the art business would
have to be sold, she didn't have the knowledge needed to run it
and anyway she would rather do something else, something very
different. Emily would have to go. It was such a shame that Paul
was still unable to get his divorce. He obviously was very in love
with Emily, a sweet twosome, a rather tragic situation. Ann
decided to wait until the New Year to tell Emily. Why spoil her
Christmas, it would be difficult enough to tell her! How in the
world was she going to tell her!*

Ann and Mama were going to stay in St Helier with friends
over Christmas. I was invited too, but I had been invited to stay

with Pierre and Françoise at their farm.   They wanted me to have a typical island Christmas on the farm, roast goose with all the trimmings for one thing and, they told me, the big fire would be roaring, lighting up the whole room.   Both grannies would be there, Pierre had already made all sorts of delicious things to eat. Paul would be there too, part of the time.   I was really looking forward to it all.   Mother had sent me a lovely dress for Christmas.   Soft, fine, dark-green wool with a high neck, a fitted bodice and a flared skirt, most becoming;   I was thrilled with the present.   I really missed mother, but Aunt Ann had filled what would have been a huge gap in my life.

Pierre picked me up in the afternoon of Christmas Eve.   The house smelled of baked bread, there were trays of nuts and dried fruit on the sideboard and small tables.   Christmas was everywhere in the house;   it looked so festive with the holly perched on tables and hanging in bunches in the windows and the large Christmas tree sparkled with many lights and coloured globes - and smelled wonderful.   Pierre asked me to come into the kitchen and talk to him while he rolled out some pastry. Before long, the pastry trays were filled and everything was in the huge oven.   Already one could smell the aroma of the mince pies. "Since it's Christmas," he said "we'll have a little drink right now, even although it's a while 'til dinner."

He poured us a large sherry (he called it a schooner) and sat across from me at the scarred, scrubbed, wooden kitchen table. "Well here we are Emily," he said, (looking very serious), "drinking sherry and soon to be eating a traditional Christmas dinner with all the trimmings when only a short time ago most of the people on this island didn't have enough to eat - in fact many of the inhabitants were actually starving you know.   You can't imagine how thin everyone became."

As Pierre quietly told me a few of the horrors of the German occupation, his face became tense and there was pain in his eyes, sadness in his voice, "Some of our people died but we were a little luckier than some because the farm went on producing, not a lot, but it was a help.   Of course the Germans took most of the food, we had to hide as much as we could for ourselves and without being suspected.   If we had been found out we would have been shot.   We were able to help one or two of our friends a little, but even to do that was dangerous -

frightening really, with the German soldiers snooping around looking for trouble, suspicious of everything. I guess I shouldn't be talking of all this right now, but sometimes when I look around and see how much we have today, it's good to remind myself of just how lucky we are. Anyway Emily, it's nice to have you with us this Christmas."

"It's wonderful to be here Pierre; thank you so much for inviting me, but you know, I just can't imagine all that - it's just too horrible to think of and someone told me that there was no salt and that some people craved it so much they snuck down to the beaches which were out of bounds and got salt water and evaporated it to get the salt they craved so much. They could have been shot for doing that, I was told."

"Well that's true, but you must remember that the Germans were following orders and that not all of them were bad chaps, in fact some were really quite humane. Anyway, we are fortunate to be here and still alive, I reckon. Now then, how about another drink! I think I need it, I do hope that you enjoy our Christmas, Emily."

"Oh I will, I will! I'm already enjoying it! Françoise seems so happy bustling about - it must be a great help to her that you are such a good cook!"

"Yes it is, a great help, as she won't cook at all! She is so restless, she would like to be dressed up all the time and truly hates it here on the farm. There's nothing I can do about that - this is where our money comes from and this is what I am trained to do. The pity is, I don't think that Françoise is going to change, in fact she seems to get more restless as time goes on. There now - enough of me! What about you and Paul? I met his wife when she was here. I can't say that I liked her much. A pity she was so stubborn, I think she planned to come back and give the marriage another try."

"Oh, please Pierre, don't say it! Do you really think that would happen?"

"Yes Emily, I really think that will happen. I can't see what will happen with you two - if she won't give him a divorce you'll most certainly have to give each other up! I don't know how you'll manage to do that, but more than likely you'll have to. I do know he loves you very much Emily. Well my dear, we had better not talk about it anymore. Time will tell, I guess. I wish you luck all the same! Now then, let's eat!"

We talked, drank and ate until late. My eyes were closing with the heat of the fire and all the food. "Please would you excuse me if I go to my bed now?"

"Of course - Françoise will take you up. It's very cold up there! I hope you brought your woolly nightie!"

As we went into the entrance hall, through the first landing window we could see snowflakes falling. Françoise exclaimed "Oh how wonderful, Louise will be thrilled! I do hope it lasts until the morning!"

We said good-night, I pulled the curtains back, and in the light from the barn I could see large snowflakes falling in the night darkness. How lovely - I snuggled into bed and tucked my feet up into my nightie. The bed was icy, but I was full of happiness and very sleepy.

A gentle knock on my door awakened me, I opened my eyes to a bright, dazzling light! Snowlight! I could see the heavily-laden trees against the blue sky, oh, it was wonderful! I felt so good, so happy.

"Come in! Come in!" I called, watching my breath billow out.

"Emily, you *are* lazy, everyone is up!" It was Paul with morning tea.

He put the tray down on the bedside table and sat on the edge of my bed then pulled me to him. He started to kiss and caress me and I could feel myself giving to him, wanting more. "Lovely Emily, I want to make love to you. Let me just slip in beside you now and make love to you."

I shook my head, "no, no Paul please, you must stop, please don't!"

Suddenly I was frightened. He seemed so insistent, his arms so strong, pulling at me; horrible memories came flooding into me. STOP, I nearly screamed, but caught my breath.

"Alright, alright, I have stopped, you do make an awful fuss Emily - after all it is very natural to make love when one is in love and it is difficult to stop when I want you so much.

"What are you afraid of? I won't hurt you Emily darling. I do love you, you know that."

He started to move closer to me on the bed and then his fingers began to undo the buttons on the front of my nightie, suddenly I was really frightened. "You must stop Paul, you must." I started to cry. "Don't you understand that if I became pregnant the shame would be unbearable! Nice girls don't get pregnant before they are married. A friend of Madeleine's had an abortion and now she can't have any babies ever and she is married to a very nice person."

"But Emily, if that did happen I would marry you."

I looked at him, had he forgotten that he is already married, then he became quite flustered as he realized just what he had said.

"Of course of course, that's terrible and I can't marry you yet can I, but I shall, I shall. Well, we will just leave things as they are my pet. Now then - I have your little present here - would you like it now?"

I sat up and looked at him, wondering if he was cross, but no, he just smiled at me. The room was absolutely freezing and I was very pleased I had on my high-necked, long-sleeved Viyella nightgown.

"I would, if you would like me to have it now." I rubbed my hands together and blew on them to no effect. He held a small velvet box and then he opened it and turned it towards me. "I wanted you to have a ring, Emily. I know we cannot be engaged yet, but perhaps you'll wear this as a token of my love for you."

Tucked in the velvet, was an emerald, set in a slender, tapered, gold band. My birth-stone. It was exquisite. "Oh Paul, a ring! I love it and I shall wear it forever!"

I was so surprised, so thrilled. So very thrilled. The feeling was almost too much. It gave my heart a tight feeling when I saw it on my finger. "Paul, Paul - thank you, thank you."

"You are welcome, darling. I wish it could be your engagement ring, but perhaps it will do until that time comes."

He put his arms around me and gently held my head close on his chest. "I do love you, my pet; you know that don't you? More than anyone ever."

He felt her head nod. He gently removed my arms from around his neck and took my hands in his. "Happy Christmas, my darling! Now drink your tea and get up! Lucky it snowed some more last night - it's a rare commodity on this island! Not a lot, mind you, but enough to make it all very pretty. I'll see you downstairs. I'm sorry if I upset you, you did seem terribly upset and you know Emily, I wouldn't do anything you didn't want me to do. You should know that by now."

I knew that to be true, but I just couldn't help that horrible feeling that came over me sometimes. Would I ever get over it?

Downstairs the festivities had begun. Louise was opening her presents. There were hot croissants on the table and the delicious aroma of coffee filled the room. Outside, the flakes were falling softly. The meal was to be at 2 o'clock; by that time the grannies would be there.

Pierre was busy in the kitchen most of the morning. Paul and I decided to go for a walk and Louise said she would like to come too. Outside we could hear the church bells ringing. Paul held me around my waist as we walked. "Are you enjoying it, Emily?"

"Yes, it couldn't be more lovely."

"We, darling, we will have many lovely Christmases together and the child walking with us will be our child. It will be."

I was beginning to think this would never be, especially after my conversation with Pierre. I turned to look at Paul. He saw there were tears in her eyes. "Oh, my pet, don't cry, don't be sad! Like I say, life is full of surprises. We have to be together, it has to be. Now we had better get back."

Back at the house we helped to bring the many dishes of food to the table. The grannies were settled at the table, napkins in place. I noticed that Françoise's mother spoke very little English but she smiled and laughed heartily at Pierre's jokes. Pierre's mother was less jolly, spoke perfect English, praising Pierre for the delicious meal. "When, Françoise, are you going to learn to cook?" she asked with a slight tone of sarcasm.

Françoise shrugged her shoulders, "Why would I cook, when Pierre does it so well - better than I could ever do it!"

I guess Paul saw the need to change the subject so he suggested we sang - some Christmas songs. "How about 'I'm dreaming of a white Christmas'?" This got us all started and then of course we sang as many carols as we could think of.

It was getting dark when Pierre took the grannies home. Paul and I cleared up with Louise's help. Françoise had disappeared! When Pierre returned there was little left to do, so we all settled in front of the fire. "How about some brandy, would anyone like a brandy?"

Françoise and Paul accepted but I didn't like brandy so I told him about my uncle introducing me to Cointreau. "If you have that I would like that!"

"I have everything!" he said.

We sipped our drinks and chatted about Christmas and how good the goose was - things like that, then Paul jumped out of his chair "I think it's time to get you home, Emily, don't you?"

I agreed, although I was very comfortable where I was. "What a perfectly wonderful Christmas it has been. I love your Christmas!"

The snow had stopped; there had not been much, so the roads were clear. Before we got to the house, Paul pulled up and took me in his arms and whispered into my ear, "I would love to have been in that bed with you this morning, I want to make love to you very much you know that, won't you let me pet, I will be very careful not to get you pregnant."

"I can't do that Paul - if anyone found out I would feel terrible, It would be a disgrace."

"But who would find out?"

"Someone would - I know it. Anyway I am going to be a virgin when I get married, nice girls are supposed to be. It is wrong to make love without being married, every one knows that really."

"I am going to marry you someday, Emily so it won't matter if you are not a virgin."

"I wish it could be true, Paul, but Pierre thinks that your wife will come back and that she will want to try again to make the marriage work."

"He told you that?"

"Yes he did and he could be right. What if I got pregnant! My mother would disown me! She would be so disappointed in me. I would hate to do that to her. Mother has always been so proud of me. And my brother! Please try to understand, Paul. It's not that I don't want to, I do want to, in a way I do, but I would know I was doing something I shouldn't be doing - not until I am married! I would feel guilty, horribly guilty and afraid."

"Afraid?"

"Yes, afraid of getting pregnant and guilty about making love without being married. I like to feel happy and free. Not guilty and afraid. Don't be cross, Paul, I do love you, but I can't do that. I just can't imagine what would happen to me if I became pregnant without being married; it would be unbearable and I would be so ashamed. No, I could never do that and of course I would never ever have an abortion, never, no matter what! Please Paul, don't ask me again.

He held me close, "Never mind, my pet, I believe with all my heart that we will have the rest of our lives together. I know we will and I am not cross Emily."

He kissed me lightly good-night, got in his car and drove off, waving to me out the window.

The house was empty! The phone was ringing! "You are there at last!" my aunt was saying on the phone, "Please Honey, be a dear and fill that wretched AGA will you, before it goes out - we won't be home until tomorrow! Are you alright? Honey - you don't sound too good!"

"Yes, yes, I'm fine, I'll fill the AGA now. Have you had a nice time?"

"Lovely, but truthfully we'll be glad to get home. How about you?"

"I had a wonderful time, thank you!"

"We'll see you tomorrow after lunch then. Will you be there?"

"Yes I'll be here."

"Night, night - then Sweetie, sleep tight!"

I admired the pretty ring on my finger, it really was lovely, but I wished it could have been an engagement ring. It was sort of sad to have a ring and it not an engagement ring. I snuggled into my bed. It would be nice to have Ann back - I needed to talk to her. Some nights we talked for ages and it was often very interesting the things she told me about her life and about love, the things she thought were important about loving someone. Then she would get up and bring bowls of cornflakes with thick clotted cream for us to eat in the middle of the night. I thought she was really more like I imagined a sister to be, than an aunt. I guess that was because she was so young and yet she had so much understanding and was so sympathetic. There was always a brightness and sparkle about her - the way she looked at life and laughed at it! I loved her, this woman who had somehow become my aunt, my "sister aunt"! It was hard to go to sleep with so much to think about, churning around in my mind. It was wonderful to be in love, but I did wish it could have been different. It would have been different with Stanley, but there was no use thinking about Stanley now and anyway he never asked me to marry him. Perhaps I should write to him and tell him about Paul, but he hasn't written to me for ages so maybe he was already taking someone else out. It might be better to leave things as they are.

It felt so good to have Ann back! I managed to tell her how I really felt about the ring and everything, she listened and agreed it might be better to leave things as they are.

As I went to sleep I thought about Paul and how insistent he had been and then without wanting to, memories invaded my mind and my body suddenly shook and shuddered as those memories took hold of me. I must have called out in my sleep – I woke up, with Ann calling my name over and over, my face was wet with tears and I couldn't stop shuddering.

"What in the world is the matter honey? Tell me what the matter is!"

So at last I was able to tell someone, because I decided at that moment that I would tell her the whole sordid story. I knew I could tell her, that it would be alright to tell her and it was, as I knew it would be, a huge relief to tell her. As I talked she kept saying "terrible, how terrible, you poor girl, oh sweetie I am so sorry", then she said, "you must forget it now, put it out of your mind forever, you are a lovely young woman and life is going to be good to you, so forget it, make yourself forget it forever Emily!"

I did try very hard and sometimes I would go for ages and never think about that terrible time, but I wished I could forget forever. Maybe someday it would be gone.

Winter was now nearly over and still things had not been sorted out. Before much longer, Ann was going to have to tell Emily what the plans were. She hated the idea of Emily leaving. They had become so close, practically every thought they shared - all except the thoughts of Emily having to leave! Fancy Paul giving her a ring. The affair was bound to come to an end when Emily leaves - she was pretty certain of that!

It was very late and I was still awake. I knew Ann was too, I was thinking how unusually untalkative we were, and then Ann asked me if I was still awake.

"Yes Ann, I am."

"Emily," she said rather hesitantly, "it is difficult for me to tell you this - "

"What do you mean? What have you to tell me?"

"Honey, you knew all about our finances, that things were not going well - well, the accountant said the only thing to do is to sell the house as well as the business and of course he is quite right; we simply don't need this huge house, all the gardens! Really we never did! All these bedrooms for one thing - and then there are all the outbuildings - and on and on. We would have to sell and I couldn't really run the art business - anyway I don't want to! I would like to do something different now, take a training of some sort. Honey, I hate to tell you this, but you are going to have to go home! I really don't want you to go but there is no other way. I had a letter from your mother a while back. I didn't tell you then as I thought I would wait until the situation was clearer; anyway, she says you must go home. She knew that Paul had been married but it seemed that she thought he was very nearly divorced Emily, perhaps you didn't tell her the whole story? She thinks you should go home and get right away from him altogether and forget about going to London. She suggests you could carry on your studies in New York or Toronto at some point when you are ready. She is right, it will be the best thing for you. I know how terrible it will be, I really do, but I'm afraid it has to be that way - perhaps you have already realized that."

I was listening, not wanting it to be true but knowing that it was true.

Ann thought that Emily was still so young she would no doubt recover quickly, or would she? Emily's mother certainly thought this was the case and had told Ann that Emily would be getting a very strong letter from her and that would be that. There was still no sound from Emily. Ann grasped Emily's hand "Oh sweetie, I'm so sorry." Tears filled Emily's eyes. "I knew this was coming," she sniffed and wiped her tears, "I knew it was coming but I didn't let myself think about it, that's all. Oh Ann, I'm going to miss you all so much!"

"We will miss you too, Sweetie."

"When should I go?"

"Well, we will have to talk about that tomorrow. There will be a lot to arrange. I'll go and make us a nice pot of tea, and then we must get some sleep. We'll talk some more in the morning."

Oh dear, she really was going to miss this girl ever so much! As she made the tea, she got her emotions under control - won't do to have us both crying our eyes out!

By the time she was back with the tea, Emily was sitting up, mopping her eyes and blowing her nose. Ann thought she was remarkably composed.

"I'll make all the arrangements Ann, you have enough to do. I guess you would like me out of your hair as soon as possible – I mean, if you sell the house quickly you won't want to have me to worry about! So it would be best if I got a move on, wouldn't it."

"Yes, I guess it would, Honey. Now let's have our tea, have a sleep and then tomorrow you can work out when and how! And Emily, you know how much I wish it didn't have to be like this, don't you."

"I know Ann, I truly do!"

In the morning I felt calmer, more in control. "Shall I drive this morning, Ann?"

"Oh do, yes do. When are you going to tell Paul?"

"I think I'll wait until this evening. We were going out to the yacht club, but I think I'll suggest somewhere else. Maybe I'll tell him before we go anywhere!"

At the art gallery shop, Ann suggested that I stayed and looked after everything. "You will be able to make some calls about your trip" she said. "You'll have time to do the deposits for me, I hope, as I have to see the accountant and you know how long that takes!"

"I'll do everything, don't worry - and the banking is my favourite job, everyone is so friendly and chatty; it's always kind of fun!"

As the evening drew near, I felt myself getting tense and emotional. I dreaded telling Paul. When he arrived at the house I could hardly bring myself to look at him.

"Paul, do you think we could park along the side of the road by the fence there - I have something I want to tell you?"

"Of course Emily. Now what could you have to say to me - you sound so very serious? Have I upset you in some way? You have scarcely looked at me since I arrived."

"What I have to say is very serious, Paul! And no, you have never ever upset me."

He pulled up and turned towards me and held my hands. "What is it, my pet?"

"I have to leave, Paul."

"Leave?"

"Yes - I have to return to Canada."

"Good Lord, NO!"

"Yes I do."

"Why? What has happened?" *His heart sank. His throat felt as if it had closed up.* He choked out, "What is it?"

I told him what the accountant had said and also what Mother had said. "So you see, I have no choice, I do have to go."

"And if I were free, we would be married and you would never have to leave, oh God, how could this happen. What can we do?"

Paul's mind was whirling, He can't let her go - he'll never see her again. It is too much. He pulled her close, "You can't go, you can't! Emily!"

"Paul, I have no choice."

I felt calm, I knew it had to be, there was nothing to be done. I knew this.

Suddenly Paul jumped out of the car, he paced about, there must be a way! He jumped back into the car, "I know what – I'll come out to Canada just as soon as I can. I'll follow you in a few months! That's what I'll do, yes I can do that. I'll look into it right away. That's the good thing about being an accountant, one can do that anywhere. When will you have to go?"

"I expect in a month or so. I'll be staying in London for a few days before the ship leaves. Nothing is absolutely definite yet about which ship. I'll travel by train across Canada. Do you really think you would be able to come to Canada?"

"I see no reason why not, a wonderful adventure."

"What about your wife?"

"What can she do? She isn't going to come to Canada to get me, now is she?"

"Something I have never asked you, Paul, how was it that you were only together a few months? You said it had not even been a full year?"

"I thought I had told you? Actually I was tricked into marrying her."

"Tricked?"

"Yes, tricked, she was working here for the summer and I took her out a few times. Unlike you, she was quite keen to make love. I wasn't her first. Anyway she told me she was pregnant and of course she was not! I was a fool at the time to believe her, but I did, so I married her. After that I could hardly bear to look at her, I was so angry. I had never been in love with her and here I was married to her! After a while she was homesick and fed up, so she left. In her letters she keeps saying she will come back some day, but if I am in Canada it will be a different story! She certainly won't come to Canada and then with me so far away I'm sure she will realize that the whole situation is ridiculous and agree to the divorce and then of course we will be married immediately!"

What a strange story, imagine tricking someone to marry you, what a dreadful thing to do. He sounded so sure that he would be able to come, I couldn't help feeling relieved and excited too! I knew everyone at home would like him. "But that would be wonderful Paul, truly wonderful!"

"It will, it will, my pet. I shall start soon and get references and then my passport. It will all take time but we must be patient. I'll write as soon as you leave and there will be letters waiting for you, Emily."

Her head, buried in his shoulder, nods, "Will we ever come back do you think, I do love it here?"

"Yes of course we will, you have your aunt - and my mother is here, so we would be bound to return, but let's not worry about coming back yet! Now then, shall we go to the club or what would you like to do?"

"Let's go for a walk! It's such a lovely evening. Then we can go home and tell Ann your plan."

Ann and Mama were in the morning-room, reading. Mama was always so pleased to see him! "Come in, Paul, come in!" She always made quite a fuss of him, then she jumped up and said she was going to make a nice pot of tea!

When she came back with tea and biscuits, Paul got up and said he had something to tell them. After his little speech Mama put her cup down and gave Paul a long look. "I hope it works out, I really do - you two get on so well together. We have grown very fond of Emily - we want her to be happy and we think that you make her very happy, Paul. She is an easy person to live with too, isn't she, Ann?"

"Yes, yes, it's true she is very easy. We've had such fun - haven't we, sweetie?" Her voice was low, her eyes smiled into Emily's.

The days passed quickly, soon it would be time to go. Ann

arranged a going-away dinner party for me at the Grand Hotel. It was a lovely party, but every time I looked up from my plate I saw Paul's sad eyes looking at me, he gave me a little wink and half a smile. My menu was passed around and signed by each guest.

Lawrence phoned to say goodbye. Although he had been at the dinner I had not really been near him to chat. My Aunt had arranged it that way. "I'm sorry you are leaving Emily. I'm very fond of you, you know. We did have some nice times together. I enjoyed being with you very much. If you write and give me your address I'll send you some of those last photos I took, the ones on the beach, with you wearing my swim costume and towel - remember the ones?"

I said yes I remembered and yes, I would write to him.

"Please do that, Tink!"

"Oh I will! Lawrence? How is it you're not Peter Pan if I'm Tink?" I laughed.

"Yes - it's a pity that!" There was no laughter in his voice. "Good-bye Tink! I shall miss you." When he said it like that I felt sorry and sad; I didn't know what to say, so I thanked him for the nice times we had together and then I said good-bye.

He would miss her and wanted her more than she would ever know. If he could follow her to Canada he would, but it just was not possible now and even if he could, would she accept him, probably not, as she seems pretty taken with that Jersey chap. Pointless to even think such thoughts at the moment, he has a lot of catching up to do financially before he could possibly go all the way to Canada. It must be very expensive, a trip like that.

It was not at all jolly at the airport. Ann had tears in her eyes the whole time and so did Mama. Paul looked miserable. Ann and I hugged each other, we had run out of words. I gave Mama a gentle hug and then Paul's arms were around me, holding me, stroking my hair. He gently let me go, still hanging on to my hands, looking into my eyes. "Dear Emily, if only I could come with you." I took a last look at him then I hurried away. I went up the steps and turned at the top, and waved. I called out to Paul, "goodbye, goodbye!"

I found my seat and sat down, I waved and waved as the aircraft took off and then there was nothing to wave at, nothing. I really had left them all - it really had happened. How would I manage without Ann, my sister aunt. How would I live without my love. But he will come, he will.

I was to have two full days in London before travelling to Southampton to embark. I had decided to travel second class, hoping to meet people of my age on this trip - different I hoped from the SS Media where it was so grand and very few young people on board. I checked into the hotel and telephoned my great-aunt that Aunt Ann had arranged for me to meet whilst I was in London.

"How will I recognize you, Lady Lambert?"

"Oh my, first of all, please dear, don't call me Lady Lambert - Aunt Julia is much friendlier don't you think? After all, I am your great-aunt, you know! I shall recognize you I am sure, as I have been told you look just like your grandmother. We will have lunch at your hotel dear, you say it is the Park Lane?"

"Yes it is. I will be waiting for you in the lounge, Aunt Julia."

"Lovely, dear. Until tomorrow then."

I decided to wait outside as I needed some fresh air and I thought it would be nice to greet my aunt at the entrance. On the dot of one, the car drew up and the chauffeur helped my aunt out of the car. She looked up and waved to me. "How very lovely, dear, to meet you," she said, "and it is true - you do look like your grandmother and not at all like your mother."

During lunch, Aunt Julia wanted to talk about my mother whom she had met in 1926 when my mother and father spent one year in London, an entirely social year, mother had said. "We had some pleasant times together, your mother had a great sense of humour too and my, how she did love clothes and the theatre! Is she still pretty, she had beautiful hair, I remember? And how is she these days?"

"I think she is fine Aunt Julia and she is still very pretty."

"Yes I can imagine she would be, such a shame that the marriage didn't last. We all felt so sorry for your mother you know. Your father leaving her for another woman and your mother with two little children and you just a baby! Your great-aunt Mary was very upset and was absolutely furious with your father, she never would have anything more to do with him you know. When he came over once for a visit she wouldn't see him and neither would the rest of the family. Your uncle Cedric was civil to him but he also wanted nothing much to do with him. It was lucky for your mother that Mary left all that money for you children and none to your father. We were all very pleased about that. It certainly was a cruel thing that your father did, he definitely deserved the cool treatment he got here and from his own brother too."

I heard what Aunt Julia was saying and I was pleased to realise that this side of the family was in full sympathy with Mother's plight and had not resented the will being totally in favour of our family.

"Now dear, enough of that history, I am going to take you shopping. How would you like that? To Harrod's."

I was really surprised, "I would love to go shopping!"

"Good, I had a suspicion you might like that! I remember how your mother loved shopping in London! After that we will go to Simpson's for tea. I do wish you were in London longer - we would have such a delicious time! Now then, off we must go – I told William to be at the door at 2:30 sharp."

I had never been to Harrod's, but I knew all about it from mother. "I think a lovely handbag might be useful, dear - a really good one will last you for years" she said, as she led the way to the handbag department. "Now I'm going to sit down and you just choose one you like. Take your time."

I had never seen such a selection! I finally chose one in black leather with a soft leather lining. It was very smart, very London-looking, was what I thought. Aunt Julia thought so too, "A perfect choice, dear. Is there anything else I can tempt you with?"

"No, no thank you Aunt Julia! This is lovely!"

"Well dear, I'm so glad to have had the chance to meet you and give you a little treat! Now off we go to have tea."

After tea Aunt Julia suggested we have a drive around London, "such a lovely day dear and you must have a last look at London Town because it may be a long time before you return. I have plenty of time and William loves driving, would you like to do that?" Of course I was delighted with the suggestion.

Finally the drive ended and we were back at the hotel. Aunt Julia turned to me and took my hands in hers, "Give your mother my love dear, a very charming woman. I hope your journey is pleasant, such a very long one!"

"It was a perfect day, Aunt Julia, perfect, thank you so much."

"A pleasure, dear, a pleasure. Remember now, my love to your mother!"

HOME – 1951

Settled on the train for the last lap of my journey, it was a very nice feeling not to be bouncing about on the ocean! There were several people travelling to Canada for the first time, emigrating. I enjoyed chatting and telling them about Canada and listening to them exclaim about the scenery which certainly was spectacular. When the train stopped at Banff, I got out for a stroll and bought a postcard for Stanley. I thought it would be a good way to let him know about my return and I remembered that he had been to Banff with his parents once and had loved it.

When at last the train pulled into Vancouver, a surge of excitement filled me as I looked out of the window; I was home! As soon as I got off the train I saw mother and how wonderful she looked. She was wearing her fur jacket and one of her pretty hats - and then she saw me and waved and started to walk towards me, but I ran to her, "Mother! Mother!" I called and realized I was crying. I had missed her - missed her so much. I got to her and hugged her; oh it felt so good, that hug with my mother, but did she feel thin? She felt different - I could feel her bones! It was wonderful to see her and inhale that familiar fur and scented-powder smell that I had known forever. At home I did not like to ask right away if there was a letter, it seemed rude so I held back, but I was longing to know. As it turned out, I didn't have to ask, as mother told me, almost as soon as we got in the door, that there were two letters waiting for me.
"Oh, I did hope there would be! I did."
"Well you just sit down and read your letters, I'll get busy and finish making the dinner."
"Thank you, mother." As I looked up at her I thought maybe her face was thinner too, yes, she definitely looked thinner altogether.
"Have you lost weight mother?"
She turned sharply; "nooo, well yes, I have a bit, but it is coming back now, do I look terribly thin?"
"No, not really, but I couldn't help noticing, especially when I hugged you at the station. Why have you lost so much weight? Have you been ill or something?"

"Yes dear I have, but it turned out to be not so terrible as everyone thought it was going to be and all is well now."

"Oh mother, what was the matter? Why didn't you tell me, I could have come home and looked after you?"

"Now dear, I arranged it so you wouldn't be here, as I thought the whole business would be too stressful and disruptive, but, as it turned out, it was all over much sooner than was expected and not nearly as serious as it was thought to be, thank goodness."

I put my letters down, "oh mother". I got up and put my arms around my precious mother, "is that why you were so keen for me to go to England? It was, wasn't it, of course, now I understand, it was a bit of a puzzle because at times you seemed determined to get rid of me! After I got there I didn't think much more about it really. I wish you had told me. It's terrible to think you were so ill and I didn't even know! Oh mother, did you tell anyone?"

"Yes of course I did. Your uncle certainly knew and if things had taken a bad turn they would have sent you home but don't be upset, all is well and I am fine. Now dear don't cry - there's the girl! You just get on and read your letters."

I sat down. "Are you really alright now mother, really?"

"Yes I am, now let's not talk about it any more." She laughed then, "I feel so good these days and it truly is wonderful to have you home, now I must get on and make our dinner." Mother did sound happy and obviously very relieved. She made me feel happy too and very glad to be home.

"By the way dear, before you start and before I forget, someone with the name of Brian telephoned asking for your telephone number or address in London or he said Jersey, I told him you were on your way home. He seemed very surprised and pleased somehow. Then said he hoped it would be alright if he contacted you. I said it would and it would, wouldn't it?"

"Of course it would but I would have thought he had forgotten all about me by now!"

"He did telephone a while ago as well, but I told him that you wouldn't be in London until the Fall. Which at the time was what I thought was going to happen. He said that if his business took him that way again he would ring then. Who is he, dear?"

I told mother about the unusual meeting. She chuckled, "cute story, I guess he felt he knew you after watching you for such a long time, he did sound very nice on the telephone. I wouldn't think he is married?"

I knew what mother was thinking so I agreed that he seemed

nice to me too and I expected that he is not married. Although I did think he seemed rather old.

I hoped that was the end of the conversation as I was dying to read my letters.

I sat down. I picked up the letters again, the blue airmail letter was like tissue paper. I unfolded it carefully.

My dear Emily,
After you left I went back to the house with Ann. She was very sympathetic. She too, was sad. She is going to miss you, Emily. It is terrible for me to think of you so far away. To think I can no longer pick up the phone and hear your voice. Watching you leave that day was quite devastating. I already felt lonely just watching you go. How empty the days are now without looking forward to you. Just to wake up in the morning and to know that you are no longer near.

I have already been to see about my passport, but it will take some time, I have been told. After that I will write to Canada House. As I say, it all takes time.

I am enclosing a book list for you as you asked! If you read all of these it should keep you out of mischief for a long time, darling!

I love you and miss you with every breath I take.
Paul.

My dear Emily,
Maybe after this letter I will have one from you. I long to hear from you, Emily.

I finally received the forms to fill for the passport. I have sent them off.

I have been spending quite a bit of time with Pierre and Françoise. Pierre is starting to work on the boat to get it ready for the sailing weather. I said I would help him this year. Give me something to do. I need a distraction. I bumped into Ann the other day; we had coffee together. She has many troubles and struck me as being very worried and tense. We commiserated with each other about you! You were great companions, weren't you! I expect you'll be hearing all her news before long.

Have you started on the books yet?

I am waiting for your letter my pet, don't keep me waiting too long will you!

I miss you so much and I love you more than you can ever know.

Paul

I was so pleased with the letters, they reassured me of his love.

I wanted to talk about my love but mother had other news and other things to talk about. It was apparent to me that mother was not at all interested in Paul - she was polite when I mentioned him but quickly changed the subject. I decided to keep my thoughts about Paul to myself although it was difficult and unnatural for me to hold back with mother.

I was beginning to realize that to have a love so far away was very lonely. I wrote to him but it was not enough. I missed the physical presence of him, the warmth of his kisses, the warmth of his arms, his voice. The lovely afternoons out in his open car. I remembered what fun it was with him at my uncle's house when we all played whist together. At night I cried for him, it was terrible this feeling, I felt I just could not bear it. There was no one to talk to about it. I was alone with this awful longing.

A letter arrived from Stanley thanking me for the postcard and then he said, "please come and visit, come at the end of June. I'm so glad you are home at last Emily and I am longing to see you." I wrote back to say that I would go and visit, although in a way I dreaded the visit but it would be nice to see him again, we could still be friends - we had known each other for a long time now. After all, he had never said he loved me, not in so many words although in a way I sort of knew that he did. It should be alright to visit and I really wanted to see his parents again. The more I thought about seeing them all again the more I wanted to.

There were more letters from Paul, full of his love and our future together. I read them over and over trying to believe what he said would be true.

I went to visit Stanley; he met me at the train as he used to do. He came towards me with that sweet gentle loving smile, sort of lopsided. It was lovely to see him again.

He loved to see her again but sometimes when he looked at her, there was something about her, it eluded him, he didn't know what it was that was different. When he finally kissed her, her kisses were not the same as his. She was sweet and loving in a gentle friendly way but where he felt passion she seemed a little cool and somehow remote.

He kissed me at last, I had wondered when he would; he took so long to go about it, but when he did, it was exciting and it felt so good to feel him holding me again - a familiar, lovely feeling. I knew I liked him still, I hadn't been entirely certain how I would feel being with him again because of Paul but I knew I still liked him; suddenly I knew I would always like him. He would always be special for me, very special. I felt confused and rather upset I hadn't thought I would still feel so full of love for him. It somehow felt right to be with him again. Every time I looked at him I felt more and more certain that my life just wouldn't be right with anyone else.

I went to bed that evening and I cried for so many reasons, I knew I would never be as I had been before I left, I couldn't be. Memories crept into me and took hold of me, horrible memories, spoiling my love, would I ever be able to talk about it, would I ever be able to tell anyone? If I ever told Stanley would he believe me, would he understand? I thought he would but I didn't know for sure. I felt that so much had been spoiled for me for ever.

Another letter came.

Dearest Emily,
Your mother, I see, is giving you great doubts about us. She says I should not come if I am married to someone else.
We cannot be married. But what I say is that if I am in Canada, my wife will give up - she would never come to Canada. She will then give me a divorce and then we will be married. I'm sure of it! Don't you believe it darling, don't you? What really could be simpler. Please tell me that you believe in me, that what we want will be. I love you more each day and I appreciate you

for so many reasons even more now than I did when you were here.

My passport is here. Now I await the news from Canada House. I will write as soon as I hear, my dear Emily.

My love for you is forever.

Paul.

P. S. Have you heard from Ann yet? I met her in St Helier the other day and she was with a nice-looking chap about her age, seems that they are in love and moving to Australia, I expect you know all this already though. I understand that their plans are very much in the future at the moment.

Paul.

It was the very next post that Ann's letter came. She was all enthused about her new life to begin in Australia with her new husband-to-be. She didn't have an awful lot to say about him but certainly she seemed thrilled about the whole thing. I knew that Ann hated cold weather so I imagined that the climate in Australia would suit her well and it would be lovely for her to be married again.

Australia was such a long way from everywhere; I wondered if I would ever see her again. I couldn't help feeling sad, even though I knew Ann would be happy with a new love and a new life. I only wished it were not to be so far away.

Even though my mind was often in a turmoil, I needed to do something, get a job and earn some of my own money again. I applied for a job in a bank. I had never thought of working in a bank but it was advertised and so I thought, why not? It turned out to be quite pleasant work, with friendly girls to work with, but it was not at all exciting. My days were not like those when I was dancing. At the barre I had enjoyed the total exertion, the concentration, perfecting each exercise. Then at centre floor! Dancing! Putting it all together. At the end of each day I had felt satisfied, exhilarated, excited and looking forward to the next day to do it better and better! Yes, I remembered and felt so disappointed with my life and surprised that I had let it all go. How had it happened? It certainly had not been a deliberate decision and yet I had let it happen. My life now so empty, so meaningless without dance.

Another letter came.

My dear Emily,
How can I bear to tell you this, this which I prayed would not happen has happened. Simply, I cannot come. I am unable to get permission from Canada House because I am married and separated from my wife. If we had been divorced it would have been a different matter altogether. As you know, my wife will not give me a divorce. My hands are tied, there is nothing I can do. I have written to my so-called wife again and again, she will not relent. It is really unbelievable that such an unhappy situation could arise because of one stubborn selfish woman whom I do not love and have never loved. Darling, the best thing is for you to go on with your life. I will not write to you again. I must not be selfish. You must put me out of your mind. That is the only sensible thing that we can do under such circumstances.
I do love you, as I have loved no other and it is likely that I will never love another as I have loved you. Try to remember this. We at least have had something that many people perhaps never ever have. Good-bye, my pet, my dear Emily. I shall miss you for the rest of my life.
Paul.

I read the letter. Oh it was awful to read it! I read it again. I knew it already. I knew it could never be. I knew it! I put the letter under my pillow. It was something I would have to bear alone, oh, how awful! I looked at my pretty ring, I had been so thrilled and yet I had been sad too because it couldn't be a proper engagement ring, yes I remembered the feeling I had then. I would send the ring back now - I really didn't want it anymore - it would just be a constant reminder of the sad ending of it all. I told mother. "Well I am sure it is all for the best." she said, "You are young dear, you'll get over all this very soon. Don't forget how fond you are of Stanley. You must go and see him more often - and he can come and visit us. What about that Brian chap? He sounded very nice. He might telephone you. He said he would. Keep busy, that's the answer. It's such a good thing you have that nice job at the bank."

I knew I would get no sympathy from mother and she certainly was not going to talk about it at all. Anyway, talking about it probably wouldn't help but I did wish I could have had Aunt Ann to unburden myself to, so many times I thought of her and missed her.

I wished that the nice job (as mother called it) at the bank were more interesting. Banking was not going to fulfill me; what would? It was difficult to know what to do with my life. I was bored and dissatisfied.

I decided to go and see Grace, my dancing teacher who had taught me for all those years. My idea was that perhaps I could teach some of the very young children. I realised that I would have to get into training again, perhaps even for a year; go to the studio every day as I used to do. I certainly liked the idea of being back in the dance world. Hopefully, after the additional training, I would be good enough to join the ballet company as I had originally planned.

As I approached the ballet school, happiness filled my heart. I ran up the steps and in the front door. The wonderful sound of the piano thrilled me as I dashed along the corridor. A class was in full swing. The sound of ballet shoes swishing on the wood floor accompanied the music, it was all so wonderfully familiar and filled me with that marvellous joy that I had when I danced.

I walked to the office where my teacher was waiting for me. As I knocked and went in she jumped up and rushed to meet me. We hugged each other, laughing with pleasure. It was so lovely to see her again.

We sat down and caught up on each other's news. When I told her about my long visit in Jersey she was fascinated, because she remembered it well from being there on holiday just before the war, before she came to Canada. I told her what I hoped to do, she responded with enthusiasm but was adamant that I would have to spend quite a while getting fit. She did not think it would take too long if I took classes every day, three hours in the morning, starting at eight-thirty, finishing at noon, with various classes in the afternoons. She suggested I began on Monday at eight-thirty. I left the studio feeling better than I had felt for many weeks. I knew I was doing the right thing.

Every day I went to the studio and every day I enjoyed. It was several months before I was forced to face the fact that I really did have a problem with my back and it was not getting any better. My left leg didn't seem very strong and ached off and on. At first I hoped it was because my muscles were weak from lack of use and it was true to some extent as it did improve a little for the first few weeks. Gradually each day became a struggle with this constant pain. I tried wearing an elastic girdle thinking that the support would help. I took a few Aspirins, to no avail. I finally told Grace because the pain had become very difficult to bear every day and my leg ached too much to do any pointe work. She was surprised to learn of my distress, but she remarked that she had noticed I had not seemed as enthusiastic or as energetic as I had been at the start. Then she guessed that would come back, that we all have these little phases from time to time. Now that she knew what the problem was, she thought I should go to the doctor as soon as possible.

It seemed that my dancing days were over forever. After Xrays, I was told there was a malformation of my lower spine which was causing problems with three lower vertebrae. The doctor said that there had been some dislocation in that area and that there had been several small cracks in the vertebrae at some time (which was true, as I had had a riding accident when I was at boarding school a few years ago and had been in hospital for several weeks). There was also major disc deterioration. Of course I didn't mention the terrifying fall I had in New York; I knew however that this really was what had triggered the whole problem. I was loathe to think about it. A fusion of the lower spine, grafting bone from my hip, would be the only way to deal with it; that, of course, would mean no more dancing. After the fusion I would have to adjust my life to accommodate a stiff back. My leg would strengthen with walking and swimming and some ballet exercises. How mistaken I had been – all this time thinking that I had got through that hideous experience so easily – when actually it had shattered all my dancing expectations. I was devastated.

I had the operation. It was much more horrible than I thought it would be. It was many weeks before I could get about and even then I needed a walking stick and a steel brace which encased my body and protected my spine. It was all very tiring and although I wouldn't have a backache anymore which would be quite wonderful, I would have to live without dancing. That special feeling I experienced when I danced, I would never feel again. I found it very hard to accept that this had really happened, to never dance again! Ever! I had been dancing since I was three years old and dance had always been such an important part of my life. I did my best not to think about it during the day but at night in my bed all my thoughts were of dancing and what might have been and what could never be and quietly and silently I cried until I fell asleep. Mother kept telling me things would sort themselves out. I tried to believe her and share her optimism.

Stanley invited me to go and visit him. "Mother and Dad both send love and hope you will come soon. Mother has your room ready now.

"We are all very sorry about your dancing, I know how important it was to you, I remember you talking about it the first time we met, you had been accepted at some dance academy and were very excited about it. You even danced for me once on the beach with the tide 'way out, do you remember? You just loved to dance didn't you! It must be awful for you. I wonder what your plans are now. Do come soon Emily, I have missed you."

Stanley was there to meet me at the train station. He helped me so gently. He was so kind, so sweet. I looked at him. It was lovely to see him, to feel his arm around me again, to hear his voice beside me. There was his mother, waiting at the door. "Oh, my dear Emily, such a relief to see you walking about, you look really well, dear."
"Thank-you, but I do hate this stick!"
"Never mind dear - soon you won't need it I'm sure." She called Stanley's father, "Come dear - she's here!"
There he was, all smiles. "Lovely to have you here, Emily! Quite a relief really, isn't it, dear."
"Yes, yes it really is. Quite a relief!"
Alone, Stanley was loving, tender. I felt his kisses excite me the way they used to do, but he said nothing of the future. He

was still at university. We didn't talk about what we would do or when we would be together, not like we used to do. We were alone all the time, but he never said anything. I knew I loved him again, perhaps I had never really stopped loving him. But he said nothing. I felt that I was ready for him now. It seemed in many ways that he did love me but he said nothing. He told me how sorry he was that I couldn't dance anymore, he wondered what I would do. When at last I started to cry about it he held me and kept saying how sorry he was and he was sure things would work out. I was puzzled and disappointed. I wanted him to say more. I appreciated his caring words but I wanted more. I wanted him to claim me. I left him with a heavy heart.

It was shortly after my visit to Stanley that the letter arrived, air-mail from England. When I opened it and read the first line I was quite taken aback.

My Dear Emily, (Tinkerbell)
In my mind I still call you Tinkerbell! Remember? Do you remember the first time we went swimming and I called you that? It suited you so! I thought so.
I have recently been back to the island. I left shortly after you did, as I had a very good position offered to me in London.
I went to see your aunt - it seems I was lucky to find her still there as she is leaving soon, as I am sure you know. I went to find out all about you and of course your address which you never did send to me. (I still have those photos of you.) I was always so fond of you and have found myself thinking of you more and more, so I thought I would just go and find out, combine it with a little holiday. I was very upset to hear that you have been so ill with a serious back problem! I always think of you as being such a healthy young thing. So full of life. What a terrible shame. However your aunt seemed to think that you were on the mend. It would be lovely to see you again. How would you feel about us writing to each other to explore our feelings. I know that you always gave me great pleasure. You could tell me about yourself and how you are managing at present. Would you like to do that?
I look forward so much to hearing from you Emily.
With love,
Lawrence

I read it again, I was really quite astonished, I hadn't thought about Lawrence for a long while. Not really thought about him. I told mother.

"Well dear, why don't you write to him. You seemed to like him. He was quite a nice man wasn't he?"

I said that, yes, he was and maybe I would. I was not immediately sure. After I gave it a little thought I decided there would be no harm in writing a letter or two. Funny he went all that way to find out about me! I was flattered.

I answered the letter, replying to the things he had asked about and told him that yes, I wouldn't mind corresponding with him for a while anyway. I told him about my swimming, ballet exercises and walking to strengthen my leg and back and that I had been taking a French conversation course. I saw no harm in the letters.

After a time the letters took a different turn.

Dear Emily,

Now that we have been corresponding for all these months I feel sure that I would like to marry you and I would be quite prepared to come to Canada, in fact I would like to come. I'm not certain if I would like to live there forever, but it would be an interesting experience for me. The fact that you are not quite back to your old self is not a problem for me at all - I would enjoy helping you. I think I always knew that I would like to marry you although at the time I did worry about being that much older than you, but perhaps now it might be a good thing for you to be married to someone older, to someone who can support you and if need be, look after you. What do you think now? I do not wish to rush you Emily, but if you say yes I could arrange to be in Canada by September. Please Emily, be my wife.

My love,
Laurence

I was not terribly surprised at this letter, but, should I marry him? I was not in love with him now but maybe after a time I would love him. He was very nice, cultured, a good profession, sophisticated. His letters indicated that he would be kind and gentle. Apart from that, he was very handsome - although this was really not terribly important to me.

I decided to write and ask him if he would be prepared to come here and then see how we liked each other after he was here for a spell. Maybe that would be sensible, I suggested.

In his next letter, he said he would do that but only if I really felt optimistic about the end results. If I had great doubts already it would be silly for him to consider such a thing. To show me good faith he would like to send me an engagement ring; that way he would know I was not going to slip through his fingers before he even got here.

I had to make a decision. I 'phoned Stanley.

"What is it?" he asked, "Is something the matter?"

"No, not really!"

"Why are you phoning?"

"I don't know, I thought I would like to talk to you that's all."

"Oh, well, I'm in the middle of exams, Emily, otherwise I would come up."

"I understand" I said. "It's alright."

"Are you sure? Are you really sure?"

"Yes, I guess so."

"Well then, good-bye Emily, I'll see you before long." He still said nothing, he did not speak of love. I put the phone down. I could wait for him forever and in the end he might not want me at all. I thought I would like to wait for him, I really wanted to but only if he asked me to - and he had not. It was a deep, painful disappointment to me. I had wanted to love him, I had wanted happiness with him. But he had not offered it to me. I decided to accept Lawrence's offer. I had had enough of wondering what to do. I wanted my life to be settled, to have one person, one person to be with, one person to know and love. I believed in this sort of happiness and of course I loved the thought of having children; family life was what I wanted now, that suddenly seemed to be the only thing that could take the place of my dancing, the only way of life that would fulfill me.

I wrote back, that, yes, I would marry him and I would accept his engagement ring.

A telegram arrived.

DEAR TINKERBELL,
LOVE AND CHERISH ALWAYS STOP RING ON WAY STOP
HOPE YOU AGREE 23 OCTOBER SPECIAL DATE BATTLE OF
ALAMEIN WHERE I WITH MONTGOMERY 1942 STOP VERY
MEMORABLE DAY STOP LOVE COMMA YOUR FUTURE
HUSBAND LAWRENCE

It was the evening after I received the telegram. There was a knock on the door and, standing there smiling, was Stanley. He looked so young, so young and healthy, so lovable. The boyish, tender, lopsided smile. His eyes that looked into mine. I felt guilty to see him there. Why had he come? I could not have him. He came further into the room and sat down, I sat down beside him and he took my hand. When he turned to look at me I thought I would die of longing for him, for his arms around me again, I knew I loved him, if only he hadn't come it would have been alright. Then he said, "I had to come, I thought you sounded so strange on the telephone and I couldn't stop thinking about you. I'm in the middle of my exams, so I have to return to-night. What has happened? Something has happened, what is it? Tell me, I know there is something?"
I felt suddenly sick. My stomach churned and my face was burning. I had to tell him. Well, I thought, I don't care. He didn't ask me, it's his own fault. I wished he didn't look at me that way, right into me. *I couldn't bear it. My whole being ached for him.*
"I'm going to be married" I said.
"Married? How do you mean married? You can't be going to be married, who on earth to? I thought you were *my* girl. You are my girl! You have always been my girl. What on earth do you mean Emily. What is this all about?"
"Well - I am. I am - and I am sorry, Stanley. He was someone I met in Jersey and he started writing to me months ago and now he wants to marry me and I have agreed to it."
"You have agreed to marry him?" He still kept the question in his voice. But still he did not talk of love. He looked at me, then put his head in his hands. "I had better go," he said. His voice was low, then he mumbled, "Better get home. So you are to be

married. I'd better go, Emily."
He got up and walked to the door, I stood there with him.
I couldn't look at him. I kept my eyes down. He took my chin in
his hand and tilted my head then he looked into my eyes. He
said it again. "Married?"
"Yes."
"Good-bye then." He turned and ran down the stairs.
I wanted to run after him, stop him from going, stop
everything. I ran to the window, I couldn't see him. I opened the
window wide, leaned far out and looked, crying and calling his
name. I ran out the door and down the stairs. I didn't know
which way to run. I ran to where I thought he would have been
parked, he was not there. I stopped, I thought what was the use,
he had gone. I would never see him again. How could I have
done this?
I had to tell mother what had happened.
"He came here - and has gone home? The poor chap, he
must have been very upset. Did you know he would feel like
that? You told me that you didn't think he was very serious about
you Emily, not serious enough for marriage. You have hurt him.
You didn't warn him what was going on at all? You just blurted it
out like that? Oh Emily, you should have written to him and
warned him about what you were doing. Why didn't you?"
"I don't know, I don't know! Oh I wish that I had! I do I wish
that I had! Maybe he would have said something if I had! I know
he liked me a lot but he never told me it was anything more than
that, he never said he loved me, so how was I to know what he
was thinking. I can't mind-read, mother!"
"No dear, that's true, but you should have learned by now that
men don't expose their feelings quite as readily as women and
I guess he was reluctant to say too much; maybe he wasn't
ready to make such a commitment and then when he saw he was
going to lose you he realised that he did love you. Don't forget
he still had a long way to go before he would be ready for
marriage, he isn't even half way through university yet!"
"But mother, I would have waited for him forever, why
wouldn't he say he loved me if he did! Why not! That was all he
had to say and if he had asked me to wait for him, well of course
I would have, forever!"
"Well dear, like I say, men are different to us girls! They don't
discuss feelings and things, anyway he obviously does care
much more about you than you thought. It certainly was not a

nice way to go about what you did and I am sorry you did it like that. I do hope you are doing the right thing? Should you call it off with Lawrence?"

"Oh no mother - I just couldn't do that, that would be a terrible thing to do now that I have agreed to marry him and he is so delighted about it all and he has probably already bought his ticket! No, I just couldn't do that; I said I would marry him and now I must."

"Well dear, you could break it off you know, it wouldn't be the first time an engagement was broken - it does happen from time to time."

"Well yes, I suppose I could, but no mother, I just couldn't do that, not now."

I felt quite sick. I certainly wished I could change everything, but now it was too late, I knew I couldn't do that. I would never see Stanley again. I dabbed at my wet, swollen eyes.

A week later there was a letter from Stanley's mother. She was upset. She said she didn't know what had happened, but she knew something had - as Stanley was upset and withdrawn, he wouldn't tell her anything. "What have you done, Emily? I would dearly like to know what the matter is. We are all so fond of you. But what have you done to my son? Please tell me, Emily. I don't want to cluck like a mother hen, but I must know."

I would have to write to his mother and explain. Oh how awful, it was all far more difficult than I had ever thought it would be. I wished I could go back and change everything back to the way it was.

In the mail was my ring. My engagement ring. It was very pretty. It fit my finger exactly. It suited my hand perfectly. In another packet was a tiny gold magnet with a tiny golden heart attached. It was on a chain. I put it around my neck. But I knew it was the wrong heart.

I had to go through with it, so I thought I would just make the best of it. I sent a telegram "Rings on her finger, bells on her toes, she shall have music wherever she goes, Love Tinkerbell." There was no music in my heart.

I was actually dreading the day of Lawrence's arrival and when the day did come I had to pluck up all my courage to meet his train. A great wave of relief swept over me as I saw him get off the train. He looked fine, he looked the same as I remembered. Tall, nice smile. He came to me and held my hand then gave me a little kiss on my cheek and whispered "Tink" in my ear. Out loud he said, "You look lovely, Emily, just lovely, the illness hasn't altered you in any way that I can see!" I was surprised to hear him say that as I had not thought of how I would appear to him - I had been so concerned about how he would appear to me - if he had changed or was different from my memory of him.

I had found an apartment for him to live in - and where we could live after we were married. It was a little old-fashioned, but pleasant. It was on the edge of Stanley Park and had lovely views of the ocean and mountains. I had put a few pieces of antique furniture in it - some my mother could spare and a chair and lamp from Nellie and Lily, a set of curtains from Madeleine. I thought it looked quite pretty. (I hadn't known that he did not like antique furniture, I was to learn that later of course.)

Lawrence didn't notice how the apartment looked, he looked at me all the time. He wanted to hold me and kiss me and kiss me, persistent kisses that I was not at all used to. Suddenly his kisses frightened me. Stanley had been so tenderly gentle and loving and I had wanted his kisses. At last he let me go. My lack of enthusiasm had cooled his ardour, (temporarily). I tried not to think of the fear I had suddenly felt. Was he going to be rough and terribly insistent? What was it going to be like? I was very afraid. He had never been rough or unpleasantly insistent before.

"I have brought you some gifts" he said as he rummaged in his case. He handed me an elegantly wrapped package. I opened the box (Harrod's) and lifted the tissue away, I was surprised to see a black cashmere pullover with a very high neck and short sleeves. "Will it suit you?" I knew it would and was quite amazed that he could have chosen something so perfect for me. I held it to my body and looked in the large mirror.

"It will be perfect." I took the one off that I was wearing, I slipped on the new stylish one and turned to him "It's marvellous! What else?" He came to me then and held me. "I prefer you without the sweater" he said, as he caressed me. I broke away. Was there something else I asked.

"Perfume, 'Je Reviens' the one you always used. I hope you still use it?"

"Of course I do Lawrence, thank you, it's nice you remembered." He looked at me and smiled, "yes," he said, "I remembered."

Of course he remembered, he remembered everything about her. He hadn't been able to get her out of his mind, he had certainly tried.

"I brought a Liberty scarf for your mother. How about a cup of tea?"

I went to the kitchen and put the kettle on. I thought it a lovely little kitchen, however, Lawrence did not even come in the door. He sat down on the antique chair and waited to be served. I poured our tea into my pretty china tea-cups (which he did not notice). He then told me about his trip across Canada, how wonderful it was, the breathtaking scenery and how he saw some Mounties and took a photo of them. At last he looked out the window. "My, my - there'll be some wonderful sunsets to see from this window. That'll keep me busy taking photos to send to my parents and brothers. Now then, I think I would like a nice walk in that park you told me about."

My limp was nearly gone by this time, I felt strong and energetic as we walked along together. He told me about his parents, his brothers and nieces and nephews. I was very interested in his family and of course he did have a very attractive English accent that I enjoyed hearing. I thought that maybe I had not made such a terrible mistake after all, it was true I didn't love him, I knew in my heart I loved Stanley but maybe we would be alright together, he seemed very pleased with me. Back at the apartment he wanted to make love, again he held me and kissed me.

"No! No! We will wait until we are married." I truly didn't want to, I wasn't at all interested in making love with my future husband; I knew that it was because, although I was fond of him, I didn't have that aching love for him that I had felt for Stanley or Paul. I wasn't longing for him at all.

"Even now?" He let me go.

"Yes. We will wait."

"Why?" He was greatly surprised.

"Because I prefer it that way. I really do. I would not feel right

if I am not married. I would feel guilty. I think it would be terrible to feel guilty about making love. I am sorry if you don't understand."
He laughed a little. "Silly girl, after all we will soon be married - in a matter of weeks actually."
"Well I could still get pregnant before the wedding and everyone would know once the baby arrived and that would be terribly embarrassing! Think how awful we would feel with everyone knowing! Mother would know immediately and so would my brother and Madeleine, they would be quite horrified."
He shrugged his shoulders, smiled a little "I guess it wouldn't really matter an awful lot Emily, however, if that's the way you want it, that's the way it'll be." He clasped me around the waist and kissed my cheek.

He wasn't really surprised, she did fuss about being pregnant and her virginity, silly really, especially now that they will be married in such a short time.

As I was leaving, he gave me a small package, "This is my present for you, it would be nice if you would wear it on our wedding day, but you don't have to of course."

On our wedding day I opened the package. Lawrence had given me a tiny gold bell on a fine gold chain, the inscription read "Tinkerbell, my love" and the date of our wedding. Of course I wore it, it was lovely, sweet, unsophisticated and lovely, it had a special meaning for both of us and it suited my very simple, cream velvet wedding dress.

MARRIED

I had long dreaded our wedding night as I knew I would have to tell Lawrence all about my horrible experience in New York. Would he believe me? I had told him long ago that I was a virgin when I was fairly certain I was not! I had never been really totally certain if it had actually happened, I had been so scratched and so sore everywhere; however, I knew I would have to tell him. Also I was still very apprehensive about sex, nervous and worried about the whole thing.

"This is for you" I heard Lawrence say as he passed me a tissue-wrapped parcel, As I undid the ribbon a beautiful nightie slithered on to the floor! I picked it up and held it to me, a delicate pink and white silk with an over-veil of lace, it was exquisite.

Lawrence took it from me and gently slipped it over my head. I felt the silk slither over my body, I looked down at myself as I saw the lace and the silk all mixed up together falling over my breasts in folds to the floor. I looked up to see Lawrence smiling at me. "So beautiful" he kept saying. As I lay on the bed I began to tell him my ugly story, suddenly I began to sob, "you will be disappointed" I said, maybe you won't believe me! I'm not really sure whether I am still a virgin."

"No Tink, no matter what happened, you are you, and of course I believe you, of course I do, I am not disappointed - your virginity is not nearly as important as you think. It is sad that such a terrible thing happened to you, my poor Tink, shocking and terrible. I love you and hopefully that horrible memory will soon be gone because I love you and it is love that will make our union a happy one.

I *knew from what she had said that she of course, technically, was not a virgin, but I knew also that she was, without a doubt.*

I enjoyed the settled feeling of marriage, the weekends, the lazy Sunday morning, the leisurely breakfast, the long walks in the park. I enjoyed cooking the meals, it satisfied me, to see a nice meal I had prepared and the table with flowers on it, all nicely set. Lawrence liked the way I did things and was especially pleased when he saw that I could darn his socks and without any bumps or lumps! He also enjoyed the meals I made and told me so. When friends came for dinner he was very pleasant and courteous, I felt quite proud of my new husband.

I was not always as well as I thought I was. Sometimes my whole body went into a spasm and I was unable to move. I had been warned that this might happen from time to time. On these occasions, Lawrence had to lift me and carry me to our bed. I would lie very still for many hours and then the spasm would go away, I would be fine again.

The park was beautiful that spring and we spent all our free time among the flowers and feeding the ducks and geese. We went for long walks in the evenings and sometimes hired a rowboat and rowed in the evening light.

As the weather got warmer we swam and sunned ourselves on the beautiful beach that was right beside our building; I often made a picnic lunch to have on the beach. It was such a glorious summer we were outdoors at every opportunity, swimming, walking, rowing. Lawrence enjoyed all these things the way that I did. He would have liked to play tennis but I was not ready for that yet. My health was improving in leaps and bounds with this physical activity but I still had to be careful.

I began to love him, not with that special aching love, but he was nice to me, kind when my legs and back ached, he told me I was beautiful, he admired the way I dressed, the way I walked, things like that. He took many photographs of me to send home, he said he wanted to show all his family his lovely wife, we were peaceful together.

It was during that summer he told me that although he liked Vancouver he felt he would rather live in England. He wanted his parents and brothers to know me and me to know all of his family. He asked me if I would mind leaving. Without thinking about it I quickly replied that I would love to go to England! I was sure I would like living there. "When did you think we would go?" The adventure, the excitement, the wonderful ocean trip, were thrilling to think of and England had a special fascination for me.

He thought September would be a good time. He was going to write to someone he knew at university because his father had mentioned in a letter that this chap was looking for a partner for his architectural practice. "Would that suit you?"

I told him it did not matter to me - anytime would be fine as far as I was concerned. I felt a little guilty at my enthusiasm to leave as I knew that mother would miss me and of course I would miss her. We would write letters and keep together that way, we had done that before and then, someday, mother would visit us in England. We would have a nice house by then.

Mother was far more upset than I imagined she would be. "How could he come and take you away from us like that? He must have planned it that way. Why, he has been here hardly any time at all, how can he know whether he likes it here or not?" She sniffed and wiped her eyes. "I'll never see you again - never!"

"Oh mother - that just is not true; please mother, don't be upset, you'll come and see us I know it. Think how lovely it will be to visit us in England."

"You say that dear, but you know very well I am not as well off as I used to be. Things are not the same as they were. Well, there is nothing I can do about it - if you are to go, you are to go, but I hate him for taking you away from me like this - and not just me either, what about Nellie and Lily and your brother and Madeleine?"

I was truly sorry mother was so upset. I knew in my heart that I probably would not see Nellie and Lily again as they were so old now and not well; they were being looked after all the time by a private nurse. I would have to say goodbye to them forever and it made me very sad because they were so important to me and I loved them. I was pretty certain that I would see my brother and Madeleine again, I could come back for a visit or maybe they would visit us in England some-day. I didn't think of the move the way that mother did. I pictured her visiting us in England and there would be a baby and everything would be wonderful. Mother's anger took the pleasure out of our plans.

We were to take the train across America to New York, then after a few days in New York we would sail to England, landing in Southampton. Lawrence's father, who had bought us a new car with a pull-down roof for our wedding present, would be in Southampton to meet us and deliver the car. Then we would be staying in the hotel with his parents at Eastbourne where they were holidaying for a few days before we travelled north. Lawrence had accepted the position with his friend in his architectural practice, with the prospect of becoming his partner. I was excited about the whole trip and believed that once we were settled I would soon become pregnant. I was longing to have a baby but every time I brought the subject up Lawrence would tell me he was not ready. He said it was too soon - "You have me to look after; is that not enough for now? I don't want to share you yet."

I was sure he would change his mind once we were settled and he was back in his own country; I was sure of it.

ENGLAND – 1954

Mr Love, Lawrence's father, was waving to us as we left the ship. He had a round, rosy-apple face. His smile used his whole face - everything crinkled and lit up. His eyes, like shiny blackberries, were warm and welcoming and his manner was one of happiness. A tall, nicely-made man. He kissed me well and firmly on the cheek. "My word, it is grand to have you here, love! Grand! Well son, shall we take a look at this car!"

The car was dark green, a Morris Minor with a cream-coloured pull-down roof and green leather upholstery; it was a lovely car. We admired it and thanked him for his very generous gift.

At the hotel Mrs Love was waiting to meet us. She was a small woman, very small, but not thin. Neither was she fat, she was a little stout. She appeared to be an old lady, whereas his father was still a vigorous, enthusiastic man. Not old. She had a quiet face, with bright twinkling eyes. Her hair was white and gently curled in a neat little roll at the nape of her neck. She held out her hands and I grasped them in mine. "How was your journey, dear?"

"Oh, very lovely, calm sea and lots of sunshine. Yes, it was very nice."

"I am so glad you did not have rough weather, that would be most unpleasant, I think. Are you tired?"

"Oh no - not at all."

"Well dear, it is lovely to see you and to have you here! Come then and we will have tea."

Her son stooped, kissed her on the cheek and patted her on the shoulder. Waiting to have tea, were Uncle Geoffrey and Aunt Alice. They were all holidaying together - a yearly foursome. Uncle Geoffrey got up from his chair and rushed over to shake my hand. He too was rosy-cheeked, healthy-looking, jolly. Aunt Alice, moving slowly, joined him; they both greeted me with warmth and enthusiasm. It was a pleasant gathering. I felt very welcomed.

The drive north was beautiful. The English villages were lovely and the pub where we stopped for lunch was picture-post-card perfect! When we were ready to stop for the night we found a wonderful old hotel, the bedroom was enormous, furnished with antique chairs and a desk in dark wood. The dining-room was very formal, with glistening white table linen and heavy silver. At night we left our shoes outside our door and in the morning they were returned, all polished. The English countryside delighted me with its rolling hills, the oak trees, the hedgerows, the small, green fields tucked inside low, stone walls. The houses looked so solid in their brick or stone coverings - and the chimney pots – I had never seen so many chimney pots before! Every town we went through had a church or a clock-tower. It was like opening a huge picture book, sitting there in our car with the roof down and all this in front of me and around me. The out-door animal smells I inhaled with child-like pleasure. We passed cows being taken home to be milked. They mooed and took their time strolling down the lane. The sheep, baaaaaed and I copied them, their baaaing! Lawrence laughed at me, enjoying my nonsense.

She was so happy, he thought, so young and unspoiled. Everything was new to her; he loved her like this, no, he wasn't ready for babies, he didn't want to share her, not yet.

The parents' house was larger and more impressive than I had imagined: built with stone and brick, it sat tall, solid and imposing at the end of a long driveway. Stone steps led up to the large, heavy, oak door. There were gardens of flowers and lawns of brilliant green everywhere I looked. Inside, the rooms were spacious, but not huge. From every room there was a garden view. It was a family house, but was formally furnished with polished wood and brocades. Mrs Love explained that the winter velvet drapes would be up in the next week or two, then she explained that the gardener came every day. "The maid doesn't live in anymore. With just the two of us - and it is so much nicer not having her around all the time, she comes most days mind, but it's not the same as having her live with us somehow!" She chuckled, "Dad has to bring the morning tea now, but he quite likes doing it, you know. He even makes our breakfast on some mornings. Very good it is too!"

"Do you like pheasant, love?" Mr Love asked me.

"Yes I do but I've not had it often."

"Well, you'll have it often here! We have a "shoot" and usually one or other of the family shoots at the week-end, in the season of course. We have partridge as well as pheasant and sometimes a hare or a rabbit. You'll have to learn how to prepare 'Jugged Hare'. Delicious! Must be done right, mind you! The game bag will be sent to you by train every fortnight or so, I expect."

High tea was cold roast pheasant, bread sauce, two plates of bread and butter - one of white bread and the other of brown. A small bowl of lettuce and a bowl of tomatoes, all home grown in the kitchen garden I was told. A Victoria Sponge cake with cream, little lemon tarts and butter tarts completed the meal. It was a leisurely meal with many cups of tea. The brothers came to join us for more cups of tea and cake at the end of the meal. "You'll soon be meeting everyone else. We thought that could be next week after you have settled into your flat."

Presently the brothers left; they all lived in the same area - and all worked for their father.

It was time for us to go as well, our flat was in Sheffield, an hour's drive and we wanted time to get settled before we went to bed. The flat, the brothers said, was the ground floor of a Victorian house. It was fully furnished and equipped so all we had to do was unpack our clothes. I thought it sounded lovely as I loved old houses, that is what I had grown up in, and I had always been surrounded with antique furniture so I knew I would love the flat and of course I knew it was to be only temporary. I assumed we would be buying a house pretty promptly.

I ran up the steps.

Lawrence opened the front door. Excitedly I rushed into the sitting room, as Lawrence turned on the light. "There," he said, "our little home!"

And here it was! A dark-brown leather sofa, old and split on the arms with the stuffing bursting out, was the first thing I saw; there was a matching, ugly chair opposite. Even the curtains that hung unevenly and dejectedly at the sides of the small windows were a rusty-brown colour - like dried blood! The walls were beige and the woodwork was dark brown. The carpet was brown and beige, faded and threadbare. We went into the bedroom. It was nearly the same as the sitting room - the same brown and beige colours - the bedspread was beige with bold dark-green and mustard-coloured swirls. It was a very shiny satin and quite the ugliest bedspread I had ever seen. The small netted window looked on to a concrete yard with a wash-line, at least it was not a busy road. The kitchen was the brightest room as the ancient gas stove was white and there were no curtains to block out any light that did come in. The window was small and also looked on to the concrete yard. Everything about the flat was depressing and ugly, I hated it. It was just too horrible to think of living here. "Do we have to stay here for long?"

"Yes, why ever not? Can't be moving about you know, all costs money. Quite cosy when we get the fire lit, you'll see."

"But I don't like it here at all."

"Oh - you will - and there's a lovely botanical garden just around the corner, you'll love it there."

I tried to cheer up. That did sound lovely, "yes, I would like that." I thought that I would walk in the park every day. I would have to, to get away from this ghastly place. I tried to smile and said I would unpack our overnight cases. The others I would leave until the morning. As I unpacked I cheered myself up by thinking that soon I would be unpacking all my china and linen and pictures, and that would make a huge difference to the flat, thinking these thoughts made me feel much better.

"Well, you seemed to take everything in your stride alright, quite a lot of family to meet all in one go, but you managed just fine, I must say."

"Oh yes, I liked everyone, they were very pleasant and so welcoming and I am looking forward to meeting the rest of the family - especially the children."

"Lovely children, lovely, couldn't be nicer! I bought them a puppy once you know, what fun that was! It was a surprise! They were absolutely delighted. Yes, we had a lot of fun with that dog."

"Don't they still have it?"

"No, not that one, No, it became ill and died, very sad, but my brother quickly got another for them. He uses it for the shoot too. Nice animal. Now then - time to sleep, I shall have a rather busy day tomorrow. Good-night love."

"Don't I get a kiss?"

He laughed, "Yes yes, of course, I guess my mind 's on other things, forgot about that I did! Sorry love."

He kissed me then, but it was just a kiss, a rather empty sort of kiss. My mind flashed back to the days before we were married when he couldn't leave me alone; he was always wanting to make love but, more than his kisses or making love, I would have liked to be held lovingly in his arms to gather some comfort from his male strength. He seemed to be unable to give me that sort of loving. Stanley had often put his arm around me,

I remembered that summer when my girlfriend had died of polio and he had held me close and stroked my hair for ages, he had always been so gentle and kind - he had kissed me with such tenderness, enfolding me in his arms. I knew I shouldn't be thinking of him, it was wrong – I was married to Lawrence, but I couldn't help aching and longing for my gentle, loving Stanley.

In the morning light, the flat looked even worse. There was no colour anywhere - just dark brown and beige, everything thin, threadbare and ugly. I put our clothes away and moved a few cushions around and re-arranged the table and chairs. It was slightly improved. At noon Lawrence came home for his lunch. "I'll be able to get home most days - the office is only ten minutes from here."

After lunch he took me in the car to show me the botanical gardens.

"There you are! A lovely place to walk. You could even bring your book and read here on a nice afternoon. Of course it will soon be too cold to sit in the park but it is never too cold to walk, is it?" His very cheery voice irritated me, I started to make some remark about our horrible flat and how I had to get out of it no matter what, but he brushed my words aside, "Have a pleasant walk!" He rushed away, not listening at all as he got in the car and drove off.

I was very glad to be out in the bright air, out of those gloomy, dark, depressing rooms.

My life in England was very different from my life in Vancouver. It seemed to me that everything was different. I made my grocery list and went to the grocery shop - the one Lawrence had told me was suitable for us. There I was given a chair to sit on while someone took my order. The shop assistant invited me to taste different types of cheese or a cookie (of course, a cookie was called a biscuit), a tiny snippet of ham. When I inquired about a specific item, the assistant brought the item and showed it to me. Everything was then delivered to the flat. "Is this the way everyone shops here?" It seemed a very luxurious way to do the grocery shopping.

"I don't think so, but that is the way my mother shops and everyone in my family. You'll shop the same way at the greengrocer and the butcher. That way too, if you want to go and have coffee or do some other shopping you won't have to carry any groceries about with you. Much the best way, don't you agree! Anyway, ladies don't carry groceries about, you know, it isn't quite 'the thing'."

Sundays we went to Lawrence's parents for the family Sunday lunch. I loved these family Sundays, with everyone there, all talking and enjoying the good roast beef and Yorkshire pudding. Someday I thought I would like to have a large family and have gatherings like that.

Lawrence did not want me to work. I had suggested that maybe I would find a job of some sort, maybe part time, but only until I became pregnant of course. I thought it would be a good way for me to meet people and make some friends. A dance studio I thought would be perfect, helping with the very young children. Lawrence, however did not think so, "No Emily, wives in our family do not work."

"Don't any wives work then?" It seemed strange to think of. I knew that in my mother's era, wives didn't work, but all of my friends worked or planned to work until they started to have children, which usually meant about one year.

"Perhaps some do, but not in my family and you are certainly not going to, ever."

I wasn't terribly upset about this as I hoped I would soon be pregnant and once I had a baby there wouldn't be much point in me having a job anyway as it would be for such a short time, although it would have been nice to meet some people my age and make some friends. One certainly did not work once one had a family. Family life was important to me, as it was to all of my friends, a young woman's goal. We had all been nurtured in the family environment and believed in this sort of happiness and fulfilment.

I thought this would be a good time to talk about starting a family. I was quite surprised to hear him say, "I don't think so - not yet. I like having you to look after me and like I said before, I am not ready to share you yet."

He had told me in his letters that he definitely did want a family. Hopefully he had not changed his mind - I couldn't bear it. I was longing for a baby. I constantly saw mothers in the park with babies in their prams and I was truly envious. Oh, how

I wanted a baby. I asked Lawrence when he thought the time would be right? "We'll see," he said, "we'll see. Cheer up love - you have me, don't you!" I suddenly realised that if there were to be no babies, I didn't see the point of being married, I didn't need his money; what I really wanted from him was a child, family life, the whole thing. He knew I wanted to start a family now; why was he the one to make the decision of when it should be? Shouldn't we discuss it together and decide together? Immediately I thought all of these thoughts, I was annoyed, horrified and depressed.

He was bound to want children, he said he did. I would just have to be patient; after all we hadn't been in England long at all. Oh well, I thought, I would just have to go on using that horrible contraceptive every night the way Madeleine had told me to do ('Just put it in every night' she had said, 'it gets to be a routine just like brushing your teeth'). Maybe I wouldn't bother with that any more, at the clinic the nurse had said that the contraceptive was not one hundred percent safe anyway, so he would never know. Maybe I would make the decision after all. If he asked me if I had put it in I might have to lie, but hopefully he wouldn't do that. I would not like to lie to him, although it would be deceitful not to say anything, but on the other hand I should have some say in the matter and, doing it this way, I would! It would be my decision, not his!

I tried to keep cheerful by telling myself that I would probably feel better when my things arrived, familiar things: my own pretty china and linen, some lovely crystal that had belonged to my great-aunts, plates too, Limoges, white with little blue flowers on them, perfect for afternoon tea. I was lonely and disappointed with my life, I missed mother, Madeleine and my friends, life seemed dull and empty. It would have been better if we had lived closer to his family; I would have liked that, I could have invited them over for afternoon tea or they would have perhaps invited me for tea and a visit. If only I could be pregnant I thought, then I could be planning and getting ready for the baby, this lonely aching sadness would suddenly be replaced with a feeling of joy, I was sure of it.

When the tea chests arrived from Canada, Lawrence put them in the sitting-room for me before going to the office. I could hardly wait to tidy up after breakfast so that I had a clear morning to unpack all of my things. I noticed that my dinner service was the first to be unpacked as I could see a bit of the pink china that had come loose from the wrapping. Quickly I unwrapped a plate, but as I picked it from the paper it fell apart. Oh dear! I hoped it was just the one. But as I pulled out each dish, each one was broken, each one fell apart in my hand. Every water glass was a mound of crunching, broken, glass. All of the wine glasses. Everything of china or glass was either completely broken beyond repair, or chipped or cracked. The pictures mother had given me and the ones that had been in my bedroom forever, the ones from my girlhood: the glass in every one was broken - smashed, even some of the frames were broken or damaged. I wouldn't be able to use any of them, not now. I sat in the mess of paper and broken china and glass and started to cry. I couldn't stop, I didn't want to stop. I looked around me, what was left? One decanter, four of my aunts' sherry glasses. One small jug from my china set and three demi-tasse cups. Four chipped and cracked Limoges plates, one dish, with a cracked lid and two tea cups and saucers - out of the 24 given to me by friends at a tea cup and saucer shower, each one had been special, now I had only two left, that was all. I went on crying, picking and stacking the broken bits of china and glass. The gifts from my friends, the treasures from Nellie and Lily and mother; I had been so looking forward to having these things around me to create our home. I had imagined it all, the table set with my china, the pictures I knew so well to hang familiar and pleasant on our walls. I must have been sitting there a long time when I heard Lawrence come up the front steps. He saw me sitting there, with the crumpled paper and broken china, bits of glass and smashed pictures, as he came towards me he realised that I had been crying.

"Whatever is the matter?"

"Look! Look! Just look at this! It's all your fault too! I knew that those people who packed for us were no good! I knew it!"

"How do you mean you knew it?"

"They were the cheapest and the worst! See! Look! All my lovely china is broken!"

He was undisturbed. "Don't be so silly, love, it's only china! Not worth getting so upset about. We can buy some more on Saturday. I didn't like it much anyway!"

"But I loved it, it was so pretty!"

"I would prefer something more modern-looking - Denby Ware is nice - nice clean lines and subtle colours."

"But I can't stand Denby Ware - and I don't want modern-looking china!" I shouted at him.

He had never seen Emily in such a state. He didn't know what to do with her as she went on about her aunts' glasses - that she had looked at all of her life in their china cabinet. How she had loved those glasses and plates; that they reminded her of her aunts whom she loved so much and missed so much! Why didn't he understand! Why! Why! She shouted louder and louder. "Please Emily" he tried to calm her " - don't make such a noise. What will the lady upstairs think!"

Anger and disappointment burst out of me "I don't care what she thinks!" I shouted at him. "I don't care!"

"Come, come now Emily, I'll make some tea" he said as he propelled me into the kitchen and put the kettle on.

"Now," he said, in his calm, unemotional voice, stirring the tea "stop crying and have a nice cup of tea and I am sure you'll feel much better."

I sipped the tea, but it *was* his fault, it *was*, if he had spent a little more money and had a more reputable company do it, this probably never would have happened. I was furious with him, I didn't want to look at him sitting there unperturbed, not caring at all about how upset I was.

"Look, do cheer up - we'll go shopping on Saturday."

I did not want to shop, I was not interested in new china! Never before had I felt like shouting at anyone, and I couldn't even remember ever feeling so unhappy. My, how I loathed this dull, depressing, horrible flat. If only I could have had my pretty, bright dishes and my pictures to brighten up the ugly, brown place. "Everything is brown!" I said, "Everything! Even the dishes are a sort of light brown!"

"You are exaggerating, Emily - calm down, it isn't as bad as all that!"

"It is to me! It's awful!!"

We went shopping and bought the Denby Ware that Lawrence liked so much. I really didn't care because I knew I couldn't have my lovely Enoch Wood china anyway. He did buy me some pretty little coloured-glass, ice-cream dishes. I wasn't sure whether he liked them or not, but he did buy them for me. He actually took me to have lunch at a health-food restaurant; he chose it because he told me he had eaten there a lot during his university days as it had been relatively inexpensive. When he noticed that the prices had gone up since he had last eaten there he called the waitress over and asked for the old menu, she thought he was joking of course, but he was serious! Anyway the waitress just told him that wasn't possible, that these were the new prices and had been for a long time. I was so embarrassed I couldn't look at the waitress at all and was really quite shocked that Lawrence would do such a thing. It was actually a very nice restaurant. I had a salad with hard-boiled egg, all on one plate, nearly the way we had it at home. Lawrence went on about how expensive it was but I enjoyed it all the same. They had that lovely English white coffee too. I tried to cheer up.

At home, we put the dishes away. I kept wishing we did not live in this flat, the sun didn't come in any of the windows, there was no brightness, nothing pretty - nothing to give pleasure. The stove was gas and I could smell the gas smell all the time. Lawrence told me it wasn't natural gas – it was gas made from coal and that was why it smelt so unpleasant. There was no washing machine; I washed the clothes in the kitchen sink. There was no refrigerator - I had never lived in a house without one. There was no heating - just the fireplace in the sitting-room. The only way I could get the bathroom warm was to run a hot bath, but I had to be careful because the hot water was in short supply. In England, both electricity and gas were very expensive. There was a pay-meter for the electricity and another for the gas and they seemed to swallow a shilling in the time it took to boil an egg!

I longed to have a house out in the country in a little village like the ones we passed through when we were out driving on a Sunday. A house with bright, sunny rooms and a garden. I asked Lawrence when he thought we would be buying a house.
"We need to save a lot of money to do that."
"In Canada, it is possible to buy one with a down-payment and take on a mortgage. Is that not possible here?"
"I dare say it is - but I do not want any debts. It is something I will not consider doing. We will have to save the money. Maybe when you are 25 and come into your inheritance we can buy one, but we will have to wait and see."
I was surprised to hear Lawrence speak of my inheritance.

It bothered me. I had always thought I would keep my inheritance invested so that I would have my own income for treats and holidays, little extras that I would be able to provide. I had always understood that my husband would buy the house - this I knew was the usual procedure. I didn't say anything, but I was surprised and my heart sank to think that I would have to buy our house. I thought that maybe I could persuade him to move from here, even if we couldn't buy a house yet. But every time I talked about moving, he said he did not want the disruption. He was busy at the office, I would just have to make the best of it for now. My unhappiness enveloped me, there was nothing to look forward to and the life I was living was dull and disappointing. I had no life at all.

Why does she go on so about a house, one would think she would be happy here in this little flat, warm and comfortable, just the two of us to look after. It is tiresome with her nagging about this flat and wanting to have a baby so soon, too soon, far too soon.

I decided that I was going to have a baby. I would not use my contraceptive. I couldn't wait forever for him to decide. I wanted to have my children while I was still young. I didn't want to be an old mother! Also, having a baby would change Lawrence. He would certainly want to buy a house then. I was convinced about that. I stopped using the contraceptive.

There was a doctor not far from where we lived - I had seen his brass plate on my walks, "Dr Johnson, Family Physician". I decided to go to see him as I was having terrible headaches and I had never been troubled with headaches before.

"How long have you been married?" I told him a year and a half.

"Maybe you are pregnant?"

"Oh no - I couldn't be pregnant doctor, you see, I am still having my periods".

"Really? Do you bleed much then?"

"No, not a lot."

"How else do you feel?"

"Not very good," I told him, I felt nauseated most of the time and couldn't eat much at all. I guessed it was the headaches.

Doctor Johnson examined me and told me that I was pregnant - but that I would probably lose the baby.

I was thrilled for a second, then the remainder of the sentence sank in.

"Lose it?"

"Yes my dear, it is likely. However, if you go to bed and stay there for three or four months, you may be lucky and keep it. I will come and examine you every week and you must telephone me if you have any discomfort at all. Any heavy bleeding. If you wait in the waiting room I'll drive you home in a little while as I live quite near you. You shouldn't walk that distance in your condition."

Lawrence wasn't really thrilled that I was pregnant, he didn't say that it was lovely and exciting for him. Nothing like that, but he was nice enough about it. He was surprised that I had to stay in bed all the time. My head ached, but worse than that was the nausea, it never left me, day or night. Lawrence had to prepare some of his own meals; he tried to tempt me with little tastes of what he was eating. Sometimes I could eat a little. He asked why it was that I was so ill - he thought that young, healthy women bloomed in pregnancy.

"I can't help it!" I cried. I cried easily then. "I don't know why either, I hate it, and your cigarette smoke doesn't help either. I hate being in bed too!" I had started to cry and shout at him about his smoking.

"Well, I smoke and not much we can do about that is there? I guess you will just have to get used to it. Your nausea couldn't be all my fault I shouldn't think. I suspect you aren't suited to having babies."

Now she is pregnant one would think that would make her happy, not sick. A pity she is pregnant so soon, yes a great pity. I liked our life the way it was, very nice it was. I expect she will get over the fuss about the smoke, everyone smokes, can't do anything about that.

It was summer, but there was no summer in our flat; it was the same as the winter - dark and gloomy, but instead of being cold and damp, it was hot and stuffy. There was no garden for me to sit in, just this dark bedroom all day long. Sometimes, when the doctor came, he would make me a pot of tea and bring it to me. "There," he would say, "not the nicest place to be on a lovely summer day, is it!"

He sat on the edge of the bed and patted my arm. "Maybe in another month you'll be past the danger. Then you can get back to normal. Have to be careful right through the whole pregnancy, mind you. How is your husband bearing up?"

"Oh fine" but I knew it wasn't that fine, as Lawrence was already fed up. I couldn't really blame him, with me in bed all the time and always feeling so ill. One more month didn't sound too bad. The next time Dr Johnson came he told me that if I was careful I could sit in the sitting-room for a short spell.

"It seems a little brighter in there, I think this dark bedroom is too depressing for words. Not good for you. Just remember to walk slowly - no jerking about - and get your legs up."

August came, a brilliant month with hot, heavy days. The sitting room where I now spent my days was not very different from the bedroom but it was a relief to be out of my bed with a slight change of scenery.

My hair was now long and hung in depressing, damp strands but, however much I tried to make it look better it still looked terrible. I was completely disheartened with the way I looked. There were two black blotches under my red-rimmed eyes, my face was thin and white. Sobbing quietly, I looked down at the small bulge under my limp nightie. Could I really stand this for another two or three months? Maybe when I am out of danger I would stop feeling nauseated, maybe I would look and feel wonderful, blooming and well. No one warned me that being pregnant could be this awful. I hated looking at myself, it was really better not to look.

As I prepared to get settled on the ugly brown sofa I looked outside, to see a taxi drawing up. Out stepped a tall, slim, elegant, young woman wearing a smart suit and very high heels, her chestnut hair fell in soft waves around her face. I watched her with envy. Oh to look like that! When the young woman turned around, I was shocked to realize it was my girl friend from Vancouver. Our families had been friends for years and years and we had attended the same expensive private school. Although she was a little older than me we had been very good friends all of our lives, since babyhood really. As I watched her come up the path I was excited to see her but I couldn't help feeling that it was a pity that she had chosen this time and place to visit me.

Just going to the door made me perspire heavily. I took a deep breath, opened the door and there was my friend, all smiles with such a healthy glow! She looked marvellous!

"Daphne! Come in, come in, what on earth are you doing here?"

"Emily, (she looked very embarrassed) I am so sorry to barge in on you like this, I didn't know that you were pregnant! What is the matter - you don't look well either?"

"That's because I'm not!" I laughed. "It is good to see you Daphne, really good. So tell me why you are here? I had no idea you were planning to come to England - what's all this about? Come and sit down in my smartly decorated sitting room! Mind the stuffing doesn't puff out at you when you sit on the beautiful sofa!"

Daphne looked around and laughed, "Yes I see what you mean - it is all rather ghastly Emily, isn't it? How come? I thought that you and Lawrence would be living somewhere rather nice, this doesn't look at all like you."

"No Daphne, it doesn't look like me and I hate the place - however, before I explain, you must tell me what you are doing over here, is it just to have a long holiday?"

"Well no, it isn't really - actually I got myself into a spot of trouble and, well, mother thought the best thing would be for me to get out of Vancouver for a spell."

"What sort of trouble? You don't mean real trouble do you? You weren't pregnant were you?" As I said it, Daphne was nodding her head quite vigorously and smiling as well!

"Oh Daphne! Oh how terrible! Not Ron was it?"

"Actually Emily, it was and it was terrible, all very dramatic! One would have thought the end of the world had come! Mother nearly had a fit - as you know, Ron wasn't exactly 'top drawer' and anyway, I didn't ever want to be married to him - I just liked to have fun with him but of course one night the fun got out of hand, we were at a party and one of the chaps started mixing up these fancy drinks and honestly Emily they were delicious! I don't know how many I had, but as I say, the fun got out of hand and bingo! I just couldn't believe my bad luck. After saving myself for Mr Right for all that time too! I was a fool, of course I was drunk and I was furious with myself and Ron, but I never told him –

I couldn't blame him really, could I. It wasn't all his fault – I didn't exactly ask for it, but I certainly did not find his advances repugnant. Well of course there was no question of me having the baby. I suppose I could have disappeared for a few months and had it in secret and then put it for adoption like so many girls do. To be truthful, I had no interest in having the baby. I certainly did not and do not love Ron - it was just a horrid accident. Well, I had the abortion, I know how much you disapprove of abortions, but I just couldn't have that baby Emily.   Anyway, mother arranged it all and it cost a fortune! I stayed in a private nursing home for two whole weeks! She thought the best thing after that would be for me to stay here for a good while - get away from Ron for one thing and to sort of change my life, if you know what I mean. So I am and I am loving it and hope to stay here for a few years if I can find an interesting job to do, although I don't suppose my degree from little old U. B. C. in Vancouver will get me very far over here.

"Now you know the whole sordid story. I am waiting for these friends of mother's to return from holiday where I shall stay for several weeks and hopefully by the end of that time I will have found an interesting job, a flat to live in and a happy life to live!"

I was shocked by Daphne's story, I could understand her not wanting to marry Ron, but to have an abortion was a pretty horrible thing to think of. Well, what was done was done and at least Daphne did not seem bothered by the episode. I gathered that she had the abortion as soon as she knew she was pregnant.

I was not keen to have a guest (not even Daphne) for two whole weeks - not in my condition, but what could I say - she, after all, was my dear friend. So I told her that of course she could stay with us. It would be just fine.

"You are sure, Emily? I'm really sorry to take you by surprise like this."

"Yes, of course I am sure," I told her, "but you may have to do some of the cooking, it's not something I can do at the moment. I do get up and do a few little things - but not much, not yet. I can't go out anywhere with you either, so it won't be very exciting for you."

Daphne smiled kindly, "I don't mind at all but I am sorry you are so ill, I don't suppose you have a sewing machine do you?"

"Yes, I have my mother-in-law's - why?"

"Well - what I would really like to do, is sew. I bought some wonderful fabrics in Scotland and if I could use your machine I could make them up while I am here! That would be a great help. You see, these people live in London and are very social, they go everywhere and do everything and I want my clothes to be just right for every occasion. You know how very smartly everyone dresses in London."

This suited me perfectly! It was a relief as I wouldn't have to bother with entertaining her at all.

When Lawrence arrived home that evening he was very surprised to find that they had a visitor, a rather gorgeous one at that. He remembered her vaguely as she had been a guest at their wedding. At the time of course he had eyes only for Emily, but this past while had been unbearably dreary with Emily so ill and depressed all the time and she certainly didn't look attractive anymore either. This Daphne girl looked quite scrumptious with her voluptuous figure, she could be quite a pleasant diversion. He thought that he was going to enjoy her visit. Perhaps the girl might brighten Emily up a bit too.

After dinner he invited her to go out with him for a little drive and a drink, "Emily can't go anywhere yet, can you Emily?" (he said this with confidence), she would have to stay in her bed you know, "but there is no reason why we couldn't go, is there Emily, I mean you wouldn't mind would you?"

"No, no! Go ahead!" I said. What could I have said? It wasn't that much fun watching them go out together, but as much I was longing to go out again I knew it was impossible and even before I was pregnant Lawrence never invited me to go out in the evening. I couldn't help the tears that came, I felt so ill and miserable. What I managed to eat of my evening meal did not agree with me. I went to bed and cried some more. I didn't hear them come in; I was sound asleep.

The days went by peacefully with Daphne sewing nearly the whole day. Occasionally she went to the shops for some thread or ribbon. Sometimes she brought home something to help with the meal. Most evenings, Lawrence and Daphne went out together. I felt quite jealous to see them going out together in the evenings while I went to bed. Lawrence was very attentive to Daphne. "My word that's a smart outfit, did you make that? Such lovely hair you have Daphne, I do like the way that you wear it. Where would you like to go this evening?" He was always looking at her admiringly. I couldn't blame him for not looking at me anymore but all the same it would have been nice if he had paid me some attention. In my heart I thought he was pretty mean to ignore me the way that he did.

At some point I decided to mention to Daphne that Lawrence was a "breast man" and the way that she wore her cardigans open in a huge "V" might just be tempting fate - it seemed to me that his eyes were magnetised to her very voluptuous form. She laughed at me "A Breast Man! Oh come on Emily, anyway I thought all men were "breast men" as you call it. He couldn't be worse than the average chap!"

"Well," I told her, "it is just a thought and you do look rather fetching you know, bursting out all over!" She giggled and I laughed too as I guessed I sounded pretty silly. On the other hand I could see that Lawrence was very attracted to her and there was quite a lot of her exposed.

He was a bit concerned that Emily was getting suspicious of his attentions to Daphne, he couldn't help admiring her but he guessed he did it too much in front of Emily. Perhaps in a way it was a good thing that the two weeks were coming to an end as he was very attracted to her and that could become difficult. He was going to miss their little excursions. He got the feeling that she wouldn't really have objected to a little kiss and cuddle, however, with she and Emily being such great friends it just wouldn't have been worth taking that risk. Maybe she was a real prude the way that Emily had been, although she does give rather a different impression than that, one way or another and of course she is older.

The two weeks were nearly over. It had been nice to have the company of Daphne; she was always so cheerful and busy with her sewing. The number of clothes she had made in two weeks was amazing. Lawrence was impressed too.

"Why don't you sew, Emily? It must save a lot of money!"

I couldn't be bothered to tell him that I could sew and quite well too (but not as well as Daphne!) and that I probably would sew again but not now! "Yes" I said. It was the easiest.

Finally Daphne was leaving and I was sorry to see her go. I wasn't looking forward to being alone all the time. At the door Daphne gave me a hug, "I'll write and tell you where I am. I'm not sure what I'll be doing after I stay with these people. I expect I'll be going back to Vancouver before long unless I'm lucky and can find some interesting work in London. I would love to live in London. I hope you start feeling better soon, Emily. I sure hope I don't get ill like you when I start having children, but then maybe I won't get married anyway! I'm not sure whether I would really want to be married - and as for having children, I'm not keen on that either.

"Well you probably wouldn't be ill like this, Daphne, so don't let that put you off. I don't know why I am and no one else seems to know why either. Another couple of weeks and I should be able to get about again, thank goodness!"

Daphne got into her taxi and I waved her off. I would miss her. Even if she did eventually live in London it was a long way from here.

That evening Lawrence said he thought he would go out on his own. "You don't mind do you, Emily?"

He had to get out. He couldn't sit here for the whole evening with dreary Emily.

I would have really liked him to stay at home and talk about where we would live when the baby was born. I wanted to make a list of things we would need for the baby. Most of all I wanted him to tell me that we would move soon. Whenever I asked about moving and having a room for the baby, he said that the sitting-room where they were would be just fine. "Babies don't need anything special to start with anyway."

He didn't want to stay home and talk to me - he wanted to go out and get away from me. So I said "No, I don't mind."

"Good, good! I'll be off then."

He usually enjoyed a pint or two chatting to whoever was about. There were a couple of young women who were always at the pub when he was and liked to chatter with him and flirt a bit. Once he managed to give the blond one quite a cuddle, she certainly didn't object. Quite fun. It was such a relief to be out and away from the dreary evenings with Emily.

He managed to get out most evenings.

At last the doctor told me that I could get up. He told Lawrence that a little holiday would do me the world of good; it would cheer her up, "it has been quite a dreary time for her this past while" he told Lawrence. "Anyway, let me know what you decide to do and, don't forget, I will have to keep seeing your wife on a regular basis. She must be very careful for the whole pregnancy, you understand."
"Yes, yes I'll keep you posted."

I had thought that, maybe with some elastic, I would be able to do up my skirts as I had not put on any weight but I had a small bulge that had to be accommodated. I put the elastic around the button and looped it through the button hole, I could see that the idea worked but I had nothing to wear over the gap at my waist - everything I put on looked awful. I told Lawrence, "I'll have to buy some maternity clothes right now, I can't go anywhere with nothing to wear."
"Maternity clothes? Is that necessary? Can't you make do somehow?"
"How? How? How do I make do if I can't get into my clothes? How do I wear stockings?"
"Wear ankle socks."
"Ankle socks? Ankle socks!" I screamed at him, "Ankle socks? I am not going to wear ankle socks ever! I have my own money and I am going shopping!"
"That money was to be saved, not spent!"
"Well, it's my money and I am going to spend it! You have no right to tell me what I'm to do with it Lawrence, it's *my* money!"
I shouted at him. I was furious. Did he really think he could tell me what to do with my own money.

He was not pleased with this new Emily, she had quite changed, arguing and shouting all the time.
She was not the person he thought he had married, not at all. What has happened to his lovely Tinkerbell? Maybe after the

VANCOUVER

Mother was there to greet me as I came off the aircraft, it was so good to see her - I felt better already as her soft cheek pressed against mine. Madeleine rushed up and hugged me, "Oh Emily, are you alright?" I told her I was feeling much better, better than I had for months! Edgar hustled us along to the car holding my arm, telling me to watch my step and to be careful, have to look after you and your precious cargo you know!

At the house, Madeleine took me to my room, which was large, with large windows. It was so bright, even on this November day! "It looks heavenly, just heavenly! Thank you, thank you Madeleine. Oh it is lovely to be home, I know I'll feel better now, I know I will."

Mother wanted to know what had happened. She knew from Emily's letters that things were not going too well, but she certainly did not expect her to come home! "Do you think it was wise to leave like that, now when you are going to have the baby?"

Edgar piped up, "Maybe it's a good thing she left. That was no life for a young mother-to-be! She'll be better here. Perhaps that man needed a bit of a shake up! Anyway, it's great to have you home, sis. You should get out a bit and see your friends. Perk you up! Get you back to your old self! Put the roses in your cheeks again."

Mother brightened up, "Maybe Edgar is right! Now I must go, up early you know! I'm still busy with those hats!"

Lawrence's letter arrived:

Dear Emily,
What on earth has made you do this most ridiculous thing. You are a silly girl. You had better get back here right away - the very first flight you can get. I telephoned the bank and after much persuasion the manager told me that you had emptied your account. Fancy you wasting all that money, a terrible waste. Now Emily, be sensible, you can't stay with your brother, you belong here with your husband. If you come straight back I will forgive you for your foolishness and I am sure my family will turn a blind eye to this most peculiar behaviour.

I read his letter and I was furious, how could he write such a letter! I was not going back, not now, not ever! How was it he did not understand how unhappy I was! He didn't mention that he missed me and loved me and wanted me back! No, just how foolish I had been! And of course, always about the money! It was my money and I was glad I did what I did; it was the first time I had felt like a normal human being in months. No, I was not going back! It was bliss to be here in a happy atmosphere. I wrote and told him.

In his reply he was not just angry, he was hostile! He said if I didn't come back now he may decide he did not want me back at all, so I had better get off my mark and get home while he was still willing to forgive me and have me back. I should be home for Christmas at the latest!

I felt very disappointed with his letters - they were bossy and unfriendly. I thought that if he really wanted me to go back he should have written me a nice letter, not these horrible letters. I simply could not go back to him if he had no idea why I left and did not want to know why. He knew how much I loathed that flat and being alone all the time, but he didn't mention any of those things, any of the things that were important to me. I knew I should not have left my husband, but he should have tried to see why I did it and try to help me and make me happy - not keep going on about the wrong I did. No, I really couldn't see how it would work out. I didn't like to admit it, but I should not have married him. Maybe if I had waited, Stanley would have married me and everything would have been very different. I wrote and told him that I did not want to return to the miserable life that I had been living with him.

I decided to write to Stanley. I told him how wrong it was for me to marry this man. How unhappy I had been. I asked him if we could be friends again, I told him about my baby, and I told him that I still loved him. It was not a long letter. The letter was returned unopened. I looked at the returned envelope in disbelief, how could it be, that he had not even opened it! How could he do such a thing? Didn't he care about me at all? Here I had been, hoping that at the very least we could be friends. I knew it was a bit of a fantasy dream to think that there was a chance that we would return to our previous relationship, but on the other hand I had thought it possible that he still cared for me. I never dreamt that he would just send the letter back like that, unopened. I put it away, I knew I must never think about him again, never. The pain was physical and excruciating, I knew I had to get over it and move on quickly.

I started collecting things to furnish an apartment or maybe a little house. I did have my own money and my full inheritance would soon be in my hands. I was not dependent on Lawrence.

Mother was a little dubious about me staying. She knew it was difficult to bring children up without a husband. She knew all about it, as that was what she had done - her marriage had lasted only seven years. She would like to have her daughter near, but the fact remained, her daughter was going to have a child and the child needed a father. Emily had never had a father in her life and she had felt that Emily had missed a very important relationship and was regretful about it although it had not been her fault; she hadn't left her husband, he had left her and the children for another woman, and Emily had just been born when the whole sad story began to unfold. Even after all these years she felt the pain and sadness of that terrible time.

At last there was a letter from Lawrence that was a little different, not as hostile. He said he really wanted her back, would I please think carefully about what I was doing. This baby was his baby too! He wanted to help bring up this baby. He wanted to be the baby's father and help look after it. He also said at the end of the letter in his very bossy way that he had no intention of returning to Canada - England was where he belonged, so if you have any ideas like that, put them right out of your head.

I did not answer.

It was a cold January night, the snow was deep and as I looked out of the window I could see the sparkle of ice on top of the snow. It was clear and bright. I went to bed.

In the night when everyone was asleep, I was awakened! I was going to have my baby! I knew it was coming even though it would be many weeks early, my water had broken and the pains had started. I went downstairs to the kitchen and made a pot of tea. It was still very early so I sipped my tea waiting for my brother to get up. I didn't like to wake him too early in the morning. It seemed a long time before I heard him rise, I called to him. He ran down the stairs, "Now?" he asked, "Now?"

"Yes I said - now - and I think I should be going soon."

The snow was thick and the car window iced up. He had to get out to clean it every few minutes. At last we were there! "You'll be alright, Emily?" he asked me as he turned to leave.

"Of course she will be alright!" said the nurse as she bustled in. "You left it a bit late getting here, didn't you, dear" she said as she finished examining me.

Left then, on a hard, high bed with a burning face and a shivering body, I was told to call if the pains got worse. Alone and frightened I started the long and painful birth of my child. I cried out and was told that a doctor would be along soon. "Soon", seemed an eternity to me that morning, but at last a doctor and nurse came to me and with my legs held high and uncomfortable in stirrups, my baby was born, small but healthy. A tiny baby boy. I had to go home without my baby as he needed an incubator for the beginning of his life on this planet. It grieved me to leave my baby, I wanted to have him and feel him next to me but he must stay at the hospital for several days. At last I was allowed to bring him home. Because he was so small, he had to be fed little and often so I was up and down the whole night through. Something about giving birth had disturbed my back and I was in terrible pain most of the time. The doctor came and looked and probed, "It will settle down" he said. I took my pain-relief tablets and hoped the doctor was right.

The letter that came from Lawrence congratulated me on the birth of our baby boy, but he wondered why he was so small. It was probably because you took that flight, he said, it probably did not do the baby any good at all. He blamed me for the baby's size! After all the trouble I had carrying it! It was probably a miracle I had a child at all! Why did he say such hurtful things, I wondered?

The next letter said that he had a position with an architectural firm in the Midlands of England and he was looking for a flat out in the country. He had been looking at washing machines for her. Perhaps a small refrigerator would be helpful too. You will need these now, won't you? He would let her know when he had moved. "But Emily please come back. I do want you back and when we are together again we can sort things out I am sure. Be a good girl and see that it is important for all of us that you return. We are a family now Emily. Do be sensible."

This letter touched my heart. It was the first time he had sounded at all like a caring husband. He really did want me back, and he really did want to please me! If he did really want me and we could have a nice life together that was what I wanted more than anything. With our baby, our little boy! How lovely to live in the country - maybe now, with my money, we could buy a little cottage in a village. That would be lovely. A Family life. I thought about Lawrence and how it was when he was nice to me. Maybe now it would be alright, maybe I should try again. I asked Edgar what he thought. "Yes, perhaps you should if you feel you want to, but it would be wise to always keep enough money in the bank in case you find you want to leave."
Madeleine agreed. "Yes, give it another try - then if it doesn't work, well, you'll just have to accept it. But maybe now things will be different."
They all thought it was a good idea to give it one more try.
I wrote and told him my decision.

Dear Emily,
At last some sense has come into your head, I must say it is about time! Now don't go wasting any more money, just get the most economical flight you can and get back here. As soon as I know the day and time I will be at the airport to meet you. I have found a little flat in the country. I am already moved in. It is a pretty area with plenty of places to walk with the baby. Now for goodness sake don't delay any longer.
Take care of that baby! Don't drop it!

Love to you both,
Lawrence.

This letter did not please me at all. The tone of it bothered me - however, I had made the decision. I certainly hoped it would be better with him than it sounded. At least we would be living somewhere nicer and that should help. Did he really think

I would drop my precious baby! That remark made me angry - even if it was meant as a joke, I didn't think it funny.

It was hard to say good-bye - I would miss everyone and, in a way, I hated to leave. I was quite apprehensive about my return. Hopefully Lawrence would be nicer than his letters and happy with me and the baby. Of course the flat had to be better than that ghastly one in Sheffield. I pictured it bright and cheerful with the pretty countryside all around. I wondered how Lawrence's family would receive me; I realized some things were going to be difficult.

The baby was sound asleep in his carry-cot on the floor in front of the seat beside me as I daydreamed, looking out of the window at the clouds passing below. I was so proud of my baby. It was thrilling to have one's own child. I closed my eyes and pictured him as a toddler. I was going to take him to parks and show him all the animals. We would go on lovely picnics. I would teach him how to swim as early as possible. He would be very good at all sports. And when he is older he must go to a proper English public school, one of the really great ones and then to Cambridge or Oxford. Yes, I would make certain he had an excellent education. I wanted him to speak with an English accent like his father. Maybe he would be a doctor like my grandfather. But of course there would be other children; I would like four children. Four would be lovely, a real family. Dr Johnson told me I probably wouldn't be as ill with the next one. Sometimes it's just the first one he said, so that's good. I certainly hoped he was right - it would be awful to be ill like that with every baby.
    I was looking forward to living in the English countryside. So green, and the fields all about, and the horses. I loved to see the country folk horseback-riding in the country lanes.
    I picked up my baby and wrapped him tightly, looked at his perfect face, his perfect hands, then felt his little feet. So beautiful my baby, I lifted him to my neck and felt him nuzzle there, I stroked his little head, so tender. My heart ached with so much love. I put him back in the carry-cot; he slept on. The nurse had told me that premature babies slept a lot and he did.
    The stewardess came to tell me that we would soon be

landing. "I'll help you. You carry the baby, I'll come with all the paraphernalia!"

I thanked her very much. My stomach was churning with excitement and apprehension. I was excited to show Lawrence our child; he looked lovely all in white, wrapped in the exquisite shawl that aunt Ann had sent. I liked that English way of dressing babies in white. Anyway Lawrence was bound to love him, fathers like to have a son.

I hoped Lawrence wouldn't want to change his name - a family name, it had been in my family for nearly two hundred years, a good solid Scottish name, Maxwell; well, he didn't criticize her choice in the letter so maybe it would be alright.

BACK TO ENGLAND – 1956

There was Lawrence, it had been a long while since I had seen him. He came to me, lifted the shawl and looked at the little sleeping face. "So this is him!"

"Yes, this is your son."

But the things I had hoped he would say, he did not say. He looked at me, then he said, "Emily, you have a spot on your face! You've never had a spot on your face - it must be the food you've been eating - couldn't have been good for you."

I was hurt and angry. "Is this all you can say? Aren't you pleased to see me? What about my hair, don't you think it looks nice, and look - I've got my figure back! My waist is exactly the same as before I was pregnant!"

"Yes, yes, you do look very nice, Emily. Perhaps I shouldn't have said that. It's just that you have always had such a beautiful skin, perfect really. It is nice to have you back Emily and I have missed you."

It was true he had missed her, not the ill, miserable Emily but the one he had married, his Tinkerbell, yes he had missed her alright, perhaps now things would be more normal and she would be her happy self again, after all this upset. She actually did look very attractive, however he hoped she hadn't gone and spent a lot of money on new clothes - he certainly didn't recognise what she was wearing.

We drove into a large yard with many outbuildings, a rambling old stone cottage stood in a meadow. "This is it!" he said, all cheerful!

We got out of the car and Lawrence led the way to the door which was around at the back of the cottage. He had difficulty lifting the latch as it was old and rusty. Eventually he managed to open it and we stepped inside. Immediately to our right was a tiny, rickety, wooden staircase; we went up the stairs through a narrow passageway and into a small sitting-room with a fireplace, a worn old sofa with no discernible pattern, two similar chairs, a card table, no carpet, the floor was unfinished wood, a dirty grey colour. There were no pictures on the walls. There was one small window. A door beside the fireplace led to a large, dark, bedroom, with one very small window. There was an old bed and a cord strung across one corner with some hangers on it and that was all. Through the door of that room was another dark, little room with nothing in it, a very small window threw some light on the drab, dusty, dirty, grey floor. Every breath I took I could smell dust and dampness. A stale musty smell.

"This will be for the baby!" he said. There were no curtains anywhere.

"Where's the kitchen and bathroom?"

"We share those with the lady who owns the cottage - she is here only occasionally during the week, and sometimes at the week-ends."

"Where are they?"

"Downstairs."

"Downstairs?"

"Yes."

"Do we eat up here?"

"Yes - when the lady is at home, but when she isn't here we can eat in the kitchen."

"So you are saying that I take everything down to cook and then bring it all up to eat and then take it all down to wash up and then bring it all back up the stairs to put away?"

"Yes, when she is here."

"What about the washing?"

"You may be allowed to use her machine, but I have not yet asked her about that."

I looked around the sitting room, I could see the outside through a crack in the wall. It must be very cold here in the winter and all the coal for the fire would have to be carried up that narrow, rickety staircase. I wondered how that small fire would heat three rooms. I decided not to say anything, but I was not going to be the one to carry the coal, no, I was not going to do that! We went downstairs into the kitchen which didn't look clean, the way a kitchen should look. The table was covered with faded, worn oilcloth - we used to have that on our table in the basement but it was bright and fresh-looking as that was where the gardener ate his sandwiches. I hadn't seen tables covered in oil-cloth since then. In the corner was a coke boiler covered in soot. Some unpainted wooden shelves which were fully occupied, took up one unpainted wall. There was a large pot sink with a small, soggy, wooden draining-board. I looked around at this very unpleasant kitchen, where I was going to live and there was nothing I could do about it.   I had come back expecting something very different and Lawrence wasn't being all that nice either. It was so disappointing, I was sure he was going to have things nice for me.   His letters had led me to believe that he would. Looking through the only window, I could see a beautiful green meadow with sheep and a few cows; my spirits lifted a little, at least it was beautiful outside! I did have my baby now, that made a difference to everything. I looked around again - the kitchen really was awful, the fact that I would have to go up and down that narrow staircase a million times a day was not something I wanted to think about.

Where was the bathroom, I asked.   He led me through another dark passageway and opened the door to a large, dark-green bathroom. "How do we heat it?" Lawrence hummed and hawed then and said that we wouldn't heat it as there was no provision for heat in the bathroom. "But," I said, "it's freezing in here and so dark!" I really couldn't see how this place was much better than the Sheffield flat, excepting of course that we were in the country and that would be lovely. Maybe (I dared to think) we wouldn't have to stay here for long. Hopefully the owner of the house would be pleasant.

I fed Maxwell and afterwards showed Lawrence how to get his wind up. He was very patient and effectively patted the baby's back. In the evening we put baby and carry-cot in the little bedroom. We went to bed.

"I'm sorry you went away like that, Emily." he said.   "You should not have."

I lay still and didn't say anything.

"Well," he said, "we'll say no more about it."

"Thank-you." I said. I put my arms around his neck. He held me close for the first time since I had returned.

"Emily, my Emily, my Tinkerbell."

"Yes." I said – and tried not to think of the refrigerator and the washing machine that he had not bought for me.

The early morning was lovely in the country. I opened the back door and could smell the freshness of the pure spring air and hear the birds singing and chirping, I stepped outside and took deep breaths. Lawrence came down and made a pot of tea. He watched me feed Maxwell and we chatted, then we had our breakfast together. It was nice, having breakfast together again.

With the owner away, we could eat in the kitchen, but when she returned it wouldn't be as nice having to cart everything upstairs - and downstairs, a bother, it would be. We had one more day and then Lawrence would be back at work and I would be here on my own. He said he would try to get home for lunch to keep me company.

"That would be nice!"

"I probably won't manage it every day but I will do my best."

"Thank you. I'll be fine here on my own so don't worry. I'll be busy with the baby. So don't worry if you can't always make it."

"You'll be alright then?"

"Yes - I will."

"Good - I'm glad. We'll be going to see the family at the week-end, Emily."

"We will?"

"Yes, they are longing to see the baby you know!"

"What will they be like with me?"

"Fine - fine. Not to worry, they are very pleased you are back. The main thing is that you have come back with the baby of course, that is all that counts, you know."

I wasn't sure just how meeting them would be, just how forgiving they would be, no matter how confident Lawrence was. Still, I had to accept the difficult situation. Like he said, I did come back and the baby was the important thing - they would love the baby!

As we pulled up at the end of the driveway, Lawrence's father came out to welcome us. All smiles, he gave me a nice kiss and patted my shoulder, "Hello love, now how about this baby!" I held Maxwell for him to see. "Meet Maxwell, your new grandson!"

"My - what a fine little chap! Come mother," he called, "come and see! A lovely little fellow he is!"

"Yes," she said, lifting the shawl a little more, "a bonnie wee chap he is, bonnie."

We moved into the drawing room. "Shall I hold him for you while you get settled in a comfortable chair? Now then, how about a nice cup of tea!"

The trolley was all set. Mr Love went off to boil the kettle again and make the tea. We discussed the weather.

"And is he sleeping outside?" Mrs Love asked.

"Not yet, but he did in Vancouver. I haven't a pram you see."

"We'll see to that, love." Mr Love said. "I expect you would like one of the large posh ones, wouldn't you. I'll see you have the money before you leave and first thing Monday you get to the shops and choose one. Now with the lovely weather, you'll want to get out and about with the baby."

"Yes."

"And it's lovely to put them in the pram and have them sleep in the garden. Very good for them too."

Mr Love chimed in "Perhaps now would be a good time to pop over to the others so they can see the little chap. They would be very disappointed if you don't get him over there on this visit you know, love."

"My, my," Simone, Lawrence's sister-in-law said, when they met me at the house, "isn't he lovely! Do let me hold him, such a long time since I have had a baby to hold!"

Edward, Lawrence's brother, looked him over. "What a wee smasher!" He held Maxwell's finger and smiled and clucked at him. Everyone was thrilled with the baby! No one mentioned that I had been away, it was as if I had never been away at all. In a sense, I would have preferred them to acknowledge the fact that I had been away, that I had been that unhappy. It might have been better. But it was fine, it was not difficult and I was glad to be with them again. I liked the family, they were very pleasant with me. "You must come to see us often," they told me, "we want to see a lot of that little chap."

I was pregnant again and glad about it. I told Lawrence.

"I hope you are not going to be ill like you were before." His voice was light and jokey, but I knew he was afraid.

"No, no, I'll be fine this time."

I was already feeling nauseated, but it wasn't all the day long this time. So I could manage that. I was not bleeding, so I thought that this would be an easier time altogether.

I told Lawrence that I would use my own money of course but I was going to have the baby privately - I wanted the doctor to be there with me when I had this baby - not like the last one, left all alone on that table. It had seemed to me I was there for hours and hours but of course it hadn't been much more than three hours. All the same, I didn't want that sort of experience again.

I would never forget it, how cold I was, how frightened, with nobody about, nobody to talk to, I had felt so alone with no encouraging words to comfort me. When I had told Simone how awful it had been she had been surprised. "That won't happen here." she had told me, "You just tell your doctor you want him with you and if I were you I would have a nice private room, just you say what you want and everything will be arranged the way you want it to be."

However, when I told Lawrence, he did not react as Simone had imagined he would. "Is all that fuss necessary?" he asked. "It will be very expensive you know."

"Yes, it is necessary, and it is my money don't forget, *I'm not asking you to pay.*" I was definite - telling him, not asking him. "We will have to move. It will not be suitable to be here with a baby. We should probably move soon, before I start to get heavier. All this up and down with dishes, groceries and laundry and this little one, is tiring and dangerous too. The ghastly smell of that woman cooking her dog bones is really something I can't stand much longer. It permeates the whole house and it takes days to get rid of the smell, I'm amazed Lawrence, that it doesn't bother you at all."

"Well of course it isn't pleasant I must admit, but it is her house so I guess she can do what she likes in it. You fuss far too much Emily and they are not dog bones Emily, they are bones for the dog!"

"You always say that I fuss too much, Lawrence, but what about the bathroom - even *you* complain about that freezing, dark, miserable room! Anyway, I've had enough of the place and we will just have to move. I never liked it here anyway."

"Yes yes Emily, don't go on so, I will start to look, I shall look at the advertisements during lunch and then if possible go and inspect right after work. How will that be? Will that suit you?"

"Yes, but you be sure now that it's all on one floor and that there is a garden, I want a nice place to live. Don't forget that I am in it all day!"

He had not thought that they would have to move again so soon, but he could see that the stairs would become more and more of a problem as time went by so he would have to find something. He just hoped he could find something not too expensive and that would suit her as he just could not stand more complaining about their accommodation, so tiresome.

The new flat was better, much better. It was at ground level, looking on to a pretty garden. There was a lovely lawn and plenty of space for Maxwell to play. There were lots of sheltered places to put the pram when the baby came. No longer would we share kitchen and bathroom. There was only one bedroom, so we gave that to little Maxwell and planned to put the new baby there eventually too. The sitting-room was to be our bedroom. There was plenty of living area in the dining-room with easy chairs and a big window; it was a large room, very bright. I was quite pleased with the flat - it was not perfect, but at least he had found somewhere reasonably pleasant for us; it was a relief. Until we could buy a house this would do - and the garden was pretty. Quite near, was a small park with swings and a see-saw. There were some pleasant little shops in the village that I could walk to. In every way it was an improvement.

It was June and very warm when my second child was born. He was small, but not as small as Maxwell was. He was a little early but not difficult to bring into the world. A blond baby boy, his skin was white, delicate, tinted gently with pink. I knew at once what I would call him. There was only one name that would do. David. I couldn't have explained to anyone why I felt so strongly about this name for this baby, but I did. I thought his middle name should be Samuel after Lawrence's father. I was pretty certain Lawrence would approve of that.

Because the baby was small we had to stay in the hospital longer than was usual. Two long weeks, but at least we were together – I didn't have to go home without my baby the way I did with Maxwell although two weeks was a long time to be separated from Maxwell. I longed for my little boy, I missed him so much and wondered if he was missing me too much. I knew it would be hard for him to be without me. I felt sad thinking about him. I worried so much my milk dried up. I didn't worry about Lawrence, in fact he seemed quite content with the routine. The lady who looked after Maxwell prepared the evening meal and Lawrence picked up the meal and Maxwell on the way home from the office. I didn't think he missed me really, he didn't say anything when he visited me and he didn't kiss me or bring me flowers either. Simone brought me some lovely flowers but he didn't. I tried not to think about Lawrence, how unloving he seemed to be. Each time he came to visit us I kept hoping he would show pleasure and affection.

At last the doctor said I could go home and maybe my milk would come back when I was re-united with my little boy and my husband.

Maxwell was thrilled to have his mummy back! He didn't let me out of his sight for long. I piggybacked him around the garden and played with him on the grass tickling him and chasing him until he fell down giggling with glee. He was full of kisses and hugs. Oh how I loved my little boy, so handsome, so joyful. He chortled and giggled "more, more" as I twirled him around and around. I loved to feed him his supper, he was such a hungry little chap, gobbling everything up. He sometimes had two baths in the one day, one after his nap if he was very wet! And always one at bed-time. He loved it and so did I! His little sleeping suits were blue and matched his dressing-gown that had a little woolly lamb on the pocket. In his cot he had a blue quilt. He looked so perfect, all clean and sleepy, while I told him bed-time stories.

I loved being a mother, reading stories, singing the nursery songs, taking them for walks, teaching little Maxwell his numbers and letters. I liked the whole thing, cooking nice meals, keeping the flat all sparkling clean. The washing on the line gave me pleasure. There were always clothes billowing out on my wash line.

When the week-end came we went to visit grandma and grandpa and the aunts and uncles. I enjoyed the visiting, it was so lovely to be with family. We had tea in the large garden and Maxwell could play with his toys and I thought it perfect. Sometimes we stayed for a meal, or overnight and the cousins, being so much older, took turns feeding Maxwell and playing with him; they loved the little boy. Little David was loved too and passed around to be looked at and cuddled. He was beautiful. He never cried, he was a quiet baby, smiling and gurgling at everyone. I always dressed him in white silk rompers. Aunt Simone knitted him a delicate blue matinée jacket with bootees to match. Mrs Love knitted a set in white. I didn't like knitting, so it was especially lovely to have these hand-knitted garments for him. So soft and pretty.

Lawrence seemed quite happy with his little family, occasionally he would unexpectedly hold my hand or put his arm around my waist. Or he might say, "I must take a photo of you in that dress" but loving words or gestures did not come easily for him. He didn't want to discuss emotions or anything to do with physical love at all. I had no-one to talk to about it, but once or twice I did mention it to Lawrence, he said it was not something one discussed and he said, "I hope you don't go discussing anything like this with my family - that would be most improper". Of course I wouldn't think of doing that! Even Madeleine hadn't said very much about it, I knew it was not a subject for chatting about and certainly my mother had never talked to me about that aspect of marriage. At school we just learned the mechanics of the procedure, there was no discussion of how often married people made love or anything else about it. I didn't know what was proper but I would have liked more loving words, more warmth, a few hugs and kisses would have been nice just to have that feeling of being loved and cherished.

The lady (Mrs Morgan) who owned the house where we rented our flat had said that the rent would be going up. She had also complained that Lawrence did not cut our portion of the grass often enough to suit her. Lawrence and she argued and Lawrence complained about the rent.

"We will have to move." he told me. "I'm also going to leave this practice - I don't see eye to eye with the to-be-partner. First we'll move from here and then I'll start looking for a different post."

I did not want to move again. It was pleasant here, but Lawrence had made up his mind and once again paid no attention to what I wanted.

He went ahead and found another flat, another upstairs flat with no garden, ugly and horrible. I thought I was done with places like that. I was upset and told him so. "Now don't fuss so Emily, it is only temporary I shall have the owner paper the sitting room walls and that will brighten it all up for you. Once we are in I shall leave you here and go up north and see what the situation is like there, then as soon as I find somewhere I shall come and get you, how does that sound!"

"That sounds terrible! Leave us here? No Lawrence - and what's more I don't want to live in the north! I don't like it there with all the dirt and fog. We have lived there and I know I don't like it."

He paid no attention to me. "I've heard there are some interesting positions there. New buildings to be built, lots of them, a new development, upgrading a whole area, even housing to design, good salaries too, might be very interesting.

I understood that I must not complain if this is what he has to do to find a post that suited him. He was, after all, the bread-winner. It would mean another move after this one. Oh, but it was tiresome, all this moving; I dreaded the move north.

We moved in, but I was very surprised to see that the walls had been re-papered and the sitting room walls were done in a very pretty ballet print! The bedroom in a sort of faded floral design, quite sweet. My goodness, Lawrence really had tried to please me for once! We did not have a telephone, so I had no word from him at all. I was lonely in the evenings. I had my books and I had made myself knit, although I still did not enjoy knitting.

At last, Lawrence came back, he had found a practice he thought would be suitable for him and it seemed they were keen to have him. He told me that he would go and live there and look for a place to live and then he would come and get us like he had said.

"But I don't want to do that! I want to come too. I don't want to be left alone all the time like this. I also don't want another up-and-down flat. I'm tired of carrying children and prams up and down - and the groceries and all the washing! I'm tired of it, I won't do it anymore - I won't!"

Lawrence was not pleased. "It would be too expensive if you came. We would have to stay in a hotel of sorts."

I had thought about this and told him that I had decided that I was going to buy a house this time - I had had enough of these flats. We could stay in a small hotel while we looked and I would pay for it.

"I don't want any debts you know Emily - you would have to pay for the whole thing - you realize that?"

"Yes I do and that's exactly what I am going to do."

What was wrong with renting? He asked.

"Money down the drain!" I told him.

He thought that perhaps she was right, but with renting it did mean one could leave a job one didn't like without worrying about selling a house. Still - he had better give in to her this time.

We found a small detached bungalow: two bedrooms, living room and kitchen - brick walls and slate roof, newly built, not quite finished, with a nice size garden; a fine little house, the rooms were a good size and bright. The garden was still a pile of rubble, but we would clear it and plant grass. I would make a flower garden and we could grow some of our own vegetables. It would be safe for the children as it was fenced all around. The kitchen floor was concrete, we would have to put tiles down and put cupboards up. It was a little cheaper that way. Lawrence had also finally agreed that I should have a washing machine and he said he would buy it for me.   All the hard work of doing the laundry by hand in the kitchen sink was going to be over! The nappies were such a time-consuming part of my life, soaking them in buckets, rinsing and then washing them and rinsing them the specified three times. Drying everything in the winter had been so difficult especially as hand-wringing the laundry did not really get enough of the moisture out.   It was quite exciting to think that this chunk of my daily life was to be so much improved.

At last I was in a house again and it was ours. I no longer had to worry about noise, or pleasing the person who owned the house, or smell a pot of boiling bones. It was a relief.

I got busy making curtains and painting the rooms. We laid the tiles at night when the children were not about. Lawrence's parents gave us a bed, a discarded sofa and chair and an old beige and brown rug. (I planned to dye the rug). Edward gave us some chests of drawers and a breakfast table of mahogany with chairs. This was useful, because it folded away, in between meals. We did not have a dining-room. There was only a small sitting-room. Lawrence told me that we would not be buying any furniture because anything we needed, his parents would probably have in the cellar, discarded things they no longer used.

We were all settled in time for Christmas, our first on our own with the children in our own house. We bought a Christmas tree. Christmas Eve, when the children were asleep, we decorated the tree, we put branches of fir and holly about and tinsel on the pictures. Christmas morning we woke very early and lit the whole house with candles, the children in their room were awake waiting for Christmas to begin. We took one child each by the hand and showed him the house all alight with the candles, the smell of the fir branches was in every room. After the children had filled their eyes with all of this, they saw the tree. With the sparkling angel on the top, the lights in all colours, the silver and golden balls hanging as if suspended in the air. The tinsel edging every branch. They saw the parcels all wrapped and ribboned waiting there.

Maxwell stood so still, with eyes wide, whispered "Santa has come! He has come!"

David's little face was full of wonder, he had travelled in those few minutes to a different land. He turned to be lifted to see more of this magical tree, he wanted to touch the golden ball.

"Did Santa really come down the chimney?" Maxwell asked, "Did he?"

"Oh yes!" we said, "Oh yes!"

"Are we to open the presents? Now?"

"One each now - then when you have had breakfast and are all dressed for this special day, we will sit and open the presents all together."

Such fun it was getting them dressed, as I had bought them new, red, woollen pullovers and little, red, woollen socks. They both loved new clothes and liked the bright colours. They ran about admiring each other.

Breakfast was special too as I made pancakes! They sat eating and looking at the tree. I knew that this was going to be a wonderful day. The turkey was already in the oven - and there was ice cream I had made for the children and also a small Christmas pudding, to please Lawrence.

Watching the excitement as each present was opened, the thrill they had with each new toy or book, it was wonderful to watch, everything was perfect and I felt so happy. I could see that Lawrence was enjoying everything, as I was. The fire was warm and cheery and the house did smell wonderful with the fir - and the turkey. Outside it was grey, damp, and ugly, but inside it was lovely. Apart from my own childhood Christmases, I thought this was the loveliest I had ever had - and I was pregnant again. I had not told Lawrence yet, but by next Christmas there would be another child! Three children, a real family! It was wonderful to think about, I was thrilled. I planned to tell Lawrence over the holiday. Perhaps it was too soon to tell the grandparents and uncles and aunts, but I might anyway.

"I thought you looked a little pale lately, ill already are you?"

his voice had an angry tinge to it.

"No, no, I'm fine!"

"Good, good!" He said it with obvious relief.

He had a feeling she was pregnant, something about her, and of course she really has looked pale lately, come to think of it. I hope this isn't as bad as the first one.

But I was ill, I got worse and worse as each day dawned. It was terrible; there was nothing that I could eat, or drink. The smell of Lawrence's cigarettes was almost more than I could bear. I carried with me a towel to retch in each time I went to the little kindergarten Maxwell attended. The doctor kept telling me that it would pass shortly. But even in my sixth month I was still feeling very ill.

Saturdays, Lawrence often went to Sheffield for the day. He went shopping or for a shave, shampoo and haircut. He had a number of excuses to get away. I would just lie on the bed, feeling too ill to read. The children bounced about on the bed. I usually managed to read them stories but it was a huge effort. Sundays, Lawrence went off in the car to visit a friend from his bachelor days. I could not go in the car - it made me worse. I kept wondering if this would continue the whole of the pregnancy. I thought Lawrence was mean going off like that, leaving me. He knew how miserable I felt. Why didn't he stay and help me. Make me a cup of tea, read to the children, take them for a walk, or make the meal, something simple like beans on toast, or poached eggs - the children loved poached eggs. That would have been heaven, but no, off he went.

Perhaps I shouldn't leave her but I can't see what good it would do if I stayed home, it really is better for me to be out of the way. I can't help her in any way that I can see. Too bad she is pregnant again. Too bad.

The doctor came to the house to see me. "You're not doing too well, are you my dear? Well, there is a new drug out that may be a help to you. It is supposed to be very good for cases like you."

"A drug?" Ill as I was, I didn't like the sound of it.

"Yes, it's very new, just the thing for your nausea: Thalidomide it's called. There are no side effects, you'll be fine."

"Well," I said, "I don't want to take a drug - not when I am pregnant. I don't smoke and I don't drink. I don't even take coffee. Not when I am pregnant. I've read that these things could affect the baby. I've never even taken an aspirin."

"Well my dear, it is up to you of course! But the fact is, this drug will not affect the baby and it most certainly will put an end to this nausea you have. I strongly recommend it."

"All the same," I said, "I don't think I will have it. I don't like the idea of taking a drug when I am pregnant, perhaps the nausea won't last much longer."

The next visit, the doctor told me that the baby was the wrong way around and would have to be turned. I would have to go to the clinic; the gynaecologist would do it. A van would pick me up in the morning and deliver me home later that day.

I arranged for Maxwell to stay at the kindergarten until their father picked them up in the afternoon. The teacher agreed to have David as well. The van picked me up at nine-thirty. The clinic was crowded with pregnant women, some with children. It was noisy, not very clean. The lavatories were unpleasantly smelly and messy. It was all quite ghastly and of course I felt ill. I waited and waited - my name was not called. I finally saw someone to ask. "You'll just have to wait, like everyone else." the woman told me. "Your turn will come!"

I returned to my seat. It was now four o'clock! "What time does the doctor go home?" I asked.

"Five," the nurse said, "five on the dot."

"I must see him! I must!"

"Well, love, if he doesn't see you to-day you'll just have to come back won't you! Like everyone else!"

Five o'clock came and still I had not seen him. The nurse came and stood at the front, "The doctor is going to leave now," she told us, "so everyone can go home. Be sure to come again next week at the same time."

I got up and rushed over to the room where the doctor examined the patients. I was desperately tired and rather short of breath. Almost crying, I told her "I won't go home until the doctor sees me!"

"But you must - the doctor is not seeing any more patients today!"

"He has to see me! I have been here the whole day! I have to see him!"

The doctor came to the door, "What is your name?"

"Emily Love", I whispered, "Oh well, let her in." he said, wearily, "I'll see her."

He was not pleased.

I climbed on to the bed. The nurse put a sheet over me - it was very cold in the room, I was very cold but my face was burning. The doctor was tired and wasted no time with pleasantries. "Open your legs Mrs Love. Now you must relax." How could I relax? I was terribly nervous and I too was very tired but I did my best. "There," he said, "I've turned the baby around, should be fine now."

I got down from the bed and wobbled beside it. His back to me, he said, "Go home now and rest, go to bed - that would be best. Get your husband to make the evening meal."

I thanked him for seeing me and said I would try and do that. He turned around then, "Surely your husband can see to the meal this evening? You should go to bed - tell him I said so!" I said I would do that and thanked him again as I wobbled out.

In the van, I would not allow myself to cry. I was unbearably tired and I hurt. I would never go to a clinic again, never, no matter what, it was too awful. It was wonderful to get home. The children ran to hug me. Lawrence made me a cup of tea while I told him all about my horrible day. I sobbed out my story.

"Now Emily, it couldn't have been as bad as all that, surely. Have your tea now, you'll soon feel better."

He did not believe me and thought I exaggerated.

He thought Emily was a fusser; no doubt about that - and just not suited to having babies. He had always thought that - she probably shouldn't be having another baby. Perhaps this should be the last. It is very unpleasant with her being ill so much. Tiresome.

I could see the look of disbelief on his face so I said no more about my ordeal.

"The doctor thought I should go to bed, do you think you could get the meal ready?"

Lawrence looked at me, "He did, did he, well I guess we could have eggs and bread and butter. Yes, I daresay I could get that ready."

At last, towards the end of eight months, I was no longer ill. I felt fine and I decided to have my baby at home. I thought it would be more pleasant and I wouldn't have to be away from the other children. I remembered vividly how unhappy I had been when David was born, not being able to see Maxwell for those two weeks. I bought Maxwell and David beautiful, new tricycles for when the baby was born; I knew they would be absolutely thrilled with them. One was blue and the other red. This would keep them busy, out in the garden. It was a lovely summer; there were gardens of flowers and grass all around the house. Yes, I thought it would be lovely to have the baby at home. I didn't like hospitals. The way they brought you your baby only at certain times of the day. I didn't think that was quite right somehow. I arranged for a midwife and for Maxwell and David to stay with Simone and Edward for the first two nights.

This baby signalled its readiness to arrive on the appointed date but it was three in the morning. Lawrence went to fetch the midwife, she didn't have a telephone, nor did we. He threw pebbles at her window, not too heavy nor too hard as he was afraid of breaking the window. There was no response. He hurried back to see if I was still alright.

"Go! Go! I need her now!"

He hurried back and kept on throwing the pebbles. At last the midwife's head popped out of the window. "I'll be right there!" she called, "You go back."

When he got in the house he found Emily busy getting the bed ready for the birth, she was sweating and her face was flushed. "Are you nervous?" he asked. "Are you alright, would you like a cup of tea?"

He didn't know what else to say, he suspected that tea was not appropriate but that was all he could think of. He felt terribly sorry for her as she grabbed the bed post and moaned. He had never seen this part of the procedure before, it made him feel most uncomfortable. He watched her putting the papers on the mattress, carefully laying down the rubber sheets, he saw that her hands shook, he wished he could do something, say something. She looked over to him and he could see the fear in her eyes as she clutched her stomach and moaned softly. He wanted to comfort her but he was frightened too and didn't know whether he should try to hold her or not so in the end he decided it was best to leave things as they were.

"I'm going to lie down now Lawrence, I'm fine", then she let out another cry and quickly got on to the bed. Finally the midwife arrived, she did not have a car, she had cycled and, although she had hurried, it had taken her longer than Emily had anticipated.

It was quite a relief to Lawrence when the midwife told him go and boil some water.

From the kitchen he could hear Emily groaning and then shouting and crying all at once; then he heard the midwife tell Emily to push, he hoped it would all be over very soon. He certainly couldn't understand this latest trend he had read about where fathers attended the birth, he definitely didn't want to witness any of it and he knew Emily didn't like the idea of it either. Just hearing her was more than enough for him. His poor Tinkerbell - if only he could help her, but what could he do. He never seemed to have the right words for her or feel the right thing at the right time. Difficult - all very difficult. It seemed that loving her was just not enough - there had to be so many things to go with it and he didn't seem to have these words of comfort or love although he did love her so very much.

I heard Lawrence but his voice was distant, offering me tea, when all I wanted was a hug and some loving words of encouragement. He was always such a disappointment to me.

Another little boy arrived, a better size than the others. The children came to look at him, David stroked his head. They were fascinated and picked up their new brother's little hands and feet, and held them. They watched the nappy being changed. They ran off. Soon they were back, they wanted to see him again. They ran in and out, happy and busy with their new trikes in the fresh summer air.

The baby slept in his pram under a shady tree. The grandparents and the aunts and uncles came to see the baby. "My," the Grandmother said "he is a big boy, so bonnie - and what are you calling this little fellow, Emily?"

"Joseph is his name, Joseph Edgar, Edgar after my brother. If he had been a girl we would have called her Josephine as that was the name of the yacht Lawrence and I crewed on and where we met, anyway we decided on Joseph as a compromise, I have always liked the name.

I was very busy with the children and the baby and visitors, but I loved it all, I liked to be busy, I had always had an abundance of energy. One certainly needed an abundance of energy - there was so much to do all the time, there was hardly enough time in the day to get all the chores done. In the mornings, the ashes from the fires had to be emptied and the hearths cleaned, all the food including baby's had to be prepared. Lawrence came home at lunch time and liked to have his main meal then, as was the custom in England. I usually ironed in the evenings, everything laundered had to be ironed of course. Darning, mending, turning shirt collars and cuffs, were also evening jobs but not unpleasant, sitting by the fire chatting, or listening to music. Being a mother certainly was a full-time job but I thought it to be a wonderfully satisfying one.

I had decided long ago that my children would have nice manners; Lawrence felt the same about this so we began at the beginning to teach proper table manners, as well as the, "please" and "thank you" and "excuse-me", all those things. The children liked to please us and enjoyed the praise they received when they did and said things the right way. It made them feel grown up. They could both eat properly with a knife and fork and knew how to use a table napkin, they dabbed at their mouths and carefully replaced the napkin on their knees.

"My," the grandmother said, "isn't it lovely to see little children with such nice table manners and so polite!"

The children smiled smugly, very pleased with themselves.

The summer was over and Maxwell and David were back at their private kindergarten. I joined a badminton club and played one evening a week, I enjoyed the exercise and the socialising.

Lawrence did not come; he looked after the children and said he didn't mind at all, this pleased me very much. At the kindergarten I became friendly with some of the other mothers and was invited out to tea with the children. Samantha, one of my new friends, had a tennis court and invited me and two or three others to play tennis at her home. It was more a social occasion than tennis, chatting and laughing, sipping tea in the garden. Sometimes my new friends came to our house for afternoon tea and brought their children to play or we walked together to the park and pushed the children on the swings. At last my life seemed settled and it was pleasant enough; Lawrence was not a very demonstrative husband and I realised that this was not going to change - but sometimes he could be quite sweet and in his way he loved me.

I was pleasantly surprised when one evening Lawrence told me he had bought a ticket for me, a ticket to the ballet in Leeds for the matinée on Saturday. He said he would be quite happy to look after the children for the day. It was thrilling to be going to the ballet and it was "Carmen", one of my favourites too. I left in the morning and did some shopping, had lunch and settled myself in the theatre. It was thrilling to see it, hear the wonderful music, the exciting story danced so perfectly and excitingly, it made me remember how much I had loved to dance.

At the time when I had to give up my dancing I had been very upset, it had been so difficult to accept the actual fact of never dancing again, I had wondered if I could ever be really happy again. Now with my children, my little house and friends and my husband, I felt content and happy. Although my husband had been a disappointment in many ways, I did love him and, in his way, I knew that he loved me.

Then the unbelievable happened. It was one of those pleasant evenings, the children asleep and our meal was finished and all cleared away, I put a record on and sat down. The fire was crackling comfortably as I sipped my coffee contentedly. I had just been to the library and was wondering which new book I would start, I was looking forward to a good read when suddenly Lawrence got up from his chair and turned the music off.

"Emily," he said, he cleared his throat, and hummed and hawed, "Emily, I must talk to you."

He lit another cigarette.

"Yes?" I looked up. He looked very handsome standing there, in the firelight, in his very smart dark suit, sparkling white shirt and colourful tie, he made my heart go bumpity bump.

"Emily, my job isn't turning out as I had expected you know. There is bribery and corruption in the office and I don't want any part of it, so I am going to be looking for something elsewhere."

I stared at him. No! I thought, No! "Do you mean away from here altogether?"

"Yes, I do - we will have to move. But first of all I will be leaving to look for another post - in the Midlands somewhere, I thought. You can stay here until I get it all sorted out. We will sell the house of course.

He could see her face changing, first it was red, now it was white, she looked up at him, her eyes wide in disbelief, he had known it would be difficult - he only hoped she didn't fuss too much, no, he just couldn't deal with too much of a fuss.

"Do look on the bright side Emily, at least you won't have to clean out the children's noses and ears every time you come home from shopping in town!" He laughed, "And don't forget how much you dislike the fog! Remember the time when we couldn't see a thing and I had to get out of the car and shine my torch on the road so you could see the road!" It was true of course about the fog; although we had fog in Vancouver I had never seen anything like it was here, thick yellow fog, absolutely horrible. I had even had to have David's powder-blue coat and leggings dyed navy-blue because the soot in the air discoloured everything - and cleaning their noses was unpleasant for the children it was true. "What's more," he went on, "you won't have to clean the soot from every window-sill in the house every morning!"

I heard him, but in my mind I knew these things wouldn't really compensate for all the nice things I was going to miss. I had so enjoyed having friends again, knowing all sorts of people to chat to, even knowing the shops had been pleasant.

"Do we have to move? I don't want to move again - I have just made some friends and the children are settled and they have friends too. It would be an awful shame. Do you really have to go so far away? Oh Lawrence, please don't say that we will have to move again! Please." I started to cry, but I knew it was no use. I knew that we would be moving again but still

I cried, my beautiful new world that I had thought was going to go on was nearly finished and there was nothing I could do about it.

"Yes, well I'm afraid it is so - yes it has to be. I shall be leaving in a few weeks and I will leave you to sell the house. I won't be back more than once a month probably, too far to come back any more often than that, I'm afraid."

In bed I couldn't sleep, sadness and anger filled me. Must I always be told what was going to happen without ever being asked what I would like. Did I have no control of my life or the children's? I would be left once again and Lawrence would choose where we lived and what sort of place we lived in and I would have to do as I was told. Anger flowed through me. I knew that this was not right, nor fair, I should be consulted, I should be a partner, not a pawn. My anger was sharpened with resentment. I said no more. What was the use. I went to bed.

He knew Emily was upset but he did not know how to comfort her, what words to use. He thought also that she tended to be contrary, he thought she should be more understanding, more helpful, instead of always thinking of the difficulties. Well, she would just have to get on with it. Nothing he could do about it, he was not going to be part and parcel of the corruption that was becoming more apparent in the office. He may not be making a lot of money but dishonesty was not going to be part of his life, ever. He pretended not to hear the little sniffles beside him although he would have liked to comfort her, hold her close, but it would do no good, it wouldn't change anything, it might get her hopes up, no, it would be pointless. He felt rather tired, he turned over and luckily went straight to sleep.

Lawrence left. It was lonely without him coming in, in the evening. No one to have dinner with, to talk to, no one to discuss the children with, she missed that.

Before he left we made a "For Sale" sign and put it at the end of the drive. A few people knocked on my door to ask the price. I set the price rather high as I had decided to buy a car with the profit. Lawrence thought it was too much to ask, but, after all, it was my house, bought with my money.

When I told Jackie (one of my new friends), she was quite excited as she thought it would be perfect for her parents as they had been looking for a house near them. When I told her the price she said she thought the price was about right for her parents. Jackie's husband Trevor was a lawyer with his own practice, they were settled and well-established. They had a lovely home and had no intention of moving. I would miss her as we had hit it off right from the start. She asked me if it would be alright to bring her parents around?

I was surprised and pleased at how interested she was and told her to come anytime. They wanted to come so soon, I had no time to do anything special to the house, however, the minute they were in the door they knew they wanted the house. It was a small house and took no time at all to show it to them. They loved it and said it would be perfect for them. Later that evening they came back with a cheque for the whole amount, they wanted to move in as soon as it could be arranged. "Let's go out for a drink to celebrate!"

Jackie's husband seemed as thrilled as his in-laws. We all got into Trevor's car and went to the local pub to celebrate the transaction. Everyone was in good spirits. Although I was dreading the move I had got my price and I fully intended to buy a car.

When Lawrence came back, he was surprised I had sold the house so quickly and got exactly what I had asked. We went together and bought a second-hand car, a powder-blue Mini. This was a marvellous step for me. Suddenly I felt very different, liberated, independent! The feeling was exhilarating.

The next time Lawrence came back, he told me he had found a position and a place to live, to rent.

We set the date and ordered the movers. It was a long drive to the new location and I didn't know what to expect, except that Lawrence had said he had rented a house not a flat.

We finally drove into a very uninteresting housing estate - rows and rows of brick houses surrounded us, they looked as if they had been stamped out of a machine. At last Lawrence pulled up.

"This is it!" he said.

"This? You mean this house?"

"Yes Emily, this house."

I stared at this drab, run-down-looking, semi-detatched bungalow with weeds sprouting through the uncut brownish grass, there were no flower beds, just brown grass! "This is where we are going to live? Look at the front door - the paint 's all peeling off, the whole place is a mess Lawrence, the garden, everything! Oh Lawrence - couldn't you have found something nicer than this? It's an awful looking place!"

"Yes, I must admit it isn't quite what I had hoped for but it was the best I could do - and you must remember it is only temporary."

I looked again at this sad, tired-looking, semi-detached bungalow with peeling paint, situated on this dreary housing estate and now I could see at the end of the driveway beside the totally overgrown garden, a rusty old wreck of a car. My heart sank further. I was so disappointed I could have wept. Because of the children I said nothing more. We unloaded the cars and waited for the moving van. I took the children to show them their bedrooms - there were three. Maxwell was to have his own bedroom for the first time and he was thrilled. I thought the house was the most ordinary house I had ever set foot in. In fact, it was squalid, with peeling wall-paper and worn, linoleum floors. There was no privacy either as the sitting-room faced right on to the street. A terrible design. It always surprised me that my husband, who grew up in such lovely surroundings and was an architect, could live in such places. He, who was so fussy about design, about finishes, quality.

"How long will we be here?"

"I'm not certain - depends on whether or not I like the job. A year anyway I expect."

"A whole year! Oh, how awful. A year in this depressing horrible place. You'll just have to get hold of the owner and get that rusting rotting car removed, I can't have that here and that is final!"

I was raging inside, but I had to contain myself because of the children.

"Yes, yes." Lawrence always so calm - he didn't get rattled the way that I did. His voice was always controlled.

He thought she was far too excitable - after all, it wasn't that bad and it was only temporary. It was too bad he couldn't have found something more to her liking - he did feel sorry about that but she would soon fix it up no doubt. She was good at painting walls and making curtains, that sort of thing. No point in crying over spilt milk.

I thought, with hot anger, that it was easy for him to stay calm and controlled! He would walk out in the mornings and never have to deal with any of it. He was out of it all day. He didn't seem to care what he lived in. But I did! I really did, it affected me terribly. I needed nice surroundings, I had always hated ugliness. Well, I would just have to buy some paint and do the children's rooms. It would be a shame to waste money on a rented place, but a year is a year and the children should have a pleasant bedroom as they always used their room a lot for playing in. Yes, I would set to and make their room attractive with pleasant bright colours - and all that grey wood-work I would paint bright white, red curtains and lots of white paint - that should do the trick.

Having my own car made a difference. After school, on fine days, I took the children to a huge park to play. Sometimes at the week-end we drove right into the country and at tea-time I cooked sausages over an open fire for a picnic. There were lots of places to take the children with the little car at holiday time too.

After we had been moved in for a few weeks I thought I should make myself known to the local doctor, one never knew with children when a doctor would be needed. I asked a neighbour for his name and made an appointment. "He is a very busy doctor" the neighbour told me, "Dr Sinclair, nice chap though, yes, very nice, has a large practice, a lot of young families in this area."

The doctor looked up immediately and gave me a friendly smile as I entered his office. He had dark red, curly hair, like a woolly rug on his head. His eyes were deeply set and dark. "Sit down, sit down! Well," he said smiling, "I know who you are."

"You do? I don't see how you could!" I laughed.

"E. B. That's your number plate isn't it?"

"Yes - it is!"

"I've seen you about!"

"I haven't been here long."

"I know, I know. Now, what can I do for you?"

"Nothing really. I just wanted to make myself known and register with you. Just in case!" I laughed again. I was a little embarrassed.

"Yes, a good idea. Now then, tell me your name."

I began to say Mrs ---. "No, No - what is your first name?"

"Emily."

"Well Emily, tell me about your children, names, ages and so on."

My previous doctor never ever used my first name. I felt my face colour. I told him about the children. He told me that he had a boy about the same age as Maxwell. I registered Lawrence as well.

"There we are then Emily, all done."

He got up, he was tall and slim, young. About my age, I thought. He shook my hand, "Lovely to meet you Emily!"

He ushered me to the door. I was pleasantly surprised, it was such a nice encounter. He was so informal and friendly. A rather unusual-looking man with that hair and those deeply-set, dark eyes.

I was surprised and rather horrified to read in mother's latest letter that she was planning a trip to visit us! It had been many years since I had seen mother and her proposed visit was a dream come true. I thought it would be so nice for her to get to know the children and what fun it would be for us to be together again. However, for the visit to take place in this awful house on this depressing housing estate was not how I had ever imagined the occasion. I felt that mother would be greatly disappointed to see me living in such a manner. Her expectations for me had been high, the expensive schools, the riding lessons, music lessons, skating lessons, dancing lessons, swimming lessons, all of this I am sure was supposed to have made me very accomplished, which in her view should have brought me a successful husband, which would have meant that we would live in an attractive house in a pleasant neighbourhood.

"Couldn't we move?" I asked Lawrence. "Couldn't we? I don't want my mother coming here!"

He was unperturbed. "There is nothing to be done! If she is coming, it will have to be here."

Lawrence didn't seem to have any pride, one would have thought he would want to show that he was a good provider and did things properly. But no, he seemed not to care at all. It was so upsetting – I was horrified that mother was going to actually see this awful house that we lived in. I was humiliated and embarrassed.

I wrote and explained that the house was a temporary place, but of course we would look forward to seeing her.

I booked at the Strand Hotel for mother and me, thankful I had my own money for this. The thought of seeing mother after so long, filled me with pleasure and excitement. The anticipation too of mother meeting my children, I just hoped that she would think them as wonderful as I did. They sometimes were pretty noisy. Unfortunately mother still believed that children should be seen and not heard! That might be a problem?

Shortly after mother arrived, David contracted chickenpox. I contacted Dr Sinclair and he said he would pop over Saturday morning.   "My," said mother "it is nice of him to come on a Saturday, isn't it."

I agreed; actually I was rather surprised, but I supposed it was because he lived fairly close and it would be convenient for him.

"You should offer him a glass of sherry, seeing it's Saturday", suggested mother.

Lawrence interjected quickly, "Oh, no - he wouldn't stay for a sherry - he would be far too busy for that!"

I thought I would offer it anyway. After all, as mother said, it was a Saturday.

When I opened the door to the doctor, he moved quickly through to the bedroom. I said I was surprised he knew the way. "Well, all these houses are the same you know Emily."   Of course, I had for one brief glorious moment forgotten that we lived in this awful house and that there were row upon row of them differentiated only by the colour of the front doors.   He looked at David's spots and then tucked him in. "You'll be fine, old chap! Drink lots of water, I expect your mother will read you some nice stories and before you know it you'll be all better. Not too much noise you two -" he told Joey and Maxwell, "David 'll want to sleep quite a lot. You understand don't you, he's a sick little boy and must rest and not get excited."

He smiled and patted them on their heads, "I'm sure you'll help your mother make him better."

As we came out of the bedroom, he chuckled, "Sometimes a little lecture from the doctor makes quite an impression on the siblings you know."

"Oh, yes" I agreed, "I am sure you are right doctor, they certainly listened to you. Would you have time to have a sherry with us since it's Saturday!"

"Oh, what a splendid idea! I should love one!"

We sat for a few minutes and chatted. He asked about mother's trip and about Vancouver then he jumped up, "Must press on, riding lessons this afternoon for Anthony. Call me if there is any change in that little chap, Emily. Anytime is fine."

Very suddenly and most unexpectedly, mother was ill with a bad cold and cough and, as the days went by, she became worse, with vomiting and fever. She was a difficult patient, edgy, any noise upset her, no food appealed to her. She wanted to go home.

"Emily," Dr Sinclair said after he had examined her, "as soon as your mother is well enough to travel, you should get her off home. This medicine I am prescribing should work fairly quickly. It's a good thing you called me when you did or it could have developed into pneumonia."

"There's nothing else the matter is there doctor? I mean she does look very ill and she seemed worried that it might be something else?"

"No no, just a very bad cold; really more like influenza, but rest and medication should do the trick."

Just as he was going out the door he turned "By the way Emily, you look lovely to-day. Let me know how she gets on." and he was gone! I felt myself flush with pleasure, a pity Lawrence never said anything like that.

"Do you know what that doctor said to me, Emily?" Mother asked in a very cheerful voice. (I wondered what could have made her so cheery all of a sudden?)

"No, what was that mother?"

"If you can believe it! He said 'Mrs Brompton, how can you be ill when you have such a lovely daughter!' Now really, what has that got to do with my being ill or not being ill! He hardly looked at me! Every time you walked by, he was watching you! It was quite amazing he knew what was wrong with me at all!" She laughed, "oh well, it doesn't matter. Fancy him saying that though! A very nice man, so very pleasant! He certainly seems to like you, doesn't he!"

I knew that mother did not find Lawrence very easy to get along with or much fun. It had seemed to me that Lawrence had been more dour than usual since mother's visit, but then I knew he was not overly fond of my mother and he also did not like the disruption of her visit. The fact that mother had decided to be ill as well, did not help matters except that he didn't have to make conversation with her at the table. In fact he didn't have to be or do anything special for her once she was ill. He had even asked me if she would be going home sooner than planned because of her not being well. So I guess one could say that her illness was a blessing for Lawrence and in a way for mother as well!

Actually mother began her recovery much sooner than we expected, she was more than ready to go home. Her bag was packed and ready before the tickets were changed!

The trip from Canada was very expensive, mother had been saving for a long time to come and see me so there would not be another trip probably for several years, if ever. I realised that she had not derived a lot of pleasure from the visit although we had enjoyed being together, talking and laughing like we used to do. The children had pleased her, but I think she found family life tiring and at times a little boring. Because the house was so small, one was unable to get away from the children at all, so that made it difficult for mother who was not used to having the constant babble of children around her all the time.

Although the visit had not been idyllic, when the time came for mother to leave we both felt sad, knowing as we did, that there may never be another visit, that it could be years before we saw each other again. The day that we said good-bye we both tried to be cheerful but, as I walked from her, a feeling of sadness overwhelmed me, seeing her leave - that we couldn't chat or laugh together again for a very long time. Telephoning was out of the question, the cost was prohibitive.

Lawrence told me he was going to leave his job. I wasn't really surprised, not anymore. He had already given in his notice.

"Why didn't you tell me?"

"You were busy - and things happened rather quickly, so I just got on with it. If this turns out to be what I think, I shall go into digs, for a while, leave you here and then work something out."

"Why would you leave me here this time? There is no house to sell - we could rent something for a while, while we look around, before we buy a house."

"No, no, Emily! I'll go first; that way I can decide where we should live and things like that."

"Don't you think I should help decide where we should live and if we are to buy a house I am going to help choose it, don't forget that, Lawrence."

"Yes, yes of course Emily; after all, it is your money and I know that, but I will be much better than you at choosing where we live because I have been to Cambridgeshire where this post happens to be, many many times and know the area reasonably well."

I couldn't really argue with that, but I still didn't like the idea, I would have much preferred to go with him to look around, I would have enjoyed it.

"How often will you get home?" I asked as he was packing to leave.

"I shall try for the week-ends, maybe every other week-end but more than likely it won't be as often as that. I shall see though."

Alone again. I spent a lot of time with the children, teaching them to read. I had bought the school readers to have at home so that I could bring them along quickly. I wanted them to be good readers and to enjoy reading, the way that I had always done. At lunch time we had games of spelling. Maxwell loved arithmetic, so I set up sums for him to do. The only time I felt lonely was occasionally in the evenings, but even then I was happy listening to music and sewing or reading. Television had not entered our lives yet.

It was time Maxwell had swimming lessons; he loved the water and was fearless at the seaside, which could be dangerous. I was very surprised to be told at the local swimming baths that they could not teach Maxwell - they didn't teach children that young, so I decided to teach him myself. He immediately became an enthusiastic pupil. At the end of each lesson we jumped about together, splashing each other, laughing and having fun in the warm water. We hadn't been at the baths many times when, one day, I looked up to see Dr Sinclair and Anthony jumping in beside us!

"Would you help me with Anthony?" he asked.   "I was watching you with Maxwell and you seem to know what you are doing which is more than I can say for myself! I could come the same day as you and we could teach both together which could be quite fun for us all?"

" It would be fun, I'd love to!"

We made the arrangements for once a week. At the end of each lesson we played and chased in the warm water. I was still calling him Dr Sinclair.

"Please Emily, for Heaven's sake call me Scott. We are friends after all, aren't we!"

I said that yes, of course we were. At some point I mentioned that my husband was away.

"Aren't you lonely? I could come and visit you in the evening, would you like some company?"

"That would be nice - but what about your wife?"

"She, Emily, would not know whether I was at home or not. She, to put it plainly, is not interested. Mind you, no one should know. You understand don't you?"

That evening there was a knock on my back door. There he was, wearing a light-coloured mac with the collar turned right up. On his woolly head was an old man's soft hat and he was carrying a walking stick! "My disguise!" he laughed. "I walked over."

I made coffee and put a record on, we listened but soon the music was forgotten as we became engrossed in our conversation. He left at midnight; he held my hand for a minute at the door. "Would it be alright if I came over again?" he asked.

"Yes do! It was lovely to have the company." I had really enjoyed the evening with him.

I sometimes invited Anthony to come with the children and myself on outings and often for tea. When I took Anthony home after tea one afternoon, his mother was there on the driveway to meet us. She came over. "I have been wanting to meet you –

I have heard so much about you from my husband. He talks about you rather a lot you know. Won't you come in - I would like to talk to you."

I followed her into the house.

"Do sit down, Emily." Somehow I didn't like the tone of her voice, certainly it wasn't friendly.

We sat down at the dining-room table. "My husband seems to admire you and, as I said, he talked about you rather a lot, so I have been curious to meet you."

I laughed, "Nothing very special about me! I'm just a mother and wife."

"What did you do before you were married?"

"Well, I was supposed to be a dancer - that's what I trained for, but things didn't turn out quite the way I wanted them to. Other than that, not much, I'm afraid!"

Mrs Sinclair gave me the edge of a smile, "I see. Scott said he saw you at the baths and that you swam very well."

"Yes, I guess I do - but then I should. I grew up by the sea and had swimming lessons at an early age."

"You have apparently been helping to teach Anthony how to swim?"

"Yes - I love children and it is fun to teach them. I enjoyed it."

"Well, thank you for your help Emily," she said icily "but, you see, we can easily get a proper swimming instructor for Anthony, so really I don't know why my husband bothered you about it. I shall arrange it immediately. Well - I won't keep you any longer, Emily, but don't you worry, I shall see to Anthony. We don't really need your help any more, you do understand, don't you?"

Yes, I thought, I did understand very well!

The woman was most unfriendly and rather rude and the meeting was unpleasant. After all, Scott and I were friends - nothing else! And anyway, the woman didn't even know about the evening visits!

I told Scott.

He laughed, "She really was curious! My fault, Emily! I guess I talked about you a bit too much. Don't worry, she won't do that again!"

"Your wife is very lovely Scott - so tall, with such fine features."

"Yes I suppose that she is, in a cool sort of way, but Anthony and I don't see much of her you know. Her career is the important part of her life. Doctors shouldn't marry doctors I guess."

I woke up in the middle of the night sweating and very nauseated, my head pounded and there were terrible pains in my lower abdomen. I remembered having those pains in Jersey that time when I had such a heavy painful period and at that time I certainly didn't realise what was going on! I knew this time what was happening! I rushed to the bathroom and was violently ill. I had not told anyone yet. I had thought it too early to mention, but if Lawrence had been here I would have told him. I had missed Lawrence even though he was not the husband I had hoped for. I loved seeing Scott, but it was not the same as one's husband. It was terrible being so sick, the pains were awful enough, but the vomiting was exhausting. All of a sudden I felt what would have some day been a baby, leave me. In the morning, still feverish, I went to my immediate neighbour who had a telephone and asked if she would call the doctor for me. The neighbour was a young woman and on her way to work. "Now?" She asked.

"Yes please, if you would - I don't have a telephone and I am too ill to go and see him."

"I see" - but she did not hurry!

"Could you do it now - before he gets out for his rounds?"

At last the woman went to the telephone and arranged for the doctor to come.

I got Maxwell and David off to school and Joey fixed up with his colouring books. I left the front door unlocked and went back to bed.

Shortly afterward, I heard Scott's car pull up and then his knock at the front door; he opened it and came in. "Emily?"

"Yes," I called, "I'm in bed, Scott."

He rushed into my bedroom. "What is the matter?" He paused then, inside the door, "You look terrible".

I tried to lift myself but I felt dizzy and ill, I flopped back. He put his arms around me, under my back and gently lifted my head on to the pillow. "What happened Emily? When did you become ill?"

I told him. He arranged my hair away from my face, his fingers stroked the strands into place behind my ears. "Poor girl."

His face was very close to mine. He looked into my eyes. "Emily, Emily" he whispered. Then he said, "My God, Emily, I will have to find you another doctor." He held my shoulders for a minute, then gently he let go of me. He got up from the bed and walked to the window. "Emily," he said very quietly, "I can no longer be your doctor. I simply cannot, you do understand, do you?"

I understood. I felt it too. "Yes." I whispered.

What could there be between us? We were both married, with children. I imagined It would have been marvellous to be married to a man like that - so young, so vibrant. He would have been the type of man who would hold your hand when you went out walking. He would probably hug you and be admiring and affectionate. Yes, I could see these things, but the fact remained that we were both married to someone else, so any such thoughts or feelings must not be allowed. There was nothing to be done about it. I was glad that he saw this and was being sensible. I knew there was no other way.

He came away from the window and sat again on the bed, "I'll send someone in to attend to you as soon as I can and I'll get some home help for you."

"What about now?"

"Yes - I have a sedative for you and some pills you should take. Emily?"

"Yes?"

"Although I can no longer be your doctor, I can still be your children's doctor."

"Thank you." My eyes filled with tears.

"Emily, Emily, please don't cry. Please." He pulled out his handkerchief and dried my face, looking into my eyes the whole time. "You will feel better very soon, the medication I gave you will work quickly. I'm sorry you lost the baby, Emily."

"I am too. Will I see you swimming?"

"Yes, Emily, as soon as you are well. Anyway, I shall be over next Wednesday evening? Alright?"

"Please."

He left me, I heard the door shut as I closed my eyes, sobs gently shook my body as the sadness of what had happened sank in. My baby, my dear little child, oh how I would have loved you, oh what a shame, what a terrible shame, why, why! Gradually a calmness began to envelope me - I could feel sleep take control and I was relieved and let it do so.

Lawrence returned. I decided not to tell him about what had happened, about the baby. I just said I had not been well for a few days and the doctor was kind and got a home help for me. "It was a blessing, I had such a bad head and upset tum, it meant I could take a couple of days in bed - and he sent someone over the same day as he saw me, so I didn't have to worry about the children at all."

"That's good - so you're all better now then?" I told him that I was and wondered how he had got on. Much to my surprise he told me he had found a very pleasant village and there was a house for sale, would I like to go down and see it?

"A proper house? Not another place like this? This temporary house where we've lived for two whole years!"

My voice started to escalate. I pulled myself together and calmed down. Why am I so edgy, I really want to cry and here he is offering to take me to look at a house at last!

"Yes," I told him, "I would love to look."

When Lawrence stopped the car and said "this is it, Emily", I was amazed, it was a real house, made of brick and quite large, sitting well back from the road, surrounded with grass and gardens of flowers. There was a sunny, stone terrace all along the back of the house; a path at the side of the house led to a garage and even a garden shed. At the other side of the house was a spinney which backed on to a field. When we went inside I saw that the inside of the house was lovely as well, with three bedrooms, a playroom, large kitchen with an AGA stove and beautiful living room with a stone fireplace. There was a dining room as well.

I was thrilled, but I wondered if it was a house we could afford. I certainly didn't want to use all of my capital as I liked to have my own separate income. Lawrence said that if I paid for the house he would carry any extra expenses associated with the sale and move. I agreed to this arrangement and fortunately the cost of the house still left me with plenty of capital invested.

The children were so excited, "Would this be our own garden?" they asked, "All of it?" They ran all around exploring the little spinney at the side of the house. In the field, there was a

horse! They ran and talked to the horse. When can we move?
They wanted to move that very day. I couldn't blame them,
I would have liked to as well.

    The time came to say good-bye to Scott. He had been over
for the evening; we stood together in the hallway. Then, for the
first time, he held me to him and kissed me. "You are the one
really bright spot in my life Emily, don't go!"
    "I'm so sorry, Scott - so sorry. We both know that I have to
go. We both know too, that it's for the best. It has to be this
way!"
    He let me go, "Yes." he said, "You have to go. I know that."
    He took my hand in his. "Dear Emily, I won't see you again.
I shall miss you Emily, very much. Take care of yourself, and
remember what I told you! Don't take that birth control pill yet,
give it a few years, wait until it has been tested longer and known
to be perfectly safe."
    Then he was gone!
    I thought about Scott: all the things I liked so much about him
and felt the sadness of leaving. We were very attracted to each
other but in my heart I knew that it really was a good thing I was
leaving. Our relationship was definitely dangerous. Maybe now,
I thought, Lawrence and I would have a better life together in our
new house; maybe it would make a difference. Maybe now
I would be more of a partner. Lawrence had been such a
disappointment to me. I had wanted so much more from my
marriage. I had expected to share all of my life, all of my
thoughts. I had wanted to give him my whole self and had
expected him to do the same, but he kept himself from me. He
closed in on himself and would not let me in. What I wanted was
not possible with Lawrence.
    I was ready to move, I needed to break away from here, this
sad parting with Scott, this horrible house. I was going to have a
happy life, I was determined. The children would love living out in
the country; I closed my eyes and could see it all. We could
even put up a badminton net. Or there is croquet; I did love that
when I was a young girl, in Nellie and Lily's garden. And the
terrace - we could have our meals there in the fine weather. Yes,
it would be lovely, I was going to love living there.

Moving day finally arrived. I took little Joey in my car and Maxwell and David were to go with their father. Just as we were leaving, David came running up the drive, "Mummy, Mummy - please let me come with you!"

"Of course, my sweet!" I said, "But if you go with daddy you'll get there sooner - his car 's faster than mine!"

"But Mummy, I want to come with you! I want to sing!" He hopped in. He was such a dear child - so loving, so blond, that white hair always touched my heart. I turned and gave him a kiss and one for his brother. I had a good look at them there, all bright with expectant smiles. It was wonderful to have children, a family, I loved it. But before I turned around, there was Maxwell "Can I come with you too?"

"Of course pet!"

"Are you going to sing?" he asked.

"Yes!"

"I thought so, that's why I wanted to come with you!"

We didn't sing in Lawrence's car, he didn't like it.

As we pulled up in front of the house I felt I was still in a dream - that we were actually going to live in this house. The children jumped out of the car and ran down the drive and into the house as soon as the key had turned. In and out of the rooms they ran, and up the stairs to the bedrooms where light was streaming in from the many windows. There were huge windows in the sitting room and dining room and French doors to the terrace. Oh it was marvellous! The kitchen with the AGA stove and masses of cupboards, counters and a double sink. I looked around and still it was like a dream. Through the kitchen window I could see the fields beyond our garden, no houses. The little playroom next to the kitchen with windows on every wall. The children were already running all around the garden, laughing and chasing each other.

It did not take long to move in as we had so little furniture. Lawrence's parents had promised a few more cast-offs if we found ourselves short of anything. I planned to buy some rugs for the oak floors. Of course it all needed decorating, but I would do that in time. Joey would be going to school now, so I would have time to strip the walls and paint. It would look much better then, there would be such a lot to do! Oh but I was happy, so happy!

After I had put the children to bed I walked slowly through the house. I could picture it as it would be, after I had decorated and with the curtains and the rugs. It was going to be a pleasant place to live, comfortable, a pleasure to live in. I looked out the window and could see the large trees, the green fields, the grassy slope with the autumn leaves lying there and the charming little spinney. It was lovely. Lawrence came to stand beside me, "Quite pleasant, isn't it?"

"Oh yes, I love it! I love the garden, the house, everything!"

"Happy, Tink?"

"Yes - I'm happy."

"Good!" he said, "Good!"

He had not called me Tink for a long time! It was lovely to hear it again. It warmed me, I felt some love return and was glad for this.

Thank goodness, at last she seems to be pleased and I won't have to hear her constant complaints anymore - it really was tiresome. Quite expensive all this, it is good that she has her own money - quite lucky really – anyway, it is nice to see her all happy and pleased for once I must say. More like my Tinkerbell.

Summer would soon be over. It had been pleasant, lots of sunny days when I had taken the children to the pool and often to the river nearby with a picnic lunch. We went camping for two weeks all together. Lawrence was more relaxed and easier with the children. Our tent was right at the beach and the children were in and out of the water all day. It had been a good holiday - even Lawrence enjoyed it. It was fun when we went swimming together and that day when I had skipped off, running, leaping and diving into the water. In bed, Lawrence had said how he had loved to see me do that again.

"It reminded me of when I first knew you!" he said, as he put his arms around me. "You know, I used to love to watch you, it was part of the fun of taking you swimming. Just to watch you. That was when I first loved you, remember? When I first called you Tinkerbell?"

He hadn't said anything romantic or loving like that for such a long time. It was lovely to hear him say that. It was good to feel his arms around me again. If only he could be like that all the time, but he couldn't and I knew now that he couldn't. Maybe he wanted to be, but for him it was impossible; perhaps boarding school from an early age, with no loving mother to talk to or to give him a hug and the warmth that children need as they grow and develop was responsible for his reticence to express feelings. When he was at university, he had lived in "digs" alone. He had been an officer during the war so there again he had lived alone. He never learned how to give warmth in words or small gestures. He did not know how to share the good or the bad with anyone, he had never had an intimate relationship before. There had been a girlfriend for a short time but I understood they had never become very close. I kept hoping that eventually Lawrence would be able to give more of himself.

MORE CHANGES – 1965

Fashions had suddenly changed, the mini-skirt had taken over from the sedate mid-calf length. My new skirt was suede leather and it barely covered my bottom. I let my hair out of its chignon and wore it loose to my shoulders. When Lawrence saw the length of my skirt he was horrified!

"Do you know what men call those short skirts? Do you, Emily?"

"No, I do not and I don't care what they call them!"

"You would if you knew!"

"Well then, tell me!"

He looked at me, right into my eyes and quietly he told me, "They call them pussy pelmets, Emily! That's what they call them!"

I tossed my newly released long hair, "I told you Lawrence, I just don't care!"

"But I care Emily, I care." He walked away from me.

I knew he was angry, but he never really showed it, he wasn't like me, he never flared up, I had never heard him shout, never. I longed for him to react, I would have preferred him to really show his anger. His cool, controlled attitude was very hurtful.

Martha, my new friend, taught art in a near-by village primary school and told me that there was a position open for someone like me who could teach swimming, dancing, music and rhythm and generally assist the other teacher as well as Martha. I thought that this would be perfect as I would always be at home when the children were at home and I liked the thought of having an interesting job, also I thought it would perhaps help our marriage, make me more interesting and give us a fresher outlook somehow.

Without mentioning it to Lawrence I went along for the interview and was accepted there and then. I was very excited! I could hardly wait to tell Lawrence, I was sure he would be really proud of me.

At last, after dinner, I told Lawrence all about it. I told him the salary I would be getting and how convenient the hours would be and how Martha and I would go together, sharing petrol expenses. The more I talked about it the more excited I was about the whole plan. Lawrence sat listening, he said nothing. No questions, no comments. Finally when I finished, he got up from his chair and said "I told you long ago Emily, that wives in our families do not go out to work - they never have and as far as I am concerned, you won't either, apart from that aspect it is a crazy idea! How could you possibly run this house and do all the cooking that is necessary, look after all the children's needs, attend to all the church functions, flower arranging, fund raising and so on - who would arrange the "Harvest Supper" - things like that? Your work in the community is very important, it is very different for Martha, she leads a different life and she is not involved with any other activities. You have to be available to attend the opening of buildings, formal dinners and such, whatever made you think you could take on a teaching position! You obviously didn't think it through, impulsive as usual. It's a pity you put everyone to all this trouble for nothing."

I looked at Lawrence, there was absolutely no expression on his face. I knew there was no point in arguing with him, I was not going to be able to accept the position. I knew I wasn't that important in the community; I was sure I could have worked something out, maybe even work part time, but Lawrence was not going to discuss it. I got up from my chair and left the room. Perhaps I had already known I would not be allowed to do this, perhaps I had given up and had accepted without realising it, that, like it or not, my husband was a very controlling man and he wasn't going to change.

Eventually Lawrence told me that he would be working on a new, rather long project in London.

"Will we be moving then?"

"No, no!"

"But won't it be a long day for you?"

"Yes, it will. I will be leaving in the mornings at 6:30 and arriving home at 8:00. I shall be too tired to do anything in the evenings, maybe on a Saturday occasionally, it would be alright."

"But what about us? You won't ever be here. Will you have dinner here?"

"Yes of course, but not with you and the children, I shall be too late for that you know."

"Don't you think it would be better if we moved closer to

London? We would soon settle somewhere else if we bought a nice house. Like we have here."

"No, no, we won't be moving. The train trip is only an hour or so and I can read or do paper work on the train, it will be fine."

I still thought it would be better to move. Not that I liked moving - or really wanted to move - but I would be alone all the time and it could stay like that with him working in London. By the time he got home and had his meal there would be no evening left. Even if we didn't get on well I didn't like the prospect of being alone like that, never doing anything together, maybe for a whole year or even two. The children wouldn't be having any meals with their father anymore and I didn't think that was good for them. Again I asked, "Don't you think it would be better if we lived closer to your job? So that you would be with us more for meals and evenings?"

"No Emily - I prefer to leave things as they are." His voice had become irritated.

He was not going to consider moving.

He didn't want me to get up with him in the mornings - no, he would rather have his morning tea on his own and take breakfast in London. Dinner he liked served on a tray in the sitting-room so that he could watch TV.

Week-ends, Lawrence was tired, lethargic. Everything was too much for him. He was more and more critical of the children, especially Maxwell. He did not like the longer hair, the flowered shirts. He used to like the Beatles but now he seemed not to. "Turn it off" he would say if he heard the Beatle's music.

He came home later and later, I suspected he was having an affair in London. We lived in the same house but we were separate.

Maxwell was his constant target; he was obsessed with his dislike of this son. The boy was growing nervous and withdrawn. He spent too much time on the river in his kayak alone. I worried about him. I tried to keep the house a happy place, but dreaded the sombre presence of Lawrence. The loving household I had thought was within my grasp, had evaporated. I loved all of my children, all so different from each other. Didn't Lawrence love them? Why was he so unloving, so critical, sometimes even mean.

Maxwell was so interesting, so different. I enjoyed listening to his plans of becoming a pilot. "You must be good at Math to become a pilot you know", he told me. He was good at nearly everything he did. He was a handsome boy as well - I was proud of him.

Lawrence said he would take the children for their haircuts as he required one himself and it would fit his Saturday schedule quite well. "Not too short!" I had said before they left. "You know boys are all wearing longer hair now. Even the Prince of Wales!"

Trusting him, I stayed at home. When they came back they had the shortest haircut they had ever had! Maxwell had run up the stairs and got under the bed. "I'll be laughed at!" he cried, "Everyone will laugh at me! It'll take months for it to get longer!" He had cried hard and long. He wouldn't come out of his room. He was affected the most, but certainly the others were not happy either. I had felt so sorry for them. Why did he do it? It had been a terrible week-end; everyone was upset, except Lawrence of course, he thought the fuss was a lot of nonsense. "It's really your fault Emily, all this fuss. You make too much of silly issues. Just leave them alone, they'll soon get over it, ridiculous."

How could we go on, every day there was something. When I saw Lawrence grab Maxwell and shake him so hard he ripped his shirt, I was frightened. Maxwell was more upset that his father had torn his flowered shirt that he treasured, rather than the fact that he had irritated his father so much.

I tried to talk to Lawrence but it ended up with me shouting because he wouldn't answer me. He wouldn't talk to me. I shouted, "Answer me! Talk to me! Please Lawrence."

He said nothing but walked away and closed the window. "I don't want anyone to hear you Emily, what would the neighbours think?"

"I don't care what they think Lawrence, I really don't."

"Well Emily, you should."

The next time I approached him, I had made up my mind not to get upset.

"Do you think we should get some counselling? We need

some help. What is the matter? Don't you love us anymore?"

He did not answer that. "There is no need for counselling."

"Why do you say that?   None of us are very happy these days. You are constantly picking on the boys and you hardly speak to me. You certainly aren't a loving husband or a loving father in words or gestures! A loving hug would be nice now and then and a word of praise or of love even! Not exactly a happy family life, is it! And of course - you are never here!"

He got up from his chair and walked away.

I followed him "Maybe it would be a good idea for us to separate for a spell - it might help to sort us out somehow?"

He looked at me, "We are a family unit and family units do not separate."

"I thought it might help us."

"Well, you thought quite wrongly then;   we will not discuss such a thing, Emily."

Of course she grew up without a father, one must remember that; she has some strange ideas about family life. How could separating possibly help us, boys need a strict upbringing - none of this namby-pamby that she finds so important, they have to learn to toughen up. Why isn't she happy, three healthy children, a nice house, a husband who provides everything, silly girl. I work hard and am tired - why can't she understand these things, being a provider is a serious business. I have real worries, deadlines to meet, difficult clients to please, difficult builders to deal with and I am not a young man anymore. She has always been too romantic, does she really think couples are telling each other they love each other after eighteen years! I never ever saw my parents even hold hands, and this hugging that Emily thinks is so important is not something I really think of doing, not very often anyway.

Autumn was in the air and so was school. Shopping with the children was fun as they were so enthusiastic about their new uniforms which did look very smart. I liked the crisp, white shirts, the polished shoes, the neat blazers.   The thought of the resumed routine pleased me.

I liked the autumn altogether. The changed colours outside, the mornings with that nip in the air, the sharp wind when I hung out the washing, the thought of Christmas, of snow, the fire burning in the sitting-room, Guy Fawkes night. Yes, winter was rather nice, I liked it.

I wished that Lawrence would be a kinder, more understanding father and a more loving husband, like when we were on holiday. I had tried to hold on to those pleasant times in my mind, to help me, but they had slipped away. Oh, how I had wanted our lives to be like that all the time, but no, it was not like that, not at all.

It was perhaps a good thing that Lawrence was away so much, since he found the children and myself so tiresome.

David, my, blond, blue-eyed, cuddly little love bug was sick. I heard him calling in the night and rushed in to find him all hot and vomiting. He vomited all the night long. Early in the morning I telephoned the doctor - he was new in the area, he said he would come at once. After he examined David he told me it was appendicitis. "Your little boy will have to go to the hospital - now. I will call the ambulance."

At the hospital the doctor told me he would have to operate at once. I looked down at my sweet, poorly, little boy. His body so tender. I hated the thought of a knife going into that little soft white tummy. I held his hand, kissed him, then he was whisked away. It was hard for me not to cry, I swallowed hard and dabbed my eyes. He looked so defenceless, almost frail because of his fair skin, white hair and very light build, so different from the others.

"There is no need to wait," the doctor told me "he will be a couple of hours. Come back later."

I left reluctantly. As I walked away, the doctor caught up, "He will be fine, not to worry." He gave me a big reassuring smile.

At home I rushed to let the dog out and write a note for Maxwell and Joey, they were not used to coming home to an empty house. At last I was able to return to the hospital.

In the ward, David was awake, all smiles, waiting for me. I had brought some of his books. I sat on the bed and he chattered about the other patients. One, across the way, was brought in with an asthma attack; he looked really sick and they couldn't save him - he died. The nurse told me that the parents had not got him into the hospital quickly enough.

"Isn't that terrible" he said, "that he died?"

"Yes - it is terrible, I am so sorry."

"I am too. Isn't it good that you got me here soon enough?"

"Yes," I said "it is."

"I might have died do you think?"

"Possibly," I said, "but you didn't, you are safe now. The sick bit has been taken away and very soon you will be all better."

"I know," he said, "that's what the doctor told me too. He was ever so nice and so was the nurse."

I was relieved and happy that they had been so good to my little boy. I could go home and not worry about him.

When Lawrence arrived home I told him how the day had unfolded. But of course he could not visit David - there was no visiting late in the evening and he was in London all day, "But" he said, "if he's still there on Saturday I could try and get over - if I'm not too tired, that is."

Just as I was leaving for early communion the telephone rang, I ran to answer it, briefly wondering who on earth it would be on a Sunday morning so early. I was shocked to hear the operator say it was a long distance call from Jersey - a Roger Brown.

"Emily? Is that you?" The voice was vaguely familiar. "This is Roger, you remember me? I was a friend of your Aunt's and also her solicitor."

"Yes of course I remember you, Roger." I did remember him but it was well over twenty years ago since I heard him speak and certainly twenty years since I had even thought of him.

"Well I am afraid I have very sad news for you Emily," he said, "very sad. I am so sorry to have to tell you this, but your aunt has died suddenly, very suddenly. She got back only two days ago. I thought it best to phone you at once, I knew you would want to know as soon as possible, better than a letter I thought, just in case you wanted to come to the funeral. It has been a terrible shock to us all, her heart you know. I'm so sorry, I know how close you two were, Emily."

"Oh Roger! How sad. Oh dear."

"I know it's a shock, but I really did think it best to let you know as soon as possible because of the funeral being so soon, you understand."

"Yes, and I am so glad that you called right away, thank you,

Roger, thank you."

I put the phone down and sat looking out of the window. It was hard to comprehend. My wonderful Aunt, my sister-aunt. Oh, what fun we had had together. How I had loved to be with her all those years ago. She really was a marvellous person. Now gone. I had missed her, with us living so far apart but we had always planned to get together again someday. Now I would never see her again. The Sunday morning noises suddenly disturbed my thoughts, the noisy chatter, who was coming to play? Who was in charge of the toast? Whose turn for the cream from the milk? Lawrence was there reading the paper, oblivious to all that was happening around him. I went to him and sat near to tell him.

He said he was very sorry, "I didn't know her at all well, but I am sorry. I know how fond you were of her. It is a pity you cannot go to the funeral. With me in London all day it would be impossible for you to go - you know that, don't you?"

I said yes, I had realised that and anyway there really would be no point. I would send flowers.

Oh Ann, Ann, how I shall miss you. Now you are nowhere, absolutely nowhere. Oh how awful, simply awful to think of.

Any secret thoughts I had of leaving Lawrence faded.

When I picked up the letter lying on the hall floor I immediately imagined it was from Roger. The envelope was typed.

As soon as I opened the letter and saw the writing, I knew that the letter was from Paul.

My dear Emily,

It was so sad about Ann. I am very sorry, dear Emily. I went to the funeral; I had hoped you would be there. I prayed you would be there, Emily.

I asked Roger if he knew where you were, your address. So here I am writing to you after all these years and here you are in England married to that chap you used to sail with! That was certainly a surprise! He told me that you were unable to go to the funeral as your husband was away a lot and you had children to look after. How many children do you have, Emily? As you know, I used to see Ann from time to time, but when she was in Australia I lost touch with her. I liked her very much, as you know.

You perhaps are wondering why I am writing to you. I will fill you in a bit before I go any further. I think you knew through Ann that my wife did come back and we lived together (not very successfully) for a few years. You may not know, however, that we had a little girl. I named her Emily. My wife could not understand where on earth I had got that name from! She, of course, was never to know. You were and always have been and always will be my number one love, Emily.

Well, after several years my wife and daughter left. They went back to Germany. Once again she would not give me a divorce. I didn't really care as I had no plans for marriage anyway. However, recently she agreed because she wants to have her freedom to marry now. So after all this time I am at last free, although I am not planning on getting married!

This past year I was diagnosed with cancer. Every month I go to London for treatment. So far they have kept it at bay. I probably will not make a full recovery and if I do there is no guarantee that the wretched illness won't hit me somewhere else. But, as I say, I do go to London once a month.

Emily, please come into town and have lunch with me! You live quite close to London so you probably go in reasonably often. Can I talk you into doing that, Emily? I should so much like to see you again. Let me know by return post, dear Emily, I will then give you a date if you'll agree.

Always with love,
Paul

I read the letter with a pounding heart. It was marvellous to hear from him, just marvellous! But how sad, for him to have that horrible cancer. The poor man. And he all alone with the horror of it too. It really was sad.

Of course I was going to go and have lunch with him! How could I not! I would write immediately. It would be so exciting to see him again! Mind you, he is ill, so he is not going to be the same - and also, so many years had gone by. We could both have changed in every way.

At Paul's suggestion we arranged to meet at Simpson's for lunch at 12 o'clock. I decided to wear my tailored, cream-coloured linen dress with my black straw boater and cream shoes. It was really quite a stomach-churning thing to be doing! I was very nervous.

As I arrived at the restaurant door I saw Paul stand up; slim, straight and elegant, he strode over with his hands out towards me.

We stood looking at each other still holding hands, he smiled, "Perhaps we should sit down darling?"

He held my hand across the table. It suddenly did not seem like such a very long time since we had been together. He really looked the same. The lines were deep where once they were shallow. His hair thinner - but he never did have thick hair. He was still slim.

"Good Lord, Emily, isn't this marvellous, absolutely marvellous! You look wonderful, darling. A bit on the thin side though! Your hair is so dark, Emily, a very different colour than I remember? Your hair was golden - remember how Pierre called you the golden girl?"

I explained that, in my family, light hair usually was dark by the time one was thirty and then it matched up with our eyebrows and eyelashes. "Also, I don't spend a lot of time out of doors now."

I asked about his treatment. He was not keen to talk about it. "Let us just say that all is under control for the present, I hope for the best. There are many worse off than me - I see them every month. You said you had three boys Emily, how old are they?"

"Well, I'll start with Maxwell who is 14, then David who will be 13 shortly and then Joey who will be 10 this summer. I always thought it would be nice to have a girl but it wasn't to be and the boys are wonderful."

"Funny Emily, how you had the boys and I had the girl. I won't talk about what might have been, not a good idea."

I laughed, "no Paul, it wouldn't be a good idea."

I asked about Pierre and Françoise and, somehow, nearly two hours had disappeared.

"My goodness," I said, as I looked at my watch, really surprised at the time, "I must be thinking of catching my train - it is getting late. It really has been lovely to see you again Paul and an absolutely lovely lunch too. I always love Simpson's, a perfect choice."

"Would you be able to come next month Emily?"

I did not hesitate, "Of course I will, certainly."

The boys hovered about me in the kitchen, hungry and impatient for their dinner.

I felt quite wonderful, uplifted.

I wondered if I would find the meeting next month as enjoyable, or was it just the excitement of seeing Paul after such a long time.

But no, it was just as lovely and I felt wonderful again after our afternoon together. He suggested I brought one of the boys next time.

"Perhaps during school break," I told him, "I could bring David and Joey, not Maxwell, he is far too busy with his kayak. We could go to Hyde Park or maybe to the Natural History museum. They would like that and they wouldn't be bored. It would be nice for them to meet you, but I would have to tell them not to tell their father, which could be difficult. I shall have to think about it. I will let you know."

Although we chatted all through lunch, I never mentioned that I had been thinking about leaving my husband, which recently had been very much in my mind. I had tried unsuccessfully to chase the thought away. I knew I would tell Paul, but not yet. I wasn't sure why I was so slow in telling him; I guess I felt he was not really very interested in that part of my life. He didn't ask much about Lawrence. Mainly he asked about the children, about what I did with my time and about the years in between, in Canada. Things like that. Of course we reminisced, which was always enjoyable. It was nice to have someone to talk to who knew Ann. I looked forward to the visits more and more each month.

It was getting close to the last of Paul's treatments for another six months. He had one more, maybe two.

I was going much earlier, this visit we planned to spend the day in Hyde Park. I was a little apprehensive about telling Paul my plans - for one thing, once I had told someone it made the plan a reality, something I really was going to do. I still hadn't thought the whole thing out but I knew I was going to do it. So I was going to tell him on this visit.

It was a beautiful day and we had been walking along arm in

arm, chatting about this and that. "Shall we sit here Paul, at least this seat looks clean and it would be nice to sit in this lovely sunshine for a minute or two and I do have something I want to tell you. You see Paul," I said, not looking at him, as we settled on the bench, "I am planning to leave my husband. It's a long story of course, but I am." I waited in the silence, still not looking at him.

"But Emily," he said, "why on earth didn't you tell me this weeks ago? Are you truly having such a difficult time? You certainly didn't let on, did you? I gathered from snippets of your conversation that you didn't have a great marriage, but not too many people do, I have found. So I didn't think there was any real problem. I am so sorry. But, tell me Emily, just where were you planning to go?"

I told him my idea about a village not too far from the one we lived in at present.

"Why do you want to be so close to where you're living now?"

I told him that I thought it would be less disruptive for the children and they could still see their father. "Maybe," I said, "if we're not too far away, Lawrence would see that he missed us, would want to talk about it and put things right between us."

"Haven't you tried to discuss the problems at all? What makes you think that if you move out, that suddenly Lawrence 'll change?"

I said that I didn't know. "It was just a hopeful thought, that's all. I guess I'm frightened of being on my own with the children and all that it means. I am frightened of actually doing it!" I was very frightened and spent a great deal of time wondering what I should do; in my heart I thought it wrong to leave and yet our lives were becoming unbearable a lot of the time and I was worried about Maxwell.

"Well, it is a big step to be sure. If you have thought it out and are really certain that this is what you want to do and are going to do, why don't you come and live with me on Jersey, Emily?"

I looked at him, "With you?" I was stunned.

"Yes, Emily, with me! I would enjoy the boys, and as for having you with me, it would be a dream come true!"

"Have you room?"

"Yes of course I have room. Lots of room. Would you consider it? You would have to take into consideration that my health is not good. It is not a subject I dwell on, but that is the fact. The treatment is finished now for six months. So far, I have done very well and I hope for the best. I have no guarantee that I am to be your life-long partner, but we could have a few pleasant years together, God willing. What do you say to that?"

I had only considered going a short distance from where we lived and had not thought of making it a step that could not be retrieved easily. It would mean a change of everything and of course it would be the end of my marriage.

"Schools?" I asked.

"Well yes - there is a very good fee-paying school there. They could all go to that. Emily, why don't you think it over? Go home and think it over! If you decide to do it, I can come over for a few days and be with you the day that you move. You wouldn't be alone Emily. I don't want to persuade you. I want you to come, but it must be your considered decision. Now let's go and find a cup of tea before you catch that train home."

We stood up, he put his arms around me and then I felt his warm love as he kissed me, really kissed me. "It makes me sad to think you have been unhappy, Emily. I would love the chance to make you happy again. Now then - tea! Then home for you - must not miss that train, my pet!"

"No one has called me that, but you. To hear you say it again, well, it makes this all seem a little unreal somehow."

"Yes, it's all a little unbelievable I have to admit, but it could be a wonderful reality."

My mind was filled with this new life that we could have, a happier life, however, there were many things I must consider. Sometimes it was difficult to keep my mind on the practicalities when pictures of us all at the beach, enjoying the warm sea and that wonderful island sunshine kept sliding into my mind. Maxwell, no longer nervous or rebellious, no one constantly criticizing him. Oh it would be so good - and the private school! I had always wanted my children to go to a fee-paying school, but Lawrence would not hear of it, not once they were out of primary school. He said the state schools were quite adequate, although he went to a fee-paying school! Yes, the more I thought about leaving, the better it seemed. I couldn't see any major problems. I imagined that happiness for us all, was just around the corner.

I made the decision.

However, as the time drew near I became nervous and again unsure. Should I? Shouldn't I? There was a relentless feeling of guilt, of disappointment, fear.

I decided to give Lawrence one last chance to put things right. I was going to tell him how I felt, really tell him. If he listened to me and tried to see my point of view and showed some understanding about Maxwell I would cancel everything; it would be a bother but I would do it. Paul would understand. It would be easy to explain it all to the children. It would be a relief really. I was quite frightened of the move - I would have much preferred to put things right and carried on, I didn't like the idea of ending my marriage, giving up, admitting failure. If only Lawrence would understand and try to be nicer, in my heart that was what I really would have liked to happen. I would have to force a conversation with Lawrence whether he liked it or not.

It was quite late and he was watching television (as usual) after dinner. "I have to talk to you Lawrence – I have to."

"Well Emily, I don't think you have chosen an appropriate time for a talk; however go ahead if you must."

"Yes, well, I must," I said, "I am fed up with being alone all the time for one thing. Then when you come in so late in the evening and sit with your dinner tray, and the television on, why, I might just as well not be here. We never go anywhere; we never do anything together, we seldom eat together, we don't even talk much to each other now. And it is quite horrible the way that you constantly criticize Maxwell, his personality is changing - where he was such a happy outgoing child he is now nervous and becoming withdrawn. You never say anything nice to any of the children - all you ever do is criticize them. You don't seem to derive any pleasure from them now. A lot of the problems would disappear if we moved, at least there would be family meals again and you would be home a lot more and then you wouldn't be as tired either. And whether we move or not you could at least try to be more understanding with Maxwell, you could be nice to him, take an interest in what he is interested in. Be friends with him instead of always finding fault with him. Telling him he is a lazy lout for example, does nothing for him. He isn't lazy and he is not a lout! He is our son and he is very clever - don't you love

him at all? And while we are on the subject of love, you never
ever tell me you love me, you never say anything nice to me
anymore. You seldom touch me now, not even a hug now and
then, I don't understand you Lawrence. Don't you love any of us
at all? It's horrible to live in a house where there is so little love.
It isn't good for us, any of us! What is life all about, Lawrence, if
there isn't love in it. Love is the most important ingredient in
family life - that's what I think, there was lots of love in my family
always. Why don't you love us anymore Lawrence? And to think
of your name being Lawrence Love, it really is a bit of a joke, it
really is."

Of course by this time my voice had risen substantially.

There was no response.

To my surprise he got up from his chair and walked over to
the window; he moved the curtain a little more to the side, then
he said, "Look Emily, there's Jupiter! Look how bright it is." he
said! "Come and look!"

He was behaving as if he had not heard me at all, I was
infuriated.

"I don't want to look at Jupiter!" I shouted, "I want to talk about
our problems. I want to solve them! I think we need counselling
– I do! Don't you understand that this is serious! This is what
makes marriages break up you know! This is what makes wives
leave husbands! Don't look at Jupiter, Lawrence - look at me!
I am so unhappy, please look at me! You never do what I want,
and you never let me do what I want - you never have! You
wouldn't even let me have that job I really wanted. You know
what you are, Lawrence? You're a very controlling man. You
won't even listen to me now! You just carry on doing what you
like, never thinking of how I feel or what would please me, never!"

"Now Emily - don't be ridiculous, you do exaggerate things
and dramatize everything. You always have."

"I don't and I have not."

"Well I say that you do. This is a family unit and family units
do not break up. The business about the job is simply of no
importance. That was settled some time ago. It is very immature
of you to expect to be told all the time that I love you, very
immature. We have been married eighteen years you know. You
should grow up! Be sensible - there are many more important
issues in family life than that! These issues you talk about and
make such a fuss about are simply not important. As always you
make an issue out of nothing. Maxwell is just going through a

JERSEY AGAIN

Life on the island with Paul was very different and difficult to adjust to. Paul wanted me with him all the time. He liked to go riding in the mornings and expected me to ride with him. I was not certain if I should ride at all, but I did not wish to disappoint him. He was accustomed to having lunch with friends quite regularly and before-dinner drinks as well and he expected me to accompany him. I thought that the novelty of my presence would cool off, that I would soon be able to get back to being more of a mother. It was lovely to meet up again with Françoise and Pierre but the only time I could see my old friend Françoise was when Paul and I went visiting together. It would be so nice to have lunch with Françoise, just the two of us from time to time, but Paul was not keen for me to do this. He liked me to be with him for lunch every day. Although Françoise had changed quite a lot, she had lost a lot of her bounce, she was a good friend, a nice woman and the friendship was important to me.

I found it strange to be with another man, to adjust to his ways. I missed Lawrence; I was accustomed to him and remembered how it had been with him at times, the good times. I was surprised he had not contacted me - nothing from him at all. I wished he had made some contact, even angry contact, but nothing; it seemed to me unnatural, cold. I hadn't ever really imagined he would race across the Channel to get us back but I wished he had made *some* effort to get us back. Maybe we could have worked something out if he had at least tried. But to do nothing at all, just let us go. Well, I thought, with a rather sad, empty feeling, I must make the most of what I have now.

There were some good things that had happened: Maxwell was more relaxed and was happier altogether and the new school seemed to suit all three. They liked living on this lovely island with the brilliant sunshine and the sea right there all the time, near. David and Joey liked the fact that they no longer had to share a bedroom. Paul had a lovely friendly dog, a black Labrador and they took him to the beach when they went cockling or shrimping in the rocks. The children hadn't mentioned former activities that they had missed, but I was sure that there were some. Still, they had their guinea pigs and hamsters which they were not allowed to have before, and of course Paul's dog, so I hoped that these helped to compensate for some aspects of their lives that they missed: like their friends in the village and the fields where they used to play and their huge garden. And of course Fluff, that we had left with friends - that was very difficult. Strange, how I hadn't thought of all those things, I had only thought of the nice changes. Well, what is done is done and I must stop thinking sad thoughts.

Christmas was coming. There had been a letter from Lawrence: the first. There was no salutation, just a line saying he wanted the children after Christmas for a few days, they would visit their aunts and uncles too. He gave the date he found suitable and that was the extent of the letter.

I thought it would be best for them to fly - I didn't like the idea of them on that long boat trip alone. They were not enthusiastic to go, they had things they wanted to do with their new friends at Christmastime. I got their clothes ready and was wishing all the time that they were not going. I had never been away from them at Christmastime, my heart ached as I prepared their cases. I tried to console myself with the thought that I was to have them with me for Christmas Day, so I had to admit that it was only fair that they spent some time with their father over the holiday period.

After the children had left, the relationship was better with Paul as I was not so torn all the time - I was not feeling annoyed and sad about not spending time with the children. He was certainly good fun and always wanting to do things. We went out somewhere special for dinner nearly every evening. Sometimes we played chess into the early hours. We visited his friends; it was pleasant, but I missed the children very much. It was not the life-style I had imagined or one that I wanted on a permanent basis.

When they returned, I sensed that Paul was not that pleased. He was nice enough but it meant he had to share me again, I knew that he would rather not. The children brought home a tape and played it for me one evening shortly after their return. It was a sort of jumble of talking, at the dinner table at their aunt and uncle's house, I could hear Simone and there were other voices laughing - and then I heard Lawrence's voice, I could hear him quite distinctly laughing and chatting in the background. I still loved the sound of his voice, I missed him, memories flooded my mind of the first Christmas in our new wonderful house and then the memory of that other Christmas in our first little house, the absolute magic of that Christmas, our first Christmas tree and the children so little; I had been so happy and so thrilled to be pregnant again. My head started to pound. I felt hot and clammy, like I was going to be sick. I excused myself and quickly went to the bathroom. I vomited violently, taking it seemed, all of my insides with it. I pulled my facecloth from the rail, wet it, held it to my face and sobbed deep, wrenching sobs into it. I looked up and into the mirror, yes here I was, what's done is done, I'll just have to get on with it, that's all. I rubbed my face all over with the cloth, dabbed and pressed the cold cloth on my eyes, brushed my hair and returned.

"What's the matter, Mum, you look funny, all white?" it was David, then Maxwell and Joey joined in "yes," they said, "you do Mum."

"Yes," Paul said, "you do, Emily, did the tape upset you?"

"No, no - I'm fine!"

"Well, he probably did it like that so that it would upset you. I'm sure his voice in the background was no accident!"

"Perhaps you are right. Anyway, I'm not upset."

As the time went on, I felt more and more tense. This feeling of being torn all the time, I felt guilty both ways and was beginning to think that I would not be able to live the rest of my life in this manner. Motherhood was so important to me. My children had to come first, after all, the main reason I left Lawrence was to give the children a happier time, they needed my attention and they weren't getting it.

It simply was not working out, not the way I had hoped. If the children had been our children, I was certain we would have had a pleasant life together. But coming together so late, with our lives having been so different for so long and of course the fact that Paul was at home all the time too, having retired so early. On top of that I was losing the closeness I had always had with my children. To be this man's constant companion was becoming too much for me.

I missed Martha, our outings together, with laughter so much a part of our relationship. I didn't go to church either or sew. My life was torn apart and I found it quite boring after a few months. It was certainly ironical, I thought, to have been so longing for companionship with my husband and now to find that I had too much of it with Paul! I would have to talk to the children, maybe I would just have to leave and accept all the complications and upset. Accept the fact that it hadn't worked out.

Paul was due for another rather long set of treatment. I would have to wait until he was back to tell him my plans. It was a pity, as it would be nice to get it over with. I had thought I would talk to him first and then the children.

At the airport he was loving and tender. I knew how he dreaded all this, but his thoughts were for me, would I be alright.

"Take the boys and have some meals out!" he told me. "Buy yourself a new dress! I'll be back before you know it!"

"I know, I know," I said, "I'll be fine. I do hope it goes well for you. Good luck, darling!"

At the house I felt the tension go and a feeling of freedom return. The boys were more relaxed too! It was fun to be with them, not always worrying about Paul's feelings. We talked for ages, just like we used to do. I was not tired, I was not up half the night playing chess. I definitely felt brighter, lighter and yes, really free again. I talked to the boys about leaving. I explained why I didn't think I could live with Paul for the rest of my life. "Would you mind?" I asked. I knew it would be upsetting to change schools and everything else.

Maxwell said that, no, he wouldn't mind and he would be happy to see his other friends again - and his new friends could come and visit us in England. "I'll miss the sunshine though! Where do you think we would live Mum, near where we were? We could all go back to our old school then, couldn't we? Actually I quite like this school except that it's an all-boys' school."

David and Joey didn't mind the idea at all but they agreed that they would miss the sunshine and living so close to the sea.

"Could we buy a dog - or could we get Fluff back do you think?" Joey asked. "What about a kitten? I would love a kitten! Would we have a big garden again and have some white rabbits in a cage? Could we take the guinea pigs?"

I told them that of course we could buy a dog and that, no, Fluff had been adopted into a lovely family, so we certainly could not have her back, but, as soon as we found a house to live in we would go shopping for a puppy. "I would have to go out to work each day." I told them, "You would have to get used to me not being at home quite as much. I think it will be fine, don't you?"

They agreed, "Oh yes we will. Will you be alright on your own, Mum?"

I told them that I was looking forward to it really.

"Don't you like Paul?" David asked.

"Yes, I do, very much, but it is a difficult relationship because it is so different for both of us. I do miss the times I used to spend with you and it is an important time in your lives and I should be more available to you. The decision is not to do with my feelings for Paul. He is a nice man and I shall always be fond of him. He certainly has been nice to you, hasn't he? However, I think I would be better sailing our little ship alone."

"When would we go?" Maxwell asked, "Soon?"

I said I was not sure about that yet, but now that the decision was made I could make enquiries and plans. They wondered what Paul would think. I told them that I knew he would be sorry, but he was a reasonable man and would never want to keep me here if I wanted to leave. He definitely won't want me to leave, but hopefully he will understand. It would be harder for him to let go of the relationship than for me. I dreaded telling him. All the same, it had to be done.

When I saw him at the airport I had that thrill I had always had with this man. It would be hard to leave him, but I knew I had to. He had a lovely way with him, there was a sweetness about him. Never arrogant or showy, pleasant to everyone. I rushed up to him. He put down his case and hugged me tightly. "My, how I have missed you!" he said.

I looked up at him - his eyes were sunken in dark hollows, his face was thin and pale. I did not remark on it, but it frightened me. He was ill; I knew this without being told. However, he said nothing about it.

"How did it go?" I asked.

"Not too well pet, not too well, but right now let us not talk about it. Let's go and have a drink somewhere. How are the boys? Are they at home?"

"Yes," I said, "they will be home by now and they are fine. Yes, of course."

He said, "You, Emily, how are you?"

"I'm fine - as always!" I laughed, "As always!"

"You look very well, Emily, lovely. I'm glad you put on that bit of flesh, you were far too thin. I knew that the wonderful milk and cream of this island would soon fix that. Yes, it suits you. I never did like scrawny women!"

"I wasn't scrawny - Paul, you are exaggerating!"

"True, true, not scrawny, but it wasn't far down the road!"

At home we had a drink while I prepared dinner. I thought it might be nice for the boys to eat first and Paul and I could have our meal alone for a change. He might like that, break him in gently to being back with a house full.

After dinner he poured me a brandy. "Come and sit with me, Emily - come and sit beside me. I want to talk to you and I need you near me."

My God, I thought, what is it? Please God, don't let it be too terrible. I sat down beside him he took my hand in his.

"It's back, only in a different place. But it's back."

"Oh my God! Oh No! What about treatment?"

"No, Emily."

"What is going to happen?"

"Emily, I am going to die fairly soon."

"Die? Die! No, You can't! You responded before, to treatment? How can it be?"

As I put my arms around him. He drew me to him and then I felt his body shake with sobs. "I didn't expect it so soon, you see," he said as he let me go and blotted his eyes. "I don't think they did either, Emily and it has spread madly. There is nothing to be done, nothing."

"Oh, Paul, this is terrible, oh I am so sorry - so terribly sorry."

"You know, Emily, I can't believe it."

I moved on to the chair opposite him, how long has he looked like this I asked myself as I looked at his sad face where the illness had now etched itself heavily. This must have been happening before my eyes, but seeing him daily, I guess I wouldn't notice the changes. How terrible to think he is dying.

"Emily, I want you to leave before this happens. It is the best thing for all of us. I will have to go into hospital before very long. I don't really want you to see all this - I would rather we parted with me still a reasonable human being. We have had a little bonus in our lives, an unexpected bonus. I know that at times it has been difficult for you. And I know I have been selfish. But all in all it has been a wonderful time. A delight. It is important to me that we part when things are still pleasant. You do understand my pet, don't you? That it is the best way."

"Of course I understand," I told him "if this is what you want.

As long as you are sure you don't want me with you for this last ordeal?"

He laughed, "I have never been more sure of anything in my life. I should hate you to see me in the state I will be in. I will be able to manage it better, much better, on my own. It would be senseless for you to stay on here. You should go back to England and get yourself organized. It is a pity I can't leave you the house, but no point in talking about that, is there? The laws here are very different from anywhere else as you know. I did open a little account for you when we arrived, so you can use that to get started on."

"But Paul, I don't want the money - I don't need it! You know I have my own money and plenty to buy a house. After that I shall find a job. You should use your money Paul, to have the best care you can get. You may need a private nurse."

"Well, Emily, I might, but hopefully I won't last too long. All the same, I want to give you a little start, so take it - do, to please me."

I was so very thankful I had not mentioned my plan of leaving before he went for treatment. Quietly I told the boys. They were saddened with the news.

I phoned Martha and told her what had happened. She immediately invited us and our furniture to stay with them until we got sorted out. "We can put your furniture in our garage, Emily. It will be fine there for a short time, so don't worry about anything."

I felt greatly relieved when she said this and was thankful to have such a kind and helpful friend. I wondered how I would feel being back. I would certainly see Lawrence from time to time; what would that be like, and the house too?

When the time came to leave, it was worse than I ever imagined it would be. Knowing that Paul was dying and I was leaving him to die alone was almost more than I could bear. He was wonderfully cheerful, keeping a bright face on it all, but he did look terribly ill. He shook the boys' hands and gave them a big smile "You are fine chaps" he told them, "and don't let anyone tell you differently! I have enjoyed knowing you. Good luck!"

While the boys were busy getting the cases and animals to the front door, he turned and put his arm around me. "Bloody awful business this. All the same, I think we are doing it the right way. Now you look after yourself - and as soon as you are settled with a telephone, ring me."

I ran down the steps. My vision blurred, I fumbled with my handkerchief and stumbled. I could hear him behind me, "Emily! Emily!"

I ran back into his arms.

He whispered into my hair, "Darling don't cry. I love you - you have always been my love - always."

"Yes I know, I do know that."

"Think of the nice times we have had, then and now. We have been lucky - think of that and don't cry darling, please! Now you must go."

And they are gone! Gone! He watched the taxi and stood staring out to sea long after it had disappeared. Upstairs he made a pot of tea. In the silent empty room he sipped his tea and prayed it would not take long for him to die. He put the cup down; no, he didn't want tea, there was nothing he wanted now, nothing. He would go to bed - surely sleep would come easily, he was so tired. The telephone rang, "Has she gone?" It was Françoise.

"Yes, my dear Françoise, she has gone."

"You get right over here now!" she told him.

He laughed. "My dear, not this day, I shall come tomorrow, I am done in, absolutely done in."

"Come tomorrow then! We will be expecting you."

"Thank you, my dear Françoise, how very kind."

He put the phone down. Yes, he is done in, God, he does hope this doesn't take long, this ending of his life.

He could still smell that perfume of hers. What was it? "Je Reviens" that was it. Well, this time she wouldn't be coming back, no not ever, not to him. Hopefully that scent will never leave his house, as long as he lives in it. He shut his eyes. It is so good that she has been here; think, old chap, if we had never had this little interlude in our lives, just think of that! In this way he found some comfort. He drifted in and out of sleep. He had no will to live, none.

CAMBRIDGESHIRE

Finally we were on the boat, all was accounted for, twenty-eight pieces of luggage, which included two guinea pigs and two hamsters. It would be a long trip and at the other end I would have to pick up my car in Weymouth and drive all the way to Cambridgeshire. A long drive. The children have been so helpful, lucky I am, that I have such nice children. I must keep cheerful for them and, for me, I'll think about the sadness when I am alone, tomorrow!

I decided to look only at newish houses. Not beautiful houses - practical houses. Not far from the school, with reasonable access to the town for jobs. Of course it must have a garden. I knew I mustn't take long to choose as it was quite a houseful to land on my friends! They, of course, had been helpful and kind, it had made the move so much easier for me.

It didn't take long to find what I was looking for, a house within walking distance to the school, not far from the town, not a beautiful house but quite adequate. It wasn't long before we were into a routine, quite settled. Now I had to find employment! It was a very long time since I had been in the work world and I had not been in it very long at that!

A dentist's surgery just outside of the town was advertising in the newspaper for a receptionist. I went for an interview. The chap was friendly and cheerful and said that certainly I could have the job if I could do some simple bookkeeping and the appointment book. He also needed me to be with him when he did extractions if the nurse was not available. "I don't like any mistakes with appointments Emily, so be very careful won't you. I would rather have a mistake with the bookkeeping!" He stood up and we shook hands, "Call me Gordon - we aren't terribly formal here".

The hours were reasonable, starting at 9:00 and finishing at 5:00, an hour for lunch. The surgery was open Saturday mornings, so I would have to work until 1:00 on Saturdays. The travelling wouldn't be too bothersome, as I would miss the city traffic. The parking might prove difficult, but I was sure I could sort that out. The pay was not marvellous, but then what could

I expect - I had no experience, I was really lucky to get the job at all!

Working for Gordon was quite demanding as I had a lot to learn and it was a busy practice. My mind was fully occupied and at the end of the day I was pleased and content to relax and read my book from the library. I thought the job would suit me quite well, although I didn't like the thought of working on Saturdays, but it was only for the mornings, so that was good.

Saturday morning, the children came running down the drive to see me off, I told them that after work I would buy the kitchen floor mop and the fruit that we needed and come home afterwards. "You have your lunch without me," I told them, "I will have mine when I get in."

They said they would and waved as I left.

It was a hectic Saturday morning, with two emergencies and a full appointment book. At twelve-thirty I looked out of the window and there, on the step, were my children! One had the kitchen mop in his hands, taller than he was - the others were carrying bags of groceries. I opened the door, but before I had a chance to say anything, they explained that they decided to do the shopping for me. Now they said, "we can all go home together and have lunch together and you won't have to do any shopping!"

"But that is wonderful! Heaven! Why don't you come into the waiting room while I finish off."

"Will the dentist mind?"

"No, not at all, I am sure."

In they came and sat all in a row, smiling, so pleased with themselves! I felt very proud of my boys, they were so thoughtful and kind. Once again I thought how lucky I was. With my coat on I went into my office to pick up my thermos flask. When I looked up I saw that there was a chap waiting at the counter. "The dentist has finished now", I told him, hoping that this was not to be another emergency and I would be delayed.

"Yes, I know, I'm not a patient, just a friend - would like to have a word with him if he has a minute, could you tell him? Just tell him it's John." He gave me a big smile and his bright blue eyes twinkled at me. He was not a tall man, rather heavy, with wide shoulders, his hair was thick and very dark. His eyebrows were like two black furry caterpillars on his forehead, he was a rather unusual-looking man.

I smiled back; "Yes, I'll call him."

As soon as Gordon came, we left. It was a nice feeling to be going home with a whole day and a half in front of me free!

Joey was pestering me for the puppy I had promised - and a kitten, he added. I said I would buy a paper and see if there were any puppies advertised.

"Not a kitten yet Joey - a puppy will be enough for now. If we see something in the paper we could go tomorrow to look, how would that be! What kind do you want?"

They weren't really sure. Maxwell was not terribly interested anyway. His mind was on music and art. What *he* would like is a girlfriend!

When we got into the house, the phone was ringing. It was a long distance call from Paul. "Emily!"

"Yes, yes I'm here. Are you alright Paul?"

"Yes my pet, I am. I was thinking about you and wondering how you were getting on; guess I was feeling a bit lonely!"

I thought he sounded worse than a bit lonely! "Are you at home?"

"No, no! Actually I am in hospital - came in last night. I'm fine though. Not to worry. How are the boys and the job?" I told him everything was fine.

"Splendid! It is so nice to hear your voice, Emily. Lovely to talk to you. Must go now, take care of yourself, my pet."

I put the phone down and phoned the hospital and spoke to the nursing sister on Paul's ward. I explained who I was and why I was calling. "Paul phoned me and he sounded so awful I just had to know what the situation was." The nursing sister told me that Paul may not last more than a week.

"Thank you for telling me sister, please don't tell him that I called, I am going to come over and please don't tell him that either."

"I won't say a word and it is good that you are coming Mrs Love." Her voice was warm.

I told the boys that the puppy would have to wait until next week "You'll have to look after yourselves for two days and we won't want to be dealing with a new puppy." I phoned Gordon to tell him my plans, he was not happy about it. "Why don't you leave Tuesday? Wednesday is not busy, come back Thursday? The sooner you are back the better; my assistant does not like having to work at the desk."

I assured him that I would not be away more than three days - three days at the most as I wouldn't like to leave the boys any longer than that. He seemed a little happier. I thought that if I wasn't going until Tuesday and there was a puppy advertised in the paper we could go and look on Sunday and a new puppy might be a good thing for the children if I were away for a couple of days.

That evening I read out all the pet ads. "How about a cocker spaniel? You know, the small dogs with the long, floppy ears!"

Joey ran to get his book on dogs. "This is the one!" He showed David. "That's it!"

Oh yes, we all agreed that would be a lovely choice. I telephoned and was given the directions to a farm about 25 miles away. I packed a picnic lunch. "We might as well take a picnic and make a day of it!" I told the children, who were already excited about the puppy and now the idea of a picnic took them over the top with excitement.

Sunday was a lovely blue day, a perfect picnic day. We found a quiet road in the country with a very grassy verge so we unpacked our picnic and enjoyed the outdoor lunch; the children were too excited to prolong the stop, so we packed up and got on our way. The farm was not difficult to find and when we got there the farmer's wife was all ready for us with the puppies out in the pen. After playing with them for quite a while we had to choose and it was not easy as they were all so playful and adorable with their long floppy ears. Eventually we all agreed on one of them. We were pretty excited, I knew we would enjoy having a dog again. On the way home we bought a basket, a water bowl and puppy food. I found an old woollen blanket for the basket. We all fussed around her and then took her into the garden to play.

"What shall we call her Mum?"

"You think of some names. Make a list and then we can choose which one we think suits her the best!"

I told them I would be leaving on Tuesday and that they would have to come home at lunchtime to see to the puppy and to come straight home after school as well, I didn't think that would be a problem!

I arrived on the island rather late, after another bumpy flight. I telephoned the hospital and told the nursing sister I had arrived. "Would it be best if I came in tomorrow or what?" I asked.

She replied with a quiet voice saying that Paul was very tired and tomorrow after lunch would be the best time. I put the phone down. I must phone Françoise and Pierre but I was afraid of all the emotion - still, I had to do it now.

"Thank Goodness you are here!" Françoise's excited voice exclaimed. "We went to see Paul today and we don't think he will last much longer. We sort of thought you would come, Emily, even though he said he didn't want you to see him in such a state."

"I'm going in after lunch, Françoise. The nursing sister advised me that that would be the best time."

"Have dinner with us, Emily. Why don't you stay here with us?"

"I booked in at 'The Ship', Françoise, so I think I will leave it like that - thank you all the same but it would be nice to have dinner with you. Françoise, thank you, that would be lovely."

Paul didn't see me as I came into the room, he was dozing and, I guessed, full of morphine. I pulled up a chair and took his hand in mine.

He turned his head "Emily? Is it you Emily?"

I very quietly told him that "Yes" it was.

"Emily dear, you are not supposed to be here."

"No, perhaps not, but I am. Is there anything I can do for you?"

"Water would be nice!"

I helped him with the glass.

"It is you, isn't it, I'm not hallucinating am I?" He laughed a little. "How very sweet of you to come, pet. But you shouldn't have."

"Would you like me to read to you, Paul?"

"No darling, I would not. Just to know you are here, just to feel you here. When I open my eyes and to see you here, Emily, then to touch your hand. I could not wish for anything more than that. I sleep a lot you know. Blessed sleep!"

The next day he looked even worse and at first did not know me. The nursing sister came in and beckoned me into the hall. "He is much worse to-day. You should perhaps stay the day if you can?"

I told her that, yes, I would stay the whole day.

Sitting beside him, I cupped my hand on his face, it felt very cool. I talked to him, I could tell he knew I was there. His voice, a whisper - "Thank you, my Emily. Thank you."

I got up and lay on the bed beside him. I put my head on his chest and my arm over his thin body and held his hand.

After a time his breathing became shallow. I lay still beside him, then I lifted my head and looked into his eyes. I thought that he could not see me. "I love you." I *whispered.* I felt a tiny squeeze of my hand, just tiny. Then *suddenly I noticed* that his breathing had actually stopped.

Now it was all over, finished, the pain had left his face, the silence of his death filled the room. I got off the bed and stood looking down at his peaceful face with the finality of his death seeping into me. The door opened and then shut, I looked up to see the nursing sister bustling over with a little tray of tea. She looked over at Paul, "Oh dear, he has gone. I am sorry, my dear." She gently shut Paul's eyes. "Here, I have brought you a cup of tea, it will do you good. Yes, he was such a charming man; a pity, a great pity. He never ever grumbled, you know."

She passed me a tissue. "There dear, when you are ready, I'll call a taxi for you."

I nodded and thanked her.

At the hotel, I phoned Françoise, "Yes Emily, the hospital rang us. Are you alright?"

"Yes I'm fine, but I am going to go straight home now - there is no point in me being here. I'm sorry I won't be at the funeral, but you do understand, don't you Françoise. I don't want to lose my new job!"

"Of course, and good luck with the job Emily!"

"Thank you, I'll write to you, thank you for such a pleasant evening! Goodbye."

Then I left my little enchanted Island and I left behind forever, my young love. It was strange, how both of us had never ever really forgotten each other. How we had both carried this unfinished love with us for so many years. Maybe because we were so young, maybe because the love had not been allowed to grow and develop, maybe that was the reason. Such a waste really. I really didn't have any regrets about what I had done. I felt almost glad that I had spent that time with him, even though it had not worked out as we had hoped. We did have some very pleasant times together - and Paul was happy - and it was good to know that.

It was wonderful to be home - even my ordinary house looked pretty nice to me as I drove up. I could hear the children running to open the door as I rang the bell. I was barely in the door when the puppy ran and jumped up at me. The boys were full of chatter about the puppy, the house overflowed with life and activity, it was definitely a happy house now.

When things had calmed down I told them that Paul had died.

"That's too bad, Mum!" they said and gave me sympathetic looks.

"Yes. It was too bad and very sad but it was not unexpected of course. By the way, what did you decide to call the puppy? Did you make that list?"

"Yes, we did, Mum, but David thought of a name that wasn't on our list! You won't guess, I know!"

"Tell me then, I do hope I like it!"

"Flopsy! Because of her long flopsy ears! Do you like it?"

"Yes I do, I think it really suits her with her flopsy ears and flopsy big paws. She is sort of flopsy altogether isn't she!"

They laughed, "Yes she is, she loves to flop on our beds too!"

At the weekend, we bought plants for the garden, some fruit trees and a maple tree for the side of the house. I would have to do some decorating and curtain alterations as well. The house certainly was not gorgeous, but bright and, because it was the end house on the street and backed on to the school grounds, it was fairly private. I liked the French doors that went into the long, quite narrow garden. It would look quite pretty when my planting plans took shape.

My job was reasonable enough, not horrible anyway - and Gordon was very pleasant. I was able to see Martha regularly, as the village was only five miles away, but there would be no puppet shows now.

The children were not crazy about the school, they mentioned that there were some quite rough children there. This was something new, I had not heard anything about a rough element when they attended the school previously. I had never been really pleased about the school, it certainly was not what I would have wished for my children; however, I watched over the homework and hoped that they would do well. Although my life was not exciting it was satisfying, sailing my own little ship with no family conflict was pleasantly peaceful.

More and more frequently the children talked about some of the unpleasant students at the school. David especially seemed to be having problems. "One had a bicycle chain in his pocket and threatened to hit me with it" he told me.

"Did you report it?" I asked, I was absolutely horrified.

"No, Mum - if I did that, I would be beaten up!"

"Is it really that bad?" It sounded terrible.

"Yes it is that bad and I get scared, I don't like it there at all now. I hate that school, Mum."

"Who is it?"

David wouldn't tell me, he was not a big, strong-looking boy, not tall and rather a lightweight. With his very fair hair and fair skin, he tended to look delicate; a bully would find him easy meat I guessed. I asked Nigel, who was David's best friend, about it. He was also reluctant to say much, but he was bigger and stronger than David, so he might have an easier time of it. I asked Maxwell what he thought, should I report the situation? Did he think that would make it harder than ever for David? He said that he thought that the best plan was for David to avoid them completely. "I'll talk to David, but he must stay away from them - that's what I do. If you report anything, someone will find out and that could be dangerous Mum. I'll talk to David - and Joey."

We began to notice things in the local paper about gangs from London coming, who were violent and caused all sorts of trouble. We were wondering if it was such a good place to live after all.

Every evening between 10:30 and 11:00 I took Flopsy for her walk. She was not good on the lead, straining and pulling this way and that way. One evening when I was pulling reluctant Flopsy along, I heard a car pull up beside me. I kept walking, only faster.

"Emily?"

I stopped and turned around, wondering who on earth it could be, when I recognized the car, it was Lawrence!

"Yes?" I walked to the car "Yes?"

"I've brought you a brace of pheasants."

"Really! How lovely, would you like me to cook one for you and drop it over?"

"No, no! You have them."

He handed them out and drove off! That was strange, he must have been around before - how else would he know what time I take my evening walk. This was the first real contact I had had with him. Not that it was really contact - he certainly wasn't friendly, driving off without a word. It would be so much nicer if we could at least communicate about the children, if we could be friends. It gave me a strange, sad feeling seeing him like that, driving off without a friendly word, painful really.

"Emily?"

"Yes?" I did not recognize the voice on the telephone.

"John here."

"John?"

"Yes - Gordon's friend. Remember I introduced myself when you were first working for him?"

"Yes, of course I remember you!"

He laughed, "Good! I remember you too! The reason I'm ringing you is that Gordon mentioned to me that you have great difficulty parking on Saturday mornings."

"Well, yes, I do, but I don't mind walking a distance - in fact I enjoy it really."

"You do? I was going to offer you to park in my grounds. I have plenty of space and your vehicle would be most welcome! My surgery is just around the corner."

"Another dentist?"

"No, actually I'm a GP. Well, if you are ever in need of a place to park, just come along."

"That is kind of you - thank you so much! Maybe I will someday if I'm really stuck!"

"You do that! There is one other reason I am ringing."

"Yes?"

"I would like to take you out to dinner one evening."

"You would? How lovely!"

"You'll come then?"

"Yes - I would love to!"

"Tell me which evening you would like?"

I laughed, "You know which night is 'the loneliest night of the week' don't you?"

"I certainly do, Emily! I shall pick you up Saturday evening at seven!"

I thanked him and hung up. What a nice surprise, it will be so nice to go out, I wonder what he is like. I must ask Gordon about him. I wonder what I will wear!

When I had a chance I asked Gordon about John.

"He has invited me to have dinner with him. I am assuming he is free?"

"Yes, yes - he is free, in a way he is free, that is."

"What does that mean?"

"Well, he is divorced. But he has had a woman friend for some time, but it has been very on and off. She spends a lot of time in Italy where she came from and where she has family still. She is the complete opposite to John. Very excitable! They fight a lot you know, not good. The trouble with John is, he's too kind, would hate to hurt her; be better to hurt her I say, then they can both get on with their lives in peace. Anyway, John is a very nice chap, but who knows what will happen. I certainly don't. Garda is a very jealous lady as well as being highly strung! Quite a combination when steam is to be let off. She's in Italy at the moment, so you needn't worry your head about it. He never knows whether or not she will come back - sometimes she's there most of the year!"

That was quite an interesting conversation, I learnt a fair bit about the chap.

I chose my long, purple, knitted dress with a high neck and matching coat for the evening. It was my most stunning dinner outfit. I would wear my great-aunt Nellie's antique cameo at the neck.

I arranged a bowl of roses in my silver rose bowl on the table under the gilt antique mirror, their scent and rich colours drenched the plain little entrance with welcoming warmth. When the door-bell rang, I took a look at myself and the roses in the mirror as I opened the door; I was pleased with the effect. "Come in John, come on in, would you like a drink before we go?"

However, he didn't even step over the threshold. "No, we'll have one there, we're already a bit late, thank you, maybe a night-cap?"

The restaurant was a large, old, country house and the dining-room was a formal, candle-lit room with polished, wooden floors.   The woodwork and tables were highly-polished mahogany. The atmosphere was rich, rather grand.

Settled with my gin and tonic, I took a good look at my escort. A friendly man. Nice eyes. Very smiley face. So dark with that heavy hair and those eyebrows. All I could think about when I looked at them was that he had caterpillars on his forehead! I smiled to myself at the thought.

"This is nice Emily, a pleasant surprise. Gordon didn't think you would come out with me. So I was ready for rejection!" He laughed.

"Oh, why did he think that I wonder - are you very bad?"

"Perhaps! Anyway he said you were always so busy with your children. That you had been decorating your house, digging holes for trees and I don't know what all, a very busy lady!"

"I am never too busy to go out for dinner - I can tell you that right now! Never!"

"How about next Saturday then?"

"Wonderful! Here?"

"No, I don't think so - there are so many places to choose from, maybe London would be a good choice. Do you like Indian food?"

"Yes I do - as long is isn't too hot! I had some once and nearly choked to death, rather embarrassing it was."

He did not come in for a nightcap. "A bit late, my dear, next time I'll come a bit early and have a drink with you. I would like to meet these boys of yours. I shall ring you during the week and set a time. Don't forget, your vehicle will be most welcome in my garden!"

He gave me a little peck on the cheek and ran off.

I decided on the following Saturday to park at his place, as I was curious to see where he lived. When I drove through the gateway I saw that his surgery was in his house! So he lives here too, what a beautiful spot. John saw me and waved as he ran down the steps. "So you finally gave in!"

"I wanted to have a look! I was curious."

He laughed, "Miss Honesty!"

"It is lovely - a lovely house and a beautiful garden. I love the garden! Now I must run!"

"About five then?" he called!

I waved and ran. If there was one thing I hated and that was to be late. It rattled me and I was inclined to make mistakes if rattled. Gordon was just unlocking the door when I arrived. I told him where I had parked the car.

"Sorry if I'm a little late."

"That's alright, Emily, no one is here yet anyway. Lovely house he has, isn't it, really lovely. Georgian, you know. He is having a lot of work done on it. Inside and out."

"Yes, I could see that. The garden is lovely too and right on the river like that, it is pretty idyllic, isn't it?"

"Yes, it is. Going out with him again this evening are you?"

"Yes, I am. He mentioned that we might go to London for dinner. I had better get moving - here comes your first patient!"

The Indian restaurant was on the outskirts of London and was well known for its delicious food.

"I'll let you choose for me - but do remember, not too hot!"

It was too hot - I had to order water! He didn't find it too hot! He ate my portion and ordered something much milder for me. After dinner we went into London, parked and walked around Piccadilly watching all the vendors selling and talking up their goods. He nearly ran, he walked so fast. I had a job to keep up with him in my high heels. Everything he did, he did quickly. He talked quickly too.

He held my hand, "Take your shoes off! This is London! No one will notice here, you know!"

I kept my shoes on. I didn't fancy having dirty feet! When we finally got home to my house I invited him to come in and have a drink with me.

"I won't come in Emily, but would you like to go to Cambridge tomorrow, feed the ducks and have tea? I can meet the boys when we get back. I would like to meet them, but I don't seem to have made it yet, do I!"

"Yes, to both! Thank you, sounds a nice way to spend Sunday!"

"I'll pick you up right after lunch then."

Off he went, running! He turned around and ran back, "What is it?" I asked, "Did you forget something?"

He rushed up and put his arms around me and kissed me properly. "That is what it is!" he said. "I didn't forget - I was just a little afraid you might think it too soon. But then I thought I would risk it anyway! Thank you for another lovely evening Emily."

"I'm glad you risked it! And thank YOU for another lovely evening, John!"

After our Sunday outing John came in and I introduced him to the boys. He was easy with them and seemed comfortable chatting to them and thankfully he didn't ask them about school, like most adults.

"Seem like nice boys. Quite a job to bring up three on your own, don't you think?"

"I guess so, I'm just getting on with it the best I can. My husband made it clear that he did not want us back."

"Did he say so?"

"Yes, actually he did. I plucked up courage once and asked him. I telephoned him. I was constantly worrying about the children, bringing them up without a father. The other thing was that I had thought he would be more of a participating father if we lived near like this, but it didn't work out like that, he rarely sees them, never asks after them or anything, although he did take them on a little holiday. I thought that perhaps if we all lived together again he might find he liked having a family about after all, I was ready to give it a try for all our sakes. Anyway he was adamant. He definitely did not want us back. 'You made your bed now Emily, you can lie on it!' I guess he couldn't have made it more clear than that! He won't give me any financial help either, so far, but I expect that when the divorce comes through he will be made to give me something for their keep and then he will have to settle with me, for the house, as I bought it. Anyway, I have made up my mind to get on with it and do the best I can. The boys are good, thank goodness! The school isn't too brilliant though! And now there are gangs of rough teenagers coming up from London - they hang around the school at times. There are some rather rough boys at the school too, so this is a huge worry. We're wondering if we chose the right place to live after all, especially as now I realize that my plans of the 'father being a help', has not and is not, going to happen!"

"You aren't thinking of moving are you?"

"Not yet, but we may do just that at the end of the summer term. It would be a good time as they will all be making big changes anyway."

"Where would you go do you think?"

"Not sure - maybe Devon. It is so beautiful there, and peaceful, far from London, 'Far from the madding crowd'! We have read about areas there that sound enchanting."

"I do agree, it is lovely - I wouldn't mind living there myself! Not that I could! We should go down together and have a look around. We could go sailing, Salcombe is lovely for sailing - if you would like to, that is?"

Each time we went to Devon, I was more and more convinced that it would be a beautiful place to live. A cottage in the country somewhere. Exeter was a lovely city, it would be a nice centre for all of us.

I decided to take the children to have a look too; we drove around the countryside just getting the feel of it.

"Do you think we would move here?" Joey asked me.

"I don't really know; there is so much to think about. Selling the house, new job for me. School for you, Dental Lab for David, college for Maxwell - all in an area I am not familiar with at all. I don't know one single soul in the south of England, not one! I'll have to think about it carefully."

It was a Sunday morning when the phone rang.

"Emily?"

"Yes?"

"I guess you haven't heard yet about the accident have you?"

"No, no! What is it, Martha?"

"David's friend has been killed!"

"Killed? Nigel? Oh no! No! How simply awful. What on earth happened?"

"Well, a gang from London went to a party where Nigel was; by the way, where was David?"

"With me. We went to Devon for the day and were late getting home - anyway, what happened?"

"Well," she said, "this gang came and started a fight. Nigel tried to stick up for one of his friends and a boy from the gang kicked him down and kicked him and kicked him until he was dead!"

"Oh my God! How terrible! How will I ever tell poor David! They were such great buddies. I'd better go and tell him straight away. I should hate anyone else to tell him."

I put the phone down. That settled it, at the end of the summer term, we leave! It could have been David!

Telling David broke my heart. He sat looking at me. "He's dead, Mum?"

"Yes, dear, he is dead. It is very tragic."

"But, he was my best friend!"

"I know dear, I know. I am so sorry. It is just too terrible."

I put my arms around him and felt his sobs, big, heavy sobs. I took him over to his bed. "I'll bring you a cup of tea, you lie down if you like."

When I brought the tea, I sat and had a cup with him. "His poor mother and father, it will be terrible for them." I said. "Oh, thank God you were not there, David, thank God! I think we will plan to leave, dear, at the end of the summer term, how would you feel about that?"

"I'd like it, Mum. I'd be glad to leave here - I think all three of us would."

"Well then, we can talk about it tonight at dinner. I'll go now, dear. Do you want to be alone, or is it alright if Joey comes up?"

"It's fine, Mum. Have you told him?"

"No, not yet."

"He will be upset too, you know, Mum. He really liked Nigel a lot. I can't believe he's dead Mum, I just can't."

"I know dear, it's such a terrible, terrible thing to happen. I'll tell Joey as soon as he comes in."

At dinner, I told them that I was seriously thinking of selling the house and moving to Devon.

"Have you thought any more about it since we talked about it before? Are there things here that you think you would miss too much? Friends? What do you really think?"

They were keen, even Maxwell! They found the idea exciting.

"What about you, Mum? Won't you miss Martha?"

"Perhaps, but we can still visit from time to time - and now that I work, I don't have much extra time anyway."

"What about your job?"

I didn't admit that this might be a problem although I still had a little money left and I was sure I could find some sort of employment. "Oh, I'm sure I can find something! So we are all agreed then? I'll put the house up for sale after Easter. If we sell, we can move as soon as school breaks up after summer term. I'll put the furniture into storage and only take some clothes and picnic gear in the car. Then rent something until we find a house to buy. We can go exploring Devon! It will be fun!"

Maxwell said that he was planning to work for the summer;

he had written to his friends on Jersey and they had told him about some farm work and if he liked he could stay with them and work on the farm too.

"Oh Maxwell, what a splendid idea! You will be able to earn money and have some fun as well! I'm sure that Mike and Ron will enjoy having you around for the summer."

At the surgery I noticed that Gordon was not his usual self. He seemed on edge and looked tired.

"Is there anything the matter? You don't seem yourself somehow, Gordon?"

"Well, actually, my girl friend and I are going through a little rough patch. Can't talk about it now, another time maybe. We were very late last evening and I am tired."

"That's too bad Gordon, I'm sorry. Any time you feel you'd like to have a chat, just give me a call."

That evening when the phone rang, I was hoping it was John, I wanted to tell him about our plans. I hadn't yet told him about David's friend either. It was John!

"How nice that you called! I was hoping that you would – I have something to tell you."

Just then the door bell rang, "Could you hold on a minute please John – there's someone at the door."

When I went down I was surprised to find Gordon there!

"Come in, come in!"

"Are you sure it's alright?"

"Yes of course. Do go in and help yourself to a drink, there on the sideboard. I'll only be a minute or two - I'm on the phone."

"Hi John, I'm back!"

"Who was it?"

"A friend of David's." I told him, surprised I told him such a lie. Except that he had asked me from time to time about Gordon in a jealous way. I thought it safer not to tell him that it was Gordon. I suppose I didn't want to have to explain.

Suddenly John said "well, I'm in a rush. I'll call you later, Emily."

"Oh, alright but you didn't tell me why you called - and I haven't told you my news yet."

"It can wait Emily, I must go now." He sounded impatient and rather cool, so I said alright again, put the phone down and went to find Gordon.

I could see that he had already had more than enough to drink. He told me that his girlfriend wanted to get married, but he would rather leave things the way they were for the present. I listened and tried to understand his difficulty, when all of a sudden there was a huge thump at the French door! In barged John! He was wild with anger!

"I knew you were lying to me!" he said. "I could tell by your voice!"

He grabbed me by the shoulders and shook me!

"Emily! Emily! How could you!"

I turned to Gordon, "Tell him for God's sake, tell him!" But Gordon had disappeared!

"John - calm down! I can explain everything! Phone Gordon, he will tell you. Why are you so upset! I haven't done anything! What is the matter?"

"Emily, don't you know, haven't you realized that I love you! And now I find you are two-timing me! Your behaviour is unspeakable!"

I was angry with him and myself, "I have done no such thing! And what is more I didn't know that you love me, you haven't mentioned it before! Oh, do leave me alone, go on, this is ridiculous, you've even upset Flopsy! (Who had been barking and running around excitedly in frantic circles!) Please go, John!"

I ran upstairs, I took Flopsy with me. In my room, I banged the door shut and bolted it. After a few minutes I heard him leave. I phoned Gordon, but he was stupidly drunk! So there was nothing I could do about it for the moment! What a horrible evening! I decided to take Flopsy and go for a nice long walk. I kept asking myself why on earth I had lied! So stupid, I never do that, I know it is stupid. But then I had really sensed that jealous streak in him. What a mess! Oh well, I shall do my best to convince him. Gordon certainly should do so when he is sober again. He must have seen Gordon's car in the drive. Gone to the side of the house, climbed the fence and jumped on to the terrace! What a nerve! The thought of him being so possessive infuriated me. He had no business doing that!

Sunday evening, the door bell rang and who should be there but John.

"Please can I come in, Emily?"

"Of course you can."

He had, clutched in his hand, a Harrod's shopping bag.

"Sit down John - are you going to let me explain now - or are you going to fight!"

"I am not going to fight, Emily, I have come to say how deeply sorry I am. I truly don't know what came over me. Why on earth did you lie?"

"I don't know, except that I felt that you were a little jealous of me working for Gordon and if you thought he was visiting me, you might get the wrong idea, which of course, you did! I guess I thought it would be easier to say what I said, that's all, simple really."

"Maybe you were right, Emily! I have been a little uneasy about you working for Gordon somehow, it is true. It is stupid of me and I am sorry. Here, I went down to London, bought you a few things you might enjoy."

I opened the bulging bag and took out the various treats: chocolates, marzipan fruit, an assortment of cheese, fancy tea, fancy coffee. "Do I deserve all this? Have I been very good?"

"Actually Emily, it's bribery, I hope you can forgive me."

"Of course I can, you didn't have to go to all that expense you know, you really didn't."

"Perhaps not, but I did enjoy buying the things for you anyway. Now then, can I take you out for dinner?"

"No - I think you should have dinner here with us. We have something to tell you. But first I must tell you what happened to David's friend."

When I told him, he was horrified. "But how terrible, Emily! That poor boy - and poor David! How sorry I am."

"Well, John, I might as well tell you now. I have decided to leave. I'm going to put the house for sale. Hopefully we will sell it before the end of summer term, then we will pack up and go."

"Really? Just like that? I somehow had thought you would stay here permanently, why, you really haven't been here very long at all. I guess I had never taken into the equation very seriously the idea that you might leave! My goodness Emily, I don't want you to, but I can't ask you to stay on my account. The situation with Garda is still not resolved, although I have a feeling it will not be long before it is. Then, as you know, the house is still in a horrible state of renovations which could take a full year to complete. I am in no position to ask you to stay, I know that."

"I think I would have to go anyway, because I have told the children the plan and they are already excited about it. It's sort of a fantasy we have talked about quite often and when I said I was serious about it, they were pretty excited. So I couldn't possibly disappoint them now. And as you say, you are not ready for me anyway, John! Even if you were, I don't think I could stay. You can come and visit us - and if and when you and Garda sort things out, I could come and visit you, so it need not be a real goodbye, do you think?"

"Yes, yes of course you are absolutely right, Emily, and, who knows, you may not like it there!"

"I will, you know!"

"Well, I hope you have considered it all carefully enough, it is, after all, a huge step to take, with you not knowing anyone at all there and you don't know the area really either, not really. I mean it's one thing to visit Devon and enjoy the beauty of it, touring around in your car as you do, but to sell here and move to everything that is different and all aspects of your life unknown to you, is a very different matter isn't it! Aren't you worried that it could be quite difficult for both you and the children. New job, new school, new everything for everybody, no friends, rather more than a little challenging I would say! Have you really thought it through?"

I listened with my ears, he was right, but my heart wouldn't listen; I knew we had to leave. The whole episode of living here had been a disappointment, Lawrence as usual had disappointed me, the school too, had been a disappointment, with the children being so rough and then the invasion of gangs of tough teens hanging about with nothing better to do than cause trouble. I enjoyed my job but I was pretty certain I could find another. We needed a little more from life than the life we had taken on here.

I was determined to go ahead with my plans.

When I put the house for sale it sold within the week! I decided to buy a new car for the first time, to have a trouble-free car would be pleasant indeed!

DEVONSHIRE

The cottage I bought was a converted stable that had served the Georgian house across from it. I arranged for a builder to come and discuss the possibility of changing the garage into a sitting room. He told me that it was certainly possible and not an expensive job to do. I went ahead with it, although financially it would have been better not to do it. The boys would be thrilled to have their own bedrooms and for that reason I felt it would be worth it.

The time had come to buy David some clothes for his new life as a dental lab apprentice in Exeter. "How about this?" I asked as I held up a Harris tweed jacket for him to look at.

"Really, Mum? Are you sure we can afford it?"

"Yes, yes - we will afford it! Try it on!"

He put it on and went to the mirror to have a look. "Feels great Mum." He checked out the pockets and turned this way and that. "Look, Mum, the buttons are leather too! Isn't that great. It's a great jacket Mum. I really like it."

"Now, grey flannels." I handed him a pair, he put them on and came back in front of the mirror.

"They're great, Mum! Are you sure though?"

"I am absolutely sure! Oh David you do look quite handsome you know." And he did.

He thanked me, his pleasure shining out of his eyes.

The next stop was to find a scooter for David to travel to and from Exeter with, as his hours turned out to be different from the college that Maxwell would be going to. He would buy himself a car when he earned enough money, but not before he was eighteen. We chose a bright red one, a thrilling purchase. We managed to get it in the car, adding that to a car full of packages. As soon as we were in the door at the cottage, David put the kettle on and Joey rushed in to hear all about our shopping expedition. Maxwell joined us and we all sat in the kitchen drinking the tea and enthusing about the beautiful countryside, how lovely the drive in to Exeter was and the city with its ancient architecture, how beautiful it all was and how interesting. We were definitely pleased with our choice of location.

In bed that night, I kept thinking about the children, our relationship, the closeness. We spent a lot of time together talking and drinking tea. I had enjoyed buying David those clothes. How handsome he looked in them; they would give him more confidence, which he needed, going out into the work world for the first time.

After all the excitement of moving and getting the boys organised I had to finally face the reality of looking for work before all of my money ran out. Where to start! Checking through the advertisements in the newspaper, there were plenty of jobs, but only one that I thought might do, with a dentist in Exeter. This would be hard to fit in because I had to drop Joey off at his school which was in the opposite direction.

Nancy (who with her husband lived in the Georgian house) came to see how we were and how we had settled. "Do come in, Nancy and have a cup of tea with me."

"Yes I'd love to." She settled in a chair and looked around. "Looks nice the way you have done it all Emily."

"Oh thank-you. Now I must get busy and find employment. There is a job going in a dental clinic, but it's in Exeter which is in the opposite direction from Joey's school, but maybe I will just have to put up with that."

"Actually I think that would be making life rather difficult you know, all that driving this way and that. I have an idea: do you have any particular skills?"

"What sort of skills? I studied dance, music, things like that."

"Well, they might be interested in you at the hospital for mentally-handicapped people. You could phone and ask for an appointment. I can give you the name of the head of the occupational therapy department. Have a chat with her, you never know - and it would be closer than driving all that way to Exeter every day. You could tell her I sent you."

"Do you know her then?"

"I don't know her well. We know each other because of me being the matron in the cottage hospital here in the village, that's all, but I could be a useful reference for you."

"Oh my, that is kind of you. That could be quite interesting."

This sounded worth a try! We went across the garden to Nancy's house for her to get the number. "It would be best if you rang her in the morning about 10 - you can use our phone."

"Oh Nancy, thank you so much, but I can use the pay phone up the street. I might just as well get used to using it as they told me it could be a whole month before mine is installed!"

The next morning I rang the hospital and asked for the head of the OT department. When she came to the phone, I told her about Nancy mentioning that there might be a place for me in her department.

"Well yes - I just might be able to use you! Come tomorrow at 12, just ask for the OT Department, Mary Moore's office, I'll be somewhere there."

Off the main road at the top of a steep, winding hill was the hospital. Nancy had told me that it had been a TB sanatorium years ago. Supposed to be healthy air up there she had said.

Walking along to the office, I saw many different types of mentally-handicapped people. It gave my heart a sad twist to see all these people with such huge problems.

I arrived at her office right on 12 and Mary was waiting and watching for me at her office door. She held out her hand and ushered me into her office. "Do call me Mary, it's all first names here you know." She explained to me that they had been looking for someone to teach music and movement and to take some of the patients in an exercise class as well as teach some of the more able ones to swim and also help with the spastic children in the water - of course this would be with a doctor in attendance. There would also be duties like taking them for walks in the countryside near the hospital. I would be expected to supervise some crafts.

"Now, tell me about yourself."

So, after a rather long interview, I was offered the job and I accepted.

That evening the boys wanted to know all about it. As I talked about my duties I became a little apprehensive about how I was going to react to being with the terribly handicapped people.

"I don't know whether I can do it. Maybe I shouldn't have accepted. Maybe I will change my mind? I just don't know." I said all this, thinking aloud really, as suddenly all sorts of doubts formed in my mind.

David looked at me.

"Well -" he said, "you did accept, so why don't you give it a try, Mum. Just try it." Maxwell agreed.

"Yes you're both right, - I'll give it a go! Let's have a cup of tea, shall we? Now I've made up my mind I can relax."

One Saturday when we were driving out of a small town, David exclaimed, "Mum, Mum! Stop if you can! I saw some marvellous old bottles in a shop! I'd love to go in and look at them!"

I pulled in and told them to go on in - I would wait in the car for them. It was not long before the boys were out. "Mum, come on in with us! There's a very nice man who owns the shop! Come on, Mum."

"Oh, Joey - I'm a little tired and it really is time we got home."

"Ah, Mum, the shop is full of interesting furniture as well as the bottles. Please, Mum!"

"Oh, alright." They knew that I could never resist looking at interesting pieces of furniture.

I followed him in.

"This is my Mum!", he said as we squeezed into the crowded shop. The chap held out his hand to shake mine, he laughed a relaxed easy laugh, "I'm Alan. How do you do. Enthusiastic boys you have, very keen on my bottle collection!"

He was a tall, slim man, rather stooped, with dark curly hair. Blue eyes.

"What would you like to look at?"

"Nothing special, really." Then an old-fashioned gramophone caught my eye. A wonderful old one. We didn't have any music machine. This would be fun!

"How much is your gramophone?"

He laughed again, "Would you want one?"

"I think I would love one!"

"You would, really? How about ten pounds? How does that sound?"

I looked inside the machine. "Not many needles?"

"I can get you some of those easily - I can have them for you in a few weeks."

"What about records, do you have any?"

"I have hundreds - and you can take your pick - I won't charge you for those."

"Well, that is kind of you, how nice. Well yes, I think I can manage the ten pounds. A bit extravagant, but I think we would have fun with it."

The boys thought so too.

"Do you think we could get it into the car?"

Alan said he would come out and have a look.

"Easily!" he said.

He told me that if I gave him our address, he would deliver the needles when he got them.

"Well, that would be kind of you. Thank you."

The gramophone was a great success! We had fun playing all the old records. Even Maxwell thought it quite an amusing thing to have.

Saturday morning, we were just finishing breakfast when there was a knock on the door. Standing there when I opened the door was a tall, smiling man.

"Did I, or did I not, hear music coming from an old-fashioned gramophone?" he asked me.

"Yes indeed you did, why don't you come in?"

He ducked his head, "These old cottages were not made for the likes of me!"

He held out his hand, "How do you do! I know you are Emily. Nancy told us about you. News travels fast in this village. I'm Jack - I live just down the road - and I've an allotment just up the road! I was coming back from my allotment when I heard the unusual sound. So this is it! I have one, too, but it is much older than yours. The horn is made of paper maché. I make the needles myself, out of bamboo. It's a very pure sound, very pure. I collect old records, you know. I may have some that you would like to hear."

"Shall I play something for you?"

"Lovely, yes do, lovely!"

"Do sit down, Jack, and have a cup of tea with us."

"Well, well, I don't mind if I do!"

He sat down, smiling all the time. He had a wide smile as he listened carefully to the sound. "Nice, very nice, something a bit special about that sound, isn't there. Yes indeed there is."

He got up to go, "Would you like some fresh vegetables? I left some at the door. Here!" and he handed me a big bunch of carrots. "Do you like cauliflower?"

"Oh yes, we do."

"Then you have this one - I'll go and get another one for us."

"Oh, I don't want you to do that!"

"Yes, yes, you have it! You must come over one evening and listen to my music. And," he chuckles, "meet my pretty wife. I can bring you all the vegetables you'll need! Don't you go buying any now! We always have more than we can use!"

"Well that is so kind of you. Thank you Jack and yes, I would love to hear your music and meet your wife."

It was sheer bliss to have a telephone again! It was such a nuisance having to go up the street every time I wanted to use the telephone!

I was surprised to hear Daphne on the phone as we usually did all our communicating by post as it was so expensive to telephone from London where she now lived.

"Emily, oh Emily, I've something awful to tell you....."

"What is it? You sound terrible Daphne?"

"Well first I must tell you that I have had to cancel those tickets for the Bolshoi Ballet - remember you were going to have that weekend here with me at last?"

"Yes, yes of course I remember, it simply doesn't matter about the ballet, what is it Daphne?"

"I've been diagnosed with breast cancer."

"But how awful Daphne - oh dear - how terrible, what's to be done? Are they going to operate?"

"No no, The doctor said there was some new treatment in Plymouth that may save me from having surgery. I was so upset about having my breast removed he said I should try it. Honestly Emily, I just don't want to have my breast removed if I can possibly avoid it."

"You say it is in Plymouth? When?"

"It'll be two weeks before they can take me apparently."

"Why don't you come and stay here with us until then - I can drive you to the Plymouth hospital when it's time for you to go? I don't think it's good for you to be there alone with this to think about - why don't you?"

"Oh Emily, I would love to, actually I was going to ask you if

I could, you know. I have been so depressed, all I do is think about having my breast off and how awful it would be."

"I'm not surprised, but maybe you will be lucky. Anyway, let me know when you will arrive and I will be at the station to meet you."

"Thank you so much Emily. Yes I'll call you as soon as I have it arranged, thank you."

When I put the phone down I sat thinking about Daphne. She had always been very pretty. She was a vain woman but then she had a lot to be vain about. Her lovely figure, her porcelain-perfect face framed with beautiful, shiny, brown wavy hair and those warm, mossy-brown eyes. She really was a lovely-looking woman. It was no wonder she felt the way that she did. Well, maybe she will be lucky.

I thought I would ask for a few days off so that we could go for walks and drives - it would be good for her to relax before going into hospital, yes I would do that.

When I saw Daphne at the station it was hard to imagine that there was anything amiss with her. She looked her usual healthy self and was full of flirtatious smiles as some chap helped with her case.

It was good to see her, the boys were pleased to see her too and, as a special treat, Joey made crêpes for breakfast - it was his specialty and Daphne's favourite. As we sat drinking tea and chatting there was a knock at the door and Jack popped his head in.

"Come on in Jack and meet my friend who 's from Vancouver but lives in London. Daphne, this is Jack - he has an ancient gramophone with a paper maché horn he tells me; I haven't seen it yet though."

"Yes, that's right I do, nice to meet you Daphne, that is exactly why I am here Emily, to invite you over to hear it, a little concert for you, would you like to come? Seven o'clock sharp!"

We arrived at the tall, dark, Victorian house at seven. Betsy, his wife, came to the door, she was all dressed up, with every button and bow in place. The large gramophone with the paper maché horn was in front of our chairs which were in a little row. It was a long concert and quite extraordinary how beautiful the sound was; we clapped and exclaimed. Betsy brought us a small glass of wine each and savoury biscuits. All the way home, Daphne chatted away about the unique evening and the friendly hospitable neighbours.

"Such an interesting evening, such a treat to meet people like that. It must be fun living here, Emily! I do envy you!"

"Well, don't! You wouldn't like all my responsibilities!" As I said this I knew I sounded a little resentful, but I wasn't. I would hate to be without my children. For the most part, we had a lot of fun together. However, there was a financial strain and this was difficult for me to deal with.

"You know Emily, I sometimes used to think it might be nice to have a family, with 'Mr Right', but now I think it is a very mixed blessing, from what I see of the people I know with children! Actually I haven't found 'Mr Right' yet, perhaps I never will, I don't really think I am the marrying type and certainly as the years have gone by I've realized that I'm definitely not maternal. I somehow can't imagine being married and living with the one person for years and years - it must get very boring! I've always been so glad that I didn't get trapped into marrying Ron! To think what I would have missed! I've had some wonderfully exciting love affairs with gorgeous men and I've had interesting jobs too. I honestly would not have wanted my life to have been any other way.

"I do think your boys are awfully nice though Emily. Anyway it is a good life for you here, isn't it?"

It was good to hear Daphne talk that way, she obviously had no regrets about that baby. I had heard of girls having huge problems with that sort of past, even to the extent of committing suicide or becoming alcoholics. It is not something I could have ever done and this aspect of Daphne's personality had always surprised me because she is such a kind and thoughtful person, loves dogs and cats and other people's children but she is on the other hand very "down to earth". Realistic about herself which is certainly a good way to be.

Too soon, it was time to take Daphne to Plymouth. I told her that I would visit her but it would have to be after work. "I'll come straight from the hospital, I won't go home first. I'll come as soon as you call me and say it's alright for you to have a visitor."

"Oh Emily, thank you - it will be lovely to see you."

It was a long drive over the moors to the hospital in Plymouth. Coming home late at night was not pleasant. The Dartmoor ponies loomed up unexpectedly out of the mist and it was difficult to avoid them. I had heard that sometimes prison escapees from the Dartmoor prison were hiding in the moors looking to get a lift to a main road. So far, the only bad thing that had happened was that my lights failed me. I was too nervous to get out and see if it was a simple wire that needed connecting! I had to rely on the moon until I got off the moors. It was a scary place to be alone late at night, but I became braver towards the end of Daphne's treatment.

The radiation left Daphne weak and tired, she was advised to rest and told what to eat and what not to eat, for a short spell.
"Daphne, I think you should come home with me. I can look after you until you're well enough to return to London." I did not like the thought of her going home, being all alone and feeling poorly.
After several days with us, resting and taking gentle walks, she was feeling a little better and ready to return to London.
There might be more treatment in a few months. Time would tell.
I took her to the station, she still seemed weak, but she was determined to go home and I could understand that.

One grey, wet, miserable Sunday, the door bell rang and, standing at the door, was the chap from the antique shop. "Here, I've brought you the needles!" He fished in his pocket for the little tin and handed it to me.
"Oh my!" I was taken by surprise. I'd completely forgotten about them. "That was nice of you to bring them over. Come in, Alan!"
He stepped in, ducking through the doorway.
"Come into the kitchen! Would you like a cup of tea?"
"That would be lovely. Nice little cottage you have. Do you like living here?"
"Yes I think so, rather a lot of travelling I'm afraid, but it was

the best I could find at the price I could afford. I've become used to compromising these days!"

"Are you a widow then?"

"No, no - I'm divorced. Nasty it was. All over now though."

"I expect that most divorces are unpleasant - ours is yet to come! I would really like to get it over with as soon as possible - so would she. We have agreed about that at least!"

"What about the children then?"

"We never had any. You certainly have your hands full!"

"Yes, I guess so, but to be honest I don't see it like that. The boys are wonderful company, they are not at all difficult. Of course we have some arguments about what they want to do and what I won't let them do! That sort of thing. It's to be expected."

When Joey made an appearance, Alan, making conversation, asked him where he went to school. When he heard which school it was he was surprised because it was quite a distance from here. I explained that I had to take him in the mornings but that there was a bus that brought him home.

"You have a long wait for that bus don't you? It seems to me that there's only one every hour. The school and the bus stop are not far from my shop - why don't you come into my shop and wait for your bus? My sister looks after the shop some days, so if I'm not there, just go on in and tell her who you are. A bit warmer and drier in there! You do that now, alright?"

Joey, I could see, was pretty pleased with the offer and thanked Alan.

"You're welcome Joey, well, I had better be on my way. Actually, I don't know your name you know, your son introduced us, but all I got out of that was 'Mum'."

"Yes that's right I guess, anyway I'm Emily. It was kind of you to come over, Alan - I do appreciate it. It's been fun having the gramophone. It's a pretty piece of furniture as well - come and have a look - I put it in the sitting-room.

"I had to add this room to give us enough bedrooms. It has made a difference, but our finances have suffered because of it! Well, anyway, what is done is done! I have to admit I don't always make the best decisions! It might be more truthful if I said I rarely did!" I laughed at my honest observation!

"Look," he said, "because I have a shop, I have access to a wholesale shop - you know, for groceries and household items. I have the card here, why don't you have it for a while, get stocked up! I seldom use it since I have been living on my own.

Actually even when there were the two of us we seldom used it. But for you, with those boys to feed, it might save you a fair bit."

"Well, that is nice of you, are you sure? I would love to accept your offer!"

"Here," he said, "you can give it to Joey when you are finished with it - or - I think a better plan would be for you to just keep it - if I need it I will ring you, how's that? In the meantime, how about having a meal with me sometime? I do live alone and I am close to being divorced."

I said I would love to. "It would have to be at the week-end though. During the week I'm too busy - and sometimes I'm required to go back to the hospital in the evenings."

He said that anytime that suited me was fine with him.

"How about next weekend then?"

"Saturday?" We agreed to that.

I was hoping that John Jones was not thinking of coming down. Even if he phoned and I was out, he would be wondering what I was up to! Not that it was anything to do with him, he certainly has no claim on me yet and I can do what I jolly well like! And I would like to go out for once.

Alan was a quiet, gentle man. As time went by, we would go for a walk together or a drive in the countryside. He was always thinking of ways to help me. He even brought me a sewing machine after I had told him that I used to sew. It was an antique one but it certainly worked just fine. We shared a passion for antiques, I loved snooping about in his shop! I sort of wished his sister didn't work there - maybe then he would employ me. Perhaps, though, he didn't pay his sister very much, so it wouldn't do for me anyway. All the same, I would have loved to work there! We got on well together too, he was so easy! I had never seen him angry or short-tempered. Oh well, silly to think of really. I had to work for money, it wasn't just a hobby for me. I needed even more money than I got now. It had been a help with the boys working on Saturdays but the cost of living was jumping up rapidly. I didn't like using what was left of my capital after buying this house. Now I was nibbling at it and that was not good. And that mingy maintenance money the solicitor squeezed out of Lawrence was not enough to feed a fly on. I had never heard of anyone receiving so little. How the solicitor ever came up with that number was quite beyond me! I hated to think about it,

I knew Lawrence should be giving me more. It just was not fair. However, it did no good to think about that - it only upset me. Just have to get on with it all - make the best of it.

The last time I spoke to John on the telephone, I was sure he was beginning to suspect I was getting serious about Alan - which of course I was not. I enjoyed the company, the new friendship. It was a pleasant way to spend an evening or the occasional Sunday afternoon. Actually, John hadn't been down to see me for quite a few weeks now. That last time he phoned, he wanted me to go up to London and meet him for dinner and a show and I had to work. It was a shame as I really enjoyed those excursions. It was a lovely trip on the train. Coming home on the overnight mail train worked well for me too - and it was less expensive! Most people would think it a waste of time, but for me it was perfect. Arriving in Exeter early, picking up the car and going straight to work. It had been a great help since that teacher at Joey's school had been taking him to school in the mornings. It was a bit of luck when he moved nearby.

I told Alan about John.

"Are you going to go on seeing him?"

"Yes, but I don't see him that often now, with him living so far away."

"But Emily, you can't go on having two. You'll have to decide which person you prefer."

"Why? I don't see that I have to, after all, you have your life mapped out, John has his and I have mine. It shouldn't bother you that I have someone else I see from time to time?"

For the first time, I saw that Alan was quite angry.

"Well it does bother me, Emily - and I think I will stay out of the picture until you make up your mind who you want!"

I was a little surprised! "Oh, come on Alan, you are being a bit foolish, don't you think?"

"No, Emily, I don't think that I am, I think that you are. You can't have one there and one here sort of style, you are being very foolish if you think you can do that."

"Alan, I am really sorry if you feel that way!"

"Well I do. So I'll leave you to sort yourself out. Let me know who wins!"

He turned to pick up his jacket, when I heard a sports car pulling up outside! I was sure it was John! Oh my God, now what! I grabbed Alan, "You'll have to go out the kitchen door Alan, you'll have to, I am certain that's John here now and he is a very jealous man!"

"Out the back door? Emily - I shall do no such thing!"

"Please Alan, just do it for me! Please be quick about it!"

I stood there holding the door open, he went through the doorway without looking at me! I knew he was furious!

Just as I went to the front door I saw John rush up with a huge bunch of flowers! He turned, and ran out the gate! I ran after him, as he was parked across the street. I ran across, but he was already in the car with the motor going. "Wait! Wait!" I called.

He jumped out of the car, rushed over to me, "Emily, I know you are seeing someone else! I know you are, but you are going to marry me! You are! I love you Emily and you are going to be my wife!" Then he put his arms around me and gave me a romantic kiss in the middle of the road! In a flash he was back in his car and gone!

I picked up the bouquet and went in the house. Oh my God, that was awful, what a situation. I laughed a little, it was awful but rather funny too! I will have to give Alan up - after today's episode! He has probably given me up anyway! I was so glad I got him out of the house. Poor Alan, he really was furious. It was so embarrassing for him, but what else could I do? I certainly didn't want another scene like the one when Gordon was visiting me!

Anyway, I had other things to think about and worry about. I must decide what to do. With all the labour strikes that made the cost of living rise all the time, managing on my small income was becoming impossible. A pity that the stove was oil-fuelled - that last batch of oil had doubled in price! Impossible to heat the house, because I really couldn't afford to buy the oil. Such a pity it wasn't coke, which was so much cheaper. Those shoes I just bought for Joey, that was what Lawrence used to pay for his shoes! It was everything, just about everything - and petrol and meat! Looking at my account book, I was more and more aware of how difficult it was becoming to manage. I had been thinking that it might be a good idea to sell this house and find a less expensive one - and one not heated with oil.

At dinner I told the boys my thoughts.

"I could put it on the market and see what happens? If we buy a less expensive house it would free up some money and also a coke stove would be much cheaper to run than this oil one. We wouldn't have to go to bed so early!"

We had recently had to go to bed shortly after dinner to keep warm! There was nowhere warm in the house and our small electric heater was too expensive to use. Anyway, it wouldn't heat the sitting-room.

After thinking about it for several days I decided to try and sell it. It might take several months to sell, because it was so near the road and the garden wasn't established. Bringing rocks down from the Moors to make little flower beds had helped and of course the tubs and hanging baskets were very pretty but that is not a garden; the house certainly had its drawbacks - more than I cared to think about.

Quite a few people came to look at it but it was not selling quickly! Eventually the estate agent told me that there was an offer in. An older couple, just retired, they wanted to live in a small village and this was just what they were looking for! He told me that they were prepared to pay the full price. I was thrilled and very thankful, it had been quite worrying not being able to sell. The boys wanted to know when I was going to look for another house! I told them I had already heard about an old miner's cottage which was for sale in a village about seven miles from here.

When I phoned the agent about the cottage, he said I could look at it any time because the lady who had lived there had died and so it was empty. We arranged to meet the next day during my lunch break.

The house was the first house in a row of four. Inside, it was old-fashioned, as nothing had been done to it for many, many years. It had four bedrooms, three of them with fireplaces. A large bathroom, which probably was a bedroom once upon a time when there was no indoor plumbing. There was a good-size living-room and dining-room and a kitchen with no cupboards at all. The stove was coke-fuelled. The garden was tiny but private. The whole house needed decorating. All the rooms were dingy, but apart from that I thought it would do nicely - and the price was right. I could even walk to work; it would only be about three miles, then David could have my car.

I took the boys to have a look. They loved all the fireplaces! Maxwell said he would stay in it for a couple of weeks before we moved in and paint it right through. "You choose the colours, Mum and I'll do everything!"

Joey said he could cycle to where the teacher picked him up in the mornings. And cycle home from where the bus dropped him. "I can ask at the shop if I can leave my bike there - and I know it will be fine with them!"

"Are you sure you won't mind that ride every day, Joey?"

He said, he was sure.

"Well then, if everyone is happy about it I will buy it!"

Joey said he thought he would be able to make a nice garden at the back - better than what we had here as it was quite private and so was the house. It was true that having been the stable to the big house, this house was not private. Everyone seemed happy about the move! It would be a great relief to get the expenses more manageable.

Maxwell finished the painting and had done a lovely job, the house was greatly improved.

The day of the move arrived. We were ready, all packed and had been loading the van since eight o'clock, there was just the freezer left. The telephone rang; I wondered who on earth would be telephoning on our moving day. I picked up the phone.

"Is that you, Mrs Love?"

"Yes, yes?"

There was a long silence, then I heard someone crying.

"Who is this? Who is this?"

Then again, "Mrs Love?"

"Yes, yes - Emily Love speaking, what is it?"

"This is Mrs Edwards - you know, the people who are buying your house." The voice was all snuffly.

"Yes?"

"My husband is dead! I woke up very late, just a short time ago and he was dead beside me in the bed!"

"Dead? Dead! But how awful! How terrible! Are you sure?" As soon as I had said it I wished I hadn't!

"Yes of course I'm sure! What shall I do?"

Good Lord, I thought, how should I know? "What do you mean - what should you do?"

PS: I have to go into hospital here, I'll tell you all about it in my next letter when I know more myself."

I opened the tissue and unfolded the dress. I held it up, "It's lovely, lovely, but when would I wear it? I don't go to any formal dinners where people like Pierre Trudeau go!"

"Wear it when you are out with John!", David the romantic, speaking!

"Yes - but we don't go anywhere like that - anyway, maybe I will have the occasion someday, who knows!

I thought of Daphne and the sweetness of her gesture, such a sweet thing to do! I wonder what the new problems are that she is having to go back into hospital? I wish she had said more about it. I won't do anything until I hear more. I'm bound to hear before long.

Although we all loved it here in this small house right in the country, it was becoming more and more difficult to manage on my present salary. The pay rise I had was just not enough. I had also started to work more hours, staying later in the afternoon. But everything just kept going up - even the coke for the stove had gone up. We started collecting wood to use instead of the coke although one was not supposed to burn anything in it but coke. I had hoped that Lawrence would pay a little more maintenance, but he had not and apparently would not, according to my solicitor.

I began to wonder if we would be better off in Canada, Britain seemed to be in such a mess with all the labour strikes and, lately, even having to shop for our groceries in candle-light. The miners never satisfied, the situation was not improving, with more and more rising prices. From what Madeleine told me in her letters, life sounded a lot easier in Canada. Salaries were higher and the cost of living, according to Madeleine, was less.

I mentioned it at the dinner table one evening just to see what the reaction would be. Maxwell was not interested; he was enjoying his course at the College of Fine Art working towards a Fine Arts degree. "Anyway, I'm going to live on campus. I'm planning to buy a van and fix it up to live in. I've already made enquiries and I have permission to live in it on campus. It's something I have been thinking about for ages. I've seen a van that would work out. I'll enjoy fixing it up too. I definitely would not want to move, I really like the college and I like living in Devon."

David said that he would love to go! "That is, if I could carry on with my apprenticeship - only three more years to do!"

"After I finish my O-levels. I could go after that!" Joey explained. "I think it would be fun to go!"

"Well, I don't know, it's a huge move somehow! It needs a lot of thought."

I thought about it, but after a time I dismissed the idea. Of course, my family, especially my mother, would like me to go back. But it would be a huge upheaval, with another job to find and a place to live. We would have to live in a flat - I knew I wouldn't be able to afford a house in Vancouver. My British pound wouldn't go very far over there, that was for certain. Maybe it would be better to find a better paid job here, we did love it here after all.

I thought I would mention the idea of going to Canada to John anyway, just to hear his view; he was very enthusiastic. "Why don't you go over for a holiday - search everything out. I'll go to Canada House and find out if I can go. I've always thought it would be a marvellous country to live in! We could go together. We could be married before we go. I'm sure that if you went for three weeks you could find out about a school for Joey and also about David. Maxwell 'll probably change his mind when he knows you are serious, don't you think?"

I wasn't so sure, Maxwell certainly was hardly ever at home any more! His whole life seemed to be in the art world. The thought of going and looking into things appealed to me though. I could certainly check it all out, it would be the best way. If it didn't look like it would be right for us, I would at least have seen my family, so the money would not have been wasted!

I told John that I thought it would be a good idea to go and have a look.

"Fine! Good girl! Now - I am going to buy your ticket, Emily!"

"Why? I can buy my own ticket!"

"Yes of course you can - but I would like this to be my treat! Now then, you come up on the train and I'll meet you and we can go to the airport together. When would you like to leave, Emily?"

"I thought, maybe, early May - it would be nice to be there for my birthday. Mother would love that!"

"Fine!" he said, "I'll see to it."

When the arrangements were made, David said he would take me to the station. My thoughtful, capable, sensible son – I was not at all worried about leaving them. After all, Joey was nearly 16, David would soon be 19 and Maxwell was 20.

At the station, I gave my last instructions "You'll be alright now, won't you?"

They said they would be just fine and to have a nice time.

"You phone me when you arrive at Exeter and I'll pick you up, Mum. Be sure to make it a time I can be there though!"

At the station in London, John was there to meet me. "I wouldn't dare to be late today! I made sure the surgery door was locked – I didn't want any stray emergencies wandering in this morning!" In the car were magazines and chocolates, "for you, for your trip, mate. I know you love your books, but a magazine is nice to pick up for a change, I always think."

At Heathrow, he held me, "Phone me, Emily - reverse the charges, but I want to know how you make out. You are my mate, you know, darling one. Do give my best wishes to your mother – I look forward to meeting her someday. I shall phone the boys from time to time make sure all is well! I am sure they will be fine. Now off you go, I do love you."

On the plane I sat back and relaxed! Camping with the boys last summer was certainly fun, but the luxury of being waited on like this for once, was absolute heaven. I thought about the boys, what they would be doing. I often thought how lucky I was to have such wonderful children - so thoughtful and helpful. I had always been able to trust them too and they were great company; yes, I was very lucky.

As the aircraft came in to land, the anticipation of seeing everyone again was very exciting! So many years had gone by.

There was mother! She always looked the same to me! I ran up and hugged her. It felt so good to hug her, to feel her physical closeness again, that feeling of belonging, that feeling I had known forever - it was part of me. My brother always standing back, the way he did, with his head a bit to the side. He hugged me. "Hi Sis!" And Madeleine - where is she? "Madeleine said she would rather wait at the house to see you," Edgar said.

The drive down Granville Street with the fresh new green on the trees, clouds of pink and white blossom floating about everywhere. The mountains, heavy and imposing, still tipped with white, in the background. Yes, I thought, quite an impressive city. A very inviting city!

At the house, my nephews and nieces were waiting with their mother with hugs and kisses. Muffins, the children's dog, gave his greeting too.

The next day was a lazy one, talking and phoning some of my old friends. I went to see mother and we had lunch together, then we sat and talked the whole afternoon. Mother kept telling me how lovely it was to see me. "Do you think you'll come back?"

"I don't know yet, Mother, I'll have to do some research. It's such a big step. Maxwell thinks he won't come, which makes me hesitate somewhat. The truth is, we see very little of him these days. He is so wrapped up in his own world. Don't worry, I am thinking about it seriously and, as I say, there 're certain things I'll have to find out before I can make any decision."

Mother smiled and agreed that there must be an enormous amount of things to consider. "I know dear, I must not influence you - but, needless to say, I would love you to come back!"

I had a good look at mother. I was wrong, she had changed; she was looking older, she looked more frail than I remembered. Well, 77, I guess it was to be expected!

I seemed to be on the telephone for hours with all the things I had to find out. All the questions I had to ask. Luckily, in Canada, telephone rental included local calls! All this telephoning would have cost the earth in England!

I telephoned the boys.

"How are you? Is everything alright?"

"Yes, Mum, everything is fine here - how about you?" It was David.

I told him all I had found out. "Would you mind doing an extra year of your apprenticeship David, do you think?"

"No - I wouldn't mind at all - and with the pay being so much more, it wouldn't be a hardship like it is here, would it? That sounds like a lot of money to me!"

Joey wanted to know if they will be able to have a dog and a cat! "School is school, Mum! As long as I won't have to do anything extra!"

I assured him that he would not. I told him that the principal who I had spoken to had accepted a boy from England last year; he would be in the same year as Joey so apparently there would not be a problem.

"Are we going to move then?"

"I think so!"

"Oh good! We have been hoping and hoping!"

David came back on the line, "Do you think so, Mum - really?"

"Yes, I think we will. I think you would like it here, you know. There seem to be so many more opportunities for young people too. It isn't nearly as crowded!"

"I know we would like it, Mum! Joey and I have talked all about it and we're sure it would be great!"

"I'm glad you feel like that! Maybe we can talk Maxwell into the idea too. Now I must go. I promised I would ring John and tell him everything as soon as I knew. Good-bye love, see you soon!"

I did think that they would be much better off, my salary would be double what I was getting in England. David's too. The cost of living would be less too. If John came - well, eventually we wouldn't have to worry anyway, as he most certainly would be coming and hopefully fairly soon too.

When John answered the phone, before I could say anything, he immediately started with, "Emily, I want you to come back and marry me! It has turned out that it would be impossible for me to come to Canada to live. There were so many things I just had not considered. Please marry me! The house will be finished before too long so there will be plenty of room. Garda has left again - this time she won't come back unless I ask her to. I cannot come to Canada Emily."

My heart lurched. He wasn't going to come after all but I had decided to come. What have I done! I had even told mother, it would be bad enough to disappoint the boys - but mother!

I had to tell him my decision. "I didn't think there would be any doubt really - I thought for sure you would be able to come, John. I just went ahead thinking that we would all be better off here, especially the way England is now, with all the strikes and the huge jump in the cost of living. You did tell me that you really wanted to come, that the thought had always appealed to you?"

"Yes, yes, Emily, but I can't come! Will you or won't you come back and settle here with me? Please, Emily, come back here and marry me!"

"I don't think I can, John. Not now. I just couldn't do that to the boys - and then there is mother."

"Please, do think what you are doing!"

"I'm sorry John."

"Oh, my dear Emily! Don't, don't say you won't come!"

"I have to say it. I'm so sorry, John."

"Emily?"

"Yes?"

"Emily, in that case there's no point in our relationship carrying on. You do see that don't you?"

"Yes I do."

"I may even take Garda back, I would rather have someone than no one. At least I do know her and her faults. Emily, are you certain about this, really certain?"

"I have to be, John. I haven't any choice."

"You do have a choice!"

"No I don't. You should have told me sooner, John - then I would have had a choice, but not now!"

"I told you as soon as I could, Emily. Oh Emily, this is ridiculous, what a mess-up - after all our plans. Should I phone you back to give you time to consider what you are doing? This is ridiculous!"

"It won't do any good to phone again, John."

"I guess then, Emily, I won't be at Heathrow to meet you - there would be no point, now would there, mate."

"No John, there wouldn't be any point."

"Then, good-bye Emily, I shall miss you, you know."

"Yes John, good-bye."

As I put the phone down, I saw that Edgar was standing in the doorway. "Emily, I couldn't help hearing what you have done. Do you think you have been wise? After all, the boys won't be with you forever. When they have gone, you'll be all alone. Have you thought of that?"

"Not really."

I felt frightened at what I had done. Had I really done it? Had I really given him up? Just like that. Is it really over? Why, he had been in my life now for five years. Oh God!

I looked over at my brother. "I have done it. I made the decision. How could I let everyone down now? What would

said nothing. He hardly looked at me. At the end of the viewing, Mary said that she would buy it. I was astonished, as it was so quick!

The agent called to confirm the sale. Mary phoned and asked if she could buy some items like bookshelves and maybe a chest of drawers. "I thought that you probably wouldn't be taking everything with you, so maybe you would sell a few things to me?"

I told her that I would be glad to. I gave in my notice at the hospital as I would need quite a lot of time to deal with everything. I had planned to sell everything except one or two antiques. It would all take time. The car too, that would have to wait until we were nearly ready to leave.

When I phoned Daphne to tell her all about it, I was a little surprised when I heard her say that she thought it probably a good idea to leave. "It is so difficult here now with everything so expensive, I do agree. And you are right, Emily, there seem to be many more opportunities in Canada for young people! Even I have noticed that! You know how much I love living in London, but I will probably return to Canada too, in the not too distant future."

I asked how her hospital visit went.

"At the moment the tests they have done have come out negative, but I will have to have more done in a few weeks. I don't feel very wonderful Emily, I am so tired all the time. My whole body seems to ache. I guess the boys are excited about the move?"

"Oh yes, they are, but wasn't that surprising that the house sold so quickly! I mean after the last one!"

"Yes, you were lucky this time certainly! A relief too I'm sure! How is that lovely brother of yours, and your mother?"

"Oh, everyone was in great form, Daphne, just great form!"

I would miss Daphne.

I wondered who it could be when I heard someone knocking at the front door, I was unaccustomed to having unannounced callers. It was Mary.

"Come in, come in! I expect you want to have another look, was there something in particular, do come and sit down!"

The young woman came in and stood in the entrance looking absolutely miserable. "Oh, I am so sorry to have to tell you this, I wanted to come and tell you myself. I can't buy the house!"

"You can't? But why's that? What's happened?" Oh dear, I thought, how could I be so unlucky!

"My boyfriend has decided that he doesn't want to marry me after all! You see, he was going to help with the payments. I was paying the main part of it. Anyway, that day he saw the house, he became frightened and now he's called the whole thing off."

With this said, she started to cry. "I thought it would be so lovely in this house, with the girls and him and everything. I was so looking forward to it."

She was really crying by this time, her heart was broken, poor girl. I felt so sorry for her. I patted her shoulder, "Oh you poor dear, let me make you a cup of tea and we can have a little chat. Come with me into the kitchen."

"I am so sorry to have to do this to you!" she said, drying her eyes. "I feel just awful about it - but what could I do!"

My heart did bump a bit at the news, but it was not the woman's fault, "Don't worry, I'm sure we will sell it again! Now let us have that cup of tea - you'll feel better then. You know, it is much the best thing that he broke it off now, instead of waiting until you had bought the house and moved in. Maybe he wasn't suited to being a family man either? Perhaps it is all for the best for you? Try to think of it like that."

When she had gone I phoned the agent. He was sympathetic. "Yes I know, but she was adamant about coming to you herself and telling you. She felt so badly about it. How are you?"

"Alright, thanks. I certainly hope it doesn't take long to sell the house again! My deadline remember, is the end of July at the latest."

He laughed, "Oh I don't think it will!"

I never met the people who finally bought the house in July, they were from London.

I sold nearly everything, which I later regretted.

Leaving time was getting close. Lawrence wanted the boys to visit him before we left. They were going to stay with him for five days. He didn't want to see me. Maxwell was going to come up from Devon and take us to the airport in his van.

I phoned John to tell him when we were leaving.

"I will probably never see you again, Emily. If you are coming here with the boys before you go, I would like to treat you to those few days at the Black Swan - you know, the one by the river. Then I could see you a few more times and you could visit whoever you wanted to visit. You'll want to see your friend Martha, won't you, or were you going to stay with them?"

"No, no - don't you remember they moved to America several years ago! No - I thought I would ask another friend. But on the other hand, she does live quite far out from the town and without a car I would be so dependent. Your idea sounds perfect! I'll accept!"

"I'm glad you'll accept, Emily. I do want to see you again."

"I want to see you too!"

I phoned Alan. I wanted to see him also before we left and I wanted to ask him if he would take Flopsy off our hands. He loved dogs and so far we had no luck placing her. The Vet said he would keep her until someone turned up but we would rather have known who she was going to be with and Alan would be perfect. When he answered the phone and when I told him we were leaving his voice was so subdued I could hardly hear him. He sounded so forlorn.

"Are you alright?" I thought maybe he was not well or something.

"Yes I am, but it depresses me to think that you are leaving. I have always hoped that somehow or other we would get together. I always had it in the back of my mind. I wish you hadn't made this decision, Emily, it seems so final. As long as you were still here, I could hope. Will it be alright for me to come and see you soon?"

"Yes Alan, of course it will be alright - I shall look forward to seeing you."

I was surprised at how very pleased I was to see him again!

"I have something to show you!" he said. "I want you to come with me and look at the cottage I am planning to buy. I am sure you'll love it!"

"How exciting! I would love to see it!"

"Come on then, I have the key and we can see it before it's dark!"

It was a long drive into the countryside. The cottage was down a deserted lane. He parked the car and we walked along a rather overgrown path. He opened the old, rickety door and immediately we were in the living room. I could see why he was so taken with it. It really was charming with the low ceiling, exposed beams and stone fireplace.

"How lovely! Oh I do envy you! I do!"

He looked at me. His eyes wide, his eyebrows lifted, "You do?"

"Yes I do!"

"Why then don't you live here with me? There is plenty of room for all of you!"

"Oh Alan, how could I now! It is out of the question, but I do thank you for asking me."

He laughed a little, "Of course, of course - it was worth a try though!"

Finally I plucked up the courage to ask him about Flopsy. "Would you Alan? Could you? I know it is a lot to ask of you, but now with your cottage in the country and Flopsy is a lovely animal and she likes you and you know how much you like her! Do you think you could?"

He laughed, "Well, I would rather have you Emily, but of course I'll have her, I was going to look for a dog once I got settled in the cottage, so I'd be very pleased to have Flopsy. Pity about her name though! Anyway don't you worry about her, she will be fine."

"Oh Alan, that's marvellous, what a relief, thank you so much. The boys will be so pleased that it's you she is going to live with. Thank you very, very much."

Time to say good-bye to John, it was hard to realize that I wouldn't be seeing him again. He had been so special to me and I still loved him very much. He was quite brusque. He said good-bye to the boys, shook hands, gave me a peck on the cheek, a hearty hug, wished us good-luck and swiftly left.

At the airport the reality finally hit me. I looked at my son whom I was leaving behind. Now I had to say good-bye to him! I couldn't do it!

"I can't go! I just cannot go!"

I started to cry.

"It's alright, Mum," he told me, "I'll be fine!"

"Come on, Mum - we have to go now! Please, Mum!" It was David, then Joey, tugging my arm.

One last hug for Maxwell. Waving and running along, turning, waving and running, tears streaming all over my face. Joey beside me, "Are you alright, Mum? Mum?"

Finally in our seats, my whole body was shaking and heaving. What have I done? What have I done? Oh God!

David, quietly, "Mum - everything will be fine - it will. Please don't cry."

I could feel the aircraft lift! We were up! We were on our way! I had left Maxwell! How could I have done that! But I had done it! We were in the sky on the way to Canada! I had loved living in England - I had always loved it, right from the very beginning - and now I was leaving!

"Mum," David was saying, "are you going to have a drink? The air-hostess is here."

"Yes indeed I am! Thank you." I must brighten up, I told myself. After all, the reason I was doing this was because I believed it was going to be better for everyone. Although I was not sure how good it was going to be for Maxwell or me for that matter. I hoped he would be as happy with the situation as he thought he would. At twenty, he thought he had passed his need of family. He wanted so much to be on his own - and he had been for quite a while now, so perhaps it would all work out, I certainly hoped so. And anyway, he will probably come and join us when he has his degree. I must stop being miserable and think happy things or I will be upsetting the boys. They were so excited and thrilled at the prospect of the new life waiting for them in Canada! It was important I did not spoil it for them.

CANADA

Exhausted, with red-rimmed eyes and an aching heart, I marched forward to meet the family and proudly introduce Joey and David. Mother gave the boys a hug. I could see she looked a bit weepy but happy; we hugged each other, words would come later.

Sam, Joey's cat, had been procured from the dark quarters of the aircraft. He was in a beautiful, wicker, cat basket and had been sedated for the trip. Edgar and Madeleine were not expecting him but they smiled and welcomed him to Canada. They already had a dog and two cats! The luggage was assembled - all were ready to depart.

The sun was shining, the car was full and hot. The cat would like out. I had a headache. The boys were excited, full of chatter and enthusiasm.

At the house, the waiting cousins were there at the window as the car pulled up. They ran down the steps to meet their English cousins! Joey and David seemed to fill the sitting-room. I felt really tired and kept wondering off and on why I was there. I was somehow surprised to be there. It was apparent that I would have to find accommodation quickly. It would be too much to have all of us here in this modest family home for very long. It was all very jolly at the moment, but we must not outstay our welcome! Madeleine called us into the dining room for a Canadian meal; she had made hamburgers!

It was not an easy thing to find an apartment, not when one had two teenage sons. Eventually, I did find one, but the fact that we had a cat we did not reveal! It was not a wonderful place, as it was dark and a bit gloomy.

Barely settled, there was a knock at the door. "We are allergic to cats and we know that you have a cat in here, so you will have to get rid of the cat or move!" the owner of the house told me.

"But, it's really hard to get a place that takes teen-age boys and we brought our cat all the way from England you know!"

"We are sorry for that, but we are allergic and so the cat will have to go - or you must move out!"

"I see."

David found, through the Dental Technicians' school, an apprenticeship in Prince George, about 500 miles north of Vancouver; he was going to live there and was excited about the adventure, he had great expectations! I would be very sorry to see him go, but I didn't let on how I felt. The early morning was dark and chilly when the taxi came to take David to the train which would take him away to his new life. I thought he was very courageous to go off like that alone, far away in a country so new to him.

"Phone me. Tell me what the trip was like and the people you'll be staying with. Just reverse the charges. Good Luck!" I hugged him and managed to smile. Joey stood quietly, looking very mournful, but he smiled and wished him "good luck"; he was going to miss his constant companion.

I found another apartment in an old house that had been converted into apartments. It was larger than the last, dark and cheerless, but the windows did open (they didn't in the last apartment) and Joey and Sam were accepted without any fuss. Edgar, Madeleine and Mother came to see it.

"My goodness!", said Madeleine, "We didn't know it was here, Emily! You should have told us exactly where it was!"

"But why, what's the matter?"

"Actually, there was a terrible murder here, not here in this building, but somewhere on this street several months ago! You should immediately get locks and bolts on all the windows and the doors. With it near the lane the way it is, you really must!"

I was a little disconcerted by this news. Anyway I was not going to move again! Locks and bolts we would purchase.

Joey and I went out for a walk one bright sunny Saturday and I bought a car, a sports car - an MG - just like John's! Even the same colour! It was an impulse, a wild impulse, a vision I had of myself swishing around with the wind blowing through my hair and me a carefree woman. It was a fantasy vision that did not last long. I was not carefree and the car was far too expensive but since I had it, I agreed to teach Joey to drive; he of course, was thrilled with the car. I agreed because I thought it would be useful. We drove to the school and the bank together, in the mornings. I had taken a banking course upon learning that well-paying jobs were available at the bank where I had worked briefly many years ago.

Joey did not like the school at all, he didn't fit in.

"All everyone talks about are their designer clothes, TV programmes, the pubs and where to get Pot! Honestly Mum, you wouldn't believe the car park at the school - really expensive cars. Nobody takes their lunch you know. Anyway, I hate the place."

He was a displaced person with his background of cycling to school, wearing a uniform, taking his lunch and a thermos flask of milk. We didn't have TV and we didn't want it.

I really didn't like my job at the bank, I didn't want to admit this so soon, but I certainly dreaded each day. The pace was frantic; never a moment free. A constant line-up at my wicket from morning until closing and speed was of paramount importance in everything I did. It was tiring and stressful. At lunch break, all I wanted to do was get out and away, so Joey and I met in the car park and had our lunch together which helped to relax me - and he was pleased to be out of the school.

One morning as Joey parked the car, the thought of my miserable day ahead in the bank reached right into me.

"What is it, Mum?"

"Oh it's alright, Joey, I'm fine. It's just the thought of my horrible day ahead! I do hate it! It's so busy, so noisy, so hostile. Never mind, I'll have to get used to it that's all. Will I see you for lunch?"

"Yes, Mum, I guess you hate the bank and I hate the school! Are you really going to stay?"

"I don't know what I am going to do, Joey. But one thing is for certain - you have to stay at school!"

He was silent.

"See you later!" I got out of the car and headed back to work.

I did not allow myself to think any more about my problems, I had to concentrate on my work. I was training a young woman at my wicket, that was the only bright spot in my work day. The young woman was eager to learn, very sweet and had humour, which was something everyone else in this bank seemed to lack.

At dinner, Joey told me that he wanted to leave school! I was adamant he was not to leave school! We argued. He told me that he wouldn't stay at school, the garage where he applied for Saturday work said he could work there full time if he wanted to.

"But Joey, what sort of job is that! It is certainly fine for a part-time job, but it isn't a career. You must finish your education. You would have if we had stayed in England wouldn't you?"

"Yes Mum, but I am not in England anymore and I cannot go to that school. Most of the work I have done anyway, last year."

"What about trying another school Joey?"

"All the schools will be the same Mum - I don't want to go to school here and I won't!"

We argued and I got nowhere. I finally went to bed but I was very upset and I realized that this was the first time I had had an argument with this son. Sadness filled me. I could feel that familiar ache of regret, nostalgia, unhappiness. I closed my eyes, longing for sleep to take me and release me, but into my mind came the pictures of Maxwell when I said good-bye, the dog, silly as it was, who was living with Alan now, our little house and, of course, John. The early morning sun through the rising mist on the fields, as I happily walked along to work. The lambs in the spring, I remembered the smell of the hedgerows, the singing, chirping birds with their morning calls. I could see it all. Smell it all. Hear it all. The country peace, the pleasure it gave me. In my heart, I thought I had made the wrong decision by coming here. I missed everything and Joey was unhappy!

When I picked up the ringing phone, I was hoping it would be David and it was! Oh, it was so good to hear his voice! "How are you? How is the work? What's Prince George like?"

In a quieter voice, I asked about the people he was living with. The man who owned the Lab had offered David accommodation until David was settled. David, was subdued and he sounded quite emotional. "I'm fine, Mum, The job is great, very interesting. It's OK here, but they don't live the way *we* do - and the children are noisy - but everyone is kind. I am going to find a place of my own soon. When I do, will you and Joey come and visit me?"

I said I would love to.

"How are you?" he asked. "How is the job?"

I told him that I would have to leave it. All of a sudden I had made up my mind!

"We miss you David!" I laughed, "No one to make my tea anymore! As you know, Joey is not a cup of tea person!"

"I miss you, Mum." His voice was quiet, "I'll let you know the minute I find an apartment, then you'll come?"

I told him that we would and now that Joey can drive, we could take turns driving.

"Will you have enough money for an apartment so soon, David?"

"Yes yes, I will! And a car too I think! You'll love it here, Mum, it is so beautiful! I love it, but it is very cold! All the people I meet are friendly, very Canadian I guess! I had better go or this will be too expensive for you. Say Hi to Joey! Bye, Mum."

It was a relief to know that at least he was happy with his work and he was going to be able to have his own apartment soon and that would really please him. He seemed to have settled in well! Oh such a relief that was. A surge of thankfulness filled me. It would be wonderful to see him.

It was a long drive even with sharing it. When we arrived at David's apartment, he rushed out to meet us. How lovely it was to see him! He proudly showed us his little home - he was delighted with it.

"I'm roasting a chicken!" he told us with pride.

After the chicken, baked potatoes and peas, he brought out a cake! Banana cake, it had always been a favourite cake with everyone - even Lawrence.

"I don't think the icing is as good as yours, Mum."

I thought it was very good, I told him. We sat drinking coffee and talking into the night.

The next day we went on a tour of the whole area.

"Isn't the scenery marvellous! Look!" he said, "There is nobody about! Not like Devon, where everywhere there were hordes of people! Remember when we used to go to Fingle Bridge for a picnic and there were so many people there. You can come here on a Sunday and there is nobody about at all! There are lots of places like this. And the fish! People are always catching wonderful, huge fish here. The countryside is completely unspoiled, it's still wild and unused in so many places. This is what I imagined Canada to be like - I love it here Mum."

I heard him and admired his enthusiasm.

"Do you find you fit in David? I mean - you are so English!"

He laughed. "I fit in well enough. Some of the people I meet are a little rough, but they are not who I am going to spend my time with anyway. A couple of the dentists have been friendly and have asked me out on their boat with them. They are pleasant, not at all rough. Perhaps some of the people I work with laugh at my accent, but I don't mind that. I like the feeling of freedom I have here. People are more open and are freer, I think. They have fun and enjoy themselves more. It sure is nice to have enough money for once! The pay is great! When I think of what I was paid at the lab in England!"

At dinner that night he listened about Joey and his miserable school. "Why don't you come and live with me, Joey? I know I could get you a job at the Lab. I could teach you a lot of stuff."

"Are you encouraging him to quit school, David?"

He coloured a bit, "I guess so. What are you planning to do, Joey, if you dislike it that much? You can't work in a garage! I could teach you and then you could do what I am doing - at least then you would have a training and a job. Why don't you? What do you think, Mum? I mean, as long as he gets a training it doesn't matter, does it, about the school? He said he had done all the work last year in England when he did his O-levels which is like grade 12 here. Eventually he could take the exams, like I am going to do."

I listened and began to think that maybe it would be alright. Joey was so unhappy these days and he had always been such a happy person. It couldn't be good for him, going to school every day and hating it. "What do you think Joey? Would you be happy doing that?"

"I think so. Would you let me?"

"It might be a good idea - we'll talk about it."

When it was time to leave David, I didn't want to leave him. I felt so lonely without him, I always felt this way when we parted. I told him how glad I was that he was enjoying everything so much and then I gave him a big hug, but as I held him close for that second I felt the pain of leaving him wrench me, I looked into his eyes and gave him a big smile - I must not look sad. We waved as we drove off and I kept smiling. It hurt me deeply to part with him, to leave him there, this caused me actual physical pain.

At home, Joey asked me if I would let him do as David suggested.

"Well, I will agree to it if you do the training. You must have a training - and if you think you would like to do it, then, alright. You can always do something else I suppose, if you want to. Once you have settled a bit more you might decide to go back to school, or do another practical training. This dental one would be a useful one to have I imagine."

"What about you, Mum? What are you going to do?"

"I'm going to do the same as you! I'm going to leave the bank. I think I will take a secretarial training. That should get me a more suitable job. Yes, I think that will be my plan. I'll probably move from here if you leave, because I won't need as much space. But at the moment I'll stay put, I think. One thing at a time!"

At the end of the secretarial course (which I did not enjoy overly much), I was waiting in the lobby for a list of prospective employers. Wondering how it would be for me to sit at a desk all day long, I was not looking forward it. I was trying to be cheerful and look on the bright side but it had become quite difficult to do this as I felt mainly miserable. I didn't even have a cat now that Joey had taken Sam with him. I lived in an empty, ugly apartment, no children, no dog, no cat, no house, no garden. Over and over I wondered if I had done the right thing. Mind you I thought, the boys seemed to be enjoying their lives; Joey had settled in quite happily with David and now had a dog. The letters from Maxwell, although not frequent, sounded fine. He at last had found a girlfriend, which really explained the less frequent letters. So perhaps it was just me, I was the one who had not settled, did not really like it here. I did not fit in! Was that it? How could that be? After all, I am the Canadian!

ANDREW

"Hello! Hello there!"

I looked up and, standing right in front of me, was the chap who had given me the 10 dollars on the plane all those months ago.

"So you did make it!" he said! "Well well, how are you doing?" We shook hands.

"How nice to see you! I thought it was you when I walked past, but I had to come back and have a good look to be certain! You didn't seem to notice that I was staring at you!"

I laughed, "No I didn't notice - I was miles away!"

Again he asked, "How are you getting on? Did you bring the boys with you?"

I was reluctant to chat - there was too much to say, standing casually like this. After a few minutes he asked me if I would like to go out to dinner with him, I could tell him all about everything then. How nice, I thought, I haven't been anywhere for months. I would love to go out for dinner I told him. We arranged to meet in the centre of town at the Birks clock. "I haven't met anyone at the Birks clock for years and years!" I told him.

The evening was pleasant, Andrew was very attentive and listened to all of my happenings. I did not tell him that I was not enjoying living in Vancouver, that I wished I had never left England, that I missed my eldest son terribly. Instead I smiled all the while and agreed that the city was beautiful. I did not say that the traffic fumes really got to me. I agreed that Canadians were very friendly, they were (except of course the ones I had worked with in the bank)! They were helpful too, yes. We talked about London, he apparently enjoyed London too when he lived there. I, of course, loved London and had, since the first time my very young eyes saw that ancient, magnificent city! It had thrilled me.

He told me about his children and his wife who was missing her own country.

All of a sudden he looked at me, "I enjoyed the letter you wrote, it was very sweet of you to bother, I didn't expect you to, you know. I kept wondering if you would get here and if you did I wondered if you would contact me. Did you think you would, at some point?"

"Not really," I told him, "but then I might have. I don't know actually. I am rather used to sailing my own little ship and dealing with all the problems I bring on myself!"

"Well, I am glad I bumped into you like that. It was pure luck! I nearly didn't go to the meeting, as I was so busy. That building is used a lot for that sort of thing you know. Anyway I did go and I am so glad that I have met you again, Emily. I will phone you in a couple of weeks and see how things are with you. Maybe we could go for a walk on a Sunday or something like that if you would like to?"

I wondered how he would manage that, with his family to entertain at the weekend, but I kept these thoughts to myself and said that, yes, I should like that - if it is on a Sunday when I was not visiting my mother. We chatted away and suddenly the evening was over and he sent me home in a cab. I couldn't help thinking how different he was from Lawrence, such a lovely dinner (he wouldn't ever ask for the old menu I was sure of that, and then to send me home in a cab) yes - very different.

The apartment, with no one in it but me, was a dreary place. In the evening, eating my meal alone in my dark, dreary, brown apartment, my mind inevitably returned to England, to my life as it was there. I thought of the country walks, my little house - and Maxwell! I hated to think about him in England, without us. Yet, as I thought these things, I remembered his letters; he sounded happy and was in love! He probably didn't miss us at all! He was doing so well too and there were prospects of him teaching in the not too distant future.

It really was just me having such a bad time. This horrible apartment wasn't doing me any good either; I decided to find a nicer place - light and bright. Yes, that was exactly what I would do.

I felt better now that I had made the decision. Move first, then apply to one or more of the employers on my list.

"Would you like to go for a walk in the park?" It was Andrew and it was a Sunday morning. His voice on the telephone was all perky. Actually I was not in the mood for a walk in the park, but I said I would like that.

He picked me up in his tumbledown car. It was a nice feeling

have to try harder, make an effort. It was different then, I was doing it for fun, for the experience."

After reporting to the personnel officer I was taken to the department where I would be working.

Here, there were glamorous women everywhere I looked. Most of them looked as if they were going to a party, dressed in silky dresses and high-heeled sandals. Exotic perfume wafted around their glossy heads. Tinselled fingernails rang up sales. They were certainly a pleasure to look at and so friendly and helpful, the atmosphere was wonderful. However, my English tweeds, woollies and sturdy brogues were certainly not suitable attire. On my way home I stopped at a very gorgeous shop and spent more than I should on two super outfits. It was a wise decision, money I couldn't afford to spend, well spent.

The small studio apartment I had found near Stanley Park was comfortable and bright, not in a house, but in a relatively new apartment block which also had an indoor swimming pool. I was no longer living in dark, depressing rooms. I could walk to work. My life had greatly improved. I felt reasonably settled and happier than I had for quite some time. It was a relief.

When the letter came from Alan, it gave me pleasure to read it and to remember the nice times that we had together, although his letter was a little sad. He wondered how I was getting on. Had I ever thought of coming back? He would love me to come back and to marry him. "I am sure we could be happy together if you gave it a chance. All I want is your happiness, Emily. By the way, that silly dog of yours is just as silly as ever, but quite well!" I read the letter, the brief thought of returning connected, in my mind, all of my nostalgia. To be married again, all settled in that cottage in the country with a man I did like, more than a little. But the thought skipped away, I was not going to do either of those things. It had taken me a long time to get this far and things were very much better than they had been and the boys were doing fine. They were settled and seemed happy. I couldn't possibly disrupt everything now. And mother too, had become used to me being about to help her. It would be devastating for her if I left now! I was very fond of Alan, but I would have to write and tell him that I had settled at last and was going to stay, but it would be nice to keep in touch with him. I would love to hear from him from time to time. If I ever went back for a visit it would be nice to see him. I thanked him for inviting me to marry him, I didn't know quite how else to put it, but I had actually appreciated the offer, it was nice to think of.

Andrew and I had lunch together occasionally, it turned out that his wife's holiday did not help her as much as they had hoped. He told me about his disappointment and that they were both trying to recover the marriage.

Christmas was coming - and so were David and Joey, to spend it with me. I was so very pleased and excited about having them and, even though the apartment was so small, I planned to have a tree. With my newly-earned money I would be able to be a little extravagant for once and buy them some unexpected gifts as well as the usual sweaters and socks. I was really looking forward to cooking a proper Christmas dinner for them - I had even made a Christmas pudding.

With Christmas over, David and Joey had gone back to Prince George, they said they would be back for the next long week-end, it had been fun having them about again. We had talked and laughed a lot. They had fun swimming in the pool too.

When the letter arrived from Maxwell I opened it with my usual feeling of pleasure and pride. He wrote so well. He was so mature, so intellectual. I was certainly proud of him.
I read:

Dear, Mum,
I don't know how to tell you this. I can barely bring myself to write it. Victoria is dead.
It was a horrible accident. I am really to blame for her death. You see, we went down to Salcombe for a week-end. We took a tent. We hired a little sailboat and went out. It is, as you know, very sheltered there and popular for sailing. The weather was a bit changeable. However we felt confident. It was so sudden, it

caught us completely by surprise. A great gust came along and we were just not prepared for it. It was such a small craft, suddenly we were over! It had capsized! The water was pretty cold. I couldn't see Victoria anywhere - I swam around and dived under, looking and looking. She was a good swimmer, so I wasn't too worried until I looked and saw that we were a long way out. At some point I realized she was probably under the gib and she was. I should have looked there first, of course! She was struggling and cold, I got her out and off she went, swimming like mad, I couldn't stop her. I shouted to her to stop and wait with the boat, she paid no attention. I panicked and swam too, trying to catch up. I saw her slow down and saw her sort of sink with her head floating a bit. She disappeared. When I got to about where I thought she had been, I couldn't find her. She'd gone! I dived over and over, looking for her, but I was really freezing, the water was so cold, I looked as much as I could but I knew I had to get out soon; by this time our plight had been spotted and I was soon wrapped in blankets and taken to the pub to warm up. I was fine in no time at all.

Her body washed up on the beach four days later.

I know it was my fault. Naturally her parents blame me, her brother is in a terrible state. What no one seems to realize is that I loved her too, we were going to be married. I can think of nothing else. I go over and over the whole thing. I will see her swimming away from me there for the rest of my life. I will blame myself for the rest of my life too.

I can't seem to do anything. I just sit here thinking about it.

You would have loved her, Mum. She was so elegant, very slim, (too slim for that cold water). She was an art student too as you know, and so clever. We were very in love. What have I done! What am I to do!

Love from,
Maxwell

When I had read this terrible letter, I wanted to go to him now, this minute! Oh, my, how awfully sad! I sat thinking about the horror of Victoria's death, his pain, his guilt, the misery he was in.

I replied, I tried to give some comfort. How was it possible to comfort him from this distance! If only I could be there. If only I could telephone him, but he didn't have a telephone, none of his student friends had one either; far too expensive, not like here where everyone had a telephone. All I could do was write to him and hope I had some of the right words.

It was hard for me to concentrate at work. The terrible picture of the accident kept intruding on all my thoughts.

The manager (Helen - she had said to use her Christian name) of my department was a warm, pleasant woman. I decided it would be best if I told her what had happened; and it might help to talk about it with her. It would also explain my perhaps not so cheerful countenance these days. As I expected, she was a sympathetic listener, it was a relief to talk to her.

Several weeks later, there was a telegram waiting for me. I went cold with fear even before I opened it.

The telegram in its terse prose told me that Maxwell was in a mental hospital, following a severe mental breakdown. Would I be able to come? They thought it might be helpful. Although heavily sedated, he had asked for me repeatedly.

Of course I would go! There was no question about it. If the manager wouldn't allow it, I would go anyway. But the decision may not be up to her. Well, I was going. My poor, poor son. He who was always so balanced, so realistic. To be in a mental hospital, he must be in a very bad state.

The trip would be very expensive, but thank goodness for magic cards. I would telephone Nancy and Stephen - perhaps they would put me up for a short spell. They were such pleasant, kind friends and always so helpful.

First things first. I must ask Helen. Her face crumpled in sympathetic smiles "Of course you must go, of course you must. Don't you worry about losing your job, no such thing will happen. You should probably go as soon as you can."

I agreed and thanked her for her understanding, for being so kind.

I telephoned Nancy and Stephen and told them the whole story, they were shocked, quite horrified.

"The poor chap! How awful, Emily! Yes yes Emily, of course you must come here. When you get to Exeter, telephone us and we will come and get you. You can stay here as long as you like. We will be so happy to see you again."

I telephoned Lawrence, he said he had been informed about Maxwell and also had been told that I would be going to see him.

"I think you are the better one to deal with this Emily; Maxwell and I don't get on and really never have and although I feel very sorry about what has happened I wouldn't be much use. I will go at some point but I believe it should be when Maxwell is on the mend, now would not be the right time."

I listened, I agreed with his thoughts but as I put the telephone down I was filled with a heavy sadness. What a terrible shame, I thought.

I telephoned Andrew to tell him what had happened and when I would be leaving. He offered to take me to the airport which didn't really surprise me; he seemed to be that sort of person, generally helpful. I gratefully accepted. I was feeling very alone and it was good to have his support.

MAXWELL

As the train chugged slowly into Exeter station my memories rushed in and filled me with nostalgia.

I telephoned Nancy and Stephen and it was not long before they were there picking up my case, hugging me and bustling me into their car.

At the house, Stephen poured me a substantial Scotch. "There - you drink that!"

They wanted to know more about Maxwell and of course more about our lives in Canada. After I had filled them in as much as I could, they brought me up to date on all the village gossip.

It was a long bus ride to the hospital, winding in and out of all the small villages on the way. By the time I arrived I was quite jittery.

I walked through the huge gates and saw that all the hospital windows were barred, Once inside, I was shown into a sort of reception room, a bare room, a few wooden chairs - no pictures, a room without comfort. One or two people were wandering around in a zombie-like way, obviously very ill.

I was shocked when I saw Maxwell coming towards me, he walked in the same manner as the other patients I had seen. He was unkempt, his face was pale, without expression, his eyes, glazed, were in dark hollows. My God I thought, what had they done to him! He looked terrible, terrible! He came to me and I put my arms around him.

"Mum," he said, "Mum."

I let go of him and held his hands. "Can we leave here? Would it be alright?"

"Yes, we can go. Where would we go?"

"I think it would be a good idea to take you shopping for a start." I told him. "Anyway, let's get out of this awful place!"

In the city, I bought him a new set of clothes, then we went to a nice old pub and had a delicious pub lunch. That was when he told me that he had been receiving electric-shock treatment.

"I hate it, but I've not been given any alternative. I just have to get out of that place, Mum. I'm sedated all the time. I can't think properly."

I didn't know what to say, I would have to wait until I had talked to his doctor. Maybe I could get him out. I told him this and then I asked him if there was anything he would like to do before I took him back. He said he would like to visit some friends. We did, which cheered him up and his friends said that they would visit him as much as possible at the hospital.

Each day I went to the hospital, Maxwell would be waiting for me, then we would go into the city. I hoped getting him out of the hospital environment would help him to feel like a normal person again. I wondered if it would help if David and Joey and I came back to England and set up house again? Have Maxwell at home, give him support, build him up mentally and so gradually lift him out of this deep depression and get him focused again on his degree. This I discussed with the doctor.

"No. No," the doctor was adamant, "this would not help him, he would become dependent on you Mrs Love and he would weaken, not strengthen. Maxwell needs medical help now and when he is at the right point he will go to a halfway house where he will have his freedom but will be monitored. If all goes well, he can then go back to his college. You see, after that accident he did nothing at college. His marks went to the bottom. He has been very ill. Getting him better will take time, but it must be handled the right way. For you to come back and look after him would not be the right way!"

This surprised me, but I trusted the doctor - he must know what would be best.

I had to leave, my two weeks had come to an end. I went to the hospital, I gathered up Maxwell and we went for our last pub lunch; afterwards Maxwell came to the bus to see me off. I knew that the sight of him, waving to me with that sad smile, would never leave me. I ached with love and sadness.

At last, off the bus, I hurried along the lane. Out of sight, I leaned against a tree and sobbed. How could I go on? How could I leave him like this? Oh God, how could I. I should not leave him, what was I to do?

Nancy and Stephen must have been waiting and listening for me to open the gate. They were there on the step. I stumbled up the steps to them, still crying. Their arms were wide, "Come, come, dear girl, you poor dear. Come in here by the fire."

"Which shall it be - tea or Scotch?" Nancy asked.

"Forget the tea, darling - Emily needs a Scotch!"

I told them what the doctor said - what did they think? They said that surely, the doctor must know what was best. What did I think? I had to agree really because he was the one with the knowledge. In my heart I felt that I should be with him, but the way that the doctor had explained it did make some sense. All I could do was abide by his decision and then, if Maxwell did not improve as expected, I would have to think about it again. Stephen and Nancy believed that even a deep depression could and would lift. Eventually Maxwell would realize that the accident was not altogether his fault. After talking with them, I calmed down. They agreed with my proposed plan; they thought that was the most practical way to deal with the situation. After all, they said, you really would have to wait and see, maybe Maxwell will start to improve quite soon and, who knows, it may not be long at all until he is right back to normal. Just sit tight Emily, for now, wait and see.

I thought they were right.

DAVID

Home at last, I rang David, he was thrilled - he had passed his exams and had placed first.

"Imagine, Mum - me coming at the top like that! Maybe when I finish I'll go back to school and do dentistry. The owner of the lab said that he thought I should! He said that he had known a couple of chaps who had done that. Do you think I should?"

"Oh David, I think it is a wonderful idea, I really do. Anyway, you have plenty of time to think about it, don't you?"

He asked about Maxwell, I told him that he was a little better but has a long way to go. "You see he just goes on blaming himself. But it really wasn't entirely his fault. They were kibitzing about a bit, they were both taken by surprise. Victoria had sailed before too. However, I guess one does have to see that Maxwell was at fault to some degree, but not to the extent of ruining his whole life because of it. He'll have to get a lot better before he will be able to carry on with his degree. Anyway, he is a little better. His friends have been wonderful, visiting him and trying to keep his morale up. Anything like that helps. You'll write to him won't you, David? Just send it to his old address, a friend picks up his post and takes it to him."

"OK, Mum, we'll both write."

It was rather nice to be back at work with a routine to follow; plenty to occupy my mind.

Occupying my mind too at this time was the fact that Andrew and his wife had decided to divorce. He had moved into an apartment near the water in Ambleside in West Vancouver; the children stayed with him at weekends. He was sad about it, but, on the other hand, he and his wife were both dissatisfied with the relationship. Although I was rather fascinated with him and would like to go out with him as he suggested, I knew that he had a lot of sorting out to do. I was quite happy with my unexciting, peaceful life for the present.

There was a letter from David. He had a girlfriend:

"She is older than I am and has just broken off with her boyfriend. So she is a little confused at the moment, but willing to go out with me. I like her a lot, but as she was always with this other chap I never thought I would have the chance to take her out. She works for one of the dentists I work for. She is lots of fun."

When I read this I was pleased but a little concerned. David had never had a girlfriend before. I hoped this girl on the rebound did not hurt him and was not using him to fill in until she made up with the other chap. My David was so sensitive, he could easily get hurt. And, this being his first love, would make him very vulnerable.

David's letters now were all about this girl. How she was sometimes off him, sometimes on him. She couldn't seem to make up her mind who she wanted. His letters were up and down. He and Joey thought they would go on holiday together. Two weeks camping. He had been thinking he might like to come and live in Vancouver for a while - he could get a job easily and so could Joey. He needed time too to decide about doing dentistry, he had more or less already decided but it would be nice to have a job for a while first. He thought that he would finish with the girl; he was fed up with the on and off stuff.

Maybe after they have had their holiday they would come and look around in Vancouver.

I thought it would be lovely to have them so near. I told him that it would probably was a good idea to break off with the girl since she was so undecided. Coming to Vancouver would help him to make the break, I told him.

The next letter was from Kelowna where he and Joey were on holiday. He sounded happy and said that he and Joey were having a great time. They had decided to go to England for a visit and planned to stay with Maxwell now that Maxwell was so much better and had his own little place. They would visit me before they left.

Sleeping bags and backpacks littered my tiny apartment for a few days; at night their long legs and arms seemed to sprawl over my entire floor. Their deep voices with the sound of laughter in them greeted me after work. There was speculation about Maxwell, David said he was going to try to get him to come to

Canada. "I really think he would love it here Mum, once he got used to everything, don't you?"

"I'm not so sure David, not really, but do try to persuade him – it would be a relief to have him here with us. You know it will be his 21st birthday before long so I've had the family crest ring made for him so you can take it with you, much easier than posting it. He's the first one to get the ring, you are next, David - and I've already ordered it for you. Anyway for goodness sake don't lose it!"

David laughed, "I won't, Mum, but I think I will wear it, save a lot of bother at Customs."

"Yes - a good idea David, but don't forget to give it to him!"

"Oh Mum!"

It seemed no time at all before they were back, staying in an apartment in the west end. David telephoned to give me the news of Maxwell "He wasn't really completely back to his usual self because sometimes he is silent and sad but at least it is not all the time and he is working hard to get his degree you know."

Although Joey had been to see me, David had not. I kept asking Joey about David; I just couldn't understand why he had not come to see me. David was depressed again, just like he was when he had that girlfriend in Prince George, Joey explained.

"He doesn't want to come to see you until he feels better. He feels too down at the moment, Mum."

"What's bothering David so much?"

"I don't know, Mum. I don't think he really knows either. We had a nice time in England and he said he was glad he didn't live there anymore. He prefers it here - so do I for that matter!"

I would soon be leaving to spend a month with Edgar and Madeleine who were now living on one of the Gulf Islands, just off the east coast of Vancouver Island. I had asked for a month's leave of absence as I had been feeling very tired, exhausted really and I believed that a complete break would help. Edgar and Madeleine had suggested I spend the month with them.

"Tell him he can come and visit me at Uncle Edgar's on the island. Why don't both of you come? What does he do all day?"

"Not much, Mum. He reads a lot and goes for walks. He

sends his love."

"Well," I told him, "be sure and give him mine and tell him what I have told you - don't forget!"

I was bewildered. David needed to talk, why didn't he come and see me. He had always been such a talker. Being alone and depressed was unhealthy. As he did not have a phone I was unable to contact him that way. I decided to go and see him before I left, have a good long chat with him. The boys were out when I arrived. I waited, hoping they would come back soon, but eventually I had to leave. I had stayed out in the cold too long and I felt cold and very disappointed that I hadn't seen him. I went home. I didn't know how to cope with the situation; I was too tired. I was longing to get to my brother's. I couldn't remember feeling this tired in my whole life. I would write to David as soon as I was at Madeleine and Edgar's.

Not long after I arrived at Madeleine and Edgar's, I started receiving David's letters, they were strangely religious. He said he wanted to abandon the material life and thought that I should do the same. He wanted his life to be pure and to find peace. He wanted to become as one with Jesus Christ. Although his letters went on like this, I could still find the David I knew, hidden between these strange sentences. I hoped my letters to him would comfort him and be helpful but I thought the real help would be when I returned and could talk to him.

It was a Saturday morning in January when Joey arrived at my apartment; I had just returned from Madeleine and Edgar's.

"Where's David?"

"He's gone."

"Gone? What do you mean, Joey - gone? Gone where?"

"Come and sit down, Mum."

We sat down. He told me that David did not come back from a walk he was going on the day before. He had waited and waited, but no David. "I looked in his room and saw that he had left his passport, driver's license, money and family crest ring, in a neat arrangement on the bed."

"But where would he go? Where? Did he say anything before he left?"

"No, not really - but he had been a little strange lately, Mum.

ALL IS WELL WITH MAXWELL

"Emily?" It was mother on the telephone, she was now in the hospital section of a nursing home; she too had cancer, the same kind as Daphne had, bone cancer. "I know you are coming tomorrow, dear, but could you come to-day as well? I do want to see you about something."

"Of course mother, I'll come right after lunch - is there anything I can bring you?"

"No, no dear, nothing, just yourself."

When I got there, mother was in her bed, where she was most of the time nowadays. Mother would rather sit, but it was becoming too painful for her. "My, you look lovely Emily, red does suit you well, doesn't it!"

"Thank you mother. How are you, what was it you wanted to see me about?"

I looked at mother lying there so frail now; I picked up her hand, her once such strong hands, now just bones, I held it in mine.

"Well, I haven't been sleeping much, that is why I hoped you would come to-day. I wanted you to ask the doctor to arrange for me to have more morphine? I just am not getting enough. I have asked but it would be better if you asked, would you dear?"

"Of course I will. I'll go and see the doctor about it, then he can prescribe more for you, that would be the best way I think. I'll do that on the way home."

I sat on the side of the bed so that I could be closer to her. I told her about Maxwell's latest letter. "I'll read it to you."

Dear Mum,

I know you will be pleased to hear that I did pass my exams and now have my degree in Fine Arts. I passed with honours. It was hard to go back after being in hospital so long, it was hard to concentrate. Anyway, I did it!

I am much better, although I do still have spells of depression and my memory is not too good. I have been told that is due to the electric-shock treatments. One good thing though, is that I am getting to know a very nice girl. We enjoy many of the same things so it has helped me very much. It's not the same sort of relationship as Victoria and I had, but it is nice all the same. I like her a lot and I don't feel lonely anymore.

I keep thinking about David. Like you, I think he will turn up some day. We had such a great time when he was here. I got him to do some drawing, did he tell you that? He was good at it too. We talked a lot. He really liked living in Canada. He told me that he wouldn't want to live over here again. Well anyway, I think about him a lot. I told Christine about him. That is her name, by the way!

Be sure and tell Grandma about my degree! She will be pleased.

Love
from
Maxwell

When I finished reading the letter I saw that mother was dozing.

"Did you hear me, mother?"

"Yes dear, I did. Isn't that nice - that after all that trouble he did get his degree. And a new girlfriend as well. That will be good for him I am sure. I enjoyed the letter, dear and it was nice to hear your voice. I like the sound of your voice, a pleasant voice. You have been a lovely daughter, dear. I am very proud of you."

Tears filled my eyes.

"Thank-you mother, you've been a pretty nice mother, you know!"

I gave her a big hug, "Now I must away if I'm to see that doctor before I go home."

I tried hard to concentrate on Maxwell's letter. It gave me such a glow. I was so pleased with him. All the same, it was difficult to keep the sadness at bay. Poor mother, I guess she knows there isn't much longer for her. It would be strange not to have her anymore, I really couldn't imagine my life without mother.

When I entered the doctor's office, he was ready to leave.

"Why Emily, what is the matter? My, you do look nice in red, you wear too much black you know! Now, what is it?"

"It's mother, she needs more morphine. Could you possibly arrange it for her to-day?"

He patted me on the shoulder, "It is a tough time for you, I know. Maybe you would like a sedative?"

"No, I'm fine, I'll be alright."

"Well," he said, "don't you worry, I'll drop in to the nursing home and arrange that right now, I am going that way anyway."

He came over and put his arm around my shoulder.

"Poor girl. I'm sorry. No news of your son I guess?"

"No, none." I dabbed at my face and managed a smile and thanked him for his help. He had been kind and sympathetic, even though he was such a busy man.

I wondered just how long mother had left to live; each time I was with her I saw a change. Although she was cheerful I knew that she was afraid of death, I could see it in her eyes.

"Are you getting enough morphine now, Mother? Are you sleeping a bit better?"

"Yes dear, thank you for arranging that. It has been a great help having you here so much, keeping an eye on things, you know. I am sure it does make a difference to the way one is looked after in these places."

I thought so too.

Then she said "Thank you for all you have done, dear, you really are a lovely daughter."

"Oh, Mother!"

I did not visit mother on Sunday as Edgar was going to be there and the nurse had said that one at a time was enough. Monday morning, the phone rang - it was the Hospital.

"You should come this morning, Emily, your mother is losing ground."

When I arrived, mother was not conscious. I sat on the bed holding mother's hands and talked to her. I told her how I remembered all the nice times we had had together, the talking, the walking. Those wonderful summers at Redroofs. About Christmases and how wonderful they had been. I watched mother's face, but nothing happened. Then I heard her give a little groan. At the corners of her mouth, I could see a tiny smile, it was hardly discernible, but I was sure I could see one. After a while I held my head very close to mother's and talked right into her ear.

"Can you hear me Mother? Can you?" There was a little groan. "I love you, Mother," I told her, "I love you."

I put my arms around her, under her shoulders, I put my face on mother's cool face.

"Mother! Mother! Oh Mother, don't go!" But mother had died. Her breathing had stopped. I slipped my arms from under her shoulders and sat silent and still, looking at my mother who was not there anymore. Inside me, was where my mother would live now, forever.

At home, I lay on my bed trying to absorb my loss, I would miss my mother, it was a terrible feeling not to have her anymore. A strange, lonely feeling.

A WEDDING

"Mum?"

"Yes dear, what is it? You sound excited?"

"I am a bit, but I hope you won't think I am choosing the wrong time to tell you this. I mean, just after Grandma has died and stuff."

"Well, tell me and let me be the judge of that."

"Beth and I are going to be married!"

"But Joey, that's marvellous! It is a good time to tell me! It really is! I need something to rejoice about! When? Is it to be soon? Oh I am so glad, such a great girl!"

"Actually I knew right from the beginning that you would like her, Mum. We think June would be a nice month. We thought maybe we could use your garden. Have the wedding and the reception, everything outside. Usually June is a good month don't you think?"

"Perfect, dear. We would love to have it in our garden - I think that is a lovely idea. It is a good time of the year for our garden too. Well that's exciting news, very! I am delighted."

The day was perfect! Glorious! Beth's parents had arranged it all. There had been nothing for me to do. The garden was full of flowers, wafts of fragrances floated about in the summer air. Beth really did have stars in her eyes! Her embossed, pure-white, cotton dress so simple and elegant, suited her well. Her hands that she worried about so much, had been creamed and manicured to perfection. That wonderful, dark, heavy hair looked as though it had been polished with beeswax.

Joey was a little shy with all of this fuss and bother! He wasn't the type who liked a lot of fuss, however, this was really for Beth and he was certainly doing his best to enjoy it all. They were a very handsome couple. He, with his European, dark good looks and wonderful posture, they went together well. Hopefully they would start a family before too long, now that would be nice! A slight chill ran over my spine as my thoughts turned to David - wishing so much that he could have been here.

Just before they left, Joey came over and thanked Andrew and me for everything.

"It went off well, don't you think?"

"Yes," I agreed, "it was lovely, dear."

Then he said quietly, "I wish David had been here."

That was all. He quickly moved away from me. Beth was swirling about saying good-bye to everyone. She certainly had enjoyed the day. Not a thing went wrong! The sun kept on shining and the soft breeze kept everyone comfortable, made to order it was! The food was delicious. Yes, it had been one of those idyllic days.

It wasn't long before I received the good news that Beth was pregnant. It gave me a good feeling to have them so settled, so happy with each other. Soon there would be a baby, a wonderful time in one's life. I thought of my years with my babies and the pleasure of watching them grow and develop. It made me a little envious somehow. It all goes by so quickly, that's the trouble. And of course one is so busy, but in today's world there is more time to enjoy one's babies: with washing machines, disposable nappies, dryers and such. Why, when I think that I didn't even have a refrigerator, or a washing machine, no modern conveniences at all really, but I did love my life with the children, they were happy times and are for most women, I think.

DEATH

There was a rather strange phone call for me. It was Miss Foster from the Missing Persons department of the police. They would like David's dental records.

"Why do you want them?" I was taken by surprise, "Why now?"

Miss Foster told me that they suddenly realized that they didn't have them.

"Can you get them for us?"

I said that I could, but it would take a day or two. "I guess you're not in any hurry after all this time! I mean it's eight years since he went missing!"

"Yes I know, but it would be helpful if you could get them to us as soon as possible - just to get things in order, you know."

I said that I would see to it immediately, I thought no more about it after I sent them off.

Visiting Beth, I told her about it. "All the same, it was perhaps a little strange but I guess these things do happen even in the police department. Beth agreed but said she didn't think she would mention it to Joey.

"I didn't tell you, Emily, but, a few weeks ago, Joey saw a blond, young man begging on the street. Joey thought it was David! He brought him home! The guy was broke and dirty, into drugs of course. Joey washed all of his clothes and we fed him and gave him some money. Joey was convinced it was David! Thought maybe he had had amnesia. Or that he had been cast out of a religious group - something like that. I didn't think it was him and luckily I found a photograph of David and, once Joey saw it, he realized that it wasn't David!"

"How sad, Beth. I guess we will all go on looking for him and hoping he will turn up someday. Please God, that he will! I miss him so much."

At home as I ran up the stairs I was thinking about David and what a very horrible experience that had been for Joey.

"Emily? Emily?" It was Andrew - he was standing in the doorway of the study. "Emily, come in here, love."

We went in together and he shut the door.

"Emily," he said - "Emily," he said it again. I looked at him, what was he trying to say? He looked at me, he seemed sort of nervous and then he pushed his hand across his forehead, "Emily darling, the police have phoned - you see love, David's remains have been found."

I looked at him, "His remains? You mean he is dead?"

"Yes Emily, he is dead. The report says that he probably died of hypothermia; that he had planned to die that way. In other words, suicide. There was no sign of violence and he was not wearing winter clothes and it was January, a very cold January too. He has been dead for eight years according to the report."

"Dead! Oh God! No! No! No!" I shouted it over and over. "No! I won't let him be dead! He can't be dead! They are wrong! I know that they are! There must have been a mistake, there must have been. I can't believe it!" my eyes bored into him, I kept screaming at him.

"Emily love, there is no mistake - the dental records match. Oh Emily - I am so terribly sorry."

"No, no! Oh my son, don't be dead! I'll never see him again! Never! Never! Oh God! I can't bear it!"

Andrew watched her. He heard her screaming and shouting, her face wet with tears pouring out of her eyes. He kept saying, "Emily, Emily - I am so terribly sorry."

He also was crying. It was too much for him to see her. She threw herself on to the floor, then she got up and seemed to move around in circles. He put his arms around her but she could not be comforted in this way. She went on sobbing, then screaming with anger. He continued to watch her and he could do nothing to help her.

At last, she left the room.

Andrew came into the bedroom, covered me and pulled the curtains. "I must tell Lawrence, Andrew. I'll send him a telegram first thing in the morning, Oh God."

I lay there on the bed. I wished I could die too, then I could be with my son. Please God, let me die, let me die. The thought that I would never see him again was unbearable.

I must pull myself together and phone Joey. How would I do it? How? It was Beth who answered the phone. I told her.

"Oh no! I'll get Joey."

When I told Joey about his brother, he was very quiet and then he said, "Maybe it was what I thought Mum, maybe."

"I must send a cable to your father Joey, and to Maxwell. These things have to be done right away, I'll talk to you later, dear."

At last, in the dark room, with Andrew asleep, I allowed my mind to return to my little, blond, blue-eyed baby. David had come a little early, but he had not been difficult to bring into this world. He had been a quiet, contented baby and had seldom cried. He had slept under the trees in his pram, that lovely pram with the fluttery canopy. He had watched the leaves drifting and floating in the summer breezes. I had dressed him in white silk rompers. So pretty he had looked, so soft and sweet. So heavenly to pick up. In my arms with his silken hair against my face. His sweet, warm, milk breath breathing into my breast. I remembered the Sundays visiting Lawrence's parents, the aunts and uncles. How he was passed around, admired, kissed and cuddled. Love was in abundance, it had surrounded him. He absorbed it and smiled to us. He was our beautiful baby. His life had joined ours, we were a family then. Mummy, Daddy, Maxwell and then David. How wonderful it had been!

How could it be that he has gone forever! It was too awful - and then - how would it be for Maxwell and Joey? It would be so hard for them. Oh dear, why oh why did he do this to us. It seemed to me that all the sadness, all the heartbreak, was coming out of me in a torrent, a torrent I had no power to stop, it came and flowed through me, my whole being was submerged in this overpowering grief. We all loved him so much! Exhausted, sleep finally entered my bedroom and took me to a dreamless sleep. A respite.

Time went by, but I dreamed of David more and more. Sometimes I thought I heard him calling me softly, "Mum, Mum!" I could feel his presence in the room, it felt very near. I would awaken and lie there absorbing his presence with sobs shaking me and tears sliding over my face. Andrew tried to comfort me.

This grief would always be with me, part of me, until I died. The pain when I thought about David would always come and hurt me. I would have to learn to accept this and live with it.

When David's ashes arrived I had the finality of his death in my arms. I carried the heavy box close to my tummy, remembering when he was actually inside me. The day was beautiful, sunny and windy. Andrew and I planted an oak tree, David's favourite. We buried the box with the ashes in it, as I was unable to take them out - I knew I could not bear to actually see his ashes.

OH DAVID

If I could hold you one more time
If I could tell you one more nursery rhyme
If I could tousle your little fair head
If I could cuddle you and tuck you in your bed
If I could look into your eyes and see them shine
If I could tell you again that you are mine
If I could chase you to hear you giggle
If I could give you that little tickle
If I could see your body wriggle
If for one more time you could be mine
I would give you all my love - all the time.

DAVID'S GHOST

Sometimes, standing at the window looking through the trees, I would see him coming towards me, he wears a jacket - a tweed jacket, yes - and a tie. He seems tall when I see him thus - his hair still so fair but I can't see his face, not exactly, not the eyes. His blue eyes, kind eyes. He walks by - not to come in, I know! I know! But I did see him - so clearly. I have seen him often, no special time that he comes. The leaves of the trees dance and tangle in his hair, the outline of his jacket blurs with the tree bark, he walks on and away. I watch him fade and disappear into the shadow of the trees.

I wish he wouldn't go, but he will be back - I don't know when, no, I don't know when.

A BABY

Beth had her baby! A little boy! He wasn't little at all, he weighed 10 pounds! My first grandson; his name is David. I received a letter from Maxwell:

Dear Mum,
Thank-you for sending me the telegram.
I just can't believe that David is dead. He certainly was religious when he was here, talked about becoming one with Jesus, things like that. About leading a pure life. He had a book called "The Prophet". He liked to read it all the time. But somehow I thought it was just a phase and that he would get over it. Do you think he went out there with the purpose of dying? It sort of seems like that, doesn't it? January is usually pretty cold and you say that Joey told you he was wearing those sandals and bare feet and light cotton jeans and a thin shirt! And leaving all of his things like that. Is that what you think too? He didn't seem depressed when he was here.
To know that he no longer exists has made me feel very lonely. It is certainly strange to think that we won't see him again. How is Joey doing? He is lucky to have a wife and a baby now. I am sure he is happy. I guess he never gets depressed! He has always been happy hasn't he! I have to admit that I still get a bit down. I would like to get married too, but the doctor has warned me that this depression could be a chronic condition that may stay with me. Christine says that she could accept that. The trouble is that I really don't want to have children, maybe someday, but at the moment I know I just could not cope with a child, so I would have to be much better than this. Christine says that she would cope. I don't know really if I could, even if she did all the coping!
It is nice that Beth has named her baby David.
I have invited a few friends over to celebrate my birthday. Some of the friends who were so nice to me while I was in hospital. I have never bothered with doing anything like this before, but it will be nice to see my friends as I don't see them very often now. Anyway, it is a couple of weeks until then so I have given them plenty of time to arrange to come. It is for afternoon tea, I make quite good scones now!
I have written to Joey.

I hope you are feeling OK, Mum.
Love from, Maxwell

P. S. I wrote and asked Alan to come too. He sometimes pops in to see how I am and have news of you on his way to his other shop. He usually brings that silly dog too. I think he is quite lonely you know. Maybe he won't come. I always thought he liked David and Joey better than me, but he is very friendly.

I read the letter and it made my heart ache. He certainly sounded a bit down, but, after all, that was to be expected! I wished I could have been there, although it probably wouldn't be a lot of help. The best person for Maxwell now was Christine. She was the one who would do the most good. It would be nice if they did get married, I hoped they would. She seemed a nice young woman and so caring. I thought I would write and encourage Maxwell to think about marriage. Tell him that if Christine is ready to accept his problem, then it would probably work out.

I would write to Alan too and encourage him to go to Maxwell's little celebration. It is probably good for Maxwell to have someone like that to talk to from time to time. He might be able to cheer him up and the fact that Alan admires Maxwell's paintings so much, maybe he could try to sell one or two of them at his shop - which would give Maxwell a boost. Anyway, I enjoyed writing to him; it was still pleasant, to have an admirer, even if one was happily married.

AN ACCIDENT

It was lunch time when the phone rang. I picked it up and before I could say a word, a voice that was very familiar was saying "Emily, Emily, is that you?"

"Yes, it is. Who is this?"

"Emily it's me - Alan. Emily, something terrible has happened."

"What is it for goodness sake?"

"Emily there has been an accident. Emily, are you still there?"

"Yes."

"Emily, Maxwell has been killed. He was on his motor bike."

"Killed? Oh no, ALAN, No!"

I couldn't move. Oh God. Shock and disbelief filled me. How could it be? Maxwell! How could it have happened, how! Oh dear God, my son, my beautiful son. "Tell me, Alan, tell me what happened."

"Well, I'll begin at the beginning. As you know, Maxwell had planned a little celebration for his birthday. He had asked a couple from Exeter, one of his friends from college and a single girl and me. His girlfriend was not there for some reason. Anyway, we were all waiting at his caravan. It was four o'clock. The light was going, not quite dark yet. It's very cold here at the moment and icy. The young woman knocked on the door. There was no answer. She rattled the door and called and there was still no answer. His motor bike was not there. There was a light on in the caravan. The door was locked.

"At first they thought that he had gone off to the shop at the corner, for some last-minute item. The girl went to look. He was not there. By this time, I was thinking I should go to the manager of the caravan site and get a key. The young people were anxious. The young chap mentioned Maxwell's problems with depression. Of course you had mentioned that in a letter some time ago but I had forgotten. But why wouldn't he be there? He had invited us for a specific time, so why wouldn't he be there? I really thought I should go to the manager. Time was getting on and it did seem odd that he was not there.

"It was just at this moment that the police officer arrived. He told us that Maxwell had come off his motor bike on the roundabout coming back from town. The roads were very icy and that area can get terribly foggy as well you know, Emily. Anyway he skidded, lost control - the police were going to contact you of course, but I felt it would be better if I did."

"Yes, Alan - I appreciate that. Thank you."

"Emily, I'm terribly sorry, terribly."

"I know Alan, thank you. I will come right over as soon as I am able to arrange it. Will you let whoever should know, know that I am coming?"

"Of course Emily. Let me know the train time and I will fetch you and take you to the caravan."

I thanked him and that ended the call.

When Andrew came home, I was quite calm, I told him the whole story.

"How terrible, He was killed instantly then?"

"Yes."

"Would you like me to come with you?"

"No, I would like to deal with this alone". My life in Devon had been a life with the boys, a life totally detached from my present life.

Andrew was concerned - "Will you be alright do you think?"

"Yes I will. I can cope, thank you. I don't expect it to be easy. I just hope that the thought of his little celebration made him happy and that he was happy thinking about it on his way home. I wonder why Christine wasn't there? Poor girl."

I wired Lawrence and told him I would contact him when I arrived in Devon.

It wasn't until I was on the train to Devon that the realization of Maxwell's death finally reached me.

Sitting there, travelling through the English countryside, I recalled those days when my children were young and thought of Maxwell as he had been then, a joyful little boy and so handsome. The train passed schools, parks, children on their bicycles and I remembered it all. He was not a rough boy, he had always this gentle way with him - really all of my children were like that. Maxwell was so sensitive; in some ways it was a nice quality but it could cause problems. It was hard to accept that I had lost two of my sons! I thought then of wars and of mothers who lost all of their sons! Sometimes they lost their husband as well!

By the time the train reached Newton Abbott I was exhausted. Thankfully, Alan was there. He came to me and grasped my hands.

"Emily darling, I am so, so sorry."

"Yes, it is awful."

We got in the car and drove to the caravan. It was eerie, I could feel Maxwell's presence, as if he might come out of the bedroom at any minute. Alan suggested I made a pot of tea.

"Oh, Alan, I need a Scotch - tea just won't do."

I fetched my Duty Free and poured us a drink. After a short time we went for dinner at the pub. When Alan left me, I promised to call him at some point. I thanked him for his kindness; he was such a thoughtful, kind person.

There was a lot to arrange. Also I must call Lawrence, maybe he would like to come down and help with things. The paintings, the diaries, the journals with the diagrams, drawings, poems, songs. Pages and pages of text. The way Maxwell had always done this, reminded me of Leonardo da Vinci, except that Maxwell's were not mirror images.

I got out some clean linen and made up the bed, I thought that I had never been so tired, so deeply sad.

Lying in bed, I felt Maxwell all around me. Drifting in and out of sleep I could hear him calling me "Mum, Mum!" in his gentle, quiet voice. I kept very still. I remembered having the same experience after David had died - he too, had called me.

When I awoke I could see frost on the inside of the window; the floor of the caravan felt just like ice, when I put my foot down on the linoleum. The air was cold, damp and I could see my breath. I lit the gas cooker and left the oven door open to heat the kitchen.

There was bread, Maxwell's home-made bread. He had asked me to teach him how to make it many years ago and once he knew how, he never bought another loaf of bread! A cup of tea and I was ready to go out into the cold morning to the corner store to buy a few groceries. The public telephone was there too, I would phone Lawrence.

Lawrence had never liked telephone conversations so I would have to quickly get to the point.

His voice on the telephone gave me a strange feeling. I had always loved his voice.

"Would you like to come and deal with a few things yourself? It would be helpful if you were here, you know?"

He hummed and hawed. Eventually he said that he would come and would arrive in two days.

The morning I expected Lawrence, Maxwell's ashes arrived.

Lawrence arrived at noon. I was nervous to see him. I had not seen him for thirty years; I wondered what it would be like to see him again. He was now over eighty - well, I was not young now either!

When I heard his car, I opened the door and the first thing I noticed was his white hair, pure white! But then, so was mine! He was quite heavy. He came to me. We shook hands and then he patted my arm (no hugs). I was pleased to see him again.

"Come in, come in!"

"Awful business this. Such a terrible waste."

We moved into the tiny sitting-room.

"I've boiled the kettle," I told him, "so I shall just go and make a pot of tea. I expect you are ready for a cup after your journey."

"Yes indeed I am, thank you Emily. A long drive that is." Then he started to look at the paintings on the walls.

"Quite remarkable his work! Yes - he certainly had talent. Didn't do enough though, not nearly enough. A shame."

We drank the tea and I showed him the box with the ashes.

"I thought we could go and scatter the ashes together, if that would be alright with you? I think the Moors would be the appropriate place. It's where he did all of his painting."

Lawrence agreed. We were quiet in the car. At the Moors he parked and we walked right to the peak. I recognized the area, as I had been there with Maxwell. Lawrence took out his little pen knife; I remembered the little knife, he had always carried it. Carefully Lawrence opened the box. It was not a windy day. He let the ashes out, shaking them about. As he did this we were silent and afterwards he looked at me. I saw him then, really saw him; he was old, his eyes were tired and sad, his military posture had vanished. My heart ached to see him so changed. In the car, he reached over and clasped my hand. I put my other hand over his, we were both weeping. After a few minutes we collected ourselves, dried our eyes, he turned and smiled, "We had better go and find some lunch I think."

He drove to the nearest pub and ordered sandwiches and coffee. He asked me if I was warm enough, would I like another pot of coffee, had I had enough to eat, would I like some cake?

That was all the conversation we had.

Back at the caravan I started sorting things out. Lawrence went off to make arrangements for paying the caravan's rent.

The only things to keep were the paintings and the journals and diaries. There were also letters. Many letters, most of them were mine; some were from Joey and David. I decided to keep all of these things.

When Lawrence returned, I asked him to choose a painting he liked.

"No, no, Emily, I don't want one, you take them."

"No, I think you should have one - if you decide you don't want it when you get home, give it to your niece - she would probably be pleased to have it."

Lawrence said that, alright, he would choose one.

After having dinner at the pub we returned to the caravan and I made some more coffee. It was getting late. Lawrence finished his coffee. Slowly and with effort, he got up and said it was time for him to find accommodation, "I should have seen to it earlier I know. Stupid of me, really."

Without thinking about what I was saying I said, "Why don't you stay here?"

"Oh, no I couldn't do that, Emily. Where would I sleep?"

"With me, of course!"

"With you? My Emily, you have changed! But of course I do realise times have changed but......."

"Oh for goodness sake Lawrence - I didn't mean I wanted to make love or anything like that!" I said, laughing - I could feel my face flush - I was suddenly embarrassed with my suggestion! "I just thought it would be nice to have each other's company, tonight."

He cleared his throat, "Well well, yes, I see what you mean, but what would the neighbours think? I am sure there are still people around with old-fashioned views of such goings on!"

"Really," I said, I laughed, "do you care? I certainly don't!"

"Well, of course you are right, why should we care what anyone thinks - perhaps I will! I'll just fetch my case."

I went to have a shower. When I got into bed, Lawrence arrived all dressed up in his winter pajamas and I was in my winter flannelette nightgown! So all was proper. I turned out the light. I felt his hand come over to mine.

Then he said, "A nice idea of yours, Tink, very nice."

It was very quiet and very dark. Lawrence began to talk.

He talked of a depression problem he had when he was at school and especially after the war, so maybe there was genetic propensity to depression that Maxwell had inherited from his father. "But Lawrence, you never mentioned to me about a depression problem - in fact you never talked about anything like that and certainly you never talked about the war, ever! I truly would have liked to have heard about your experiences."

"Well Tink, the fact is that it was the last thing I wanted to talk about; all I wanted to do was forget it, all of it. I don't honestly think I could have talked about it at that time."

"Maybe if you had said just those few words to me Lawrence, I would have had a better understanding of you altogether?"

"Perhaps you are right, but I wasn't much of a talker; one learns to keep a lot of thoughts to oneself when one spends one's whole life at a boarding school. I was only five when I went. I had never lived with anyone, not even my parents, until I lived with you. Mainly the maid looked after me if I was at home during any holidays. At university I lived alone in Digs, then in the Army, being an officer, I had my own room. So you see, I had little experience in exposing my thoughts, sharing them. Talking about the war and my experiences during it was too difficult and very painful. I felt I was lucky to be alive, a lot of the chaps in my unit weren't; some didn't even make it out of Dunkirk! I was one of the lucky ones, but it was a pretty terrible time and I didn't want to think about it or talk about it; for me it was a chapter in my life, closed, tightly at that. I couldn't help it, I couldn't seem to deal with my war any other way. War, Emily, damages people inside as well as outside."

"Yes I know Lawrence, I'm very sorry, I do wish I had known. If only you had said. I certainly didn't know you were at Dunkirk, even I knew about Dunkirk! I knew very little about the war really, I was too young and it was so remote, but I knew enough about it to understand how awful it was and what a terrible time some of the soldiers had. I had seen movies and I had read books so I certainly would have understood had you told me. It doesn't surprise me that you suffered from spells of depression, I am just so sorry that I had no idea what you had gone through and consequently lacked any understanding of you. A great pity", I told him - and it certainly was. In my heart I thought that his rather sterile childhood as well, was a large part of his problem.

We discussed David. He said he had no idea how all of that came about. None at all. A puzzle. He said he hadn't paid enough attention to David's rather strange philosophising when he and Joey had come to England for that holiday. He had thought it was a passing phase and hadn't taken the time to talk to him about it. "Poor David, but hopefully he was happy within himself, that is all we can hope for really, I suppose." I listened to his words but there was no comfort for me in them. My feeling was that David had not been happy, he had been troubled in some way and I desperately wished I could have helped him. I could never brush it away, I would always feel sad that I had not realized the depth of David's problems, perhaps if we had been living closer to each other it would never have happened because we would have talked the way we had always done. Who knows.

I told him the dream I sometimes had. "I don't have it is as often as I used to, but I still have it. You are standing some distance from me. You say to me, 'It is our anniversary time, you know Emily.' I walk over to you. 'Yes,' I say, 'it is to-day.' I put my arm around you and my head near yours. I say 'I am so sorry our marriage was not a success. I am so very sorry darling.' You lean toward me (you are still a young man in the dream) - you kiss me on the lips, you say, 'I am too, but I have worked through things you know. Haven't you?' I wake up then. In the dream, I feel happy when you tell me this."

When I finished, Lawrence did not react but kept on holding my hand.

At last he said, "I am so sorry too, Tink. I wish your dream had been reality and that I had taken the trouble to work things through. I was stubborn and so were you - but I was very hurt and angry. You should not have left the way that you did. You were unhappy and just left. I admit I was of no use to you at that time. I was not happy with my work, I found all that travelling very unsatisfactory."

"But Lawrence, why didn't we move? That would have been the one time I would not have minded to move!"

"I don't know, Tink - I think I just couldn't face another upheaval."

"Well - I was too much alone, Lawrence. I felt so unloved. At some point I thought you were having an affair as you didn't make love to me for ages and ages."

"Well I didn't have an affair and yes, I am sure you were alone too much! I realize that now, there were many things I realized as time went by. I learned a lot of things about you, about me, but I learned them too late."

"Do you think we could have repaired the damage if we had given it a chance Lawrence?"

"Yes, perhaps we could have."

I listened, I was glad he at last had talked to me.

"Yes" I said, "I believe we could have too. Part of me imagined and hoped that someday, you might ask me to come back! And that if you did, we would live happily ever after!"

"Maybe we would have!"

"And then I would never know what happened between you and Maxwell."

"That, Tink, is a subject that would take half the night to discuss, but let me say just this. For some reason he irritated me beyond words at that time. Perhaps this phase would have vanished as he became older – I don't know. He was very difficult and, as I have said, I was going through a bad time myself what with the unsatisfactory job, the travelling and the constant fight against recurring depression, so it was not a good combination, was it! Anyway, you didn't give it a chance to work itself out, did you Tink? Impatient as always, you left."

"Well, the truth is that I missed you - and I did wish that you would have taken us back you know Lawrence, if you remember I did ask you."

"Well - it is all too long ago to worry about now. I admit I was unforgiving and stubborn. But, like you, I am sorry we didn't try to put it back together."

"I guess we were both at fault."

"I missed you Tink, I never stopped missing you. I did love you you know, even though you somehow thought I didn't. I guess I wasn't very good at telling you or showing you. I was too bogged down with problems past, present and future, stupid really. Now – I think as I am such an old man, I should go to sleep, don't you!

"By the way, one thing before I go to sleep, I often thought about how lucky it was you didn't take that Thalidomide, remember how the doctor was quite insistent about how good it was, that it would definitely make your nausea vanish? Thankfully you didn't take his advice! A miracle really, considering how ill you felt most of the time!"

"Yes, it was in a way a miracle. I felt very thankful for that miracle when the sad news came out."

"I'm sure you did! Well now, I must try and get some sleep. Good-night Emily. God Bless."

I murmured my good-night, kissed him on his cheek, gave him a little pat.

"Yes - God bless you too, Lawrence."

He patted my hand, "Sleep tight, Tink".

In the morning I walked with Lawrence to his car. I gave him a little hug and he kissed me. Then it was good-bye, we knew we would never see each other again. We probably wouldn't correspond much now that this son had gone. Perhaps the occasional letter and I always sent him a birthday card and Christmas card. Then one of us would die. I too was getting older - it could be me who went first. Mind you, he was quite heavy now and he did seem short of breath. It was sad to wave him away. I felt a great sadness about seeing him go; after all these years I was still fond of him. It was because of the shared memories, those memories of when our children were little and we did so many things together as a family. Those years. Whenever I thought of them I thought only of the nice times and that gave me pleasure.

Yes indeed, we did have some nice times. It was good that he came down, I was so glad that he did. My, my - what I needed was a cup of tea - I am far too sentimental! I must perk up and get on with the chores. It will be so good to get home, a relief really, to be back living a normal life.

I paused to think about my pleasant life in Canada. All the same, I still loved England and was sure that I would be coming back from time to time.

Before I left, I tried to contact Christine but had no luck. One of Christine's college friends told me that Christine was on holiday. I was too tired to do anything more; I would try and contact her from home, I was too tired now to bother with anything. I phoned Alan and told him that I was leaving and thanked him again for his kindness.

"You should get yourself married, Alan, you are wasted!"

He laughed, "Perhaps you are right, Emily, but I don't want to get the wrong woman again this time so I'll just wait until the right one comes my way. You were the right one, Emily, but for some reason I missed getting you!"

I laughed, "You are sweet - but I wasn't a great prize you know! Far from it! Look at all the troubles I have had!"

"Oh Emily, how sorry I am. Please keep in touch with me Emily - and Bon Voyage!"

A DEATH

Beth and Joey now had two children. A little girl came after David, their life was settled and steady, so was mine. Robert, my eldest stepson, gave me a darling little kitten for my birthday. It was lovely to have a cat again, so pleasant at night to hear her purring by the fire. My stepsons were growing into such fine young men – I was very proud of them.

Andrew and I had time to travel. I loved Italy - I thought I must have Italian blood - I felt so at home there!

Travelling was pleasant but it was always so nice to get home and to catch up on all the news from Beth and Joey.

When we returned from a sunny holiday in Spain there were two airmail letters for me.

The official notice of my ex-husband's death was one; the other was the will and, with the will, a letter.

When I opened the envelope, there was a tiny, tissue-wrapped parcel inside the letter. It was my little golden bell on a chain - his wedding present for me. I had worn it on our wedding day. I remembered leaving it behind when I left him all those years ago. I had worn it all the time we had been married, hardly ever taking it off my neck. I had decided to leave it behind as the marriage had ended.

So now he had gone. I sat down with the letter, the little golden bell still in my hand.

My Dear Tink,

It has been so sad about our two lost children. Maxwell seemed to have recovered quite well from his depression and that was a blessing but so tragic to die so young with a life full of promise. Difficult to understand what exactly went wrong with David as he had been such a happy, pleasant, loving soul. We must be thankful that Joseph seems to be settled happily with a family and seems to have escaped the torment that our David suffered.

Nice that there are some grandchildren for you to enjoy. Let us hope that all goes well for them.

Thank you for your comforting presence, you-know-when. It was pleasant to think of and I did many times. It has been sad to think we both had such regrets. A terrible waste. After our conversation that night, I realized how wrong I had been not to take you back, not to ask your forgiveness for being so unrelenting in my disapproval of your actions. You were wrong, but so was I in many ways and I am sorry for it.

A long time since I have said such a thing to you, but I have loved you very much, Tink. Remember when I first called you that? You were such a Tinkerbell! Those were certainly carefree days and I did enjoy them with you.

Lawrence.

I was glad that he wrote this letter. It was thoughtful of him and in some way it gave me peace. Yes, eventually we did, I think, forgive each other. I felt we did, I think Lawrence felt that way too.

The will was not long. A picture had been left to a niece and some china. The other niece was to receive a picture and a very pretty, antique chair. There was a set of beautiful crystal hock glasses that had been a gift from his brother years ago; I was to receive these. The nephew was to receive all the other crystal glasses. A coffee set was for him as well. The tea sets went to the nieces. The little antique gold watch that had belonged to Lawrence's mother, he left to me. The house and car and any money that was left were to go to Joey, our remaining son.

When I put the will down, I was aware that Joey would have had a copy of the will by now. I wondered what he thought of it! A house in England! A rather lovely house too!

When I rang Joey, I told him that I had the news about his father's death.

"I know you were not particularly close to him, Joey, but still, he was your father and you must have some nice memories of those days?"

He agreed, "Yes of course I do, Mum, but, like you say, I was never that close to him and it was all so long ago. Anyway, it was nice of him to leave me the house and car, somehow it was quite a surprise. I don't know what you'll think of this, but Beth and I rather like the idea of going to live in England. See if we like it. Things are so changed there now with the economy of the country so good, very different from when we left! I could have the same business there as I have here - and Beth really likes the idea of bringing the children up in England. The house would be better than anything we could possibly afford here - with that garden and playroom it would be great!"

When I heard this I was very surprised!

"Do you think Beth would like it there?"

"Well, she thinks she would and she will only know if we try it. If we don't like it we can sell up and come back here!"

Well I thought, why not! Out loud, I said just that, "Why not? I think it's a great idea! But of course I have an ulterior motive! I will have somewhere to stay whenever I go to Britain!"

He laughed, "Of course, Mum. Anyway - you think it a good idea basically?"

"Yes dear, I do. I do!"

"Good, I know Beth will be pleased that you approve of the idea."

After I put the phone down I felt the excitement of the family making the move. I remembered how I had loved that house, how excited we had all been when we moved into it. Oh yes, I thought, they would love it. The village school was near enough to walk to. They would soon make new friends - they were young and children usually adjust quickly. I could easily visit them once a year, I was sure of that and they would be able to come to Canada too. Yes, I thought it a very good idea. Lovely to bring the children up in such a pleasant area, in the country, but not too far from anything.

I was just getting the dinner ready when the telephone rang. It was David.

"Grandmother, when we move to England will you come and visit us?"

I told him that I certainly would - that I could hardly wait!

"Neither can we!" he said, "Daddy has told us about the house and the great big garden! He said that as soon as we sell this house we can move. Mummy is going to start getting things ready right now! Isn't it all so exciting, grandmother!"

"Yes dear, it is very exciting. Is Veronica excited too?"

"Oh very!"

When I told Andrew he laughed, "I guess you'll be flitting over there like a bird finding its old nest! Well - you'd better not be leaving me here alone, I'll be coming too, you know! I can always drag you up to Scotland to my old nest!"

"You know darling, I love Scotland too - I love going there!"

He smiled at me, "Yes, of course I know, dear. I know that, of course I do."

It was not long after the family was settled in England that I received a letter from Beth.

Dear Emily,

We are well settled now, although it has taken a time to get sorted out! I must tell you that I really had no idea how lovely the house is! I had seen photos, but mostly of the children playing in the garden, things like that. So when I saw the beautiful, dark wood floors and the panelling in the hall I was quite surprised at how attractive it all was. The stone fireplace is quite magnificent! Well, I could go on forever! It is really lovely - I do love it!

The children are thrilled with their bedrooms looking out on to the garden, so bright and pretty. Of course the garden with the spinney is the great attraction! Joey says it was the same when they were children. They apparently played in that spinney for hours!

There are still people about who remember Joey! There is one family here you'll remember well. The son was a pal of Joey's and David. His name is Marcus. Well, he has children the same age as ours. He inherited his father's farm so they live near us and will be schoolmates of the children. Marcus has introduced us to new members of the village and they all seem very nice.

I really think I am going to like living here, it is very different from where we were in BC as you know! The countryside around is lovely, so unspoiled and quiet! Then, we can be in London in one hour and enjoy the amenities the city has to offer! There are some things I do miss! They don't seem to know how to make a decent hamburger over here, or a decent milk-shake! Joey says that you used to make them at home and they were the best they ever had, so I guess I will have to do that too! The fish and chips are marvellous though! Joey thinks the beer here is the only beer worth drinking!

We all want to know when you are coming over!
We all send lots of love,
Beth.

The letter pleased me very much. When Andrew came in I gave him the letter to read.

"What do you think?" I said, "When should we go?"

"Well Emily, I think that this time you would enjoy it more if you went without me. You'll want to visit people you used to know and places you used to know. It would be nice for you to have a visit with Beth without worrying about me all the time. Also I have a lot on, at the moment. So why don't you discuss it with Beth and Joey and see what fits with them and then make your arrangements. I'll manage just fine."

"Are you certain?" I asked, pleased, really, that he had seen it this way. I thought, too, that it would be nice to be on my own this one time. He assured me that he was very certain and that I was just to go ahead and make my arrangements.

I thought that towards the end of the summer would be a good time. I would have some time with the children before they went back to school and then Beth and I could have a nice visit once the children were back at school.

Beth agreed that this would work well.

"You can help me to sew on all the name tapes!" she told me on the phone, as we finalized the arrangements. Such a blessing now with telephoning not costing the earth as it used to do.

"Yes," I said, remembering those evenings I spent stitching on the name tapes - it had seemed to be an endless task until I remembered that because I had been a boarder at school, mother had to sew them on bed linen and towels as well as every item of underwear!

I told Beth that I would take a taxi from the station. Not to bother meeting the plane either. Such a waste of your time and I am quite happy coming along on my own, I told her.

I was glad I had done it this way as an avalanche of memories accompanied me on the drive from the station and I was able to enjoy them without interruption.

The house of course, had not changed, being built of brick, but it all looked very different because the trees had grown and grown! They were huge! I had forgotten about trees growing and making the garden look so different. And the rhodos - they were enormous! I thought how lovely it all looked, for those few moments before there was a rush of everyone around me. As we walked down the drive, I spotted the maple tree I had bought as a Christmas present, that must have been forty-odd years ago! It was, of course, enormous now.

Inside, it was much the same as when I had lived there apart from the kitchen which Joey had transformed with yellow and white paint! I had always had it blue and white. I thought the pale yellow with the white was much prettier. The AGA had been converted to oil - no messing about with coke any more! Yes, it was much improved. The children were nagging at me to come upstairs and look at their rooms. David had the larger of the two rooms. He had bunk beds so that he could have a guest to sleep over if he wished. They hadn't got around to decorating the upstairs yet but there were new carpets in the bedrooms.

The main feature of the tour outside was to show me the fort they had made in the spinney! The tea chests that had been used to ship some of their belongings from Canada they had made into a little hide-out, one part to sleep in and the other part had some of their cars and books in it. We went right to the end of the garden, a full tour! The children chattered the whole time. They told me that they were going to be wearing a uniform to school. A proper shirt and tie and shoes, just like Daddy wears! Veronica was to have a flared grey skirt. They told me that they had been to London!

"We went to see Peter Pan! Then Daddy took us to Madame Tussaud's! Have you been there Grandmother? It's real spooky!"

"Yes I have - and it *is* spooky! Did you like London?"

They were enthusiastic about London. "Daddy said that we are going to go there lots and lots of times and see everything!"

After dinner one evening, I mentioned the panel in the panelled wall in the dining room that Lawrence and I had opened up and made into a secret place. We had used it for storing silver and jewellery when we were on holiday. It was quite cool there, so we had also used it to store wine because there was no cellar in the house. Lawrence had cut the wood close to the framing so the cut was invisible. To open this he had made two screw-holes to screw handles into. The handles were stored, they were quite small, in a wooden cigar box that stood on the window sill. A picture hung over the little holes. Now there was a bookcase in front of the panelling. The space was under the stairs. Joey had forgotten all about it.

Once the children were in bed we decided to have a look. It would be rather nice if there were some bottles of special wine still there. First of all I located the handles which were still in the cigar box on the window sill. Then we moved the bookcase which fortunately was not a large one. Joey fitted the handles into the holes and lifted the glued-together panels from the wall. It was dark of course. Joey fetched his torch and shone it into the darkness. There stood my old school trunk! Why on earth was it there - it had always been stored in the attic? Why would Lawrence bring the old thing down here? We had to pull the trunk into the dining room in order to see if there was any wine at the back of the cupboard. There was nothing at all - just the trunk. I assumed it would be empty but lifted the lid to have a look anyway. There was my beautiful book "Baron at the Ballet"; I had really forgotten about it, although once upon a time it had been a prized possession of mine, Stanley had given it to me a very long time ago, dear sweet Stanley. I picked it up and a letter fell out, I saw immediately it was the letter he had sent back unopened all those years ago. Many times I had wondered what would have happened if he had read that letter. Strange to think of that. I could see that there were quite a few things in the trunk, all carefully wrapped in white tissue paper. I had a strange, eerie feeling as I unravelled my worn old pointe shoes, my first evening dress, and then my nightie, so thin, so beautiful, fine delicate lace like a cobweb and then I remembered Lawrence on our wedding night when I told him the whole sordid story hoping he would understand and forget his disappointment and find in his heart sympathy, because in my view I was a virgin, I had never made love to anyone ever before. When I said it to him like that he had looked at me with mournful eyes "Of course you are and I do believe you - of course I do. Poor Tinkerbell, my poor lovely innocent Tinkerbell." We had comforted each other. It was never mentioned again.

Happily I returned to the present and the pleasant past enjoying the good memories as I looked at David's little silk rompers, the boys' teddy bear, my figure skates, my old evening jacket, my puppets, each puppet was wrapped very carefully. As I unwrapped the puppets I put them in a row beside me on the floor. Beth had been sitting very quietly watching me. "Did you make them Emily? What was all that about?"

"Well yes I did - or I should say, we did; Martha (you've heard me mention Martha from time to time), well, she was and is a very creative person, it was her idea to make puppets and so we made them together, we thought it would be fun to do puppet shows for children. So we made costumes and wrote little plays and poems. It was a huge project and fun too. A friend in the village made us a travelling theatre.   So we entertained at birthday parties and children's Christmas parties. We even did a show on the village green and all the village children came and it was a great success. Lawrence was not enthusiastic at all. In fact I could say he came close to hating the project! Well, it did take up a lot of time and most of it in the evenings. We used the playroom for sewing and we often were up until well past midnight - which of course irritated him greatly. Sometimes he would actually come to the door of the playroom and tell me that it was time to come to bed! Oh well - all such a long time ago!"

The last thing was the bottom half of my powder dish, the only piece of Limoges that was left, even the bottom half without the lid was very lovely, maybe Beth could use it for something or other. I looked up to see Beth still watching me. Then she said, "It seems so sad to me Emily, how do you feel?"

"Yes I know what you mean. The odd thing is, that for Lawrence to do this, one would think him to be a sentimental man, but I never thought of him being like that. It somehow strikes me like something someone would do if a loved one had died."

Beth nodded. "It is a bit like that I agree; poor man, he must have loved you more than you knew, Emily."

"Yes, perhaps - a lot of things that happened could have been avoided. I didn't really know him you know, that was the real problem. He didn't let me know him. He didn't talk about feelings or ever show much emotion. There were many things he couldn't discuss. Not much of a marriage, a great disappointment to me and probably to him. I expected a very different relationship, but I don't know what *he* expected. Certainly not a partnership as you have with Joey. That was really what I had expected in marriage but Lawrence had such different ideas, controlling ideas, perhaps because I was so much younger. Anyway it's all so long ago and times have changed, thank goodness!"

"Well Emily, it all seems rather sad to me. How did you come to leave these things?"

"I don't know really; the book was in the bookcase so I just plain forgot about it, the puppets I had put in an old suitcase in the attic. I think my pointe shoes were probably there as well; I know there was a top shelf in the linen cupboard where I kept a few of my treasures so I guess I just didn't think of these things when I was leaving - I was too nervous and upset to think of everything. Anyway, what should we do with them now do you think?"

"Well, let's just put the whole shooting match back shall we? We won't be using the space and I'm sure you don't feel like dealing with these things at the moment do you?"

I agreed, apart from my book and the letter, which I would take home with me, I really didn't care much about the other things anymore. Then I remembered Teddy, "Perhaps you would like Teddy, Beth, as a keepsake from Joey's childhood, would you?"

She took him from me, "What a lovely worn-out old bear! I would love to have him. Not even a growl left!"

Beth and the children were busy shopping every day now that the summer was nearly over. Kitting them with everything new was time-consuming. They had put everything on, to show me. The long, grey trousers for David and grey, flared skirt for Veronica, both with red blazers, white shirts and tie, looked very smart.

"We could have had grey shirts," David told me, "but Mum thought the white ones looked nicer than the grey. The lady in the shop said that the grey would be less work, but Mum said it didn't matter. We like the white ones better too."

In the evenings, Beth and I sewed on the name tapes. At last every item was named, right down to the handkerchiefs. It was certainly less of a chore with the two of us sewing and chatting the whole time.

I did some last-minute shopping and then it was time to pack up and leave the family. It was always sad, to leave people one loves but I knew that I would be back again, I looked forward to it already! It was fun being there too, in the old house, where so many of my memories of my children were.

But first there was one thing I must do - I must now make the effort to find Christine. What that girl must think of me, leaving that time without being in touch, but I had tried, to no avail and I had been so tired, desperately tired. Now I was going to find her, I had brought a painting of Maxwell's to give to her, I was sure this would please her.

I found out where Christine's parents lived, so I thought I would just go along one afternoon and knock on their door. I wrapped the painting in a tea-towel and put it in a carrier bag. When I was on the bus, I asked to be let off as near as possible to Bluebell Lane. The newsagent had given me directions from that point.

I saw the house immediately. A rambling farmhouse sitting back from the lane. Beyond it, was a field. I could see many outbuildings to the side of the house.

In the garden there was a chap working, I thought it was probably Christine's father. When I got near, I asked him if he was Christine's father.

"Why yes - I am."

"Well," I told him, "I am Maxwell's mother, I'm Emily."

"Oh, my dear woman," he said, "how lovely to meet you at last! Come, let me open the gate for you! Come in, come in! We were so upset about Maxwell - we had met him many times you see. Such a nice young man he was. We liked to have him here. Yes, indeed a tragedy. We have thought of you many times my dear, many times. By the way, I'm Clive." He turned to me and shook my hand. "Barbara will be delighted to meet you I know. She is at the church doing the flowers but she will be home shortly."

As we walked along the path to the house I asked him about Christine and explained how I had tried to find her, but in the end had given up.

"You see," I said, "I suddenly just couldn't do another thing. I felt so tired, so exhausted, all I wanted was to get home to my husband. But perhaps you'll point me now in the right direction and I will be able to meet Christine and take her this little painting of Maxwell's?"

"Well, that won't be too difficult, Emily - Christine lives with us now."

Once in the house, he went and called up the stairs.

I had no idea what sort of girl to expect, I couldn't even remember if Maxwell had ever described her. I knew she had been an art student. As I watched the stairs I was surprised to see Christine coming down the stairs carrying a baby. He looked about nine months old. Clive was quite formal and introduced me to her, gravely. Christine went all pink and told me how glad she was to meet me, how she had wanted to meet me ages ago.

I explained what had happened and then I turned my attention to the baby, "My, Christine," I said - "what a lovely baby - and a boy?"

"Yes - a boy, would you like to hold him?"

I said I would love to hold him.

"He is a beauty, Christine."

She gave me a big smile. "Yes he is - and so good!"

Just then her father came in with a pot of tea and some biscuits.

"I'll leave you two to it, for a few moments," he said, "I have one or two things I must finish off."

I admired the baby and Christine told me little things about him. I was wondering why Christine and baby were living at her parent's home like this. I didn't like to ask. After a few minutes Christine put her cup down, "I'll hold him now, Emily, while you have your tea. I am so glad that you found us you know. It was all so terrible, I just couldn't do anything. Even now I hate to think about it all. I was really glad I wasn't there that evening."

Then she looked at me. "I was ill you see - I was pregnant! This, is your little grandson!"

I heard, but I was so surprised I said, "Oh no, really? Really? Really - my grandson?"

"Yes Emily, he is."

"Oh my! My! But that is wonderful, Christine! Did Maxwell know?"

"No he didn't - that was the problem. He had told me many times that he didn't want a child. He was afraid to have one. He thought that the child might inherit his genes and those that David had, the depression problem or whatever it was. I had decided not to tell him until he was feeling really good. He had been having a bit of a bad spell. Anyway, I had planned to tell him, but I had to decide when, that was all."

After hearing all of this, I realized that I didn't know the baby's name yet.

"What is his name, Christine?"

"I hope you don't mind, Emily," she said, "but I have named him after his father. Maxwell had told me that his name had been in the family for a long time - two hundred years he said. Is that right?"

I said that yes it had and that I was absolutely delighted that the baby was named after my son.

"But tell me, Christine, how are you going to manage without a husband?"

As I was asking this, both the father and the mother came into the sitting-room and Christine's father introduced his wife to me.

"Emily, how lovely to meet you! We have hoped for so long that somehow we would meet and now at last you are here."

"I guess you have heard the news?" Clive asked me. "How do you like the little chap? Grand little fellow isn't he!"

Christine's mother went and took him in her arms as he was getting restless. "He is an absolute delight Emily - don't you agree?"

"Yes indeed I do, a delight."

"I think I will put him down for a nap, Christine - it's past his time anyway."

"Yes it is - you're right, mother."

She kissed him, "Bye bye, sweet one".

"Yes," the father said, "we love having them here. No trouble to us at all. We have plenty of room. If Christine does want to work or go back to college, we would be happy to look after the little chap. However, she has never really enjoyed being out in the busy hectic world, have you, Christine?"

Christine nodded and smiled.

"So you see, she can stay here and work here. This is not a large farm but we have horses and then the sheep - and we breed dogs. There is always plenty to do. All of these things are things that Christine loves to do. She is happiest in this life style. She can do her art when she wants to, or take another course or degree - whatever. We are just so happy to have them here and to see Christine content. Yes indeed, it is working well."

Christine got up and asked me if I would like to see the baby's room. We went upstairs and through a door into the baby's room. Both rooms looked out to the orchard. Both rooms were decorated in the same very pale yellow, all the woodwork was white and the curtains were white with pretty spring flowers on them. There were soft toys on the window seats in both of the rooms. On the walls were prints of nursery rhymes. The whole effect was light, bright, sunny, cheerful. I could imagine how lovely it must be to wake up in these rooms.

"Oh Christine, this is lovely! Did you do all this yourself? The colour is so pretty. I do love the curtains. It is a perfect choice for both of you I think. One couldn't help but feel happy and cheerful in these rooms!"

Christine said that she loved it too. "I love being back in the country you know. I love the freedom, the fresh air, the animals all about. I hardly go into town at all. The roads are still quiet in this village too. We go to the river in the summer - the park there, is lovely and next summer Maxwell will really enjoy feeding the ducks. There's a small, village primary school where he'll go when he's five. We can walk to it and he will be able to come home for lunch, which is so nice when they are little, don't you think?"

"Yes, it does make a nice break for them I agree. The whole business of bringing up children in the country is to my mind much nicer for them than in the city. You are so lucky, Christine, to be able to be here! You seem to get on well with your Mum and Dad too?"

"They are understanding - I think they are hoping that I will continue with my art, living here. I think I probably will take a bit more training at some point, but not right now."

When we went downstairs I suddenly remembered my carrier bag.

"My goodness! Look at me! With all this excitement about baby I nearly forgot the picture!"

I opened the bag and unwrapped the painting.

"This is for you, Christine. I gave one to Maxwell's father and two to his brother. I have two. There are four more which I've reserved for grandchildren. I hope you like my choice!"

Christine picked it up and carried it across the room and propped it on the piano. Then she stood back with me.

"Yes," she said, "I do like your choice - and the light in here suits it. I liked all of his paintings - well nearly - there was one I thought he had not really finished. Thank you so very much for giving me this."

Then she turned and put her arms around me and started to cry.

"Poor darling, I am so sorry. It still hurts. Right now it is still so fresh, it is hard for you. You know, Christine, it will always hurt, but time will help to lessen the pain but it will never go away."

Christine dried her eyes, and smiled at me, "Thank you so much - I am ever so glad that you came, Emily. It will make such a difference to me to know you are there. I know it will help me."

"It will help me too, to know you Christine, and to have this new, unknown grandchild!   Maybe he will be an artist like his daddy and his mummy, I know you will have great pleasure watching him grow and develop. It's wonderful for me to think of these things and to know you too, I feel very fortunate indeed. I am sure we will be good friends - very good."

Christine nodded, "Yes, I am sure we will, that will be wonderful."

Clive and Barbara were at the door to say good-bye and Barbara apologized for not having more of a visit with me, "It was a pity I was out to-day when you came, Emily. Next time you come we will have a really good visit. The most important visit today anyway, was yours with Christine and Maxwell, wasn't it!"

"It certainly was and we did have a good visit. I am just so glad that I found you!"

"We are very glad that you did too!"

I gave them all a hug and then I was on my way.

NOW ALONE

It seemed a long time ago that I was in Scotland with Andrew and yet really it wasn't. I guess it seemed that way because my life had changed so much. It was comforting now to be back, to renew my friendship with this remote, ancient, undisturbed village.

I had booked my room in the hotel where Andrew and I used to stay from time to time, it had once been a private residence. It was a large stone-built house with a sweeping curved stair entrance and the art nouveau iron work gave it a Rennie Mackintosh look. Inside, as well, had that look, with some of the internal doors having coloured glass in neat geometrical designs. The decor too, was mainly black and white which certainly added to that look. It stood high on a cliff with marvellous views of the North Sea. Standing at the window looking down at the turbulent sea, I thought of the times with Andrew when we walked together through the tall, bleached grasses, beside the narrow lochs where swans rode the tranquil water. Then, laughing at our ineptness scrambling up the stony paths that deer had made and used, long before us, we would enjoy a picnic lunch while the sheep noisily observed our intrusion. Listening to the calls of the sea-birds and the sound of the waves rushing and crashing against the rocks, life seemed very peacefully idyllic. Not so long ago in reality, but it seemed somehow, a long time since those days.

The weather was cold and stormy as it often was in this part of the world, but it would not keep me in. I wanted to be out in the weather, to walk in the wind and the rain as Andrew and I used to do.

Andrew's ashes I deposited with the grave-digger at the churchyard, he told me that he would see to it in a day or two.

There was to be a morning service at the nearby priory; it was a friendly and informal service with lots of hymn singing. Many little children were there with their parents and grannies and grandpas. It lifted me to be there, with all of these friendly people singing together with happy voices, hymns that I knew from my childhood. After the service I went to the graveyard to enquire if Andrew's ashes had been buried beside his mother's and was told that they had.

It seems to take so much longer to get home now and travelling has become very tiring. It is quite true there is no place like home! It is indeed blissful to be home again where I can read my books, listen to music in peace and quiet and enjoy the company of dear old Sophie and hear her contented purr again.

It was amazing after all these years to read that long article about Stanley. Of course, with him living in the USA, how would I ever know about all the interesting research he has done and the time and money he has given to various worthy projects. It does seem strange that all those years ago he could have been so callous that he sent my letter back without even opening it. I had forgotten about that letter until I found it in "Baron at the Ballet". Hurt and disappointed, all those years ago, I had made up my mind not to think about Stanley anymore. Now It would be easy enough to find his address but what would be the point except that it would be nice to congratulate him on all his good work. I could enclose that letter at the same time. One never knows, he might even read it, on the other hand he might do the same again. Anyway, I think I will send it, along with a little letter. Reading it now, I remember my emotional turmoil, wondering if I should write such a letter at all, but I had put aside my doubts hoping that all would be forgiven and that we would be friends again and maybe be married one day and live happily ever after. I don't think I ever really believed we would ever be married, it was one of my little fantasy dreams. Yes it would be pleasant to send him my congratulations and good wishes, maybe that would give him pleasure, it certainly couldn't do any harm!

When I saw the writing on the envelope I knew immediately who it was from, even now, after all these years, I recognised Emily's handwriting. But why would she be writing to me? I opened the envelope and read her pleasant little note which was rather sweet of her to bother, and then I picked up the enclosed envelope addressed to me many years ago, sent to our old address several months after mother died and Dad and I had moved, so obviously the letter had been returned to Emily. I sat down and finished reading her note, telling me about how upset she had been when her letter had been returned, it was no wonder that she had been so upset thinking as she did, that I had not even bothered to open the letter. So now she is at the end of her life, ill she says. Although I am not ill, I too, am at the end of my life. For some reason she wants me to read this very old letter she wrote such a long time ago.

Dear Stanley,
I was wrong to marry someone else when I love you so much. I have left my husband and come back to Canada to live and to have my baby. I have been very unhappy and know I made a terrible mistake. I know that having a baby is a very serious commitment and I am happy with that as I love children and I love my baby who is to be born in March.

Do you think we could get together again? Maybe you already have someone else but we could be friends couldn't we? I have missed you a lot.

I hope you don't mind that I am writing to you but I had to.
Love,
from
Emily.

I put the letter down, an overwhelming feeling of shock and sadness came over me, this is beyond belief, how could such a thing have happened! Oh my goodness, what an awful shame, of course I would have taken her back, I would have been delighted to have her and been pleased for her to have her baby, a start to our family as I had always known she wanted a family. Yes, I would have thought it wonderful to have her back – a miracle after the dreadful shock and disappointment of losing her to someone else. I remembered her well, of course, I could even remember the way she laughed so readily and unexpectedly, yes I certainly remembered her, all so long ago. Such an ordinary thing to happen, I guess it happens all the time and yet, on this occasion, this small mishap changed our lives totally and forever. Poor Emily, how very sad, and such a sad little letter, poor girl.

Should I answer her letter? I don't know, she says she has not much longer to live. Would it make her happy or unhappy to know the truth about the letter and that I certainly would have answered it, had I received it. I remember well, how much I had missed Emily and for a long time, I was heart-broken, I had loved Emily, my first love.

So now her life is ending, I hope she found happiness as time went on. A strange, sad, unfortunate ending to our young love.

Two years have passed without Andrew and I am tired, very tired. Nice to sit here with Sophie on my lap, a cup of tea to drink and a book to read. Yes, these things are a comfort and enjoyable. I can't say truthfully that I am ready for death as I don't really want to die - and yet I know my time has come - the pain now is tiring and constant. I know too that, with my death, peace will finally come to me with the aching anguish of my two dead sons finally extinguished.

I looked over at my old blue-metal school trunk with the very old-fashioned and quite useless lock, a bit battered but somehow most of the faded stickers had managed to stay put. It had held up well considering it had been following me around since I was sixteen going to boarding school in Victoria, which had been such an exciting experience for me. Then the sea voyage to England and Jersey and back to Canada and England again and Jersey and Jersey again and all the moves around England, sometimes exciting and sometimes sad. Rather surprising to see it sitting there after so many years, all those memories of the different places where I had excitedly packed and unpacked it with new expectations each time. I had thought its useful days were long over until it arrived filled with my lovely old rug that Beth said she didn't care for. It too, held memories for me as Lawrence had bought it on impulse, both of us having seen it in a showroom one evening on the way home from an evening out. He had gone into town the very next morning to purchase it, which was one of those lovely surprise gestures of his that were all too infrequent. I certainly have enjoyed the colourful warmth of it again.

I remember how surprised I was that evening when Beth and I opened the old trunk and found those things of mine that I had left behind, Lawrence had wrapped and packed them so carefully. What for? Had he planned to send them to me some day, or just keep them because they had been mine and part of our lives together - which was what Beth thought. Once again I had seen a different Lawrence, as I had that night we spent together in the caravan after Maxwell died.

I am glad that Stanley wrote to me.

When I think of that letter, how I felt when I wrote it and how

I hoped he would understand. To think it never reached him! That he never even saw it! Strange to think of what our lives might have been had we spent them together. Amazing thoughts to have, quite disturbing, as I cannot help the feeling of sadness that fills me when I think of what might have been, with the union of our young love.

The end of my life now, so near. I have nothing left that I must do and that is strange. I feel somehow content and happy, a feeling of love, so much love I have felt, it has given me great joy to give love to those around me - and that joy is still in my heart.

Poor Sophie, difficult for you to jump up now, here let me help you. There now, you settle down and keep me company, so good to hear your comforting purr and feel your warm old body on my old lap!

When I shut my eyes I see before me that little girl I once was, longing to dance, practising the turns over and over, with mother counting and then clapping as I finished a row of perfect turns and in my fairy costume with the silver tinsel and silver shoes with a fairy crown on my head. I remember the very beautiful Russian costume of gold-coloured beaded velvet with a matching head-dress. The Russian dance took such a lot of practising low on the floor, kicking my legs, then up quickly to turn and curtsy. At the actual performance, however, the heavily beaded head-dress fell right over my face as I did the low kicks. Having been told that no matter what happened the show must go on, I carried on doing the kicks keeping time to the music with the crown covering my eyes, not stopping to adjust the crown. Strong applause accompanied my curtsy, but mother said it was mainly because I had carried on dancing with the crown covering most of my face! "Didn't I do the Russian dance well?" I asked, "Well enough dear, but it probably would have been better had the crown not fallen over your eyes!"

THE END

ACKNOWLEDGEMENTS

I want to thank my wonderful husband, Colin, because this book would never have been completed had it not been for his endless encouragement and support.

Several good friends read various early manuscripts. Their reactions helped to further inspire me to continue. Thank you all so much.